Rift in Evil

Rift in Evil

Ken X Briggs

iUniverse, Inc.
New York   Bloomington

Rift in Evil

iUniverse books may be ordered through booksellers or by contacting:

iUniverse
1663 Liberty Drive
Bloomington, IN 47403
www.iuniverse.com
1-800-Authors (1-800-288-4677)

All scripture quotations, unless otherwise indicated, are taken from the HOLY BIBLE, NEW INTERNATIONAL VERSION®. NIV®. Copyright ©1973, 1978, 1984 by International Bible Society. Used by permission of Zondervan. All rights reserved.

ISBN: 978-1-4502-5089-4 (sc)
ISBN: 978-1-4502-5090-0 (ebk)

Printed in the United States of America

iUniverse rev. date: 08/26/2010

DEDICATION

Dedicated to the millions of young people who struggle with life and hardships and who know there is a better way!

Additional Information available at
www.RiftInEvil.com

Prologue - 1995

The huge metal jaws mesmerized Bryan Robyn as they crunched rocks bigger than a man's head. He found the dusty smell of the African air was more acrid here in the metallurgical building. Rocks splintered and burst as he watched them. He had been in this work for thirty years and never lost his fascination with the power exhibited by these huge machines.

Noticing that the jaw could accommodate more rocks he shouted to the operator of the conveyor feeding the machine, "Simon, increase the conveyor speed, it's not crushing enough. We don't want Hendrik to get mad!"

The gray-haired black man operating the controls at the top of the conveyor waved back to him, flashing Bryan a white-toothed smile. He'd worked with '*Baas* Bryan' for years and they had a mutual respect. The speed of the conveyor increased and more rock hurtled off the lip of the conveyor thundering down into the insatiable metal jaw.

It was horrendously noisy for Bryan who ignored wearing the regulatory ear protection. He found them hot and unbearable in the African heat. Others complied, but being past retirement age he felt no need to follow the company policy.

Rocks thundered down off the conveyor falling twenty feet into the jaw crusher. The splintering of rocks that occurred every time the jaws came together was a captivating and fearsome sight. Rocks at the top cracked and broke into smaller pieces that were again broken down as they moved down the 'V' and out the small opening at the bottom to drop fifty feet into the silo.

Bryan needed to fix a control box on top of the conveyor engine as it had an electrical fault. It was the foreman who had called him and told him to come in. To do the work he needed to remove safety railing that was now lying on the floor alongside him.

"*Môre!*"

Bryan swung around, surprised to see his archenemy, Hendrik, the plant foreman approaching.

Hendrik was a big man at six foot four with boxer arms atop a huge iron hard torso supported by powerful sprinter's legs. He had tousled curly black hair that was darker than most and this morning was exceptionally tidy. His countenance was morose and scowling as he climbed the incline to the top of the conveyor with a measured tread. It was a hard climb and most men were out of breath by the time they reached the top of the silo where Bryan was working. Hendrik didn't tire! The greeting they received would have been the same in his office with him sitting slouched in his oversized chair.

Bryan had always considered Hendrik evil and prayed a quick silent prayer. "Lord give me patience with this man!"

This prayer would have been more insistent and focused if he could have seen the forces in the spiritual realm, but he couldn't.

"Good morning Sir!" he answered knowing the English greeting would annoy Hendrik. Glancing at Simon he noticed his friend avoided looking at the foreman. Hendrik was a racist and hated all black people on principle, so Simon was simply being prudent.

As Hendrik arrived at the top of the conveyor incline, a rock started to block the huge jaw. Elongated and big, it resisted the clenching and relaxing of the jaw by riding up and down inside the 'V' and supporting the rocks above it. The chute started to jam with rocks.

Simon stopped the conveyor, picking up a long pry bar. It was his job to lever the rocks into a position that enabled the jaws to grip them, but now he would have to do so without the benefit of a safety railing. Both Bryan and Simon knew how dangerous it was.

"Simon! Be careful! I'll hold your belt while you lean over. Be quick!" Bryan warned his black friend.

Both men leaned over the jaw as Simon worked feverishly to lever the rock. They totally forgot about Hendrik as the activity demanded their full attention. Simon finally moved the rock slightly so it was gripped by the serrations in the jaw. It burst into five fragments with a sound like a clap of thunder just as Bryan felt a push from behind!

"What the…" he said, never completing the sentence as he collided with Simon tumbling both of them over the edge into the crusher.

Simon died instantly! His head dropped into the crusher as the jaws closed, popping it like a melon dropped from height onto concrete. Bryan who fell onto his friend's body was luckier and tried to scramble up the steep slope only to find rocks starting to rain down onto him. Someone had started the conveyor again. The third rock knocked his hard hat off and the fifth knocked him unconscious.

The ore rained down covering the bodies until nothing was seen. Nobody saw Hendrik leaving!

CHAPTER ONE – Before the "accident"

Sitting in his plush office at Zinaville Platinum Mine or ZPM as it was called, Tom Lurie reflected over the years since his mother's death. His desk displayed the piece of rock that had changed his life. It stood upright with its solid silver base glistening in the sunlight.

Tom was slightly above average in height and his stocky frame filled the chair in which he relaxed. His heavy eyebrows emphasizing dark brown eyes set in a strong angular face with aristocratic features. Well built and tanned, he exuded the quiet mystique of control, self-assurance and power that was generally found amongst the rich and powerful. This was somewhat strange to those who knew him from his early years, since he had started out life as a simple seaman.

The rock he gazed at, had been found while scattering his mother's ashes on a farm in the mountains outside town. Its irregular gray and white coloring had caught his attention and he had picked it up. A month later a friend who was a geologist had come to visit and seen it on his mantelpiece. His friend identified it as a piece of platinum reef. Tom then bought the farm where it had been discovered. Months of saving and scrimping followed, and finally he had purchased the mineral rights to the farm as well! He approached a bank, and was successful in obtaining a loan to sink the first incline shaft in return for the bank becoming a part owner of the mine.

The partnership had been useful and had helped with the mine's international finances and structuring of exports. Fortune smiled on the venture and after the first ten years Tom expanded the operation.

Tom grinned as he thought of all the heated arguments the contracts had evoked over the years. His experience as a sailor had paid off. He was tougher and smarter than his competitors. In addition, his contacts in the shipping and export world ensured that his competitors treated him with respect. Now he was a wealthy and influential man!

About twenty-five years after he had starting the mine, he started his first metallurgical plant to recover the platinum. He employed a young metallurgist just out of training. This gamble had paid off. What the youngster lacked in experience, he made up for in enthusiasm and bright ideas. The boy's father had helped with the start-up years. The father, Bryan Robyn, was an electrician from the Palaborwa Mining Company and had been only too glad to move to Zinaville to help his son. Tom had been lucky to get those two. The old man was still working for him as an electrician, but was past retirement age. They kept him on for historical reasons and because his son was so important to the success of the enterprise.

Tom looked around his spacious office. A picture of his mother hung on the one wall in a place of honor. There were others depicting the first years of the mine's existence. How unsure he had been of himself when she had died. Developing the mine had eased the ache and he had put his energies into work to escape the dull feeling of emptiness. He felt in many ways as if the mine had grown from his mother's ashes. For a while he had even considered calling it Phoenix, but the name was already used. For a while the focus and effort had worked. Making money and building the operation had taken most of his time. He was now feeling that ache again as the work became routine. He never seemed to escape the tendrils of anxiety and depression that plagued his life.

There was a knock on the door. Tom looked up calling for the person to come in. A man in his mid thirties entered and greeted Tom.

"Hi Josh," said Tom. "What brings you here? How are things going at the plant?"

Joshua Robyn was a tall handsome man of six foot with dark brown hair tinged with red. His slim, well toned body showed just a touch of tension and his normally infectious smile was missing. He was annoyed! Obviously at home with Tom, he dropped his lanky frame into the seat across from the desk. Folding his tanned muscular arms, he leaned back and frowned as he paused to ensure Tom's full attention would be focused on what he was about to say.

"Labor problems again!" said Joshua. "The workers are still threatening to strike for an increase in wages. This morning Hendrik added to this by apparently hitting one of the workers while out of sight of the others. The workforce has basically ground to a halt, and they are now demanding that something be done. The problem is that I have no proof of the situation and Kasper is swearing he was with Hendrik all morning. According to him, nothing occurred. I can't do without my foreman, but I also need the workers to continue. What do you think I should do?"

Tom leaned back in his chair and ran his hand through his gray hair to flip it out of his eyes. The workforce on his mine had always been given above average wages, so he knew he was fair in that regard and he had never subscribed to the apartheid philosophy of the South African government. Hendrik the metallurgical foreman was a different problem. He had also been employed from the Palaborwa Mining Company and had increased the productivity of the plant impressively since he had become foreman, but he was a notorious troublemaker. Tom had employed Hendrik himself since Joshua didn't want anything to do with him.

Tom was glad he had disagreed with the young man! Hendrik had improved the productivity of the workers immediately. Joshua had objected vehemently and Tom had come to understand that there was bad blood between Hendrik and Joshua's father, Bryan. Now Tom was starting to agree with Joshua that despite the short-term improvements, Hendrik seemed to have brought trouble with him in the long term.

Zinaville wasn't the quiet town it had been in the sixties when Tom had arrived. Tom realized the mine was partly to blame as it had caused an economic boom in the small town. Businesses had prospered, and the town had filled up with mining types. For several years the original inhabitants and the newcomers had coexisted happily. Then trouble had started! Tom couldn't quite place when, although he knew that it was soon after he had employed Hendrik. There were rumors that Hendrik hated blacks and was a member of the political right wing group who wanted the apartheid laws to be applied more rigidly to the black peoples. The rumors intimated he was causing trouble in the town in this regard as well.

The rumors were all based on gossip. Tom had not found any proof of Hendrik being harsh with the black people. As time passed he got annoyed with Joshua who was the reporter of most of these rumors. Possibly Joshua had a hidden agenda in continually complaining about the older man. Tom eyed Joshua as these thoughts crossed his mind.

"No proof that Hendrik was involved?" he asked.

"Not really Tom! But it's hardly like our workers to get so upset over something that didn't happen. All I get out of Hendrik is a comment to get off his back and a string of profanities each time I bring up the subject."

Tom nodded. Hendrik had the foulest mouth he had heard. As a former sailor he knew that was saying a lot! This problem was going to be difficult to solve! The black folk in the country were getting more and more upset with the discrimination against them by the white folk. Their demands were no longer based on work place complaints but on political demands as well. He thought it was time to call in the shop steward of the mineworkers union.

Tom leaned over to his intercom. "Mrs. Wold, please call in Steve Kumalo from the mine hostel. He must come over as quickly as possible. Send a car to fetch him and call me when he gets here."

Steve had started off on the mine as the hostel cook, but his excellent language skills and natural way with people had soon led to him being promoted into the personnel department. Then things had started changing in the country. Riots improperly handled in the black townships had generated angry feelings. Unions had developed and each mine was now subject to legal scrutiny by these organizations. Tom's platinum mine, ZPM, was no different. Steve had quickly risen to leadership of the union in the area. Tom had found that he got on well with Steve. Probably this was because he was color-blind in his approach to people. They clashed on economic grounds however. Steve wasn't fond of the fact that Tom took a fair portion of the mine's profit. He felt it should be distributed to the workers. Tom resisted as he felt that he had started and developed the whole community, and he knew it was his right to gain the benefit from his work. A twinge of anxiety went through him again as he thought of some of their arguments.

Joshua interrupted his thoughts. "Is it wise to have these discussions without a representative from the management staff of the plant present?"

Tom knew Joshua was referring to Hendrik and deliberately misinterpreted the suggestion.

"You're the manager of the plant, aren't you representative?"

Joshua knew better than to argue with Tom on these matters, and simply nodded.

They discussed the production figures for the last month as they waited for Steve. Despite sanctions against the country, the platinum prices were up. Cars needed catalytic converters for exhaust emission requirements and over the last while, it appeared as if more platinum was finding its way onto the world market. They both felt it had to do with special alloys being manufactured. Whatever the reason, they were doing well.

They discussed the worker situation for a while and were tentatively agreeing to increase the wages slightly, when Tom had an idea. "Why don't we give the workers part of the profits? Profit sharing will encourage efficiency and will remove the likelihood of unnecessary strikes."

Joshua agreed. "Can we afford it and should it be suggested now?" he asked.

Before Tom could answer there was knock on the door. Mrs. Wold opened the door and announced Steve.

"Send him in Mrs. Wold," turning to Joshua he added, "we will play it as the situation dictates."

A small stocky man entered. His eyes glinted with energy through his wire rimmed eyeglasses embracing his pronounced forehead. He had a grim smile on his black face and the air of an attorney with pent up energy. Not that Steve had ever been inside a courtroom. His only legal training came the hard way, from union negotiations with management. He wore a blue loose fitting shirt that "Westerners" consider Hawaiian.

Tom gestured to an empty chair and Steve dropped into it. He immediately looked completely relaxed, but his eyes belied his body language. They were sharp and penetrating! Both Joshua and Tom knew from previous encounters that Steve was far from relaxed and was annoyed by the current situation.

Tom rubbed his brow, paused for a second and then opened the discussion. "Morning, Steve. Thanks for coming. How's your dad?" It was traditional to ask of the family before doing business and Tom knew that Steve had an elderly father from Zimbabwe who had inspired Steve as a young boy to achieve something with his life. He waited for the reply.

"He is as well as the circumstances will allow," came the guarded reply. "He is well into his seventies now but still as strong as an elephant."

Tom nodded.

"Steve, you know we didn't invite you here to discuss family. We have a problem at the plant. What do you know about it?"

Steve settled back further into his chair, looking down for a minute. When he began to speak his penetrating brown eyes burned into Tom. "The workers are angry. There is a racist element on the plant that is making their life unbearable!" Steve was studiously avoiding looking at Josh. "I have been trying for the past months to calm the people down. The continuing situation is making it impossible to keep the people from expressing their anger in some way. I warned Mr. Robyn twice in the last month that this may occur and that he should do something, but nothing has been done! Today I was approached by some men who wanted to do worse than just strike. They would have knifed the main culprit on the plant if I had not intervened. I suggested a temporary go-slow until this could be sorted out. What are *your* suggestions?"

Tom looked surprised. "Joshua told me about the incidents but I didn't realize that they were so serious. I thought it was only the wage related issue that was causing some friction. I know our wages are ten percent up on similar wages in the area but I didn't know the complaints were against personnel. Why were no official complaints filed?"

Steve looked at Joshua. "Ask him!"

Joshua defended himself. "Each time I have had someone come and complain to me, I have explained that they will have to prove their charges. I explain that I have to find reasonable proof that the accused is guilty of the charges before anything can be done. If there isn't enough proof I need to reject the charge. Of course, if that occurs the culprit could be charged with insubordination. After I explain this, they simply refuse to press charges and leave. Without their input I can't do anything!"

"Yes, you could!" Steve retorted angrily. "You could remove the men who are the cause of the problem!"

Tom interrupted. "Steve, you know that Joshua can't fire a man without at least three warnings against him. That would be unjust! We need those men who have complaints to lay charges! What do you suggest we do?"

Steve looked frustrated. "These culprits are too clever," he said. "They never let anyone see what happens! Each time I get a report, it's from a man who has no witnesses. A few times they even tried to trick me with stories. You're lucky I am an honest man, or you would not be in as fortunate a position as you are now. You must do something! I agree with them! The situation is a problem. They need to know you're doing something about it!" He fell silent.

"Can I suggest a plan?" asked Joshua.

Both Tom and Steve looked at him and nodded.

"Obviously we need to show that we're taking action against both Hendrik and his friend, if we're to placate the workers. Equally, we need to show that we care for our workers! Since most of the problem comes when Hendrik is doing his inspection of the plant, there needs to be two witnesses to everything Hendrik does. We can then take action if he threatens or abuses anyone! We simply never leave him alone with any of the workers."

Joshua paused to allow the reasoning be absorbed by the men.

"I suggest that we call in Hendrik and Kasper separately and warn them they are under observation, then for the next month Steve will accompany Hendrik each time he goes onto the plant. That means that nobody will be without a witness for this next month and it will show the workers we're trying to do something."

Joshua turned to Steve showing concern on his face. "This means the only person that would be really taking a risk is you! How do you feel about it?"

Steve thought for a while. "The men are very angry. What you say may help. I agree we could try this for a month, but under two conditions. I want to be able to stop without having to justify myself, and I want this promise given to me in writing."

He stopped and thought a while. "What will happen to clear up the situation at the end of the month?"

"At that time we will ask you for your ideas. You will be the person who will know what is happening and so you will be able to advise us," replied Joshua.

"Well that's settled then!" said Tom dictatorially. He pressed his intercom, "Mrs. Wold, please write a letter addressed to Mr. Kumalo saying he is to accompany Mr. van Vuuren at all times on any plant visit during the next month. He'll also be given the option to return to his normal duties the moment he requests to do so. Type it up for me to sign and make two copies, one for our files and one to be given to Mr. Kumalo."

Tom closed the meeting and said good-bye to the men. He went back to sit in his chair and the emptiness started to prey on his mind again. He fought the depressing influence by pulling his in-tray forward and beginning to go through his work again.

CHAPTER TWO

In Joshua's office an hour later a storm was erupting! Joshua was about to give Hendrik the bad news. It was obviously second hand already, and Hendrik had a fair idea what the discussion was going to be about from the scowl that he had on his face. Joshua offered Hendrik a seat. He ignored Joshua and stood towering over the desk, obviously angry. His normally morose features were thunderous. Joshua felt uncertain on how to continue.

"Hendrik, thanks for coming so quickly," he said. "Have the workers started work yet?"

Hendrik shook his head and looked even more sullen.

"They should be starting work soon. We have come to an agreement that will help production to be re-started." Joshua suddenly tired of Hendrik's attitude and he vented his anger, "SIT DOWN, Mr. van Vuuren!" he commanded the larger man.

Hendrik lowered his large frame into the chair, dwarfing it, and still said nothing.

"Mr. van Vuuren, you're aware the workers have complained that you're not treating them correctly! I have spoken to Mr. Lurie and we have come up with a solution that protects both your interests and theirs."

Hendrik hissed, "I don't need my interests protected!"

"Maybe not Mr. van Vuuren, but this solution also protects the interest of our mine, ZPM. We have no other choice to ensure that the workers can't blame you for something you didn't do. Mr. Kumalo will accompany you to the plant every day. This continues until we see fit to stop it! Mr. Kumalo's work as a personnel officer will be to provide a report on the activities of all plant personnel on a weekly basis."

Hendrik wasn't happy. He was angry! His eyes narrowed.

"I want my disagreement noted, Mr. Robyn," he said. "I'll do as you say, but if the production slows, it will be on your head. I can't work with a spy following me around the whole time. He's not accustomed to being in the production area. If something happens to him it'll be his own fault!"

Joshua felt a pang of worry but hid it immediately. "No Hendrik, you're wrong! If something happens to him it's YOUR fault! You're his mentor in these affairs and must therefore ENSURE he doesn't get hurt or do anything dangerous. As a foreman, you shouldn't be operating equipment yourself except in exceptional circumstances. Mr. Kumalo will be expected to be out of the danger area but be able to see what you're doing. Do you understand?"

The two men glared at each other for a while. Finally Hendrik nodded reluctantly.

"Do you have any queries about this?"

Hendrik shook his head slowly.

"Then you can go. I hope this will help everyone. The workers can no longer blame you for doing things you claim you didn't do, as you will have a witness to all your activities."

Hendrik's face was a mixture of anger, frustration and hate as he left the room.

Joshua felt the danger radiating from Hendrik's retreating back and prayed that he had not made a mistake. In the spiritual realm a whole host of demons retreated with their leader. The large angelic being, Beor, who was Joshua's guardian, sheathed the sword that had been flashing to and fro only seconds earlier.

Joshua picked up his pen and filled in the disciplinary form summarizing what had been said. A long stream of expletives could be heard fading into the distance as Hendrik went up to his own office. Joshua couldn't help feeling afraid. He knew Hendrik could be really unpleasant and knew that it was likely that this was not the end of the matter.

Just then Steve knocked on the door and walked in.

"Hello Mr. Robyn, I hear the foreman isn't very happy!" he grinned cheerfully. "I suppose I'll just have to watch my back."

Joshua smiled back weakly. "Yes, but I warned him that your safety is his responsibility! If anything happens to you, he will be in trouble. I think that will help." Joshua liked Steve despite their differences. He was always honest even if they disagreed on various plant politics and union matters. He was a man you could trust! He never gave his word when he couldn't deliver and normally managed to achieve what he said he would.

Steve was speaking, "I have spoken to the workers. They have agreed! I think the plan may work. I'll start work now. Where's my office for the next few weeks?"

Joshua smiled again.

"Hendrik's unpleasant friend Mr. Kasper Prinsloo is about to be promoted sideways to the time office to help with the administration of the clocking in and out of personnel. He'll be vacating his office and you can use it."

Both men smiled, they knew this would provide further protection to Steve and the rest of the workers by separating the two men.

They chatted for a few more minutes then Joshua asked Steve to go and call Kasper to his office.

In the spiritual world Beor, protecting Joshua, watched until Poneros, Hendrik's demonic guide and his throng of foul creatures had gone. The creatures left Worry and Fear behind to terrorize Beor, and if possible Joshua. These two serpentine types found their subject less than amenable and finally left hurriedly as Steve had come in followed by another tall dark-skinned angel.

Beor greeted Libni, the large dark-skinned angel who accompanied Steve. God's planning was accurate and the expected path was developing! Beor then exited the office, rising up into the air before speeding to the Zinaville Christian Church to alight amongst a throng of glimmering angelic beings.

His brilliant white faded as he settled. The flash of light that had scribed his path across the heavens also slowly faded.

"Greetings Beor," murmured Tabitha, a lightly built angel known to move with light-splitting speed and grace. A general hubbub of welcome followed. There were twenty angels present. These represented hundreds more who were waiting hidden in the surrounding hills, valleys, rocks, trees and waterfalls. They were awaiting instructions and ready to react at the specific time.

"Glory and power to the Lord!" said Beor.

"Glory and power to the Lord," thundered the assembly. Outside Meddler and a fellow demon resting in a tree suddenly became aware that something unusual was happening. The church was radiating light. The sound of the human voices in prayer inside was accompanying the light. Meddler knew better than to approach any closer. Many times over the last months his Master, Kakoo, had attempted to send small detachments into that church to disrupt affairs. First they had been small groups and then larger. Each time the cohorts had been repelled, each successive attempt being more effectively defeated. Initially there had been no casualties, later the demonic forces experienced significant damage. The Christians were causing trouble for the demonic forces. Their prayer was most frightening.

Right now Meddler could see a large angel standing at the church entrance with a glittering sword in his hand. He knew that many angels would appear should he attempt to get closer. Standing shoulder to shoulder they would stop any attempt to get closer to the church. He would be lucky to escape with his current shape intact. Meddler shivered at the thought of the gleaming swords and pushed back into the shadows.

Inside the church Beor was reviewing the progress. "Time to recover the lost ground for the Lord is drawing near," he was saying. "The townsfolk still don't honor his name sufficiently. The growth of the enemy that is occurring is not unexpected. Evil pervades this society since Poneros joined Kakoo. There's work to be done!"

Beor looked at the prayer warriors seated in a circle in the sanctuary. Young and old were present at this woman's meeting. All were praying earnestly. Their prayers were for their men folk, God's will in the community, reduction in violence, removal of filth from television, closing down of the Priggles Bar and other requests. Now and then, one or other of them would give glory to God, to be concluded by a chorus of amen's.

Beor pointed to the group. "These Christians are our support and power. Protect them well." He turned to Tabitha. "The Lord has revealed that Joshua's mother, Karen Robyn is about to go through a time of anguish. Ensure that despair and depression don't gain a hold on her life. You may need help. Should that be necessary we will help!"

Karen was busy praying at that moment. One of the angelic company placed a hand on her shoulder but she didn't seem to notice. Beor looked around. "The rest of us must generate more prayer from the saints. The time of testing is coming and only prayer will help." A murmur of agreement followed. Spiritual light flooded the small church. Outside in the shadows a pang of fear swept over Meddler as this occurred and the demon moved further back into the spiritual shadow.

Beor addressed Mushi another more feminine looking angel. "Ensure the leader of this congregation; Jake Pankhurst encourages them to pray!" His golden brown eyes narrowed and a brilliant glow enveloped his body as he spoke. "Friends, this will be a difficult and protracted battle. The enemy must not know our planning. Be strong for our Lord!"

"For our Lord!" echoed the gathering.

Beor organized a group of three messengers to exit through the back of the church with their swords drawn and radiating light.

When the two demons saw the movement they split up after a short argument. Meddler followed the angelic trio and the other demon tried to become less visible as he watched them disappear. As his eyes were on other things, he didn't see the main group of angels leave in the bright sunlight via the main door of the church, mingled in amongst the departing women.

At the ZPM metallurgical plant Joshua was looking resolute and mildly sorry for Kasper Prinsloo, Hendrik's sidekick. He had invited him in and offered him a seat. The enormous girth of the man combined with his obvious indignation at being squeezed into a chair that was suited to a lesser sized man, made Joshua think of adults sitting in kindergarten seats. He tried not to smile at the poor mans plight. The image wasn't helped when Joshua told him he was to be promoted to the time office and Kasper pleaded to be left on the metallurgical plant like a little boy arguing with his headmaster. However, his requests were falling on unsympathetic ears.

"You can ask to see Mr. Lurie if you're unhappy with your lot Kasper!" Joshua was saying. "This move is to protect you from angry workers who seem to consider your work here more problematic than useful. While I may or may not agree, one thing is certain; you could pick up trouble if you stay here. It is safer for you to be in administration and you will be getting an increase. You want that don't you?"

Kasper glared at Joshua then shuffled out to get the personal items from his office. Over the next hour or two he went passed Joshua's office window several times with boxes as he moved to his new office. Every time he went passed he studiously avoided looking in at Joshua.

Joshua completed the reports on his discussions and sent them off to personnel for inclusion in personal files. Then he closed his door and returned to his seat. He rotated so that only the back of his chair was visible through the window and closed his eyes.

For many minutes he prayed. He asked God to build up those who were Christians that worked for him. He pleaded with God to resolve the anger and hatred among the workers and certain parts of management. He begged the Father to call both Kasper and Hendrik into his storehouse. He asked for protection for Steve Kumalo. Finally exhausted and tired, but full of a quiet peace that seemed to radiate from within, he looked up through the window where the sun streamed in. In the warmth of the day he thanked the Father for his love.

CHAPTER THREE

Downtown in the center of Zinaville in small back office of the police station, Carl Lubber, the District Detective Officer, or DDO, as the Detective was known, looked as if he would be more at home on a beach with a surfboard than in an office.

He was lounging back in his chair talking into a telephone while dressed casually in a loose fitting red golf shirt and a pair of black pants. He smiled his infectious friendly grin that caused him to be the heartthrob of many of the local girls who would have liked the non-uniformed man to pay attention to them. Carl enjoyed his freedom and so was on friendly terms with most of the girls, skillfully evading any serious relationships with the ease brought on by many years of happy practice.

Today the lady on the phone was getting the reward of these years of polite interactions. However Carl's frown and wrinkled up nose showed dislike for the conversation.

"Yes Ma'am, I understand fully. You saw a man grab a hobo and bundle him into a car outside Priggles Bar. Yes! Yes! You gave your name to the constable. Yes! Did you give him your statement? Ok! Yes, we will be working on it. No, we do *not* have any leads yet! Yes! *Thank you! Good-bye!*"

Carl's neatly trimmed moustache twitched as he placed the phone down less than softly. "Ms. Public Awareness," he muttered. "I wonder if she knows how many crimes against tax paying citizens I have to deal with?"

"Gerhard, do you know anything about a hobo that went missing?" he asked the constable at the desk alongside.

The constable smiled. He knew Carl Lubber well and respected him. Carl's gruff manner was normal when he was under pressure and he was under pressure now. The town had more than its normal share of criminals to contend with. The turbulent political change in the country had not left Zinaville untouched as it dragged citizens from the apartheid to non-apartheid era and criminals capitalized on the instability for their own purposes.

The pile of papers that were almost falling out of his in tray by their sheer numbers reflected the detective's caseload. The constable half tossed a folder across to his desk.

"Don't do that!" growled Carl. "The papers fall out all over my desk."

They hadn't this time. He grabbed the folder and flipped through it.

He paused and read one page more thoroughly.

"Hey! Gerhard! It sounds like the hobo was Brandy Bob. Did you read this?"

Gerhard looked sarcastically at Carl. "Who do you think took the statement?" he asked.

Brandy Bob was a well-known hobo. Carl knew him as a slight built man with a high forehead and long gray hair that concealed his ears as it straggled its way to his shoulder. He was as seasonal as the summer itself. When the months were warm, Brandy Bob floundered around the town sipping from a bottle that gave him his name. He was always extremely polite to everyone whose path he meandered across. A soft smile rarely left his face but the emptiness in his bright blue eyes never relinquished their hold on the pain of his life. He wore a threadbare sports jacket that surprisingly stayed clean but seemed to gather more holes and patches each year.

In winter he hitchhiked down to warm coastal weather. He was memorable as hobos go. Spoke the street slang with the rest but when he was locked up occasionally, he insisted in conducting his defense in absolutely faultless English or Afrikaans as the situation dictated. During these occasions his handling of the law was exceptional. His reason for being on the streets was unknown. Rumor had it that he was actually an attorney who had lost his family, a few tough cases and then his fight with the bottle.

Carl liked the scruffy character and felt a bit concerned for him. He knew nobody would want to forcibly remove Brandy from the town, and felt sure that he would not have caused trouble. He wasn't the type! The thought of someone kidnapping him was laughable! Brandy didn't have any known relatives and certainly had no money other than that which he got by begging and pushing shopping carts to cars in the car park.

"I'm going out for a while Gerhard. Hold the fort till I get back."

Gerhard hardly looked up to nod, as Carl went out. The police station was just a block away from Priggles Bar. Carl decided to walk. Half a block later, he saw two other hobos sleeping under a tree in a municipal park. He strolled over to them and nudged one with his foot.

"Oops sorry!" he said and pretended to trip over the elderly chap. The hobo sat up.

"Don't worry 'bout me mister," he said. "I'm tough enough. How come you didn't see me? Bad eyes? A whole park and you kick me. Humph!"

Carl grinned. "It's the only way to make sure you're alive," he quipped. "Say, I'm looking for Brandy Bob. Seen him?"

The hobo scratched in his beard and his bright blue eyes peered up at Carl inquisitively. "What might you be looking for Brandy for?" he asked.

"There's a lady concerned about him," Carl said. "Wants to make sure he'll be around to push her carts tomorrow. Seen him?" he lied.

The hobo ignored the question and poked the snoring body alongside him in the ribs. "Hey! Wake-up! You seen Brandy?" he yelled.

The other hobo was obviously the worse for wear. Only after the third thump did he roll over. His glazed eyes flickered to life momentarily and he slurred something Carl didn't quite hear. The hobo turned to Carl. "Nope! Haven't seen him since last Friday"

Carl thanked the old man and continued walking to Priggles Bar. Now he felt sure something was amiss!

The pub lunch crowd had gathered at the popular bar that reeked of beer and French fries. Carl elbowed his way through the throng to the counter and had to wait for a while until he was served. A new barmaid that he didn't know was serving drinks. Her beauty was offset by her apparent inability to smile.

Looking as if Atlas himself was sitting on her shoulder she finally got around to serving his side of the bar.

"*Kan ek jou help?* Can I help you?" She asked.

"Yes please, could I have some orange juice?"

She looked surprised, but poured some juice from a jug, took his banknote and went to get change. Carl looked around for Lofty the usual barman. There were too many people to be able to pick him out. The barmaid returned.

"Not too many people come here for juice" she remarked with raised eyebrows.

"Possibly," remarked Carl. "Some of us have rules we follow. You seen Lofty today?"

She nodded and pointed to the far corner of the room where a few alcoves were provided for the more business-oriented clients.

Carl left the coins on the counter and strolled over to where she had indicated. The noise was less penetrating in this area and he found Lofty in the furthermost alcove sitting with a friend sipping a beer.

Lofty was probably one the smaller people in the room. His small egg shaped head was topped by dark brown hair that looked like it had been shaved around a pudding bowl. His ears were far too small for his head; his thick eyebrows complemented a large bushy moustache that underlined a large and reddish nose. Lofty may not have looked the smartest but he was known for his fiery temper and sharp tongue. Very few men wanted to anger him as he was notorious with a broken bottle, the reason Carl had first met the small dynamic man.

"Afternoon Lofty, mind if I join you for a few seconds?"

Lofty's lopsided grin showed he actually did mind. He knew Carl would join anyhow, so he motioned for Carl to sit.

"Carl, meet Zack. Zack, this is our disreputable detective who is again sniffing around my bar. What are you looking for this time Carl?"

Carl shook Zack's hand.

"Lofty, I had a report that Brandy Bob was hanging around outside Priggles last week. Are you aware of it?"

Lofty sniffed and looked disinterested. "Yes, I have had such a crowd in here over the last week. He was helping cleaning the floors in the mornings. I paid him with a half pint of brandy as usual."

Lofty paused and looked a bit quizzical. "He stopped coming around here for no reason at all. I presume he either got himself locked up in your cells or had found another source of booze. Why do you ask? What has happened to him?"

Carl told him of the reported incident and got told that Brandy had last been seen Wednesday morning. Having got the information he wanted, he excused himself and left, stopping off at the home of the lady who had seen the incident. She lived across the street in an apartment on the first floor. Her only addition to her story was that the man who had bundled Brandy into the car had pocketed his half jack of booze as well. Carl could imagine how much *that* had angered the old guy.

Walking back to the station Carl pondered on what he had heard. He couldn't imagine why someone would want to abduct a hobo. "Someone had," he acknowledged. This case intrigued him. It just didn't make sense. "What value could someone find in abducting a useless drunk?" he thought.

Carl resolved to try to find out more.

CHAPTER FOUR

Later that evening the Robyn family was sitting around the dinner table having a discussion. Joshua had just recounted the activities of the day to his father and the old man was giving him advice; "Josh, beware of upsetting Hendrik. Remember my experiences at the Palaborwa Mining Company. He is an evil man who is very familiar with trumping up charges against people. Remember that when I refused to be dishonest and allow him to make illegal money from the mine, he made my life a misery there. You were a youngster at the time but you must remember how for months on end, he made sure I did all those extra shifts at night, and he even organized that my leave was canceled. It was due to him that I finally left that mine. Be very careful of that man my son!"

Joshua nodded and looked at his Mom. She was looking very serious. "How are you going to protect that black man, Mr. Kumalo?" she asked. What if he takes offense to what you did and decides to beat Mr. Kumalo? How will you stop that happening? You know he has friends that help him!"

"I have warned him that he is personally responsible for Steve and so I don't think he will touch him Mom," answered Joshua. "I agree that I'll have to keep tight control of our friend, Mr. van Vuuren. Perhaps he'll learn from this experience."

Bryan looked dubious and Karen looked hopeful. She suggested they take their problems to the Lord. They prayed for Hendrik, Steve, Tom and the whole work situation. Bryan prayed that he would be permitted to work for another two years to build up his pension. Karen prayed for her son. Standing in attendance were Beor, Tabitha and Tola. They loved to hear the sound of the humans praising and praying to God, but couldn't understand why their charges spent so little time in the activity.

A few days later, Joshua and Tom were invited for a drink in town by a salesperson selling metallurgical equipment. They ended up at Priggles sitting in an alcove similar to the one Lofty and Zack had sat in a few days before. A live band in one corner of the pub cranked out some local songs and Joshua was thankful the music wasn't too loud.

Tom and the salesperson gulped beers as Tom related some of his well-worn sailor stories. Joshua had heard them all before, but was smiling and nodding in all the right spots. The salesman was apparently eager to hear them and Tom was in his element telling them. Joshua was totally bored and after completing his third Coca-Cola, decided he would buy a round for the others and leave.

Lofty was behind the bar counter and a new barmaid that Joshua hadn't seen before, circulated, serving the clients in the alcoves and tables scattered around the room. He waved her over to their table impressed by her good looks. Her long black hair flopped across her face as she bent down to take his order. But it was looking into her eyes that startled him. He didn't expect the emptiness he saw in them. It was like looking into the cold emptiness of space, but in some way it seemed to accentuate her beauty, making it more remote and untouchable. Joshua wondered what could cause such emptiness.

He ordered a round of drinks and she mentioned that for further rounds they have to get Lofty to serve them. This was her last order of the evening. Tom caught Joshua's attention again. He was explaining how they were having labor problems on the plant and wanted Joshua to describe the situation to their companion. Joshua was half way through his exposition when the drinks came. He paid for them, leaving a large tip for the barmaid. After he completed his story he excused himself leaving a mildly inebriated Tom to deal with the salesman.

The cool night air was refreshing as he stepped outside. The stars were bright and the soft warm breeze wafting along was reminiscent of a sea breeze on a summer evening. His car was parked directly outside the pub. Climbing into the driver's seat, Joshua started to put the key in the ignition when he heard the sound of a motorcycle roaring to life almost directly behind his car. He turned around in his seat just in time to see it shoot past without its lights on and almost collide with someone who had stepped into the road.

The person stumbled backwards and fell badly. Joshua rushed to help, only to find it was the barmaid who had fallen, hitting her head on the edge of the curb. She was lying very still. Checking her pulse, Joshua looked around for someone to help. The street was deserted.

He put his hand under her head to lift her into a more dignified position and felt a warm stickiness. His handkerchief became a pressure pad to stop the blood, and realizing she needed to be taken to the hospital, he carefully positioned her head on the sidewalk so the handkerchief would still apply some pressure, and opened his car door. Reclining the seat as far as it would go, he covered it with a rug he had handy. He lifted her into the passenger seat. She was lighter than he had first expected. The car's interior light showed that she would probably need a few stitches. The blood flowed immediately he lifted the handkerchief. Joshua thanked the Lord that he had always kept his first aid experience updated and pressed down again. About a minute later she came to. For a second she almost panicked, but then she recognized him from the bar and relaxed.

"*Wat het gebeur?*" She asked.

Joshua realized that she was muddled forgetting that he spoke English. Quietly he told her what had happened. She took the handkerchief from him and held it against her head herself, peering into the vanity mirror to see the damage. She couldn't see it though!

"I think you will need stitches," said Joshua. "Shall I drive you to the hospital?"

She smiled. Joshua wondered why she didn't smile more often. It changed her whole appearance. A sparkle lit her eyes momentarily before extinguishing just as quickly to be replaced by her now familiar bland countenance.

"Thank you, I would appreciate that," she said quietly.

It took them a few minutes to get to the hospital. Joshua helped her inside to the emergency room. In the waiting room Joshua sat reading a magazine as the night staff took her particulars. Finally she gestured for him to follow her and the nurse gave them directions to the doctor's room. Joshua suddenly realized he didn't even know her name.

"By the way, my name is Joshua; you can call me Josh if you like."

The barmaid laughed and Joshua again found himself responding warmly.

"True, I did need to know your name. That nurse assumed you were my husband and I had to correct her. I didn't even know enough to explain the situation to her. I think she thinks we were having a fight and you hit me. I told her that was not the case but she looked dubious. I hope I haven't embarrassed you or got you into trouble with your wife." She paused and that smile lit up the room again.

"Thanks for your help Joshua, I'm Susan."

Joshua explained he would like to make sure she was fine before he left. Quietly he gave thanks for the unfortunate incident that had brought them together.

As they walked down the passage chatting and looking for the doctor's room they would have been amazed if they could have seen the spiritual forces accompanying them. Beor, close to Joshua, was fending off a horde of demons with the help of another angel. The demonic crowd seemed to be accompanying Susan. They taunted the angel continually, but didn't appear to want to use force against him. Their hands didn't drift to their swords and their eyes continually flicked as they watched Beor's sword hand that rested lightly on its hilt.

Beor could feel the power of the prayers Karen had offered up for her son that morning and almost wished the demonic crowd would try their luck. Picking on him could shorten their path to Hell considerably. Unfortunately he doubted they would give him that chance.

The doctor examined the wound and asked a few questions. He gave Susan a local anesthetic and then stitched the wound closed. A lock of her beautiful hair was cut away to enable him to work but it wasn't visible once she stood upright again. The rest of her hair covered the wound that was low down on the back of her head.

The doctor was concerned about a possible concussion and he tried to persuade her to stay in hospital but she reacted badly to the suggestion becoming upset. She was about to argue with the doctor when Joshua suggested that he would keep her under observation for the next few hours if the doctor was in agreement.

Susan looked much happier with that suggestion and when the doctor consented to the arrangement, the matter was settled. As they left, Joshua suggested they go somewhere for a meal. Susan agreed on the condition she could go home first to change her clothes.

Her apartment was on the second floor of a drab looking building without an elevator. Joshua offered to wait in the car but she insisted that he accompany her, using the excuse that he had to keep an eye on her. The apartment was simple but carefully furnished and he appreciated the elegance of the place. Settling into a chair he started to read a magazine as he expected she would take a while, only to be surprised by the speed with which she returned. Her red dress revealed her shoulders and he thought she looked exquisite. His complement was waved aside as Susan commented, "Well Josh, at least it won't show blood if the wound comes open again"

They went to the edge of town to a small restaurant called 'The Ox Wagon' which served traditional South African meals. Joshua ordered *sosaties* for them both. The meat arrived spiked on four sticks together with an assortment of spiced vegetables and fruit. It was delicious! They ordered some white wine and talked about the accident. However, when Joshua broached the subject of her work at Priggles, it was if she didn't hear him. After his second attempt he decided it was taboo and avoided the subject.

At eleven thirty, the staff started clearing up in an obvious manner so Joshua suggested they leave. He took her home and she invited him up for coffee. He left her apartment after one thirty feeling invigorated. He couldn't remember when he had enjoyed himself so much. He went home with a feeling of excitement that caused his mind to spin with glowing thoughts of her and the possibility of a developing relationship.

CHAPTER FIVE

The next day at the police station Carl explained his findings regarding Brandy Bob to Gerhard.

"Gerhard, this whole darn thing is worrying! Brandy Bob wouldn't have turned down the offer of a half-jack of brandy from Lofty! You know how he always wanders around with the other hobos and he almost never leaves town at this time of the year! I think he *was* abducted although I can't imagine why!"

Gerhard looked at Carl dubiously. "Do you really think that it's worth chasing after a story by an overwrought woman about a drunk?"

Carl's face showed he did. Gerhard disapproved but wasn't going to tell his superior so directly.

"Gerhard it's the manner of his disappearing that is so peculiar! Maybe it's a threat to others in the town. I think I need know where he is."

Gerhard still looked disapproving and Carl decided to ignore his bad humor. For the next hour or so he phoned most businesses in town. He concentrated on the liquor stores, hotels and anywhere hobos might hang out. Then he started to phone the local drinking clubs that were located in the black suburb out of the town. He called the *shebeens*, that was the name the locals gave the illegal clubs out of town. The owners were amused to find the police asking them for help. Not all of them helped! They had too often born the brunt of police raids and now enjoyed returning the unpleasantness. Nevertheless, after a few hours Carl was certain that Brandy Bob wasn't anywhere to be found. His last call was to the local morgue, which also turned up nothing.

Carl went out for a bar lunch at Priggles and returned about one-o-clock to find a message to contact his Brigadier. He couldn't think why such a high up person would be calling him. However, he put through the call as ordered and heard the gruff voice on the other end of the line.

The Brigadier curtly pointed out that he'd heard that Carl was not getting through his caseload effectively enough. He insisted that Carl get Gerhard to help him.

"You are not to spend time chasing hobos! This isn't helping law and order in Zinaville!" he emphasized.

When he put the phone down Carl was livid. A glance to Gerhard showed him with his nose buried in administration tasks. "A little too deeply," thought Carl.

He pondered who had known about Brandy Bob's disappearance. How had the Brigadier heard about it? Why was it such a matter of importance to drop the case? Carl looked at Gerhard again. He was sure the only person who could have brought the situation to the notice of the Brigadier was Gerhard. He wondered why? Taking the Brigadier's advice he turned to Gerhard. He handed him a third of the files from his own tray and enjoyed the look of pain on the other man's face.

"Brigadier's orders! You're to become an assistant detective for the next while. Here is your caseload. Have fun!"

Gerhard looked less than impressed. Carl grinned knowing the work would keep the constable's nose out of his business for the foreseeable future. Then he got up and walked out.

"What had happened to Brandy Bob and why is this little hobo so seemingly important?" he wondered again somberly as he left the police station.

CHAPTER SIX

The ZPM afternoon shift cleared away the leftovers from maintenance work that morning, as Hendrik was doing his rounds at the metallurgical plant accompanied by Steve Kumalo.

There were some problems plaguing the plant and causing a mess where the ore from the mining operation came into the plant on a long conveyor.

Normally the conveyor dropped its load of ragged rocks, most of them larger than a man's head, into a crusher on top of a silo from where they were redistributed. Today there were problems! Hendrik had ordered the belt delivering the rocks be sped up to increase tonnage through the plant. He was still not happy. Steve watched as Hendrik came as close as he could to swearing at the workers. He demanded more tons before the night shift came on.

Steve was at his wits end having spent the past few days accompanying Hendrik. However there was nothing tangible that he could report about Hendrik's performance. He was too clever and this latest incident was a case in point!

The production figures for the mine were better than the previous month's for the work in progress, but Hendrik was deliberately pushing the workers to produce even more. Steve knew it was Hendrik's job and if he complained about it, he would be wasting his time. Steve also knew the workers resented being stressed in this way and wanted him to do something about it. He hated the position he found himself in. He disliked Hendrik who continually humiliated him in front of management and his peers. His own position was becoming tenuous with the workers who considered him a sell-out to management.

This latest call for more tons had been a fiasco designed to make the workers work harder to achieve the same results and Steve knew it! The loading of the conveyor with more tons of rocks resulted in the conveyor starting to slip every few hours. When this happened, huge rollers that pinched the conveyor to pull it upwards lost traction and the belt either stopped or started to slip backwards. Then the motors had to be turned off and the rocks allowed to drop onto the floor at the base of the conveyor. When the belt started again, the workers had to reload the belt with the rocks that had piled up onto the floor. This was done with hands and shovels. As if the work was not bad enough, Hendrik was screaming and shouting at them continuously. The result was that despite the higher loading and belt speeds, about the same amount of ore was being deposited into the silo over the shift. The only difference was that the workers were working five times harder than normal and were being demoralized at the same time.

Steve knew this was Hendrik's way of getting back at the workers legally and he hated him for it. The workers were getting tired and accidents were likely to happen. To add to this, people had to walk long distances to go around the conveyor as the rock blocked the small bridge over it. This annoyed people and tempted them to cross the moving conveyor. This was illegal and likely to have disastrous consequences if people got frustrated and did it anyway.

The heat and dust was oppressive! Hendrik's voice urging the workers to work faster was irritating and Steve decided that he would speak to Tom Lurie about the situation when he got a chance. An informal discussion describing what Hendrik was doing would suffice. He wanted to address the amount of overseas faxes the foreman seemed to be getting. Hendrik seemed to be very secretive about them and flew into a rage if anyone even dared to look at a fax that was addressed to him. He had arranged that only he had the key to the fax room and he collected faxes himself at least five times a day. Those not for him he handed out for general distribution. This activity made Steve curious. It was a lot of extra work to deliver the faxes and not the type of activity the foreman would normally want to do. This needed to be looked into as well.

Steve reflected again on the way Hendrik dealt with the workers as he heard him shouting at another man. Possibly Tom could do something about the situation. Steve knew he couldn't go to Joshua. Hendrik would become even worse if Joshua was involved. Somehow when those two met it brought out the worst in Hendrik. The bad temper seemed to last for hours afterwards and the last thing Steve wanted was more trouble of the type Hendrik was dealing out.

Back in the metallurgical offices Joshua was trying to get a telephone call through to Priggles Bar. It seemed as if everyone in town was trying to call. The phone was continuously busy. He had been thinking of Susan all day. As a strong Christian he didn't want to get involved with a woman who didn't know Jesus as Lord but he couldn't put her out of his mind. Her face kept creeping into his thoughts. He tried praying that he would forget her but some small voice seemed to disagree, so finally he gave up the fight and had decided to give her a call.

The phone was busy and Joshua realized it was probably people betting on the horses, as he always suspected the bar had an illegal trade in that area. He then decided that rather than call, he would surprise her with a visit to the bar. Locking up the office he drove into town to Priggles.

Friday afternoon at Priggles was a rowdy boisterous occasion. A mixture of miners, farmers, gamblers and local townsmen combined to banter with one another telling jokes and stories and arguing about anything that took their fancy. The sour smell of beer and sweat mixed with cigarettes made Joshua feel queasy. He wished Susan worked in a more pleasant environment. This wasn't a place he liked to frequent.

She was very busy and didn't have time to do more than nod when she saw him. Lofty took his order and he sat at the bar waiting to get a chance to speak to her. The barman shook his head as filled the glass with coca-cola. "You want to try something a bit more exiting than Cola next time!" he asked Joshua rhetorically.

Finally after half an hour Susan slipped onto a bar stool alongside Josh and he felt that surge of excitement that she generated inside him when she was near. "Hi," she said, looking around, "I guess it's still busy but I'm glad you dropped by!"

Josh felt a rush of warmth for her and smiled. "Listen," he said, "do you want to see a movie tonight?"

"Oh, Josh! I've got to work 'til midnight tonight! I've got tomorrow evening off, though. Would that work?" she asked hopefully.

"How 'bout going somewhere tomorrow?" he asked.

They arranged a time to meet and Joshua left to spend the evening alone, disappointed but realizing that her work would probably often conflict with his free time.

CHAPTER SEVEN

A few blocks away at the police station, Carl was busy. He'd been having trouble ever since he had started to try to find Brandy Bob. That whole week his superiors had been calling to find out why there wasn't more progress with the other cases. Gerhard wasn't overly helpful and to top it all, it seemed as if the Brandy Bob file had gone missing!

This Friday Carl planned to spend his evening reconstructing the file. This way he couldn't be infringing any departmental orders and he planned to go to the lady who had reported the incident. He started by looking up reports with references to hobos, collected over the past three years on the department computers. There were many! He located a hundred and twenty three entries, most of them referring to the same events from different perspectives. A summarizing screen showed about thirty incidents. Most were of drunk and disorderly behavior that bothered law-abiding citizens.

Glancing through the records he found one other incident that might be related. A drunk by the name of Toby had been causing trouble in the street for several days about a year ago. Toby had been warned by the police to stay away from the area. Later a member of the public had reported Toby to the police again. They arrived to remove him from the area to find he had already been removed. A group of men had come and bundled him into a car. The similarity was tenuous but it was there.

Completing his search he locked the office and said goodnight to the duty officer on his way out. The station was quiet but he knew that soon it would start to get busy. It always did on a Friday! It was as if a warm breath of evil flooded the town on these evenings bringing with it minor assaults, complaints and various other incidents. Carl decided to walk to the block of apartments where the witness lived. It was invigorating strolling in the cool evening air. He climbed the stairs instead of taking the elevator and knocked at the door of her apartment, number 27.

She opened the door almost immediately but when she saw whom it was, her face changed from pleasant anticipation to alarm. Instinctively she seemed to want to close the door. She didn't however and when he asked if she would repeat her statement to replace the missing one, she refused. He felt she was scared. When he pressed her a second time, she simply said she wasn't interested in bothering about a hobo's problems and closed the door. Carl stood in the hall for a second. He was completely confused. This woman who had plagued him to do something about the incident was now acting as if nothing had ever happened. He couldn't understand why!

Carl crossed the street to Priggles to get hold of Lofty. At least he was able to give Carl a statement and helped without any coercion. Reassured, Carl slowly sipped his beer watching the progression of a dart game. He wondered again why the woman had felt it necessary to retract her statement. Wanting to take another look around, he finished his beer and crossed back to the apartment building. This time knocking on doors of the neighbors and asking if they had noticed anything the day Brandy had disappeared. They had neither seen nor heard anything unusual over the period. He was about to leave, when he saw the night watchman standing outside some garages near the end of the property. Maybe he could help? He strolled down to where the man was standing.

"Hi, a bit of a cool evening," he commented. "Are you on duty every evening?"

The black watchman smiled and his teeth shone in the dim light.

"No, Sir. I'm only on duty here every second week. This is my week 'on' Sir."

Carl smiled. "Tell me, have you noticed anything different this week? Sorry, I didn't get your name..."

"Sipho, Sir."

"Sipho, did you notice anything different this week?"

Sipho nodded seriously.

"Yes Sir, I did. It got me into trouble because I didn't see who messed up the garage door of the lady from number 27."

Carl perked up immediately. "The lady from number 27 you say?"

"Yes Sir! Somebody must have sneaked in here when I went on a smoke break. When I got back, there was a drawing in red. The red stuff was thrown all over her garage door, and they stuck a note under the door."

"Was it paint?" Carl wanted to know.

"I'm not sure sir, could have been paint but I think it was blood from a chicken or something. The light is poor in this part at night you know..." he looked at Carl as if he was worried he had said the wrong thing.

Carl was now extremely interested. "What did you do then?"

"It was early in the morning, about one thirty," he showed Carl what appeared to be a new watch. "I picked up the note and washed the garage door down with water as best I could in the dark. In the morning I gave the note to the lady when she came to the garage and told her what had happened. She was very upset! I think she told my boss because he told me I must be more careful in future or I would loose my job."

"What happened to the note?" Carl wanted to know as he noted the company name on the night watchman's lapel.

"I gave it to the lady, Sir." The watchman considered the question superfluous and it showed.

Carl nodded. "What was drawn on the door?" he queried.

The watchman went over to where there was some loose sand in a lighted area and drew the picture with a stick he found.

"Thank you Sipho, I am a police officer. I may call on you to come to the police station so that I can take your statement. Would you mind?"

When Sipho said this would not be a problem, Carl turned and started to walk back to his home, several blocks away.

He couldn't help wondering if the woman's refusal to co-operate was linked to the incident. Evidently someone was going to a lot of trouble to keep him from finding out what had happened to Brandy Bob. What bothered him was the source of the pressure. It was as if someone knew of his activities and was trying to block the Brandy Bob investigation.

Carl at least knew this red stuff on the garage scenario wasn't new to Zinaville. There had been numerous reports of it over the past few years. It appeared to be some group of kids who were mixed up in heavy metal music but he had been unable to find out exactly where they came from. They had painted it in the form of the AC/DC sign similar to the one groups album cover. Also a swastika and signs with a moon and star had been found previously. This was the first case of a note being left behind. Previously he had written off the occasions to teenage pranks. Suddenly he wasn't so sure. He got an idea that he should call in at Rev Brenan, the Anglican minister on his way home. The reverend had tried helping him with youth before so maybe he would know something! The youth of the church may be a good place to start the investigation. He walked the few blocks to the rectory.

Frank was at home and the sound emanating from the open door indicated that he was watching television. Surprise fleetingly crossed his face when he saw Carl, but he invited him in with a smile. The Brenan's home was old fashioned, but exuded an air of warmth and comfort. In the living room, Carl settled into a large armchair that sighed as it took his weight.

Carl didn't know how to introduce the subject to Frank. So he started by simply talking about the church activities while organizing his thoughts. Finally he began to tell Frank of the strange circumstances surrounding Brandy Bob's life and disappearance. The Reverend listened intently.

Frank sat for a while after Carl had finished speaking and thought. When he spoke it was in a careful tone.

"Carl, I agree the disappearance of Bob is strange but as I didn't even know him, I can't be of much assistance. I'll keep an ear open amongst my congregation for any news that may help you but I must say the change in attitude of your witness and the circumstances surrounding the change are much more interesting to me. Maybe I'm wrong, but I think a mild form of witchcraft or Satanism has influenced these people who have been painting the garages. Maybe there's a spiritual side to the situation?"

Carl found this an approach to the problem that he had not considered previously. He nodded.

"My guess is this," continued Frank. "The people who placed the blood or paint on the garage are more than just a group of teenagers having fun. Possibly it started this way, but someone in the group knows something of occult matters. Those signs that you saw are not random. I want you to tell me if the moon and star looked like this." He picked up a pencil and paper and then drew a quarter moon with a five-pointed star slightly above and to the left of it. The star was almost at the top of the curve of the moon. Carl nodded.

"This is a sign reported to be used in white and black magic cults," said Frank. "It is a combination of symbolism for the goddess Diana and that of Lucifer. The heavy metal rock group name AC/DC that was painted on some garages, is often reported to be short for Antichrist/Devil's child by those who oppose this group. The Swastika is used to denote nature out of harmony. All these signs have at one time or another been connected with occult practices. Unfortunately I know very little about this sort of thing other than what I have told you. One thing I do know however, an investigation into these types of things will be more successful if accompanied by prayer."

Carl was disturbed and uncertain. This was a totally unexpected development and could be construed to be a bit crazy as well! Frank wasn't the type of person to be crazy. This was *really* strange! The routine investigation of a disappearance of a person was now developing sinister connotations. He spent the next hour drinking coffee as the Reverend found odd articles about occult happenings and read them to him. What he heard made him feel uneasy about the reliability of the journalists that had reported them. On the off chance that they were true, he was glad that these types of practices were against the law in South Africa. He went home much wiser but more worried than when he had left the police station earlier that evening. He found himself wondering how you fight an unseen enemy. He hoped this wasn't going to turn out to be a more difficult case than he had initially imagined.

It felt like it already had!

CHAPTER EIGHT

It was beautifully sunny the next day. At ten-o-clock Joshua pulled up outside Susan's apartment to fetch her for their day together. He knocked expecting Susan and was completely shocked to see Hendrik van Vuuren open the door.

Hendrik was equally as surprised to see him. They both stared at one another in stunned amazement for what seemed like minutes. Finally Susan's voice came from inside asking who was at the door. Hendrik answered in Afrikaans and brusquely invited Joshua in only when Susan said she was expecting him. His attitude was one of mild anger and annoyance. He wasn't happy about the situation and it showed.

Susan, brightly dressed in light yellow, was ready to leave. She greeted Joshua warmly and then said good-bye to Hendrik whom she addressed in Afrikaans as 'father'. Joshua was surprised for a second time in less than a few minutes. He hadn't known of the relationship between them! He managed to cover his surprise but knew that this unintentional relationship would add fuel to Hendrik's dislike of him. By the look on Hendrik's face, problems were likely to erupt soon. Joshua dodged them by leaving with Susan as soon as he could.

Once they were in the car he pointed out that her father was annoyed. Susan looked worried but discounted it remarking that probably her father had expected her to be at home while he fixed her plumbing. Apparently the drainage in her apartment was giving problems. Susan changed the subject by asking where they were going.

Joshua had planned a day at a game reserve viewing the wildlife of Africa but he wanted to surprise her and didn't want to tell her right away. Instead he told her he had a picnic lunch and that they would be away until five in the afternoon. Susan was worried because she had to start work again at six that evening. He promised he would have her back no later than five.

An hour and a half from town they drove into a small range of hills. They paid their entrance fee at a grass roof hut serving as the reception to the wildlife reserve. Maps were provided and the next few hours were spent looking at the wild animals from the comfort and safety of their vehicle. They saw several different types of antelope, elephants, giraffes and a white rhinoceros before it was time for lunch. Most of the time they talked and as the day drifted on, the talk and their attitudes became more intimate.

Early in the afternoon they made their way to a picnic area located away from the main dirt road along a track. It had a small brick washroom, a few wooden benches attached to tables and a lonely water pump set out in the veld grass.

Joshua pulled out a metal contraption that he unfolded and it soon developed into a receptacle for wood and paper. He packed it carefully and lit the kindling. Once the fire was going, he put the metal grid over it and started to prepare the food and meat for the barbeque. Susan helped with cutting up of some of the fruit. All the time they talked and joked. Finally when Joshua considered the embers to be right, he placed the meat on the grid to cook. Susan came over and slipped her arm around his waist. They stood there quietly as he turned the meat to roast on both sides.

They were enjoying each other's company in this way when they saw the kudu. It seemed to just appear without warning. The large horns caught the sun as the large regal looking male buck stood looking at them. The drone of the insects in the warmth of the day seemed to make the situation timeless. Then, just as suddenly, with a few quick bounds, the kudu was gone and they were alone again.

This seemed to unlock something in Susan and she started to cry softly. Joshua was most confused. Initially he thought she had burnt herself on the fire or was scared of the kudu, but when he asked her she shook her head. Then he thought it was something he had done. Again she shook her head. He simply held her tight and kissed away the tears. This seemed to make things worse and she cried even more. Finally he took her over to a wooden bench and sat her down waiting for her to stop crying.

"Hey! What's wrong Susan?" he asked as the crying reduced to a few sobs. "Why cry on a lovely sunny day like this?"

Susan looked at him sighing. "Today is one of the most beautiful days I can remember," she said. "I hate my life, I hate my work and most of all I hate things I have done in the past. Josh, I am not the nice a person you think." She started to cry again. "I am not sure I should even see you anymore. Father will make my life a misery! I just know it. I could see that the way he treated you this morning. I can't go against his wishes. He is too powerful. I could end up getting hurt. You too! Oh, Josh. I do really like you and appreciate what you've done for me, but I don't want my father to get angry with you!"

Joshua was both shocked and indignant.

"No Susan! Things can't be so bad! What you don't know is that your father works for me. I only found out who your father was this morning when I came to pick you up. I think that is why he is annoyed. Anyhow, you're independent! He can't make you do something you don't want to do. You're a free person!"

Susan fingered a leather thong that hung around her neck. "There's a lot you don't know Josh." She said. "You're wrong. My father can be really evil at times. I can't go against him. He has hurt me before, and can do it again. You can't understand." She looked down avoiding his eyes. Joshua disagreed. "Susan, there is nobody that can be that powerful. The only person who is all powerful is God himself."

Susan seemed to jerk upright as he said this. Her eyes became angry and even wild. Within their depth a flame seemed to glimmer for a second. The old Susan seemed to disappear behind this harsh exterior. "Don't talk to me about God! He tortures people with guilt and sin." She spat the words out. "'God' has never helped me once! Where was he when I needed him to protect me as a young girl? Where was he when my father beat me? When my mother died? When I had to get an abortion? God is for the weak and spineless! Don't talk to me about 'God'!"

Now Joshua was really upset and worried. His relationship with God was very special to him but he could feel her pain. He felt the love of God well up inside him and felt the presence of Holy Spirit speaking into his life. This Susan wasn't the Susan he knew so far and he felt sure it was not the true Susan. He decided to tackle the situation head on.

"Oh, stop that talk in Jesus name Susan!" He said with quiet authority and then his mood softened as he tried to explain. "I have had a personal relationship with that God for a long time and I have never, ever, found Him to be anything less than loving and kind. I'm not undervaluing the horrible nature of what 's happened to you, but I do know that if you'd met the God I know, you would not be as angry with Him. He can definitely help you." Joshua put his arm around her. "Possibly you have been misled about who God is. Someone has pointed you to an imitation of God and not to God himself." Joshua's tone changed to a lighter note. "Come now! Today is a lovely day. Please let's enjoy it together?" He spoke more seriously. "These depressing thoughts are not welcome on this picnic day. Today is for you to enjoy. Chase them away and don't let them bother you again."

Suddenly he caught the smell of burning meat and had to rush over to take it off the fire. When he returned Susan had wiped her tears and was looking a little better. He put his arm around her shoulders and she relaxed against him. "Feeling a bit better now?" he asked.

"Yes, sorry I don't know what came over me" she said. "Josh, I am sorry I was so stupid. Please forgive me!"

Joshua smiled knowing he had never taken offense. "Of course!" he said.

They then attempted to enjoy their charred meal. The rest of the afternoon they spent in the cool shade of a hide, watching animals moving to and fro from the waterhole. Water buffalo came and went and warthogs played in the hot sun. Three giraffe came to drink and Susan had to stifle a laugh at the way they had to do the splits to get down to the water. It was a grand African afternoon, with heat, the dusty smell of warm vegetation and the cavorting of the animals as could only be viewed from their hideout overlooking the waterhole. At three-o-clock they left to go back to Zinaville and by the time Joshua dropped Susan off at home, they were as intimate as two new lovers should be.

CHAPTER NINE

Joshua arrived home to find his phone was ringing. It was Tom Lurie! There was an emergency at the plant. An accident had occurred on number one conveyor leading out to the silos. Being responsible for the plant Joshua immediately drove out to the mine. On reaching the gate he saw that there was a police vehicle and an ambulance parked outside. Joshua knew then that the accident was serious. The security staff waved him through without even checking his identification.

As he drove around to the conveyor he could see a crowd had gathered. Tom had obviously arrived at the scene before him as his white Mercedes Benz was already parked in the shade of the building. Joshua got out and made his way over to where Tom was talking to Hendrik van Vuuren. He greeted both men and asked what had happened.

Hendrik answered first.

"This afternoon I was called into the plant because they were having trouble with the electrics of the motor on the conveyor. I phoned Mr. Kumalo and told him to meet me here. When I got here the conveyor was running and Mr. Kumalo was waiting at the bottom of the belt. We went to the top of the conveyor where we checked the motor and found it was operating correctly. Alongside the motor was an electrician's toolbox. The silo was filling quickly. We both looked around for the silo worker and for the electrician but I didn't see them! I decided to walk around under the silos. On my way to the mill building I saw the bloodied safety helmet come out of the silo onto the belt leading into the mill and then the chute jammed. I immediately stopped all the belts and called security. They called Mr. Lurie, you, the police and the ambulance."

Tom Lurie was looking at Joshua with pain in his eyes. He put his arm around Joshua.

"Josh, there is bad news. It was your dad that was called out to fix the motor. We're not sure where the safety helmet came from but it was a blue electrician's helmet and we can't find your father."

Joshua's legs nearly buckled under him as the implication hit. Tom's steadying arm was welcome for a second. He found he couldn't think clearly. The noise of the men offloading the rock out of the silo seemed to dim and the experience of life became hazy. He was not new to accidents, but this one was too close to home. It was his responsibility to help with the investigations. How could he do it that now?

Tom was speaking. "I've got a team of workers unloading the silo one rock at a time. That part of the plant will not be starting again until we understand what caused this. Josh, would you like to go home?"

Joshua shook his head. He wanted to find out what had happened.

"No thanks! I'd rather be here. Please, I think I need to sit down!"

They made their way over to Tom's car and they sat waiting.

Joshua was feeling sick. The shock drained him. How could this have happened?

They sat in silence for a while watching the men unloading the rock. Joshua mentally went over the statistics of the situation. The silo was three quarters full when they were putting fair tonnages through the plant. The past few days they had been pushing tonnage, and so the silo could have been fairly empty if the conveyor had stopped for a while. The fall into the silo would have been sufficient to kill someone unless they were very lucky. If that hadn't killed his father, the tons of rock raining down on him would have. Joshua didn't want to think of it! He turned his thoughts to the addressing the immediate situation.

"I saw the police and ambulance. Who is the police representative?"

"Detective Carl Lubber," replied Tom pointing to the detective. "That's him over there."

The detective saw Tom pointing and so he walked over to their car.

"You must be Joshua Robyn," he said as he greeted Joshua and then turned to Tom. "Mr. Lurie I've taken a few items from the scene as evidence if you don't mind?"

Tom explained that he expected this to happen and asked what was removed.

"The railing that was removed next to the motor at the top of the conveyor, a large heavy steel bar that you chaps have a name for..."

"A *gwala*, a type of pry bar!" Joshua helped him out with the term.

"Yes, the *gwala*, and the electrician's toolbox. We might find other items, but so far those and the helmet are all the evidence we have found. We also took fingerprints before the workers started unloading the rocks."

Joshua wondered which *gwala* was being referred to, and then remembered that the worker on top of the silo used different sized pry bars to push rocks into the center of the silo if they built up against the sides. They also used them to dislodge rocks in the jaw crusher at the top of the silo. He wondered where that worker was.

"Has anyone seen old Simon who works at the top of the silo and controls the conveyor belt?" He asked.

Tom looked perturbed. "No, I'll ask Hendrik." He shouted to Hendrik who came over. "Hendrik, have you seen Simon."

Hendrik looked puzzled for a second. "No, Mr. Lurie, I haven't," he replied. "Maybe he got a fright when the accident happened and ran away. You know how these men can be!"

Tom Lurie didn't appreciate Hendrik's attitude to the people that worked for him, but knew that Hendrik's supposition could be correct. Similar accidents had occurred in the past and they often found the missing man within a few hours. Usually in these cases they were drinking back as much of the local beer at the mine hostel as they could. "Ok, Hendrik. Maybe you could send someone down to the hostel to see if they can find him." Hendrik nodded and went off to carry out the instruction.

The team unloading the silo shouted in the local vernacular that they had found something. The men from the ambulance took a stretcher up the conveyor ramp to the top. Joshua didn't want to go and look. He waited, watching from below. A body bag was loaded onto the stretcher and soon they started walking down with it, and even before they reached the bottom, there was another shout. The workers had found something else. They continued removing rocks. The body that had been retrieved was brought to the ambulance.

Anxious, Joshua got out of the car and went over. A wave of nausea swept over him when he looked into the unrecognizable face and body of the dead man. It had been smashed beyond recognition. It was evident the man had fallen into the jaw crusher before falling into the silo. Rocks falling couldn't do the damage that the deceased had suffered. It wasn't his father however! The victim was a black man. They had found the elderly worker.

Joshua started to hope that somehow his father had been somewhere else. He was starting to persuade himself of this when he saw the red helmet. His hope dissolved. Workers used red helmets and the technical staff blue. A blue helmet had come out of the chute under the silo.

The ambulance men went back up the ramp with the stretcher and after ten minutes they could be seen loading something else onto the stretcher. Detective Carl Lubber accompanied the men back down to the ambulance. They tried to keep Joshua away but he forced his way to the body bag that was open, only to see the remains of the poor man's head. This time when Joshua looked at the face of the man there could be no mistake, it was his father! The shock hit so swiftly and so painfully that those around him hardly had time to react as he collapsed. They carried him to Tom's car, placing him on the back seat. A few minutes later he regained consciousness and sat up but his face was as white as a sheet. When Tom offered to drive him home, he accepted.

They moved Joshua's vehicle into the shade and Tom drove Joshua back to his home in his Mercedes. They left him at home after calling a doctor to come in to see him. Joshua didn't want this but Tom insisted.

Cavorting around the mine was a cloud of demons. Beor and Tola stood in the distance watching.

Tola, Bryan's guardian angel, had followed the Lord's instructions exactly and had not intervened when Bryan had been struck from behind with an iron bar. Demons, spurred on by evil Poneros, had worked themselves into a fever pitch resulting in both Bryan and old Simon being struck down.

The assailant had seen an opportunity to get rid of Bryan and the deed was done before he could think twice. Simon was a casualty of the circumstances!

The shrieks and screams of delight emanating from the foul contingent as the men tumbled into the silo were horrifying to hear. Their tone soon changed to fear however! Beor smiled. Both men had belonged to the Lord and it was their time to make the transition. The angels knew that this was another victory for the Lord! Like at Calvary, the offensive creatures had misjudged the outcome. Beor was amazed that they never predicted the results of their actions for themselves.

Even as they garbled their malevolent congratulations to one another, God's spiritual light erupted forth in the place. It blazed forth with a purity that drove every demonic spirit backwards. Written on their repulsive faces was the fear of the abyss that fueled their retreat. The glorious presence swept the spiritual darkness out of the area momentarily before fading.

Tola had been drawn forward to take Bryan's spirit, leading him to what appeared to be a fiery chariot and horses in the midst of the brilliance. This chariot was to transport Bryan through time and space to a place of rest. Another angel performed the same service for Simon. The angels in attendance passed out of the world of men in this last service to their charges. The manifestation of the light had dwindled and all that had been left behind were the inanimate bodies that were steadily crushed and covered by the tons of rocks raining down on them.

Tola had returned as soon as possible to the same locality and found Beor to get new orders. He could see that God's plan was developing fast. The prayers of the saints were mounting! Nevertheless an increase in prayer was needed to strengthen the spiritual forces for the Lord. Both Beor and Tola spent some time estimating the visible strength of the enemy before Beor started the next phase of the plan. He nodded to Tola, who sank into the ground to hide the glimmer of the departing light and streaked off through the earth towards the town. Beor waited a few more moments and then followed.

Once home Joshua wanted to scream with the hurt in his life. He couldn't go to his mother, as his vehicle was at the plant. He cried quietly to himself for a while and then picked up the phone and dialed through to his mother.

Karen answered the phone in a joyful way and Joshua could hear from her voice that she had been having a wonderful day and hadn't heard the news.

"Hi, Mom" he said. "Has your day been pleasant?"

Her voice acknowledged his guess and chattered on for a few moments. After a while she realized something was wrong when he didn't cut into her monologue. "Josh, what's wrong, why are you so quiet? Is that girl that you are seeing giving you a hard time?" she asked.

"No Mom, she is wonderful! Mom, I want to tell you this in person but I can't get to you. I don't have my car with me. I am really sorry Mom! I wish I could do something...rather I wish that I had. Mom, are you sitting down?"

There was a silence on the other end of the phone.

"Mom, are you OK?"

"Yes Joshua! I'm sitting down! Tell me what has happened. Is it your father?"

"Yes Mom, an accident happened at the plant. Dad was fixing a conveyor motor..." Joshua broke down and whimpered.

"Mom, Dad fell into a silo, he's no longer with us!"

There was silence except for Joshua's sniffing for a second and then Karen spoke again.

"Joshua, are you sure?" she asked in a choking voice.

"Yes Mom, I saw Dad myself. I'm sorry Mom!"

On both sides of the telephone line, mother and son cried. Tabitha and Beor stood by empathizing with their charges but in some ways unable to understand the pain. They viewed death very differently! Bryan's death had been a glorious calling to the Lord and a furthering of the kingdom of God. They knew that nothing these humans could imagine could compare with the wonder and joy that Bryan was experiencing now. The purpose of his life was concluded in those brief seconds. Nevertheless, they could see the pain in those they cared for and so supported their charges in this time of need.

Beor knew that the time for action was coming and was waiting for an indication of what must be done next. The silence between Joshua and his mother was pre-emptive and Beor looked at Joshua.

"Mom, meet me at the church" Joshua said suddenly. "I am going to walk down there now. I think we need to see Jake and to pray together. Will you do that?"

Beor knew the time had come to contact the others. The glittering membranous wings lifted him up and off to contact his companions.

Karen agreed to Josh's suggestion and they rang off. Joshua collected himself and was about to leave when the doorbell rang. When he opened it their family doctor greeted him.

"I am sorry to hear about your father Josh," he said. "Can I come in?"

Joshua invited him in and they spoke for a short time. The doctor left Joshua some tranquilizers, promised to do the same for Joshua's mother, and was off on his evening rounds within ten minutes. Joshua locked up the house and started walking to the church.

CHAPTER TEN

At the church Meddler was getting more and more worried. The demon could see that something was awry. One by one, angels were appearing from various directions, alighting at the entrance, and going into the church.

A pang of fear shook the rotund worm and it turned to its comrade. "Tell Kakoo that something is happening. We will need re-enforcements. Go!" The creature buzzed off at high speed, dodging trees and bushes and keeping low to avoid being seen. Now and then it paused as another streak of brilliance shot passed overhead.

Beor's word had reached far and wide. The coordinators were gathering at Zinaville Christian Church. The prayer warriors had been alerted. Tabitha had prompted Karen to phone the church prayer chain and ask for support. She had mentioned that she was meeting Joshua at the church. The prayer chain had worked fast. Within minutes half of the Zinaville Christian Church community had been contacted and informed. A torrent of prayer was generating that was even now drifting into the throne room of the Father. Angels were activated knowing their purpose was being fulfilled. Various angels coordinated groups that were spontaneously heading for the tiny church building.

Although the brilliance of each angel faded as they slowed and alighted on the church steps, there were so many in the small building that it emitted a spiritual glow. Meddler had pulled back further into the shadows considering what the forces within the building represented and shivering at the thought of the potential danger.

Joshua was nearing the church, when he saw a very old couple slowly climbing the stairs. Uncle Peter and Aunt Sannie had been there as long as he could remember. Uncle Peter, who could hardly see any longer, needed his wife to guide him. He was still a spiritual powerhouse despite this! The old couple was known for their prayer, discernment, and wisdom. As Joshua neared, Uncle Peter painfully climbed the last step into the church. Joshua couldn't even understand why the couple would be at the church at this time in the evening. He was glad however. Somehow he knew they would help ease the ache that pained his soul. The thought brought a lump to his throat again!

In the church, a group of their friends had gathered. Oddly different and almost out of place was an old black man whom nobody knew. He had just entered the church a minute or two before the first of the congregation and was sitting with his head bowed at the back. Joshua thought he looked vaguely familiar. Everyone was sitting quietly together and praying. Now and then, as someone else entered, one or two people would nod their greeting and then continue praying. Jake was sitting in the back row and greeted each person that entered.

Joshua was amazed to see how many people were in the church that Saturday evening. They didn't usually have a church service on Saturdays and he wasn't expecting to see anyone. He was so glad to see Pastor Jake! The two men hugged each other and Jake expressed his condolences. He pointed out that the people that were present had come of their own free will when they heard of the accident. He didn't know what had happened in the community but explained that everyone present wanted to join Karen and Joshua in prayer this evening. He inquired about the accident and Joshua told him what he knew as briefly as he could.

Again Joshua only just managed to stop the tears. He could see the kindly faces and feel their love as he made his way to his usual seat near the front. A few folk put their hands on his shoulder and gave him a squeeze, muttering their condolences as he went past. Soon Karen joined him. She just folded up against him and cried. How long they sat there he didn't know. After a while her sobbing reduced and he just held her tight. Jake moved to the front of the old church.

"Friends," he started. "Tonight has been one of tragedy for our beloved Sister Karen and her son Joshua. Bryan passed away in a mine accident. The love he has generated in this community is reflected in those of you sitting here tonight. No-body was asked to attend. You each felt led to come when you heard others were gathering. Praise God!"

A murmur of assent rose from the group. "Joshua, Karen, as painful as it is for you, would you allow me to explain what happened?" Both of them nodded and Jake gently explained the situation to those that had as yet not heard the details. He was ending his description of the accident when the old black man at the back of the church coughed rather loudly and came walking up the isle. Most present turned around annoyed at this interruption.

He made his way down to the front very slowly as if dreading his destination. When he got there, he almost bowed his large frame in submission to Jake.

"Sir, I have something to say, may I speak?"

His large brown eyes seemed to penetrate into Jake's soul as his white hair reflected in the overhead lights, creating the illusion of a halo over him. The interruption was most disturbing to those present!

Jake was obviously confused and didn't know what to do. The evening's activities were too different for him to comprehend. He nodded his consent.

The old black man seemed to be gathering words and assembling them into his message as he began to speak slowly.

"Thank you people, I am John Kumalo. Steve, my son, was present at the accident discovery. I love God as you do!"

He paused to collect his thoughts.

Joshua felt as if he had received a jolt of electricity. Now he understood his feeling of familiarity. Deep in his spirit he sensed that what this man would say was very important. He knew this man. This was Steve's father!

John Kumalo continued. "Neither Steve nor I have much respect for what you white people have done to us with apartheid." A few people in the pews obviously felt uncomfortable and squirmed a bit in their seat, "however, that has little to do with tonight. I have forgiven all of you long ago." He paused gathering the words again.

"Tonight, I was at home, watching my television, when my Steve came and told me of what happened. I switched off the television and suggested we pray. My Steve, he starts to cry. My Steve, he doesn't cry often, and so I am upset. We pray. My Steve, he asks God to show him who murdered Simon and Mr. Bryan."

At this there was a sudden collective gasp from those present. They had only heard of the incident as an accident. Karen, startled, went pale and Jake made as if to cut the old man off. But, before he could, Joshua's voice rang out clear and strong as he asked John Kumalo to continue.

John looked very sad as he glanced at the congregation and Jake. Then he lowered his eyes again and continued. "We prayed for a while and then I got a message from God in my spirit. His quiet voice tells me to find out what church Mr. Joshua belongs to. He tells me I must come here. My Steve, he knows this church and so he tells me how to get here. My Steve, he doesn't want me to come here. When I tell him what God says, he agrees. Here I am." John paused a minute. "God says this...!" John suddenly looked up and his penetrating brown eyes swept over the congregation momentarily as his large frame unfolded to its full height.

"Mr. Bryan is an electrician at the mine." he looked around at the crowd who weren't sure of where to look or what to do. "Mr. Bryan did not die in the accident. He was murdered! He was fixing equipment on top of the silo where the rocks are thrown in and he was pushed into the silo. This was wrong! The time is coming when his death will be understood. Blood was spilt on the ground and it calls to God. You must be strong! Times will be difficult! You must be strong! Do not fear those in authority, do not hate. Love! Pray! Support those who are hurting!"

John dropped his eyes again and subsided into a round-shouldered stoop that reduced his height to a less imposing presence. "Mr. Joshua, may God bless you Sir. I am very sorry that your father is gone. He was a good man! Thank you!"

With this he turned and slowly walked down the isle and out of the church. The people sat dumbfounded as he left. When someone finally moved and went to look for him, he was no longer in sight. The church member returned to his seat shaking his head to let the others know that he had been unable to find John.

Joshua felt shattered. His mind was in turmoil. He didn't know what to do.

"Why Dad?" His thoughts turned to his Mom who was crying with the shock of the words. She turned to him, pain in her eyes.

"Josh, can it be true? Who would do such a thing? Why Josh?"

As the others present sat in stunned silence waiting for his answer, Joshua's mind spun through the events. He remembered the detective's comments. Slowly he acknowledged the fact that murder was a possibility. He nodded.

"Possibly mom," he said. " I don't know why! However, there is a possibility it's true."

A murmur started amongst the congregated people. Someone rushed out to try and find John. People were obviously concerned for Karen and Joshua. Jake Pankhurst intervened suggesting that they pray. For the next hour, one after the other, people prayed for Karen and Joshua. They prayed that if murder had been committed that the person would be found. They prayed that the community they lived in would become less violent. They prayed until they subsided into a silence, each praying silently within his or her mind.

Finally Uncle Peter stood up. He asked Jake if he could say something. Jake agreed.

"Friends," he started. "I have been in Zinaville for many years. Never have we had such violence." Uncle Peter was already out of breath. "Please excuse me; I must sit as I talk." He sat down. Leaning forward he continued, "If we don't gather together to pray more for this town, it will get worse. Brothers and sisters, now is the time! May I suggest we get together once a week to pray as we have done tonight? Tonight we all came here because we know and love the Robyns and knew it was right to do so. Will it not be right to continue? Over the next few weeks the bikers will start to come to town for their annual Easter bike rally. You know that someone always gets hurt on these occasions. Shouldn't we continue to meet, praying for the town and for the discovery of Bryan's murderer?"

A murmur of assent was heard again. Jake asked if he could see a show of hands for those in favor. It was unanimous! In the spiritual world the angels watching gave thanks to the Lord. They knew that they were being equipped and that the small group of Christians formed a much needed prayer continuum in which they could work in freedom. The glow of the Spirit radiated amongst the powerful group of humans.

Joshua and Karen left with the first group of friends who offered help and advice. Old Uncle Peter and Aunt Sannie remained seated. They were exhausted! Jake came over to offer to drive them home. He brought his car around to the church side door to make it easier for them to leave. Soon the church was empty except for a throng of angels.

CHAPTER ELEVEN

In their enclave in the Magaliesburg Mountains the demons were cavorting in pleasure. Poneros had flopped onto a throne shaped rock and was displaying his ugly mass to the buzzing hordes around him. Kakoo was sitting glowering on a smaller similar structure to the right of Poneros. Several important demons surrounded them. The cave was lit by a group of five candles that had been placed on the points of a pentagram that had been drawn on the cave floor. This was the only light.

In the shadows men and women intently watched what was happening in the center of the pentagram. Around the pentagram was a circle. Poneros smiled at Incubus, the demon who had lit the candles. The humans were so impressed by his little show of power. Incubus was a short stocky male demon with pointed ears. Poneros reminded himself that this demon must not be underestimated. He had a lot of influence with the Master.

Tonight they were planning and preparing for both the black mass to be celebrated soon, and for the initiation night that would occur at the end of April. Located to the one side were a group of sixteen men and women dressed in black. One seemed to be in charge and they were discussing something that obviously caused hilarity. While they were talking a group of men appeared at the entrance of the cave. They entered and said something to the leader who laughed. Others joined in and in the spiritual world the demons surrounding them spun themselves into an even more frenetic cloud, grinning from ear to ear. The men continued talking. Suddenly out of the demonic group that had entered with the men, a small demon was kicked out in the direction of Kakoo.

Meddler's companion slid across the floor to halt in front of Kakoo with his wings buzzing as he regained his balance. Kakoo's red eyes locked on him. He lifted his eyebrows, querying the obviously terrified creature as to why he had been disturbed.

"Your Devilship I have news..." started the frightened worm. He glanced at Poneros in fear and relaxed when he saw the huge demon's eyes had closed and that he wasn't paying the slightest attention to the situation.

"...the Zinaville Christian Church is getting more and more attention from the enemy." He paused watching the affect of his words on Kakoo. Kakoo's eyes opened, narrowed and he waited. "Beor seems to be gathering the enemy in the church and it is gleaming with that painful light!"

Kakoo nodded and with a toss of his head told the messenger to leave. Relieved, the small demon shot out of the cave. Kakoo stood up and went over to Poneros.

"Uh! Um! Your Defilement," he called in a tone that would wake, but not anger Poneros. "The awaited news on your plan has arrived at last!"

He waited as the larger demon opened his eyes and settled more comfortably. "The second phase has occurred as planned!"

Poneros grinned.

"There are however some problems," Kakoo continued. "The Pankhurst community of the enemy is receiving more reinforcements and grows stronger daily."

Poneros glared pure hatred and Kakoo knew that he had said enough.

"That useless frightened Meddler!" roared Poneros and immediately the whole area quieted. The demons present settled quickly. They wanted to see the developments but go unnoticed.

"We will need to show him how to deal with such a group!"

Poneros turned to Kakoo. "I'll personally take that group of the enemy apart, wing by wing."

A roar of agreement rose from those present.

"Tomorrow we invade that church!" Poneros spat the words out and returned to his seat. Screaming and hooting followed. Soon the normal noise level resumed, indicating that the tension was over. Poneros who was still in a foul mood contemplated his plans.

CHAPTER TWELVE

On the edge of town, John Kumalo was getting home. He lived in a small brick cottage that he and his son rented from the land owners who had a magnificent house further along on the grounds. Steve had selected the cottage for its proximity to both the town and the mine.

All the lights were on in the little cottage as John got closer and he presumed Steve was waiting for him. They had an unwritten agreement that if neither of them were at home or if they had gone to bed, they turned off all the lights to save on electricity costs. Actually, they often only kept one light on for the same reason. Tonight the cottage was well lit. John decided he would speak to his son about wasting their money when he got in.

The walk from where the taxi had dropped him was a few hundred meters and uphill. John was happy to push open the kitchen door and call for Steve as he flopped down onto a kitchen chair. He called again. The radio was playing in the living room. When he called a third time and Steve failed to answer, he heaved himself out of the chair annoyed with the young man's impertinence.

He huffed and puffed his way to the living room adding just a little extra noise for effect, hoping to make his son feel guilty for getting his old father to come looking for him. Steve wasn't in the living room. John was perturbed. This wasn't like Steve! He checked both their bedrooms but Steve was nowhere to be found! Now he was really anxious! Steve would never have left without locking the doors and turning off the lights unless there was an emergency. He went to lock the kitchen door and noticed that Steve's keys were hanging in the lock. Now he was sure Steve was somewhere near!

John walked around the house again looking for a note or something that could tell him where his son was. There was nothing to be seen. He decided to go to the landlord's home to ask if they had seen Steve. When he went to the door to go, he saw the landlord's house was in darkness. Then he knew Steve wouldn't be there. The activity had now tired him! He knew there wasn't much he could do this evening so he made himself a cup of tea and went to bed leaving a note on the door telling Steve to knock at the window to be let in. He had locked the doors.

John got up at 5-o-clock on Sunday but Steve was not home. John made breakfast for himself and by 6-o-clock locked the cottage and went down to the road to get a taxi to the mine hostel. He needed to find out if Steve had worked overnight.

On arriving he met some old friends who told him that Steve had last been seen at the silo on the plant the previous day. John was therefore the last person to see Steve. Steve had been home at the time John left to go to the church. Now John knew something was wrong! He took a taxi to get to the public telephone where he phoned Joshua Robyn. The phone rang for a long time. Finally Joshua answered and it was evident from his voice that he had just woken from a deep sleep.

John explained that Steve was missing and that he had not been at the mine. He asked what he should do. Joshua suggested that he contact detective Lubber and tell him. He also cautioned him that under the law, people weren't considered to be missing until they had been gone 24 hours. John wanted to scream! Law? Couldn't anyone help? He prayed silently asking God to intervene and find his boy. He then went down to the road to hitch a ride home.

CHAPTER THIRTEEN

For Joshua and Karen the start of the Sunday service was painful and yet comforting. The normalcy of the Sunday crowd emphasized the fact that Bryan was not there, but the love and kindness shown to them helped them cope. Jake's sermon was on support, one for another. Jake took the sermon from the King James Version of John 1:10, "He that loveth his brother abideth in the light and there is no occasion of stumbling in him."

A quarter of the way through the sermon a group of men, dressed in leather and with bike helmets, came in. They didn't seem to mind that they were causing an interruption. Joking and swearing, they pushed at one another and settled in the back pews. Some of the congregation got up and moved to the front to escape the intrusion. Joshua noticed that Hendrik was also in the church in the back right corner. He was dressed in a black suit with a gray shirt. Joshua thanked God that his dad's death had at last got Hendrik into a church.

Jake did his best to deliver the prepared sermon but was obviously disturbed by the group sitting at the back. The congregation tried courageously to follow the sermon but the flow had been broken. The words seemed flat and devoid of meaning. When the service ended, the group really became disruptive. They made comments to all the young girls present about the lack of manhood of any young male accompanying them. One of them even picked on Old Uncle Peter.

Uncle Peter simply smiled at the biker. "In Jesus name I bind your activities here. I don't know why you came into our church but in here we worship the living God. Maybe you could do with meeting him?"

The biker growled out a curse and turned away abruptly, ignoring the old man. Some of the others laughed at him. They then left the church teasing the poor individual and almost knocking Jake over on the way out. The shock of the interruption and the unpleasantness of the situation had caused Karen to start crying again. Joshua put his arm around her and led her to her car. For a few minutes she just sat sobbing and Joshua prayed silently for her. Slowly she seemed to gain strength. In the spiritual world, a glimmer from alongside the car showed the presence of Tabitha who leaned against it.

When Karen drove off home, Joshua went to greet Hendrik who was standing to one side watching the proceedings. A beautiful young woman had her arm looped through his. Joshua greeted them. Hendrik nodded and introduced Joshua to the woman.

"Nice to see you here Hendrik," commented Joshua, "first time?"

Hendrik nodded again. "*Ya*! Not that it seemed to do much for anyone!" he quipped and the young woman smiled. "When is your Dad's funeral?"

Joshua felt a pang go through him again. "We're not sure yet, the nature of the death means that there will be an autopsy. We will just have to wait and see."

"Well, let me know," said Hendrik. "I want to be sure to attend." His tone didn't reveal much. Joshua wondered why the man that had hated his father had such an interest in the funeral. A verse about not judging others passed fleetingly through his thoughts.

With that they exchanged farewells and parted company.

CHAPTER FOURTEEN

After the service Joshua walked down to the police station hoping to find Carl Lubber there. He was in luck. The constable at the charge desk gave Joshua directions to Carl's office. He walked down a small passage decorated with plants and pictures of various important government people. It had the faces of the newly elected interim government leaders prominently displayed and Mr. Mandela was in a picture together with Mr. de Klerk.

Joshua knocked on the closed door and Carl's voice called out inviting him in.

The office was large with a lot of furniture and clutter. Carl was sitting at the second of the two desks near the window. Outside in a thorn tree two brightly colored birds were playing tag in the sunlight. Carl got up, and came across to Joshua with his hand extended.

"Good to see you're out and about again Mr. Robyn," he said. "What can I do for you?"

They shook hands and Carl gestured to a chair where Joshua could sit. After a few pleasantries Joshua came to the point.

"Did John Kumalo phone you this morning?" he queried.

"Who is John Kumalo?" asked Carl. "The only Kumalo that I came across lately was Steve Kumalo at the mine where your father was found."

Joshua explained. "John is Steve's father. He called me this morning to tell me that Steve was missing and that he had disappeared last night. He was very worried and I suggested he call you." Carl nodded his head encouraging Joshua to continue. "That isn't the only thing related to John. Last night, at our church, he suddenly made an announcement that my father had been murdered and that it was not an accident. Can you tell me more?"

Carl sat silent for a while. He wondered how this black man could have come to that conclusion. Again he thought about Steve Kumalo. What was his exact involvement in the incident? He remembered Joshua was waiting for him to reply.

"Mr. Robyn, I can't say if it was an accident or not. The investigation is under way and any statement would be premature. There are definitely some things that don't fall into place. We're currently investigating them. Did this John Kumalo say anything more?"

Joshua described the detail of his encounters with John. Carl scribbled notes on a piece of paper. He asked Joshua where he could contact John. Joshua gave him the number of the personnel department at the mine. They would provide the address. Carl then walked with him to the door and they said good-bye.

Carl went back and got his jacket as he wanted to speak to Tom Lurie and ask him some questions. He had heard Tom was an attendee at the Anglican Church on Sundays

CHAPTER FIFTEEN

Tom encountered Carl after their church service early on Sunday. Tom always found it amazing how much business he could conduct after a morning service.

"Got a few moments to discuss the incident," Carl asked Tom.

"Sure if you will re-open the silo when the forensic people have finished. The plant not running at capacity will diminish our monthly profit. Can you help me get it going soon?" Tom replied.

Carl agreed and got Tom to answer several questions on the aspects of the incident and mine policy. When Carl mentioned the possibility of murder, Tom became concerned.

He decided to go out to the mine. The drive through the gentle majesty of the sun-drenched mountains gave him peace. The talk of murder left an encroaching feeling of dread within Tom. He prided himself on running a shipshape operation where people respected one another. This should not be happening!

Arriving, he went inside to the metallurgical offices. At the gate the security guards recognized him immediately as he swiped his security card through a reader and the electronic doors let him through. They greeted him warmly but knowing how Tom had insisted that nobody be left out of security checks, they passed him an opaque box containing different colored plastic marbles.

This ritual was performed by anyone who went into the plant. One marble was withdrawn and if it was red, you were body searched. Nobody was allowed to take weapons or personal equipment onto the plant. Similarly, nobody was allowed to take anything out. This had been established to stop equipment disappearing and had stopped major losses almost immediately. Tom's marble was blue and he was spared the ordeal of a body search.

Tom dropped his marble into the discard slot where it would automatically be placed in an envelope with his name, the date and time. Sometime over the next three weeks, these envelopes would be transferred to the personnel department where a clerk would open them and log the color against the person's name. A statistical check could then be made to ensure that specific people weren't getting preferential treatment. Tom made his way onto the plant.

Walking through the plant was refreshing. The familiar sounds of the motors, crushers, pumps and the workers shouting to one another brought some relief to him as he made his way to the shift supervisor's office.

"Morning, how's it going?" He greeted the supervisor.

"Good! Our silo's online and we are catching up!" he was surprised to hear. He chatted about production for a few minutes over a cup of coffee and then decided to go to the site of the incident again.

He saw Joshua's car parked outside and wondered what Joshua was doing. Walking to the base of the conveyor and then up the long ramp to the gap in the railing, Tom stopped to view the falling rocks. The gap had been spanned with a piece of red and white striped plastic tape, which didn't engender confidence and he took a step backwards instinctively.

He imagined again what could have happened and it disturbed him. Talking to his workers, he strolled through the plant and found as he expected that they all reported being happy and without problems. He knew that African folk tended to answer to please the listener so he wasn't surprised. He tried to re-assure them hoping they hadn't heard of the possibility of it being murder. He was fairly sure they weren't content.

He went through security as he left the plant and this time turned up a red marble. The security guards checked him over very thoroughly. So much so, that he found himself wondering if his requirements weren't too stringent. The thought passed away soon, and within minutes he was back on the open road on the way home.

Driving past the hostel entrance he saw John Kumalo hitch-hiking. Not being in a hurry and out of courtesy to Steve, he stopped to give the old man a ride. At first John didn't recognize him as he accepted the ride. They had only met once or twice before at mine prize giving functions and so Tom was pleased that he had remembered the old man was Steve's father. A spiritual flash of light resolved into an unseen angel that sat comfortably on the car's roof as John had climbed into the passenger seat.

As they drove Tom started talking to John, "Mr. Kumalo, Steve has told me that you stopped working?"

John nodded. "Yes Sir, one's age slows you down you know. On my last job, I could no longer compete with the youngsters. They threw me out!" He said it in a matter of fact way, without resentment. His tone suggested life was not easy but that he never expected it to be so. He paused for a second gathering courage and then asked, "Mr. Lurie, have you seen my Steve today?"

Tom glanced across at him. "No why? Was he supposed to meet you today?"

There was a moment's silence.

"No Sir, he seemed to have disappeared last night and so I came to the mine this morning to try to find him. Nobody seems to have seen him today."

Tom frowned. "That's strange, Mr. Kumalo! Yesterday he was at the accident and I thought he was on his way home soon after I left. Didn't he arrive there?"

"Yes, he did Sir," John explained. He then added that Steve had disappeared later in the evening. Tom listened to the events and the feeling of disquiet that had established itself earlier grew considerably. When John finished, he said nothing for a while. They motored on in silence through the sun filled countryside.

Finally John pointed to a sandy driveway leading onto a piece of land just out of town and asked Tom to drop him off. John got out, thanked the manager and walked away up the drive. Tom pulled away absent mindedly, accelerating too fast and spinning the wheels as he considered the events. He decided it was time to call on Joshua again.

CHAPTER SIXTEEN

At Zinaville Christian Church, a contingent of angels had gathered waiting for Beor to arrive. As a group they had been caught unawares by the sudden influx of the demonic forces at the morning service. Tabitha had been at the gate watching when she had seen the onslaught racing along with the bikers into the church grounds. This added to the small group that had earlier been let in at Beor's request. This small group had been edgy and crushed against one another, as they settled in a corner of the church. They didn't make a sound until the others arrived.

The arrival of the second group had barely given Tabitha time to alert the gathering. The angels who openly attended the church had been hopelessly outnumbered. Beor had not called for additional support. Instead, those present had protected the congregation as best they could with their limited resources. Two of their number had been injured in the skirmishes that occurred, but on both occasions, the demons drew back before inflicting further casualties. Their apparent control didn't give them confidence to mount a full-scale attack on the angelic forces. Lacking power to their blows they obviously felt exposed on the holy ground. The angels fought carefully ensuring they wouldn't provoke a full scale attack.

Uncle Peter had saved an angel from serious injury. Demons that had been attacking him were thrown backwards by the force of the light of Holy Spirit that enveloped Uncle Peter when he used the Lord's name. The demons couldn't withstand this holy attack and it had given the angel a precious few milliseconds to recover his guard. It also increased the strength of the other angels turning the attack. It was the deciding point in the occupation of the church. The demons and their hosts had left in small groups snarling profanities at humans and angels alike.

Beor's encounter with Poneros outside the church had been one of utmost control on both sides. Arch enemies, they stood their ground warily as Joshua and Hendrik exchanged words. Once as Beor leaned forward whispering something to Joshua, Poneros started unsheathing his sword to counter the expected attack. He replaced it as Beor withdrew.

Joshua accompanied by Beor then left to go to the police station. Poneros fired vile looks at their departing backs and signaled the dark forces to withdraw. The demons taunted the angels as they had withdrew a few minutes later.

The angels thought about these events as they waited for Beor.

Suddenly a flash of light descended into their midst. The glimmer faded and Beor folded his wings, settling on the edge of the church piano. A murmur of welcome rippled from those gathered around. Beor began to speak.

"Glory to the Lamb!" he greeted. "Glory to the Lamb," they responded.

"Poneros is gaining confidence. That is expected. The Lord is with the congregation as could be seen by His presence in the heat of the skirmish."

A murmur of agreement rippled out again.

"The Zinaville congregation has been disturbed. We must use this according to the Lord's purpose. Tabitha, ensure that Karen is not left alone for a moment. Help her to find the diary. We also need to get Frank Brenan to start generating prayer support in his congregation." He turned to another angel, "Jake was not prepared and I have heard that Doubt is bothering him. Deal with that problem as you see fit!"

The angel grinned from ear to ear. Obviously she had something in mind. He paused and looked across his group. They were ready. He knew that the enemy was building in strength but he knew they would carry out their tasks.

"Everyone, you will have noticed that we did not show our strength on the invasion of the Lord's ground and may be wondering why. The Lord did not want us to! Poneros is plotting and the stronghold is hidden and growing in strength. The Lord has not yet seen fit to reveal it. We must be shrewd to defeat the enemy." A roar of agreement followed. Beor then dismissed them and the group broke up.

Beor arrived at Joshua's home as Tom knocked on Joshua's door. It was half open. Joshua invited him in and told him to make himself comfortable, he was busy with a phone call.

Settling himself in a chair, Tom idly picked up a magazine that was on the table. He could hear Joshua on the phone. He was talking to someone.

"Yes Susan, I can come in a few minutes! What? OK, I'll come to your apartment. Really! He said…what? That is outrageous! He can't say things like that! I will… Ok!"

Tom heard the phone being put down and was replacing the magazine onto the coffee table when Joshua returned.

"How is it going Josh?" he asked. "You getting enough support?"

Joshua smiled and nodded. Tom found himself respecting the younger man. Judging from his attitude, without knowing the circumstances, it would be impossible to deduce that his father had just died. He looked relaxed and if anything was looking less stressed than he had looked at work last week. Possibly the pain had tightened his smile a bit and the hint of tiredness in his eyes showed sleep had not come easily over the last evening.

"There is no need to come back to work on Monday. Take a few days off!" Tom suggested.

Joshua dropped himself into a soft chair and put his feet on the coffee table.

"No thanks Tom! I prefer to keep going than to sit and stew in my own thoughts. I'll be there tomorrow bright and early as usual," he assured him.

Tom grinned. "Seeing as you're being stubborn, can I offer you a ride in the morning? Your car is still at the plant!"

Joshua nodded, "Yes, Thanks! I haven't seen the need to go back there yet."

The thought of the silo and the accident darkened his countenance.

"There has been some talk that my Dad's death was not an accident…" he looked at Tom. "What have you heard?"

Tom felt uncomfortable. He knew the information he had received from Carl was privileged and so could not confirm it directly.

"Yes, Josh. I have heard mention of the same. However, it's a bit early to jump to these conclusions. I must say, I find it hard to believe. Bryan was well liked by everyone. I can't see how anyone could commit such a crime. Where did you hear this rumor?"

Joshua told him of the events of Saturday evening and his visit to Carl at the station earlier that morning. Tom listened. When Joshua had finished he sat in silence for a while. Finally he spoke, "Josh, I also met John today. I gave him a ride back from the mine. He told me he's been looking for Steve and couldn't find him anywhere. Have you any idea where Steve might be?"

Joshua shook his head. As far as he knew, Steve had three interests in life and these were his work, his father, and his trade union affiliation. None of these would lead to him disappearing without telling anyone. They both knew that and couldn't think of a single reason for Steve's disappearance. The discussion lasted a bit longer. Tom then went home after agreeing on a time for the morning ride.

After he had gone, Joshua tried to piece the events together but couldn't. Too much was happening too quickly and now he wanted to know why Steve had disappeared? Who could have wanted to kill his father? He was certain there was a link but couldn't put it together. His mind mulled over the events as he prepared lunch. He finished, washed the dishes, locked the house and walked down to Susan's flat.

He was glad she had called to tell him she had the afternoon off. He was even more pleased that she wanted to see him. When she had told him Hendrik had warned her off seeing him it hadn't really been a surprise but it did annoy him. Hendrik was a thorn in his flesh. Whenever Joshua seemed to be achieving something, Hendrik popped up somehow and interfered. Reflexively Joshua prayed for Hendrik's salvation again. He had decided to pray for the man every time he thought of him and now it was becoming a habit.

The walk did him good, helping straighten out his thoughts and by the time he arrived at the apartment he was more relaxed. He knocked. Susan opened the door. She was dressed in a revealing but simple black dress showing off every curve to perfection. Joshua found that her beauty was captivating. For a brief second he forgot to speak. She didn't even allow him to say hello but pulled him inside and shut the door immediately.

"Josh, I'm so afraid," she said. He took her into his arms and she melted up against him finding security in the hug. They kissed and for a brief second time stood still. Joshua was intimately aware of the softness of her body pressed up against his. He could sense strength and support flowing from him to her. In the spiritual realm Beor smiled. He knew that the union that was forming was according to the Lord's purpose. Time passed and they simply stood there gaining strength from each other's presence.

Joshua spoke first. "There is no need to be afriad Susan. God is always able to help us!"

He had said the wrong thing. She pushed him away.

"You maybe! Not me!" She retorted. "Keep your God!" She scowled, then smiled. "I didn't want to argue with you, let's sit in the living room. Want some coffee?"

"Yes, let me help!" said Joshua. They went through to the kitchen. Susan got out the cups and Joshua put the filter paper and coffee granules into the coffee maker. They stood waiting while it hissed and popped, filtering the coffee into the receptacle.

While they were waiting Joshua broached the subject of Hendrik again. "Has your Dad been giving you a rough time again?" he wanted to know.

Susan in an upset tone explained that Hendrik had come into Priggles that morning. She'd been stocktaking and he had found her at the back of the store. Apparently he'd told her to stop seeing Joshua or things would start going badly for her. When she showed him the bruises on her arm where Hendrik had gripped her, Joshua felt anger flow through him and for a second he wanted to hit Hendrik. Concern for her tempered the thought.

"I'm sorry Susan, but he can't make demands like that! He has no right to control your life. Surely you can tell him that it's your life and your choice?"

Susan fingered the black leather thong around her neck and looked down.

"Not with Hendrik, Josh! He's meaner than you think." She suddenly looked around the kitchen as if someone else was there. "I'm not even sure it's good to be talking to you at the moment. He has ways and means of finding out exactly what I do. Also, he knows things about me that I can't tell anyone, not even you Josh." She looked frightened again.

The coffee had finished spluttering and was ready to pour. She poured it into the mugs and they each added their own milk and sugar. Joshua put an arm around her and they went through to the living room where they sat in silence sipping the hot coffee. Joshua noticed how many small African and Eastern art ornaments she had collected. There were carved African facemasks, small Buddas, various carved African animals and some beadwork. It made Joshua uncomfortable and he suddenly wanted to get out of the apartment into fresh air. He suggested they go for a walk together.

Susan refused. She seemed paranoiac about going outside. Joshua couldn't understand why. Slowly it dawned on him that she was probably going to tell him she could no longer see him. Maybe Hendrik had scared her sufficiently to get her to this point.

Joshua continued to talk to her as he thought how he could counter Hendrik's intrusion her private life. He took the cups to the kitchen and on returning started to open the curtains. Susan immediately asked him not to. Again he wondered why she was so afraid.

He went to her again and put his arm around. Soon they were kissing and cuddling each other. Susan pushed him over and snuggled into his side as they joked and chatted to each other. Joshua started to kiss her again and she started caressing his chest, undoing his shirt buttons. For a while they lay and talked. She played with his chest hair. Joshua could feel the passion rising in both of them. Slowly lust had its way and she started to undo the belt on his trousers.

Joshua realized what was on her mind and although his body wanted to go along, he put his hand over hers, kissed her again and did the belt up. Immediately Susan pulled away from him. "Don't you want to make love with me Josh?" she asked.

"Susan I want to make love with you but I really don't want sex with anyone until I get married." he explained. He felt immature but the strength of his convictions rising up inside him made him sure he was doing the right thing. "I believe that only the special person I choose to be my wife should be joined with me in that way. I also have a belief that the act is both a spiritual and physical joining of people who love each other."

Susan looked shocked. "You mean to say you have never..."

"Yes, I have never had sex with anyone yet!" interrupted Joshua. He almost felt a bit ashamed for a second but he remembered the biblical words on the subject and resolved that the feeling wasn't to be entertained.

Susan looked at him as if he was crazy and then got angry. "Why didn't you tell me before I went and made a fool of myself?" She was obviously upset.

Joshua reassured her, "Susan, I love you very much and your actions were a compliment! You were just offering more than I can take from you as yet. Please don't be upset! I really want us to continue to spend as much time together as possible. Thank you! It's a wonderful gesture of your love."

Susan blushed and hid her face for a while. He just held her tighter. She seemed like a young girl in his arms and again he thought of how beautiful she was. He found himself wondering what God had in store for them and silently prayed for her salvation. After a while she looked up. "What did you mean by more than you can take, *yet?*" she emphasized the last word.

It was Joshua's time to be embarrassed. He'd been thinking she might be the one for him but wanted to keep it to himself. Now the words had escaped and he had needed to explain more than he wanted to.

"Susan, I do love you very much," he said. "Maybe sometime marriage could become an option but I love God very much and I know you don't understand that. The bible I honor says a Christian should never be 'unequally yoked' and that unfortunately means that a Christian should not link himself to a person who doesn't have the same relationship with Jesus Christ that they do. You don't seem to have the correct relationship and I would like to help you get there, but until then I can't even entertain thoughts of our making love. Only after I married you, if that ever happened." Joshua smiled and tried again. "Would you like to know Jesus?"

Susan was obviously shocked and confused by his answer. For a second time she drew away from him. Unknown to both of them, Beor was really battling to keep some demons at bay. Now some of those associated to Susan turned their attention from him and concentrated on Susan herself. She went pale. Joshua could see the negativity and was worried that his answer could drive them apart. Suddenly he felt an impulse to bind the demonic forces in the room. The statues and ornaments seem to loom out towards him. Under his breath he muttered, "I bind the demonic forces in this room in Jesus name."

Immediately Beor gained strength as he saw the authority of the Spirit. He grabbed the demons that were attacking her and pinning their arms. Susan's color returned. She looked up at Joshua. Obviously she had not heard his muttered comment. She sighed and leaned against him again. "Josh, I can't do that." She said. "I don't think I can even see you again. My father will make things so difficult for me if I do. You don't understand how dangerous he can be."

Anger got the better of Joshua. "Hendrik can't stop me seeing you!" he retorted. "I want to see you and I will! Even if I have to sneak in here every day to see you, I will! Please, don't let your dad destroy these precious feelings we have," he pleaded with her as Beor tried in vain to remove the grip the demon had gained on Susan.

Susan looked so small and confused. Her mind was in turmoil and she couldn't even think clearly. His voice appeared to come from a distance, and a mentally she seemed to close down. His voice was warmth and light amongst the turmoil. She wanted to cling to him but found an unseen pressure was forcing her from him. Like a spiders web between two windblown branches she felt stretched, distorted and about to be torn apart. She started to cry.

"Josh, I am so confused! I think you should leave Josh. I do love you but I am scared of my Dad. I'll think about what you say. Please go!"

Joshua was upset, but he kissed her and left. On the way home he realized that he hadn't even told her that his father had died. Suddenly he felt the sorrow choking him. He prayed to the Lord asking for His intervention and asking Him to ease the pain. His thoughts turned to his mother and he wondered how she was coping at the moment. He also found his mind chasing between thoughts of Steve's disappearance and what Tom had said.

CHAPTER SEVENTEEN

Tom was sitting at home outside on the porch in the warmth of the evening, looking at the stars, as was his custom on clear summer nights. They reminded him of when he had been sailing across the oceans of the world. It was a clear night and the sky was awash with glittering stars. He sipped at his sherry thinking about the weekend activities.

The murder at the plant bothered him most. Death was always a problem for him. His Father's death in his adolescence and his mother's death a few years back always crept up on him in these times. Separation caused the anguish. Looking up into the night sky he saw the bright stars of the Southern Cross and remembered his Dad's words. "It is fitting that the early explorers leaving the northern lands should be guided by the light of a cross placed there by their God!" He wondered why his atheistic father had made that comment. It was strange that of all the things they had discussed together, this one should ring in his minds ear.

A radio was playing quietly in the background and he could hear that Mandela, leader of the African National Congress was speaking. The South African government had let this man out of prison four years ago and he and the government had negotiated to get the vote for all people of the country. The struggle after the ANC came into power was going on with a quiet desperation in some small enclaves within the country. Zinaville was home to a large group of right wing white activists who would rather see the blacks killed than acknowledge their vote. The election had caused a large amount of friction in the town.

His thoughts led him to thinking of the murder again. Could it have been a militant right wing supporter? It was possible! If it was true, the threat to the plant and production was much greater than he had previously thought. Tom decided to discuss the matter with Steve if he could be found.

A gentle breeze started, cooling him as he sat listening to the buzz of the insects and the croaking of the frogs. Peace seemed to evade him however. Again emotional numbness entered his body and he found himself asking what the meaning of life was. He seemed to work and work, and work. He had no social life. Weekend evenings were either spent at the pub, at a wild party, or as with tonight, alone. There had to be more to life! A wave of depression flooded over him and he sipped morbidly at his sherry.

Karen Robyn was listening to the same radio message from President Mandela where he was calling for peace and asked the police to avoid excessive violence. She missed Bryan's protection and felt vulnerable. Somehow she couldn't grasp that he wasn't there anymore. Bryan had often gone away on trips and it felt like he was away on one of them now. She was almost expecting him to come through the door any moment.

"I must get hold of myself," she thought again. "Bryan has gone, I must accept that!"

Simultaneously to that thought, there was a knock at the door. Karen got up and went to open it. Standing at the entrance was Pastor Jake and his wife. They had a picnic basket with them. Karen invited them in. The food was appreciated and Karen suddenly realized that she hadn't eaten anything since she had heard the news. The food and company was welcome. She just wanted to talk. They talked away into the night and it was 11p.m. before they left.

Karen didn't feel tired and the night seemed to stretch out before her as an invisible timeline of frustrating inactivity. She got up and walked to their bedroom. Going to the cupboard to hang up her clothes, she got an inclination to open Bryan's cupboard. Tears filled her eyes as she looked at his clothes and possessions. Alongside some aftershave on the shelf were his Bible and a diary. She picked up both and went to sit on the bed.

Hours later she finished reading Bryan's diary. The love for her husband and his love for her had moved her to tears many times as she read his words. Bryan had kept a diary all the years that she had known him but he had never allowed her to read it. Much of the diary revealed the relationship between himself and God. She featured in it most days and reading it now after his death, she realized anew his immense love for her. The emotions were bitter sweet. However, some of the entries over the past few months were disturbing. Hendrik van Vuuren featured in many of them. Bryan was sure that Hendrik was up to something and had started to keep watch on him surreptitiously. There were several entries in that regard. Then a few days before his death there was an entry that recorded that Bryan had an argument with Hendrik. The detail wasn't recorded.

She didn't know what to do. Her mind was in turmoil. She decided to phone Joshua. It was now 4a.m. and the phone rang for a while before he answered. He didn't sound too happy when he answered but when he heard it was his mother, his attitude changed. She related what she had found out and explained that she was sure there was something to John Kumalo's statement at the church.

Joshua listened to his mom. He could hear the pain, tiredness and loneliness in her voice. The comments about Hendrik that his dad had made in the diary sounded as if they could be a lead to finding his Dad's killer. He advised her to put the diary away, take a sleeping tablet and try to get some sleep. The diary would keep until the next day. She agreed and they both went to bed.

CHAPTER EIGHTEEN

Monday morning, Joshua was waiting outside at 7a.m. when Tom came passed to drive him to the mine. He dropped him at the plant. Joshua went through to the metallurgical offices to check the production figures for the weekend. Despite the accident, production was being maintained at reasonable levels, largely due to Hendrik's effort in the period before the accident.

Everyone expressed concern for him and offered to help. Joshua found it a welcome relief to the loneliness and quiet of his home. The hustle and bustle of work made it easier to cope. There were items to order, maintenance to plan, and a myriad other tasks.

It was almost reaching a semblance of completion when the phone rang and he picked it up. It was Carl on the other side.

"Joshua Robyn? It's Detective Lubber speaking. Have I got through to the correct extension?"

Joshua assured him he had.

"Mr. Robyn, I would appreciate it if you could come down to the police station immediately. I believe you can help us with some inquiries."

Joshua agreed to be down at the station within half an hour. He phoned Tom to notify him of the development, collected his car from the nearby silo, and drove into town. Parking in the front of the police station, he went inside to the charge desk where he asked for Carl Lubber.

Carl appeared almost immediately and took him into an adjoining interrogation room. They sat down comfortably across from each other with a small wooden table between them. It was attached to a white wall and there was little else in the austere room. Sunlight filtered into the room from a series of small windows set up high in one wall. On the one side of the room a mirror reflected the two of them as they sat facing each other. The bright fluorescent light buzzed quietly like a cicada and Joshua found it's flickering mildly annoying. Through the half open door the front desk could be seen. Carl looked pale and tired. He struggled to find the right words.

"Mr. Robyn, you are probably not aware of it, but there have been some serious allegations against you. Earlier today a lady came into the police station with her father to lay a charge against you." Carl paused and looked at Joshua who was looking very puzzled. "She accused you of raping her last night!"

Joshua looked at Carl incredulously. He couldn't believe what he heard. First his Father's death, and now this! What was the world coming to? He couldn't even speak he was so amazed. He wondered who this woman might be. Carl could see his confusion and continued.

"Her father was urging her to lay the charge but when she understood she would need to be examined by the district surgeon, as well as questioned by a lady constable, she retracted her charge and walked out. They both left here arguing bitterly. The desk sergeant reported this to me thinking it may have bearing on your Father's investigation. That's why I wanted to ask you a few questions. Mr. Robyn, could you tell me where you were last night?"

Joshua regained his composure but couldn't believe what he was hearing. He explained all the events of the evening from the point that Tom had come to visit until the call at 4am from his mother.

Finally, curious, he asked him who it was that wanted to charge him.

"Miss van Vuuren!" replied Carl.

For a second time in 48 hours the shock hit Joshua so hard that he passed out. He regained consciousness lying on a bed in the police sickbay with Carl standing alongside.

"I am sorry Mr. Robyn," Carl apologized. "Who is your doctor?"

Joshua sat up, his mind was spinning and he felt nauseous.

"Susan came in to lay that charge?" he asked Carl incredulously. "Susan! Susan van Vuuren?"

Carl tried to calm Joshua down. "Yes sir. There is no charge however as it was withdrawn. Sir, can I get you a doctor?"

Joshua trembled as if he had just been thrown into an ice cold bath. His mind couldn't process what he had just heard. He felt as if it was trying to disengage itself from his body. He wanted to scream but the years of hardening within a society where males didn't show their feelings choked his emotion. Carl's face seemed to swim and his voice sounded distorted. Darkness seemed to reach out to clutch him promising oblivion from pain. It was inviting. The alternative was too stressful and real. The choice of descending into oblivion stretched in front of him and the dull pounding of his heart echoed in his head.

Beor and the macabre demons were exchanging blow for blow unseen by the two men. The spiritual space was a tumultuous, heaving, straining battlefield. Neither side was winning the right to put suggestions to Joshua's mind and soul. Light flashed and darkness tried to envelop it but failed. Sulfurous clouds of smoke billowed around as Beor's sword found its mark again and again. The prayer power spurred him on and on. The demonic horde rushed in frantically only to be held at bay by the glowing white sword moving so fast it that blurred with light.

Carl was very concerned for Joshua. In his dealings with him he found he liked the man. "Beware of prejudicing your objectivity," he quietly reminded himself. His emotions shouldn't be part of the case. He pondered over his evaluation of Joshua. The man seemed to be an honest, single minded and likable individual. Looking at Joshua he realized that the man was at risk both physically and mentally. Joshua looked as if he was about to have a heart attack and Carl wasn't even sure he hadn't already had one. If Carl could have seen into the spiritual world it would have confirmed his evaluation. Gently he shook Joshua and asked him again for his doctor's name. Joshua didn't seem to hear!

Through the open door Carl could see the constable at the charge office desk. The man was not very busy so Carl called him over to sit with Joshua as he took over the desk to use the phone. He phoned called Gerard to get Joshua's work number in the mine accident file. Glancing into the sickbay he could see Joshua hadn't recovered yet and the constable was standing by looking helpless. Carl got a line to the mine on his first attempt and asked for Tom.

Tom had just finished his morning commitments and he offered to come down to the station to help out. He re-assured Carl that Joshua was fit and not likely to suffer from any heart ailment as his health had been recently checked as part of the mine "red ticket" medical. He agreed to take Joshua to the doctor.

Through the open doorway Carl could see his desk clerk shuffling from foot to foot not knowing what to do. He went back in to Joshua and sent the relieved man back to his desk.

Joshua's mind was a kaleidoscope of thoughts. Vision after vision swamped his mind. Flashes of times of when he was a boy, his mother, the events around his Father's death, the activities of last night at Susan's apartment, Hendrik at the plant arguing with his father, Hendrik at Susan's apartment, Priggles, and much more flashed through his mind. A dull pain permeated all. He couldn't gain control. Each time he started to gain a foothold on reality the scene changed and he found himself surfing a mental roller coaster.

To Carl, Joshua was just sitting inertly staring at the floor, mumbling now and again. He heard words like 'Susan', 'diary', 'Mom', and others. He listened for a while then went over to Joshua and shook him roughly by the shoulder, "Joshua! Joshua! Mr. Robyn! Can I get you a cup of coffee Sir?" He asked.

Something seemed to get through. Joshua shook his head and Carl glad to get some sort of feedback, and so he persisted.

"Tell me what you did this morning! Sir! What did you do this morning when you got up?"

He asked hoping that the link would stabilize Joshua's emotions.

Joshua made a concerted effort to concentrate on Carl's voice. The spinning scenes slowed and he could crystallize the reality of Carl's question from the contortions of his thoughts. However when he tried to relate them to the activities of the morning, he found that they eluded him. He shook his head. "Sorry," he whispered. "I can't seem to remember right now, sorry!"

Carl didn't give him a break and continued gently but insistently to ask simple questions that forced Joshua to regain his grip on reality. Within a minute or two Joshua seemed almost to be back to normal. When Carl repeated his question about the morning activity, Joshua was able to explain what he did.

Once Joshua seemed better, Carl went to get him some coffee. As Carl went out Joshua again started to succumb to the onslaught. This time he found he could select what to do before the emotions became too strong. He started to pray quietly and found that if he concentrated on talking to God, the anguish subsided and by the time that Carl got back with the coffee, Joshua was starting to feel himself again.

Beor had grown in strength and the demonic milieu had retired to a safer distance where they sat, waiting and watching, exuding hate and anger.

Carl explained that he had called Tom to take Joshua for an immediate consultation with his doctor.

Joshua felt annoyed but realized that Carl was being helpful and that he probably would have done the same in similar circumstances. They sipped coffee for a while in silence. Carl remembered Joshua's mumbling and asked him what diary he had been talking about. Joshua couldn't remember for a moment and then realized he must have referred to his father's diary in his confused state. A pang of fear seemed to reach out to touch him momentarily as he thought of his mother's feelings if the police wanted to see the diary. A counter thought intruded reminding him that it could be beneficial in deciding if his Dad's death had been accident or foul play. This motivated him and he told Carl of the phone call from his mother.

Carl listened quietly to the information. He realized the diary was important to the investigation and wanted it but he didn't want to put the family under further strain. At that moment, Tom arrived with his usual hustle and bustle mildly annoying the desk sergeant who was relaxing reading the morning paper. It was a quiet morning at the station. Tom strode in through the open door, a smile on his face and his voice booming.

"What's up here? Carl, I thought you told me this man was the worse for wear? Kidding me were you? Careful, I'll charge you for my time off work if this is a false alarm. Josh, how are you, is this dumb cop giving you a hard time again?" He smiled at Carl to take the sting out of his words.

"I'm here to take you for a visit to that fool they call our mine doctor! Are you ready?"

Carl ignored Tom's blustery entrance and smiling explained in as simple a way as possible what had occurred. Tom quieted down as he listened as Carl described Joshua's collapse and his opinion that a visit to the doctor was necessary. Tom nodded his agreement.

"I guess the old fool may have a few tricks up his sleeve that could help you Josh!" he quipped.

Joshua complained that the visit wasn't necessary but it was obvious that he wasn't going to persuade the two men so he agreed to go to be checked out by the doctor.

The medical man was waiting for them. He checked Joshua over carefully and prescribed some different and stronger tranquilizers, as well as rest. He booked Joshua off work for a week. Tom agreed and promised to ensure that Joshua would get rest. Joshua was not amused and didn't want to agree but knew that he had no choice. He resigned himself to a boring week and allowed Tom to take him home.

When they were ensconced in Joshua's living room, Tom asked him about a few aspects of work that he would have to delegate and then quizzed him about what had happened at the station. Joshua explained.

"So nothing happened between you and Susan then Josh?" Tom wanted to know. "Normally I would say you're a stupid fool and that your Christ is a pain in the butt but this time I must agree, you made a smart move. You have a lot more restraint than I have!" he commented."

Joshua smiled.

"What is this diary you're referring to?" asked Tom.

Joshua explained again how his mother had found the diary and that there were references to Hendrik in it. Tom mused over the facts for a while as the two men sat in silence. He wondered if the diary might unlock the reasons behind the trouble at the plant.

"Josh, do you think we could get the diary from your Mom?" he asked.

The sedative was taking effect and Joshua was thinking slowly.

"Tom, I really don't want to go out again. How about you fetch it? I'll call my Mom and let her know you're going to drop in and collect it."

His Mom was on her way out to do some shopping when she got his call but she said that she would wait for Tom. Joshua realized she was depressed. He knew shopping was her way of cheering herself up and hoped it would help her this time. They all needed whatever help they could get.

CHAPTER NINETEEN

At the police station, Carl was busy with administrative work but found that he continually thought of Joshua, the 'accident' case and the possible link to Miss van Vuuren, the strange disappearances of both Steve Kumalo and the hobo. He had a hunch that there was a common thread to be found in all this but couldn't isolate it. Frustrated with his inability to concentrate on the task at hand, he sat back and mulled over the facts as he saw them.

Hendrik hadn't been present at Bryan's death and Steve had testified to that. They had been together when the 'accident' was discovered. Steve had in fact been waiting at the base of the conveyor for a while before Hendrik arrived. Steve was the one that disappeared! Carl made a mental note to check this more fully. Could Steve have been the murderer? He looked at his watch and decided Steve had been missing long enough. He picked up his radio and put out an 'all points bulletin' looking for Steve.

"The facts...?" Carl considered the confusing array of them. Joshua was connected to the murdered man by birth and both of the others by work association. None of those people even knew Brandy Bob. Tom knew Steve and Joshua. It was really confusing and the more he considered the situation, the more confusing it became. The only solid piece of evidence that he had not yet investigated was the diary. Possibly it was the key to unlocking the puzzle. He opened the Robyn file on his desk and located Karen Robyn's phone number. He called, but the phone just rang and he presumed she was out. He made a note to call her again later and went back to his mundane duties.

At Zinaville Platinum, Tom was back in his office. Dealing with a few urgent tasks he canceled a meeting and got his secretary to cancel all activities for the afternoon. She brought him a cup of coffee and he started to read the diary from Karen Robyn.

Initially he found it strange to be delving into the intimate past of a man that had worked for him for so long. He realized how little he knew of the man himself, his home life and social circles. The reading was fascinating! Bryan had an intimate relationship with his God that was initially amusing to read and then became something that seemed downright captivating. It was an overriding aspect in his daily activities. A tightness gripped Tom's chest as he read. He found himself getting angry that despite having so little, this man could have been so content. Tom found it amazing to see how much Bryan had believed he had heard from God. He hadn't realized until then that a person could be so caught up in his religion and yet still be so fully "normal" in other aspects. Bryan was obviously a real man with successes and failures but also a man that cared for others deeply.

A real shocker was the number of times his own name appeared; "Tom Lurie made a wise decision today..." "Mr. Lurie asked us to ...," "I am praying that Tom Lurie can achieve..," "Tom Lurie made a bad decision but I'll go along with it and pray that we succeed..." and many more. As he read he got used to the comments and found that while he hadn't always been the best character in the old man's book, old man Robyn had continually supported him in many different ways.

Most of the initial pages only reflected positive aspects and Bryan's concern for his wife, Joshua, and the community as a whole. There was a fair bit about the church that Tom just skimmed over. Then beginning over a year ago Bryan started expressing concerns about mechanisms Hendrik was using to increase productivity. Some of the things really perturbed Tom as he read them. Most were hearsay but now and then Bryan recorded clashes with Hendrik. Tom was amazed to see that Bryan's main objective was to keep out of Hendrik's way but that it appeared as if Hendrik sought him out just to aggravate him. Tom wondered if this was the same treatment that others had been getting. There was a period that Bryan appeared to absolutely flood his prayer life with prayer for Hendrik. In the middle of this period Bryan accidentally picked up a fax that had dropped into an electrical junction box and had read it. Tom read on...

"Today while adding a 10 Ampere line into junction J175, I came across a fax to Hendrik. The words 'your payment' caught my attention and being worried that it reflected an invoice for our plant, I read on. I was really surprised to find it came from an overseas satellite company and was instructing Hendrik to check for money in a specific bank as he was being paid for 'services rendered'. As employment terms explicitly deny us any right to employment outside ZPM while working for them, I became inquisitive and telephoned the number given for the bank. It was the Toronto Dominion Bank. I looked up where Toronto was and found it to be in Canada. What is Hendrik up to?"

Tom now asked himself the same question. Anger grew as he thought of the foreman's audacity. To think he had almost trusted this man over Joshua! What the hell was his foreman up to? Anger exploded within him. He read on. The next pages contained very little information that concerned ZPM or Tom. They described church activities, an argument Bryan had with Joshua, and how Bryan loved Karen.

Reading on, Tom found a month after the first entry there was another entry referring to Hendrik's activities.

"I was most concerned to see Hendrik with another fax today. I am sure it wasn't work business. He was so surprised to see me standing there, that when he looked up he positively jumped and then immediately hid the paper in his pocket. He was harsh with me. Accused me of sneaking up on him! I am sure he is up to no good! I intend to find out what it's. This man has terrorized me for too long. Hopefully the tables have turned!"

Tom was skipping a few pages and the diary opened at another strange entry. A spiritual finger, invisible to Tom, selected the open page. Ahira, Tom's guardian angel, empowered by the prayers of the Zinaville Christian Church community was intervening. Ahira displaced Boredom, a fat sleepy eyed worm as they both competed for Tom's attention. Tom selected to force his mind back to what he was reading.

"Hendrik is getting items sent to the stores that are marked for him personally. I saw some boxes marked to 'Mr. van Vuuren, Confidential, to be opened by the recipient personally'. They were marked as transformers but as we don't use transformers of a size that would fit into that box my interest prickled. I must find out what it really is!"

The next day had the entry...

"I found out that the 'transformers' have disappeared from the store. The computer had no record of them coming in or going out. The store man remembered receiving them vaguely and claimed to have processed them as normal. I assumed Hendrik came and got them!"

Worried by what he was reading, Tom decided he had to do something. He wasn't sure of his course of action and felt an urge to put a call through to Joshua.

Joshua's voice was slurred and gruff. Tom presumed that Joshua had been asleep. Apologizing, he sketched out his discovery. Joshua immediately sounded more alert. After a short discussion, they decided to have supper together. Tom would finish reading the diary and Joshua gave him permission to copy some pages. Tom felt it was important to have some of the information for backup should he want to address matters at the plant. He marked the pages he wanted copied. They contained more references to items moving through the store. Bryan had seemed to be sure they weren't going to be tracked but made no reference to checking them again. Then his eye caught an item in February showing a possible link between Hendrik and Bryan's untimely death.

"I was in the electrician's workshop and had closed the door so that our air-conditioner could cool the place down. While I was eating my lunch, I looked out the window next to the workbench. Hendrik was reading a fax with his back to the window and I could see over his shoulder. It seemed to be the same type of fax as the one I found. Unfortunately, I knocked a spanner off the bench and it hit the wall as it fell. Hendrik saw me. He rushed into the workshop as I turned around. 'What the hell are you doing?' he screamed at me and I am sure he would have assaulted me if I hadn't grabbed a gas torch and lit it in one motion holding it between him and myself. He was crazy but fortunately not stupid. Although he is much bigger than me, this afternoon he looked bigger, meaner and more dangerous than I have ever experienced before. I am getting worried that this anger of his is getting out of hand."

The diary reflected badly on Hendrik. The two men had been enemies for years and Tom realized he had ignored it. This was now an issue he had to deal with. "Too ruddy late as well!" he thought angrily. He came across a new statement.

"Hendrik is evil and must be stopped. He has terrorized me all my working life and I am now going to put an end to this man's evil. I have found out that I can duplicate the printing of the faxes. I intend to set up a duplicate printer to the one that prints all the metallurgical plant faxes. If I can get copies of his faxes I'll confront Mr. Lurie with the evidence and have Hendrik fired! Joshua will stop me if he finds out so I'll not tell him. I pray that I get the evidence before I am discovered."

On the Friday before Bryan's death an entry read: "While Hendrik was screaming at me today, I lost my temper. I told him I knew of his illegal bank account and that I would not take his nonsense anymore. That wasn't wise! I really got scared. For the first time he didn't say anything. He just became quiet, thoughtful and walked out. Heaven knows what I have started!"

Tom felt certain the entry was significant and that Bryan had died as a result of losing his temper. Somehow the thought was sobering. Tom called his secretary on the intercom and asked her to copy the pages of the diary. Mrs. Wold came in, got the diary, and went to copy the marked pages. It was already late and Tom had to leave to meet Joshua. He finished off a letter for a shipment of supplies for the mine, and then went to get some of the copies from Mrs. Wold. She wasn't finished. She said she would put the rest of the copies in his drawer with the diary when she was finished. Tom took what he could and left.

CHAPTER TWENTY

Tom met Joshua at his home and they traveled together to the restaurant. Both men were quiet, their thoughts focusing on the events of the past few days. Other than asking Joshua about his mother's health, Tom ignored conversation.

Sitting down near the salad bar at the restaurant, Tom ordered a bottle of red wine, Joshua orange juice, and they settled to chat about the local news. They discussed politics, sport, and business before Tom broached the subject of the diary entries.

"Josh, that diary really shows Hendrik to be a tough son of a B. I guess that the police will need it in the murder investigation. My personal feeling is that we should get it to them as soon as possible. I suppose your Mom may not like that?"

Joshua nodded.

"I also notice that although you're Hendrik's boss, your Dad doesn't seem to have wanted to discuss Hendrik with you. Do you have any idea why?"

Joshua thought it over for a few seconds. "Not really Tom," he answered. "Possibly he knew that he would be putting me in an awkward situation. What sort of things did he say in the diary?"

Tom explained how Bryan had quarreled in a progressively more intense manner with Hendrik and how the friction had arisen between the two of them. He gave Joshua the few photocopies he had with him and Joshua read through them. Tom sipped his wine and waited while the other man finished reading. He could see the reading was taking its toll on the young man and reflected on the strength of character that Joshua's mother must have had to be able to read those pages. Soon Joshua finished and looking at him, Tom could see a quiet anger reflected in Joshua's eyes. He explained to him that the most important items were still being copied.

The waitress arrived with their food and as they ate, they discussed the diary further.

"How are you going to handle Hendrik, Josh?" Tom asked, skillfully handing his own problem over to Joshua. Joshua thought for a while.

"We need to get hold of that fax information my Dad was collecting. Don't you agree Tom?" he suggested.

Tom noticed that Joshua had equally as skillfully ignored his reference to Hendrik but didn't take it up with him again.

"I agree Josh. Where do you think they would be?"

Between them they decided that Bryan had probably kept them at home. So, after they had finished their meal, they went around to Karen on the off chance that she was at home.

They arrived to find she had visitors. Jake had come around as part of his pastoral duties, and Carl had arrived to visit Karen in the hope of obtaining the diary and any other information that could help in investigating Bryan's death.

Karen was very pleased to see Joshua and while the two hugged and comforted each other, Tom went through to the living room. He noticed how a sense of peace seemed to pervade the home despite the recent events. Carl introduced Tom to Jake. Tom engaged in some lighthearted banter and then suggested that he would allow Joshua to explain the key part of the day. They discussed general issues as they waited for Joshua and Karen to come in.

When they arrived, Karen brought in a delicious array of cookies together with coffee. Joshua followed with a tray of freshly brewed tea. Inconsequential discussion continued while they ate and drank. Joshua could feel the other men were waiting for him to say something but ignored the feeling, allowing his mother time to relax and get to know the group as a whole. Then he started to tell Carl of the diary contents.

"Remember the diary I told you about this morning, Carl... " he started.

Carl nodded and glanced at Karen to see how she had taken the revelation. She didn't appear to be upset.

"Well I arranged for Tom to borrow it and read it today. He suggested that you read it as well."

Tom nodded.

Carl looked pleased and asked a few questions. The available photocopies were passed to him to read and when he asked for the rest, the men explained that the remainder of the diary was still in the office, as Tom's secretary was copying them. Joshua asked his mom if she knew where Bryan had kept the fax copies he had made. His mother looked confused.

"What am I looking for Josh?" she asked.

Joshua smiled and explained that what they needed to find some pieces of paper with messages typed on them. Karen didn't seem to think that there was anything like that in their home.

"Bryan never brought anything home! The first time I actually knew what he did in any detail, was when I was reading his diary. However, I'll have a look in a few places where they may be."

With that she left the room leaving the men to talk among themselves.

"What do you think Carl?" Tom wanted to know.

"Well… the diary showed something strange was going on," replied Carl. "What it is, and if it's connected in any way to Bryan's death, still needs to be investigated. Finding those faxes would certainly help," he added.

They all nodded in agreement. Jake, Tom and Joshua discussed their suppositions while Carl listened quietly, gleaning small insights into their personalities and lives. They waited for Karen to complete her search for the faxes and when she returned empty handed they were all disappointed.

Carl suggested that Bryan may have kept the information elsewhere. Joshua remembered that his Dad had a locker in the electrician's workshop at the metallurgical plant. Tom immediately suggested that they go to take a look. Jake declined, wanting to stay and discuss some details of the funeral with Karen. The rest left as a group.

CHAPTER TWENTY-ONE

They arrived at the plant at ten-o-clock and the shifts were changing. After going through security, they made their way to the shift boss' office where they met a bright eyed, but scruffy individual who was running the night shift. Having informed him that they needed access to the electrician's workshop, they obtained the key and walked down to the shop through the orange-yellow glow of spotlights that provided pools of illumination.

The shift boss was in attendance when they broke open Bryan's locker only to find that there was nothing of value inside. Disappointed they left the plant and went to the main office to retrieve the diary. When they got there, the office lights were on, and a security van was parked outside. A break-in had just occurred! The security manager was outside and when he saw Tom, he immediately came over to report the incident.

"The front doors have apparently been forced open," he reported. "We can't see if anything is out of place or damaged, could you please come in and take a look around," he asked.

Tom nodded and they all went in. Tom did a cursory visit to each room, but as far as he was concerned there was nothing out of place. He advised the manager and went back to his office to get the diary. It wasn't there! He presumed that Mrs. Wold had not yet finished the photocopying and went to look on her desk. They all searched her desk, around the photocopy machine, and in most of the areas where they thought it could be. Tom finally decided that although it was late, he would call his secretary and inquire where she had left the papers and diary. She hadn't gone to bed yet and despite sounding amazed at the late call, was very helpful. She explained that she had placed both the diary and the copies in the desk drawer before she had left work that afternoon.

Carl asked to speak to her. He wanted to know who she had spoken to at work that afternoon, who had seen her making the photocopies and who had been into the offices that would not normally have been there.

From her reply, it appeared as if a number of people had been through the offices at around that time, including some people from the time office, a pay-clerk and some other employees who worked in the same building. Carl asked if she had seen or spoken to Hendrik van Vuuren. She hadn't. Confused, but certain that Hendrik was somehow involved; the men drove back to town, arriving home near midnight.

Joshua went to bed immediately but couldn't get to sleep. His mind wouldn't settle. Nothing made sense! It was as if the world had gone crazy. He could feel the tendrils of fear trying to attach to his soul and fought them off with a quiet desperation fueled by the memory of his problems that morning. He started to gain control over his fears as he prayed out loud against the evil attack. The whirling thoughts slowed and settled into a steady stream of incoming images.

He was sure that Hendrik was behind the activities. How could he prove it? Tired, he decided to pray, hand the problem to Jesus, and forget it for a while. This thought comforted him and was soon he asleep. Sitting on the edge of his bed, Beor's presence ensured peaceful sleep for his charge.

It was two weeks later that Joshua suddenly remembered Tom saying that his Dad had mentioned setting up a printer that copied the incoming faxes. Maybe it was still connected! The fax was locked in a small office that he knew well. It was in the same building as the main store for the plant.

Hendrik kept the key and Joshua remembered how he had justified that responsibility. "We must stop the personnel using the fax for private business" was the argument he had used. To solve the problem he would control access by personally keeping the key and distributing the faxes three times a day. Joshua considered where Bryan might have hidden the printer. He would have needed access to the telephone line or the fax itself, power, and a place to hide the paper that would be used. It couldn't be in the fax room itself, as the noise of the printing would lead to a discovery of the equipment. He remembered that his Dad knew the store man well and decided that it must be somewhere inside the store

Tom had just finished the manager's monthly review meeting when he was surprised to see Joshua enter the room. Tom ended the discussion he was having as soon as he could and went over to Joshua.

Joshua briefly told him of his idea and asked Tom if he could investigate. Tom agreed but insisted on accompanying him. They stopped off to tell Mrs. Wold of the change in Tom's activities and she set about changing his appointments for the next two hours. On the trip over to the plant, Joshua explained the rationale behind his deductions.

The store personnel were curious to see both of the men together. There curiosity increased when Tom's insisted that they take some time off and leave the store. Tom ignored their inquiring looks and as soon as they vacated the building, Joshua and Tom made their way to the back of the store closest to the fax room. This was an area where damaged items were placed before being removed to scrap.

At first they couldn't find anything. Everything was heaped together. They moved everything but couldn't find anything resembling a printer or a fax. Many of the items were relatively heavy and so required both men to lift and move them. Tom wasn't as fit as he had been in his sailing days, and found he had to rest more frequently than he liked. It was a hot day and the lack of sleep had made both men tired. The lack of success made Tom anxious and depressed. It was thirsty work and Joshua suggested he wanted some Coca-Cola from a nearby refrigerator.

He was opening the door when he noticed the refrigerator was standing away from the wall and on impulse decided to look behind it. Peering into the darkness he couldn't see anything. He tried to push the refrigerator back against the wall but it wouldn't move. Prompted, Tom noticed what Joshua was doing and came over to help him. Even with both their efforts the refrigerator didn't shift backwards and the men looked at each other. Both of them had the same idea. The channel inside which the power cable ran, to provide the energy to the refrigerator, extended from the fax room wall. Could the printer be behind the refrigerator?

"Let's move it away from the wall," Joshua suggested.

Tom nodded and they pulled the unit forward. Attached to the power cable was a smaller screened cable that disappeared up inside the fridge behind a panel secured by six small screws. Exchanging knowing looks, they went off in different directions to look for a screwdriver. One was found on a rack in the store. In a little less than a minute they had removed the panel from the back of the unit.

Inside, neatly collected in a small wire basket were many typed sheets. The faxes had been found! They couldn't wait to look at them, but after a cursory look decided it would take a while to locate the relevant information. Tom wasn't going to allow this evidence to go missing as well. He insisted Joshua leave them as they were and went to call Carl. Joshua was burning to read them but rather than destroy possible evidence, he joined Tom in the office. Tom made two calls, one to the police station and one to security control. The men settled down, each with a cup of tea and waited.

Carl arrived a short while later. He had a small camera with him and took photographs of the setup. He also got the men to sign statements of their activities. They then removed the faxes, closed the panel and replaced everything as it had been. They left without explanation to anyone from the store. As soon as they were allowed to, the workers scurried back to see what they had been doing. They couldn't see anything out of place and a rumor developed that it was a spot audit by top management.

Tom suggested to the other men that they meet in his office. When they got there, he asked Mrs. Wold to bring everyone some refreshments and they settled down to look through the faxes. Each of them took a third of the stack and silence settled over the group as they started to read.

CHAPTER TWENTY-TWO

Sitting in his plush office in the downtown area of Johannesburg, one of South Africa's largest cities, one of Johannesburg's most successful businessmen, Don Warmen, was grinning. The business deal he was orchestrating was going very well! He was in charge of one of the largest technology based companies in the country and could envisage himself as one of the more wealthy people in the world. Not that he had need for anything, it was just that he loved the power and the control the money brought with it. He scowled as he realized that the woman he was divorcing hated him for his success. She claimed his focus on these aspects was due to a hidden insecurity in himself. "What a load of garbage!" he thought angrily. In the spirit world, the huge serpent that circled itself around his spine writhed and hissed orders to underlings.

Don swung around in his chair and looked out across the metropolitan skyline. The view out over the tall buildings cluttering the Johannesburg horizon always gave him comfort. It was good to know that, in almost all those buildings, some product his company had made was busy whirring and clicking away. He was successful and he knew it! Over the past few years he had been systematically buying out shares in the communication industry. Now he was poised to conclude the biggest deal of his life. Pride filled his being and he felt a rare rush of emotion. The world was moving into a different era and he was going to capitalize on this. He wanted control. Absolute control!

Government officials were such fools he thought. He considered the current South African government. They had an almost impossible task in forging a new South Africa from the ruins of the previous political mess. Ten years ago he had known that this situation would occur and now he was reaping the profits from careful preparation for that day. The previous government had bankrupted the country, refusing to bow to world pressure to remove their racist laws. His company had profited from their mistakes. When the world imposed sanctions, he had hired the best brains in the country at the time and set them to work copying and enhancing ideas generated outside the country. While developing his industry, he had been subsidized by the government because he was 'providing jobs'. The technology developed by his companies could also be used in desirable military and police applications. This added to his growing wealth and influence. By steering his company into the gap vacated by companies leaving the South African marketplace, he skirted around a threatening situation and made huge profits. In so doing, he became identified as successful, shrewd and having national pride. He openly helped the government in its nationalistic siege mentality and he hid his true feelings towards the country and its problems.

Don smiled inwardly when he thought how the foolish government had thought they could fight the world at large forever. Amazingly, they managed until the South African youth entered the fight. Almost everyone except himself underestimated the youth of the country. The group had taken to violence and terrorism like a duck to water. At a time when the Soviet Union was glad to find a market for their arms, they had been able to buy AK47 assault rifles and ammunition cheaply. Here again he had profited, helping the police with sophisticated electronic gadgetry to track down weapons. Then the times had changed. He carefully moved his assets to non-military applications and expanded his operations into providing rural communications. Now he was about to do the deal of his life. Provided his planning was accurate, he was going to move his assets offshore using a merger with a satellite company. Anticipating years of turmoil, he sold the incoming government on the advantages of satellite technology and was therefore allowed to move the money offshore in return for services to be provided. The country needed the communications satellite his company would be part owner in.

Don smirked. This promised to be the most successful business deal he had ever concluded. Distantly he heard the telephone ringing as his administrator took a call for him. Soon thereafter the telephone on his desk rang. He picked it up and walked across to the window where he stood looking out at the sunset. The call was from a friend of his in the police force. After listening for a short while he commented, "Do it!" and said good-bye. He picked up the phone again and made a long distance call.

Sitting in his suite at the Four Seasons hotel in Toronto, Canada, David Larrel was reading a newspaper when the phone rang. He was a heavily built man in his fifties, wearing a neat gray suit but with untidy hair and glasses that were a few years out of date in their style. The call obviously pleased him and he was grinning widely at the end of the brief conversation. As soon as he rang off, he pulled out his diary, looked up a pager number and dialed.

In London, Roger Maclean, a younger man than David Larrel but with impeccable taste in clothing and women, was being driven home from an evening party when his pager rang. He checked his pager in the taxi and dialed the number on his cell phone. He paid off the taxi driver as the call was answered and unlocked the door to his home. The message was so outrageous that he simply sat down on the front step. He went pale as he muttered yes several times before ringing off. For a while he just sat there with his head in his hands, and then according to the instructions he had received, he called a Hong Kong number to complete the instructions he had been given. Fear and excitement gripped his being. He relished it for a second contemplating the extraordinary position in which he found himself. "No more taxi's for me" he thought, "from now on I'll have my own limousine."

Don Warmen had not moved from his desk when early morning hours arrived in South Africa. He sipped some coffee while he awaited his call. When the phone rang, he listened to the man from Hong Kong, thanked him for the call before driving home in his Porsche for a few hours' sleep before sunrise.

CHAPTER TWENTY-THREE

Most of the Zinaville citizens were sleeping quietly as Don Warmen's international activity was evolving. Unseen eyes watched over them. Meanwhile those from the darker side amused themselves by torturing the dreams of the ungodly.

Susan van Vuuren was not fortunate enough to sleep. Her body was hot

and flushed, and her mind would not focus on reality. Every time she closed
her eyes to sleep, horrendous images of nightmarish characters flooded her
mind. Time and time again she tried not to close her eyes, but sooner or later
she would doze, and then almost instantly she would begin the terrifying
journey again. Through her turmoil, she felt guilt. She hated her father
and wanted to escape his stranglehold on her life. He knew too much. She
knew that it didn't matter where she tried to hide, he would find her. The
consequences of that were too horrible to imagine.

She considered how Hendrik hated Joshua. This became evident a few
evenings back when Hendrik arrived at her apartment unannounced just after
Joshua had left. He had begun to rave to her about family loyalty and that she
wasn't to see Joshua. When she had tried to point out that her meeting Joshua
wouldn't impact the work relationship, Hendrik became enraged. He hit her
across the mouth, calling her a slut. She knew better than to argue or provide
resistance. The pain and suffering resulting from resisting his demands would
not be worth the resistance. Bitterly she gave up the one glimmer of light and
joy that her existence had permitted her.

He then demanded that she institute charges against Joshua for rape
and assault. As wrong as she knew it to be, her spirit had broken, and she
capitulated. The next morning he arrived and had driven her to the police
station expecting her to do as he demanded.

This backfired because when faced with the reality of the lying and
charges and the threat of a medical examination, she gained the strength to
turn against her father. Retracting the charges, she left the police station and
had run away from her father.

She had arrived home and locked herself into her apartment. Then she
had lain on the bed crying. Not long thereafter, her father had been banging
at the door. She refused to open it and when he started to hammer at it she
had screamed that she would call the police if he didn't go away. That stopped
him but not before he cursed her with some of the foulest curses she had
ever heard him utter. Immense fear came over her and she had not left her
apartment since that time. The faintest sound of a footstep drove her to her
bedroom where she lay shaking on the bed.

It had been many days since then and she had hardly slept and had
only eaten what little she could find in the cupboards at home. She didn't
answer the telephone and jumped every time it rang. She was exhausted but
too frightened to sleep. Confusion placed its tendrils around her mind and
thoughts flowed at supersonic speed. Tonight was too much and suicide entered
her mind with provocative thoughts of a short trip to oblivion. Suddenly her
mind seemed to clear as this thought descended on her. It was a way out! No
further pain, no more nightmares, no more fight for existence. The thought

beckoned her on, and she considered her options. She had no sleeping tablets in the home. She fumbled for the phone, which she had disconnected. She needed to get some sent up.

"Yes! I'll call for a doctor and ask him to prescribe tranquilizers. When I get them, I'll take them all at once!"

Proud of succeeding in a single uninterrupted thought, Susan plugged the phone in. The instrument seemed to float in front of her as she dialed and it was as if her fingers knew the number all by themselves. An unseen angel gently prompted her with the numbers.

The voice at the other end of the phone sounded very sleepy and confused. She introduced herself and then asked the doctor if she could have some tranquilizers. There was a deadly silence at the other end of the phone. Susan waited but the doctor didn't reply.

"Doctor, can you hear me? I want you to phone the pharmacy with a prescription for tranquilizers." she re-iterated.

The silence continued a while longer.

"Susan, are you sure that is the correct thing to do?" the familiar voice asked.

"Yes, please, just phone the store now please!" she sobbed.

"Susan, do you know who is speaking? It's me, Joshua!"

She struggled with the delusion. How had her doctor turned into Joshua? It didn't make sense! She burst out crying and put the phone down. What was going on? A feeling of dread hit her again. Too tired and weak even to do anything she curled into a ball and cried, and cried.

Joshua was more than amazed. It was unpleasant to get woken in the middle of the night but when it was the woman he was attracted to, whom he had been told had tried to accuse him of rape a few days ago, he didn't know what to make of it. Susan sounded distraught and irrational. Something told him he should do something immediately. He picked up the phone and called Jake Pankhurst.

Jake wasn't exactly courteous, his treatment of people who woke him in the small hours was always offhand. A pastor of a church was prone to calls from people who thought he was awake for twenty-four hours a day to meet their special needs. He found it particularly annoying when they felt they had received a revelation from God in their sleepless hours and felt they had to inform him immediately. His silent annoyance was however tempered by the knowledge of Joshua's bereavement and so he listened as Joshua explained. The concern in Joshua's voice penetrated and he started to understand the young man's situation. Advising Joshua to call Carl he offered to accompany him to Susan's apartment. He would pick up Joshua within five minutes.

Joshua called Carl who said he would meet them outside the apartment. Fifteen minutes later, the men were gathered alongside their cars outside Susan's apartment. The weather was unpleasant with a miserable drizzle wetting them as they gathered around Carl's car. He'd called for the assistance of a woman constable and she arrived within a few minutes. After explaining the situation, the group made their way up to the apartment.

Inside, Susan was lying quivering on her bed when the doorbell rang. Panic gripped her at the noise and she began to scream with fear. Carl, hearing her cry, looked at the two men and as one they all hammered the door with their shoulders until it broke open. They burst into the apartment almost bowling each over as the door gave way. An ominous silence greeted them as they entered and regained their feet. They all spread out trying to locate the source of the scream. The woman constable shouted out re-assurances to Susan. The sound of breaking glass caused everyone to run to the bedroom. As they stumbled into the room their eyes met the sight of a wild-eyed Susan who had thrown a chair through the window and was starting to climb out. The lady constable was first to react and caught onto Susan's hand while trying to calm her with her voice.

Beyond reason, Susan clawed at the other woman's face and when the constable drew back, Susan almost made it out of the window. The men rushed forward grabbing whatever part of an arm or leg they could reach and held her tightly. They pulled her back inside, but shards of broken glass had cut her jeans and one leg. They placed her on the bed and held her down until she relaxed.

Susan was like a frightened animal, almost too stunned to realize who she was or what was happening. Waves of extreme fear rolled through her mind and the pain in her leg contributed to a disturbing kaleidoscope of distorted perceptions. In the midst of this pain, she saw a smiling image of Joshua come and go. It was as if for the first time a ray of light penetrated. Glimmering recognition traced a glimmer of a smile before her expression went blank again. The two police officers directed Joshua and Jake to leave them alone with Susan. They suggested the men get something warm for Susan to drink. Joshua and Jake went to the kitchen to make the coffee. A while later Carl left Susan with his sub-ordinate to come and talk to them.

"She is extremely scared," he reported. "It's impossible to make much sense of what she is saying and she isn't capable of laying charges against anyone but my guess is that somebody wants to do her harm. Her inability to explain the situation means that I can't use police resources to protect her this evening."

He turned to Jake.

"I know this is asking a lot, but could you take her to your home for a day or two?"

Jake agreed pending his wife's approval. He went off to phone her.

"Carl, who is doing this to her?" Joshua wanted to know.

Carl shook his head.

"If only I knew! They have scared her half to death! This lady is beyond reasonable fear. I am hoping that a few days rest in safety will help her tell us who or what has done this."

Jake returned saying that his wife had agreed.

They all escorted Susan down to the Jake's car and her drove her to his home. The lady constable accompanied him and the others followed. Jake's wife helped with a shower, cup of tea, tranquilizer, and some prayer, and Susan was soon asleep. The tossing and turning showed that all was not well, but at least she was resting. Sharleen, Jake's wife, waited until their guest was comfortable and the police had left, before she asked her husband and Joshua what it was all about. They explained what they knew. It was 6a.m. before Joshua got back home. He was worried about Susan and prayed for her safety and recovery.

Around the Pankhurst home was a brilliant ring of heavenly protection that could be seen for miles in the spiritual world. The Christians were starting to make their stand. In the shadows various groups of demons were working themselves into frenzy in an attempt to re-establish their control. Amazingly, the people whose prayers had made this all possible slept on peacefully, a guardian watching each as they restored their physical strength.

CHAPTER TWENTY-FOUR

Later in the day in Toronto, Canada, David Larrel was meeting with a friend, Ronald Jackson Jr. David finished reading the morning paper and then slowly strolled down to a coffee shop near the subway, not far from the Toronto Dominion bank where he was heading afterwards. It was early on the cool spring morning and he was glad to get inside out of the cold air. The warmth of the shop and the exquisite aroma of coffee and donuts made David feel as if he had never had any breakfast. Soon he was sitting in a corner facing the door enjoying a chocolate covered doughnut and a cup of black coffee. He had been there no longer than ten minutes when Ron Jr. walked in.

Ron was below average in build, with sandy colored hair, an infectious smile and emerald green eyes that penetrated your soul from behind his thin rimmed spectacles. In his late thirties, he carried himself off as a much younger person and dressed the part. He slouched across to where David was sitting and slumped into the chair opposite him.

"How's my millionaire friend? Still too cheap to buy a friend some doughnuts?" he joked.

David grinned.

"Still too immature to have learned manners Ron?" he replied, a touch of coolness in his voice. Ron ignored it and pulled a small credit card like item from his pocket.

"Here it is! Now, where are my share certificates?"

"At the Dominion Bank as we agreed. How does this work?"

"Ever heard of E-mail Dave?" Ron wanted to know. "This is the latest form of getting information from one point to another. Thousands of computers worldwide are all connected and many of them have telephone lines into them. The department of defense wanted to use this network, but didn't think that the information was secure enough. This card answered their problems. With this baby you can get right into the satellite program control center electronically but you can't get into the satellite computers themselves."

David lost all pretense of looking calm.

"So? How is the gadget used?" he wanted to know.

Ron smiled and shook his head.

"Not until I know that I have the share certificates and that they are verified to be correct. Shall we go?"

David's grin was strained but he agreed and they both went out into the cool air again. The wind had picked up and they didn't talk as they walked. Instead they put their faces in their scarves.

When they got to the bank, a third man joined them as they entered through the revolving doors. He made some short comment to Ron who merely smiled and shrugged at David's angry look. He obviously thought that he had more bargaining ability than David.

They made their way to the safety deposit box. It had two keys and it could only be opened if both men agreed to unlock it. Ron smiled.

"So? Where are the share certificates?" he asked again.

David reached into his overcoat pocket and pulled out a long brown envelope, which he handed over. Ron handed David the credit card gadget after handing the certificates to the third man. While David investigated the gadget, Ron's companion looked at the certificates and made a few short phone calls on his cellular phone. Finally he nodded to Ron, handed the certificates back and left.

"Didn't you trust me?" David asked.

"When I'm dealing with tens of millions of dollars, I don't trust even myself!" Ron replied. "Now, let me explain how the security card works..."

David looked at the card again. It was pale blue. There were three small displays. The first had a time on it. This was not the local time and he surmised it was based on Greenwich Mean Time with a twenty-four hour clock. The second and third display both contained twelve characters in groups of three. As he watched a display it changed. The periodic changing of the pattern of numbers and letters were meaningless.

"The top display is the time that you need to synchronize your computer system. You then call the following number on the electronic world wide web."

Ron handed David a business card and a diskette.

"Use the program on the diskette. When you get connected, a program downloads and runs within 30 seconds of downloading to re-connect your computer with another via a special access number. This access number is only valid for a short period."

He smiled. "This is a tough system to break into!"

David nodded.

"The program asks for a security identification code. Type the second number to get you in. You get asked to do this every five minutes. The third number is used when you enter the Star Wars program series. The screen will change from blue to green. You will now need to enter the number in the last display on the card. Please be very careful. You must enter it exactly. Failure to do so will result in an instant dismissal from the system, an automatic purging of the program from your computer, it will also scramble as much information on your computer as is possible before you can switch it off. Do you understand the threat of making even one mistake?"

David nodded again. "End of our venture?" he commented.

"Right! Finally, when you're using this you need to be able to talk to me at the same time. The program is loaded with personal information about myself. You will need to keep a line open to me continually as questions will be asked on a random basis. These are based on my life and work. Failure to answer correctly creates a security alert and stops any further information transfer. I could get into a lot of trouble and the card would come under scrutiny."

Ron paused to ensure David understood. David looked thoughtful.

"So what you're saying is that my computer connects to a second computer. I get asked for a number periodically. While the background is blue I type in the middle number if it's green I use the bottom number. When the computer asks some personal information, I ask you, you tell me, and I enter it in before carrying on. Hell! This is more complicated than breaking into Fort Knox."

"...and more lucrative!" Ron answered. "Don't try to open the cards surface to see if you can duplicate the circuitry. It contains numerous chips each testing the integrity of the others. Hairline circuits just under the surface join these. Cut one and the card begins to give out false data after destroying some of its circuitry. In this state if you try to use it you will be connected into Interpol and from there into USA national security immediately. You would not even know this! I suggest you look after it carefully. Bending it is not advisable..." a grin crossed Ron's face. "My friends are ingenious, don't you think! Oh! Also, remember it's only valid for the next two months!"

David looked decidedly glum.

"Ruddy nasty little thing!" he commented. "Can I have the certificates back now please?"

Ron handed them over and they were locked into the safety deposit box. Each man locked it with his own key.

"Ron, I'll not be the person contacting you. When the job is done, I'll send this key to you. Meantime, let me know if anything changes at work."

On that note they shook hands and each left in separate directions. David carefully placed the card in his pocket. Now he needed to transfer fifteen thousand dollars to the account of Mr. van Vuuren in South Africa!

CHAPTER TWENTY-FIVE

Back in Zinaville, Susan was still sleeping deeply when Joshua arrived at the Pankhurst home at 1p.m. Sharleen provided him with coffee and light conversation until just past two-o-clock when Susan awoke and came into the kitchen. She was obviously bewildered, and both Sharleen and Joshua could see that she remembered very little of the previous evening's events. She went pale when she saw Joshua and almost turned away. Sharleen went to her and put her arm around her shoulders and gently led her to a chair at the kitchen table.

"Hi Susan, I hope you're feeling better!" Joshua greeted her.

"Yes, thanks!" A faint smile glimmered somewhere deep and faded so quickly that it might not have been there at all. "Where am I?" she asked.

Sharleen explained the events of the evening. Joshua just sat and listened. When Sharleen was finished he spoke.

"Susan, I don't know who is after you, or why you're so scared, or why you haven't called me earlier, but I am glad that you're safe here."

"Also, you're welcome to stay here until you feel you can go somewhere else safely," Sharleen added.

Susan said thanks, but more than that she wasn't willing to contribute. She sat in silence without looking at them until Sharleen gave her the small suitcase that the woman constable had packed with some of her belongings. Susan asked where the bathroom was and went to shower. Joshua stayed for a few more minutes and then left to go back to work.

Joshua arrived on the ZPM plant to find that Hendrik had taken over and was administering activities. He checked the plant statistics and he found them accurate. Working with Hendrik was now an immense strain for him and Joshua quickly found an excuse to leave. He physically inspected the plant activities. His mind mulled over the faxes they had read the previous day. Tom and Carl had also read them but they hadn't discussed them yet. Carl had taken them to the police station.

Joshua remembered a snippet of the first fax..." inform the B that the data as discussed for the final operational instruction retrieval can be obtained. Location of the final equipment is underway and the contact with R.J will be made within the next month" What could that mean? Who was B and who was R.J? There was some attempt to find equipment that had been referred to. A later fax had shown, "Shipment, will arrive Friday." Based on the fax date which was recent, this was referring to the coming Friday. What would the shipment be? Where would it arrive?

There was only one fax that followed the one referring to the shipment. That said..." Visitor to see Rod A. to arrive, Flight ZA 204 from New York. Meet at Holiday Inn on Wednesday 18h00 in Foyer. Yellow green duffel bag. Congratulations on dispatching problem. B. will clear problems both with dispatch and with customs(if any should arise). Inform him of bag color and date. Attempt to silence J.R. However, not overtly! Look forward to BM at Easter. Regards D.W."

What did this all mean? Suddenly it occurred to him that the Wednesday evening referred to was this very evening. All desire to work effectively disappeared as he realized that Hendrik was to meet someone tonight. He wondered if Carl had come to the same conclusion. He completed his rounds of plant activities and satisfied himself that everything was running smoothly. Then he called Carl at the station.

Carl was decidedly gruff when he answered the phone. Obviously the late night intruded on his attitude towards the world. He listened to what Joshua had to say.

"Joshua, keep clear of Hendrik," he warned. "I'll do the follow up work and check to see what this is all about. The last thing that is needed is for him to cause a further problem for your mother."

"Carl, I am involved," Joshua protested. "How can I stand back when my family is involved? Could you? What are you going to do about this meeting?"

"Joshua, will you listen to me or must I use the law to ensure you do?" Carl growled. "While you're at work, you can keep an eye on Hendrik from a distance, but when he leaves you must not follow. Do you think he'll meet the person if he sees you following him? Leave this work to us professionals! All I need you to do is provide me with the registration of his vehicle. Other than that, stay out of it!"

Joshua agreed and rang off. He was annoyed, but understood the other man's point of view as well. He strolled down to the parking lot and wrote down Hendrik's vehicle license plate number. Then, he went to look for Hendrik to ask him for the fax room key.

"I, will send your fax for you," Hendrik volunteered.

Joshua shook his head.

"Sorry, Hendrik, it's of a confidential nature and I must send it myself," he said and stretched out his hand to receive the keys.

"I must still collect and distribute the faxes," Hendrik answered, ignoring the outstretched hand. "I'll come with you."

Joshua smiled inwardly.

"I know why too," he thought as he followed the foreman to the fax room. Hendrik unlocked the door and handed the key to Joshua. He then collected the few fax sheets that were lying in the out tray and left. Joshua scribbled down the license number onto a fax header sheet together with Carl's name and rank and the word 'Urgent'. He sent the message to Carl and was about to leave when the fax started to print out a message again.

From D.W

To F.J van Vuuren

Customs fixed as required. Please take our visitor to the site this evening. Imperative that the work be completed rapidly.

Joshua grabbed another header sheet and wrote another message "Carl, this came while I was at the machine. Please review" and sent it to the station together with a copy of the fax to Hendrik. Placing Hendrik's fax back in the output tray, he locked the room and returned the key to Hendrik who was relieved to have it back judging from his grateful expression. This expression soon changed into a 'Why the hell are you still standing around here?' type of expression. Joshua left. He positioned himself at the shift supervisor office overlooking the fax room and spent the rest of the afternoon there, chatting to the supervisor.

At four thirty, Hendrik made his way over to the fax office, opened the door and disappeared inside. He re-appeared a minute later, locked the door and walked off to security. Joshua excused himself and selected a route to the office that would cross Hendrik's path. He 'accidentally' met Hendrik a short distance from the gate.

"Hi Hendrik, planning to leave early?" he asked.

The older man looked annoyed. "Yes! In fact I was!" he answered curtly. "Do you have a problem with that? My work is complete and I have an urgent matter to attend to in Johannesburg."

Joshua shook his head. "No, I don't have a problem with that." he answered. "I do however expect to be told about the fact that you're leaving early. Seeing as you didn't bother to let me know, could you bring the production figures for the day to my office before you leave."

Hendrik went red in the face. Without a word, turned on his heel and went off in the direction of the supervisor's office.

Joshua made his way to his office where he phoned the police station. He was told that Carl had left an hour previously and was expected back the next day. Joshua was worried. What if Carl didn't get to follow Hendrik? He decided that he had to do something himself. He locked his drawers and as he finished, Hendrik came in. He threw the report onto Joshua's desk.

"Anything else, SIR?" he said sarcastically. "May I leave now?"

Joshua nodded and Hendrik left immediately.

Ten minutes after Hendrik left, Joshua made his way through security to his own vehicle. Hendrik's car was no longer in the parking lot. Joshua gave chase. On the outskirts of town, he came up behind Hendrik and followed him to the first set of traffic lights. Hendrik didn't seem to see him. When the lights changed, they both headed out down the main street towards Johannesburg. The next set of lights caught both of them again and before Joshua even came to a halt, he felt a jerk from behind as a vehicle nudged into his. His heart sank! He envisaged Hendrik getting away as he settled with the driver behind.

He climbed out, and when he got to the culprit in the car behind he was amazed to see Carl glowering at him.

"Why are you not doing as I told you?" Carl said angrily. "Get your car out of my way and stay in town," he ordered.

Joshua shot him a guilty grin and did as asked. Carl's car disappeared up the street following Hendrik's towards Johannesburg.

Joshua drove to the Pankhurst home.. When he got there he was pleased to see Susan was sitting chatting to Sharleen in the kitchen. He knocked on the kitchen door and Sharleen let him in.

"Hi Sharleen, Hi Susan" he greeted them. "I thought I would drop by to see how you're doing."

They both smiled, but it was obvious that he had interrupted a woman-to-woman talk. Sharleen, gracious as always, offered him tea and cookies. He accepted and while it was being brewed, there was an uneasy silence, broken only by Sharleen's chatter. She placed the tea on the table and excused herself, leaving them alone.

"How are you Susan?" Joshua finally asked.

Susan smiled wanly. "Better than over the past few days. Thank you for helping! I am sorry for all the trouble I have caused. I don't know how to thank the Pankhurst's for all that they have done," she added.

"Possibly by recovering as best as you can," Joshua interjected. "Susan, what is this rumor that I hear of you attempting to lay charges of 'rape' against me? Why in the world would you do that? I thought we had a friendship starting. How could you do that?"

Susan looked down but before she did, he could see a flicker of anger in her eyes.

"I'm really sorry Joshua." She looked up; her eyes fiery and filled with tears. "I told you how powerful my father is. I told you there is a lot you couldn't understand. I did warn you...!" her voice trembled. "I didn't want to do it, Josh. Really, I didn't! He made me do it! He always makes me do things!" Her voice was full of emotion that welled up and stopped her speaking.

Joshua waited patiently with concern as she fought for control. "I would never want to hurt you. I had to do as he said. I didn't have an option, he's my father."

Sharleen came back into the room. Immediately she sensed that there was a serious discussion taking place.

"I can see you two have things to discuss. I'll have my tea in the living room and you can join me when you're finished."

They both smiled their appreciation. Sharleen took her cup and some cookies and went out.

"My father hates your family Josh!" Susan revealed.

Josh nodded agreement. "So, what's new? How could you think to lay such a charge? I like you very much Susan and I thought it was reciprocated. What is going on?"

"Josh, it was reciprocated. You're the best thing that has happened to me! Josh, there is a lot about me you don't know. If you did you wouldn't like me! You would despise me! My father knows things about me that he could use to destroy my life! Believe me, please!"

Joshua's anger slowly subsided again. In the spiritual world Beor touched him. Joshua looked at Susan. He saw her beauty despite her tears. More than that, he somehow saw a little girl with a tearstained muddy face looking up at someone in shock and fear. Overwhelming compassion filled his heart. He moved his chair to alongside hers and took her hand in his.

"Susan, I don't think there is anything that can change my feelings for you. I love you and want to help. However, to do that I need to know what is wrong, everything! How about starting at the beginning?"

Susan looked fearful and as if she was going to refuse and then, she started to explain. Joshua listened and realized that she had probably never told anyone what she was telling him. He realized just how broken she was. Her father had started abusing her at an early age. Twice she had actually fallen pregnant. Both times her father had arranged an abortion. From what she said, he had absolute control over her life. Her mother had died before she was old enough to remember her, and Joshua wondered if her mother's existence had also been as difficult. Susan had tried to run away once when she was in high school and had failed miserably. Her father caught her and beat her badly. So badly that he reported to the school that she was away with an aunt. He kept her indoors for two months while the bruises faded but sexually molested her during that time.

Joshua could hardly believe what he heard. He felt anger welling up inside him together with his love for this terribly scared women. As the story of her life unfolded, it seemed as if she grew younger and more vulnerable. Her head drooped lower and lower as she spoke and soon she avoided eye contact altogether. The words passed into a silence where they reverberated around his soul. Gently he took her face into his hands and turned it to himself. He kissed her and then told her that what she had said didn't make the slightest difference. His feelings towards her hadn't changed.

Susan began to sob, and he just held her. Sharleen found the two of them sitting together in this way when she came in to place her cup in the sink. She looked quizzically at Joshua who simply shook his head. Susan didn't even notice her. Sharleen left them and went back to the living room to continue praying in a quiet voice. Around her a throng of angels protected her. Now and then, as her requests were made known, one of them would depart to see the requests met. Others joined every so often to hear her prayers. Around the home, a throng of angels defended the property. This home was holy ground and from appearances, that wasn't going to change. The only demonic activity in the environment accompanied Susan. This small group knew they were hopelessly outnumbered. They had coalesced into a screaming ranting globule of hell around her, their noise and activity making up for their lack of confidence.

CHAPTER TWENTY-SIX

Forty kilometers away, Carl followed Hendrik to a small pub in a hotel in Johannesburg. Hendrik settled at the bar and looked around. Carl walked directly through to the men's room to avoid being seen. He was standing at the washbasin when a toilet flushed and a man came out to wash his hands. Carl immediately recognized Brigadier van Vuuren, the man who had given him so much trouble in the Brandy Bob case. The Brigadier was a heavyset man with an almost non-existent neck, and Carl had seen his tight-lipped face many times in police department notices. Quickly, Carl turned and entered the vacated toilet stall, ensuring the man didn't see him. He didn't know why he did this, as he was sure the man would not have recognized him. He had just felt a compulsion to do so and followed his instincts. Carl was only one of a large number of men who were under the Brigadier's command in a distributed manner. It was hardly likely that the Brigadier could recognize everyone that he controlled.

When the Brigadier left Carl followed him. Hendrik was no longer in the Pub and neither was the Brigadier. Carl nearly panicked! What if he lost Hendrik? He calmed himself and looked around the room again. Sure that they were no longer there; he climbed the staircase to the door. He was about to open it when he heard Hendrik's voice just outside.

"Gideon, just make sure to meet me at exactly nine fifteen at the usual spot. If you're a minute late, my friend will not be able to get you in. You <u>must</u> be on time! Bye! *Goed gaan, broer!*"

Carl recognized the last part to be Hendrik saying good-bye to his brother. The thought hit him like a kick in the stomach. Hendrik and the Brigadier were related! No wonder he had been getting so much trouble over the last while. Since his murder investigation, Hendrik had probably told his brother he was investigating the mine where he worked. Obviously the Brigadier had decided to keep a watch on how the work was progressing. This had probably led to his interest in the case.

The voices and the sound of footsteps led away from the door. Carl opened the door and watched as the two men walked off down the street. Hendrik waved good-bye to his brother and crossed the street. Carl was in a quandary. What should he do? Follow Hendrik or the Brigadier. He retrieved the fax from his pocket.

He read again, *"Meet at Holiday Inn on Wednesday 18h00 in Foyer."*

"I can always catch up with Hendrik later" he thought and followed the Brigadier. The Brigadier climbed into a red Honda further down the street. Carl just had time to race back to his own car and get out into the traffic before the Honda turned at the traffic lights and disappeared. Carl decided to misuse his portable police light for once. He clipped it onto the vehicle dashboard. Turning on his siren briefly, he shot out into the street and through the red light. Just as quickly, he switched the siren off and pulled the light off the dashboard. The Brigadier was one traffic light ahead.

He followed the Honda through the tree-lined streets painted orange with the glow of the setting sun. The vendors were out selling newspapers. A small half starved waif in torn shirt and barefoot knocked on the car window as Carl waited at another set of traffic lights. "Newspaper, read today's news, cheap!" He bought it to get the attention away from his car and was rewarded with a bright white smile in the happy little black face when he refused the change. *"Dankie,* thank-you sir!" the street vendor shouted as the lights changed and the cars pulled away. For a second he again felt compassion for these small street merchants and then his mind focused on the task of following the Brigadier without being seen.

The Brigadier wound his way through streets and up a long hill to where several university residences were located. He pulled up alongside one and a student came out to his car. He made a U turn and headed back towards Carl who suddenly found himself doubled over to avoid detection. His car parked at the side of the street was fairly innocuous and he hoped the Brigadier would not recognize it. The Brigadier passed at quite a speed. He obviously was in a hurry. Carl waited until he had turned the corner and then followed.

The traffic in the city was building up to peak hour and it was fairly easy to follow without being observed. They slowly curved their way to the airport and in less than half an hour approached the off-ramp that led to the arrivals terminal. Carl realized that the Brigadier was going to the Holiday Inn on the airfield property and took a chance to park in the airport car park rather than follow the Brigadier into the hotel parking. He rushed over to the hotel as fast as he could, just in time to see the Brigadier enter the foyer. Carl strolled up to a gardener working outside the entrance and asked him a complicated question. While engaging the man in the discussion, he watched the Brigadier walk up to a dark haired man dressed in jeans and with a pale yellow sweater. The man was holding a green and yellow duffel bag with a small USA flag on its side. They engaged in conversation for a short while and then both turned and headed back towards the door.

Carl hurriedly ended his conversation with the gardener and walked back to his vehicle. By the time he paid for his parking, he was sure the Brigadier would have got away. Angrily he floored the accelerator and shot out into the traffic. He presumed that they would head back towards Johannesburg and he hoped to catch-up. Good guess! Five minutes later he passed the Honda. He pulled in front of a slow truck they were following. When they passed the truck, he picked up their trail again.

The traffic was heavy but he tracked them into the city center where they parked in an underground parking. He followed but instead of parking, hung back until they entered the elevators. These elevators opened into the garage and he could see the illuminated floor indicators from his car. He drove up to where he could see which floor they ascended to, and then went to park. They had gone up to the first floor and as soon as he parked he followed.

The elevator opened into a large reception area that was decorated with exquisite paintings of wildlife, semi-precious stones, and arrangements of dried grass and flowers. It had an African flavor to it but exuded a presence of money and wealth. A receptionist guarding a set of elevators was the only person in sight. He made his way to the reception desk.

"Hello, I have a meeting with a Mr. van Vuuren and a Sir Thomas Foot. Could you let them know I am here?" he commented as he greeted the receptionist.

She looked confused.

"I am sorry," she answered, "The only Mr. van Vuuren I know of is a man who is here to see Mr. Warmen and there is no Sir Thomas Foot here. I don't think there is anyone of that name that works here. At the moment, there are very few people still available. Sorry, what did you say your name was?"

Carl told her and she looked through a list on her computer.

"I'm afraid I don't have you listed here! Are you sure you're in the correct building?"

"Is this the Carlton Center?" he asked knowing it wasn't.

"No, you're completely in the wrong place. She provided him with directions on how to find the Center and he went back down to the garage to wait for the men to return.

They were away for the better part of an hour. When they returned, the student was carrying a small laptop computer and they were arguing over something. Carl made a note of the time and gave them nicknames. The tall man in the yellow turtleneck sweater he called 'Stretch' and he called the student 'Nerd'. Nerd was arguing with Stretch, and the Brigadier wasn't looking happy. They sat in the Honda arguing for a while before the Honda backed out of the parking bay and screeched out of the parking garage.

Again Carl followed. This time he was too slow. The vehicle had disappeared by the time he got into the street. Annoyed, he turned his car towards Zinaville and decided to relax and listen to the radio as he drove.

He realized that Hendrik hadn't been at the Holiday Inn and that the fax message had not referred to Hendrik but to someone named B. It took a while for him to realize that B. referred to the Brigadier, the message suddenly made some sense. He mentally revised the message: *"Visitor to see Rod A. to arrive, Flight ZA 204 from New York. Meet at Holiday Inn on Wednesday 18h00 in Foyer. Yellow green duffel bag. Congratulations on dispatching problem. Brigadier will clear problems both with dispatch and with customs(if any should arise). Inform him of bag color and date. Attempt to silence J.R. However, not overtly! Look forward to BM at Easter. Regards D.W."*

It appeared as if Stretch was the Visitor referred to in the fax. He had been carrying the duffel bag at the right time in the right place. Carl wondered what was in the duffel bag. It made sense that the Brigadier was 'B.' as he had the contacts and influence to deal with customs. Whatever the message meant by referring to 'dispatching the problem' he didn't understand. He also had no idea who the 'Rod.A.' and the 'J.R.' referred to. He made a wild guess that D.W. was referring to Warmen and made a mental note to find out Warmen's first name.

"What could the connection be between this industrialist, a metallurgical plant foreman, a student, a police Brigadier and an American?" he thought.

The link eluded him. The more he thought about it, the more confused he became. He put the immediate problem out of his mind and started to think about how he was going to structure his report. Suddenly he realized that even this was not simple.

"What if the Brigadier was somehow involved?"

The report would provide the very people he needed to track with information that he was onto them! He was in a quandary. He already didn't fully trust Constable Gerhard. The police station at Zinaville was small and there was nobody else there that he could confide in. It looked like he was on his own! He realized that he would need help but didn't know where to find it.

These thoughts occupied his mind as he drove and as he was entering the outskirts of Zinaville, he decided that he would discuss the situation with Tom. He had respect for the shrewd way the former sailor had built up his fortune and his staff at the same time and considered that if he had to turn to civilian support, this man was a good option. His only concern was that Joshua shouldn't get any further stress from the situation. He believed he was responsible for giving the young man hope in regard to finding his father's murderer and didn't want him to think that there was a possibility of police involvement in the situation. Adding to this, he wasn't sure if Joshua would not somehow pass information to Susan. He'd call Tom when he got home! A shower and meal would be great!

CHAPTER TWENTY-SEVEN

Carl scrubbed himself under the hot water enjoying the pulsating of the spray on the back of his neck when the thought hit him! Unseen a glimmer of light flashed and the luminous trail of an angel glowed for an instant.

"What about Hendrik?" How could he have been so slow! Carl wanted to kick himself. He remembered the conversation between Hendrik and his brother.

"Gideon, just make sure to meet me at exactly nine fifteen at the usual spot."

Hurriedly he finished and toweled himself dry. Picking up his watch he realized that he couldn't get to Hendrik's home in time. There was too much ground to cover. It was already 8:30. The likelihood of Hendrik even being at home was remote. He decided to call Joshua who lived at that side of town. The phone rang but nobody answered. He let it ring a few times and then he hung up. Next he called Tom. Mrs. Wold picked up the line. Carl had a second to wonder what she was doing at the office at that time of night before he asked her if he could speak to Tom.

"I am sorry sir, but he has gone to have a few drinks at the Priggles Bar," she informed him. Carl thanked her and rang the bar. Lofty answered. He called Tom to the phone.

"What's a lazy public servant like you doing bothering an honest citizen as he drowns his sorrows?" Tom teased him. Carl wasn't feeling like idle chatter and so explained his activities to Tom in as succinct a manner as he could while being polite. Tom listened.

"I've got some good news for you mate," Tom's inebriated voice proclaimed in what was supposed to be whisper, "Hendrik is here right now! He's alone, sitting in one of the conversation pits at the end of the room. He is in a foul mood! Almost swore at me when I greeted him."

Carl experienced a warm gush of thankfulness towards this aging seaman. He asked him if he would keep an eye on him until he got there.

"Sure! You pay for the drinks though," Tom warned and hung up.

Carl dressed quickly and within minutes was in his car heading over to Priggles Bar. As he got there and walked in, Hendrik walked out. They nodded a greeting to each other, and Carl felt his heart leap into his throat. He couldn't walk out immediately. If Hendrik saw him now, he would know something was up. The thought had hardly passed when he bumped into Tom who was heading out the same door.

"Hi Tom! Thanks for your help!" he said.

The older man grabbed his arm and pulled him to one side.

"I follow him, you follow me," he ordered. "That way you can bail me outa trouble if something happens. Got it? Oh, and by the way you owe me for the drinks!"

Carl hardly had time to react and nod before the older man pushed him aside and strode out into the night. Carl smiled to himself. He wondered how many of Tom's opponents had underestimated him. He waited a minute and then followed.

Tom was getting into his car part way down the street. Carl's eyes adjusted to the darkness. Soon he was in his own car and they were driving off into the dark. The cars tagged each other down the main street and then headed out of town passing ZPM. As planned, Carl kept back from Tom's car. He made sure that the taillights of Hendrik's car were out of sight most of the time. They were 15 minutes out of town when suddenly Tom's taillights disappeared. Carl accelerated. Soon he went speeding passed Tom's car parked at the side of the road.

Annoyed with his foolish following procedure, he was about to slow and turn around when he passed another two cars also parked in the shadows. As the beams of his headlamps swept over them, it appeared to be both Hendrik's car, and the Honda of the Brigadier that he had been following that afternoon.

He kept on driving as he knew that the sound of a car stopping and turning around would notify the group of men that they were being followed. He hoped Tom would be able to see what was happening and that he wouldn't do anything stupid. Glancing at his watch, he could see it was 8:55 p.m.

The night was already dark and there wasn't much traffic on the country road. When the next vehicle passed him, he stopped and did a U-turn. He went back to where he had seen the stationary cars. They were no longer there! He continued on to where he had seen Tom's car at the side of the road. It was also missing! Again he stopped and did another U-turn. Now he was quite worried. What had happened? Was Tom in difficulty? He pulled over to where Tom's car had been parked.

Climbing out, he shone his flashlight on the ground where the car had been parked. The tire tracks were clearly visible in the soft sand. He looked for footprints but there were none. From the way the sand had been scooped up and sprayed backwards, it looked like the car had accelerated away, indicating Tom had been in a hurry.

Thinking back, Carl realized that the cars hadn't passed him. That meant they had turned off somewhere along the stretch of road between where he had passed them and before he had turned around. There were numerous farm roads leading off the main tarred stretch but there was only one other main road. From what Carl could remember, that led to an observatory. He remembered seeing a sign to that effect and he decided to take that route to see if he could find Tom and the others.

The turnoff was half a kilometer down the road. The sign actually indicated a radio observatory and a satellite station. Carl turned in and followed the road. It twisted and turned a bit and then forked. The sign to the left said 'Hartebeeshoek satellite tracking station', and the other said 'Observatory'. Carl chose the 'Observatory' as he knew that there was likely to be security around the tracking station. He had just passed the intersection when again he passed Tom's car standing in the shadows in the bush at the side of the road.

Again Carl was angry with himself. He drove on for half a kilometer then slowed, turned off his lights and did a U-turn. It was a dark night but the clarity with which the stars shone gave him sufficient light to drive by. Slowly he made his way back to the intersection. Turning off his engine before he got there, he coasted up into the shadows to where Tom's car was hidden. The crunching of the gravel under the wheels of the car was the only sound. Once that stopped, an eerie silence seemed to fill the night air. Carl just sat still for a moment listening to the silence.

A sound of the car door opening was followed by the crunching sound of footsteps in gravel as Tom made his way over. Tom opened the passenger door and climbed in. He greeted Carl, scolding him for causing a noise and failing to pay attention to events before explaining how the two cars had turned off on the road leading to the tracking station. Tom knew the station. He had been there to get some geological and agricultural photographs of the lands around the mine in the stations formative years. His negotiations with the farmers had been greatly simplified when he could calculate their yield of crops from the photographs instead of relying on their statements. Remembering the setup at that time, he knew that there was security at the gate. He told Carl he had not followed them for that reason. Instead he had opted for waiting in the dark, hoping he could get an idea of what was happening from a distance. Unfortunately, little could be seen and they sat in silence for a while.

Time ticked by. Nothing had happened by midnight and the men were getting tired. Tom offered to show Carl some of the star constellations while they were waiting and they both climbed out of the car and looked up into the heavens. The stars were bright and clearly visible. Carl was amazed at Tom's knowledge and as they were getting into the intricacies of the universe, they heard a car start up in the distance.

They went over to Tom's car and waited. Soon two cars came out of the enclosed area and headed back towards the main road. Tom waited until they were out of sight before pulling out after them. Carl climbed into his car and followed.

By the time they got to the main road, there wasn't a car in sight. Tom pulled his car over onto the verge of the road and Carl pulled in alongside. Shouting to each other they decided to choose opposite directions to follow the cars. Tom would follow the route into town as he himself took the other direction for twenty minutes or so. He would return if he didn't catch up with anyone. They both pulled off in a hurry and headed in their respective directions.

Carl was fairly sure that both car's had headed into town but used the opportunity to test the unmarked police car capability. He enjoyed high speed and the high pitched hum of a finely tuned engine driving a car at over a hundred and sixty kilometers per hour on dark twisting roads pleased him. He drove hard but carefully keeping an eye out for cattle and wildlife.

After fifteen minutes, he could see the headlights of a car in the distance. He kept going and within another five minutes was able to catch up to within a few hundred meters of the vehicle. Not sure what car it was, he decided to pass. He waited until he reached a straight stretch of road and then shot passed. He was amazed to see that it was Hendrik's car. He had assumed that both cars would go in the same direction. Realizing that to slow down now would cause suspicion he accelerated into the distance. The road was long and straight without any major turn-off and so he planned to get out of sight, park on one of the sandy farm roads and wait for Hendrik to come by. Within another ten minutes of hard fast driving, he was sufficiently ahead to do just that. He found a side road to a farm that was fairly hidden from the main road, parked and turned off his lights, leaving the engine ticking over.

Five minutes went past, and then ten. Realization that Hendrik wasn't going to pass came slowly and after fifteen minutes, Carl decided to give up waiting. He pulled out of his hiding place and headed back towards Zinaville. He was disappointed but at the same time glad that he could go home and get some rest. It had been a long evening!

Tom's attempt to follow had been even more worthless. The speed of his chase had been more leisurely and by the time he got to the outskirts of town, he had not seen a single car on the road. The effect of the beer was now weighing heavily on his bladder and he turned towards home having had enough excitement for one night. In the morning he needed to attend a sales meeting and he knew the particular kind of hell he went through when he was tired and not as clear thinking as he should be.

CHAPTER TWENTY-EIGHT

Carl got into the police station the next morning later than he had planned. As he passed the charge desk sergeant on the way to his office, he knew something was wrong. The normally friendly banter was replaced by a staid formal greeting. His quizzical look was ignored and everyone seemed to be busy. This was far from the normal happy chaos that seemed to pervade the charge office atmosphere.

When he got to the office, he could hear voices inside and they didn't sound familiar. He opened the door to see Gerhard and Brigadier van Vuuren in discussion. The Brigadier had positioned himself at Carl's desk and was slouched back in the chair with a cup of coffee in his hand. Carl greeted him, saluting as he did so. Brigadier van Vuuren didn't even respond. He ignored Carl.

"You were saying Gerhard?" he asked.

Gerhard looked at Carl nervously.

"Yes Sir, Detective Lubber was busy investigating a case yesterday afternoon and I was addressing the more general policing matters."

The Brigadier glared at Carl. His partially closed eyes glinted as he considered him. Carl felt like a rat mesmerized by an Egyptian cobra. He wanted to run but couldn't. The anticipation of the next question made him feel queasy. The Brigadier's question when it was finally asked had soft spoken words, which impacted like a staccato spray of lead bullets from an automatic rifle.

"Perhaps …you could enlighten me… as to what your activities were? Detective?"

Carl took his time to answer. His heart was pounding and he knew that he had to be extremely careful.

"Sir, yesterday I took some of my afternoon off in lieu of the overtime I have worked over the last month. I left mid-afternoon. I trust that Gerhard has brought you up to speed on what we're doing?"

The Brigadier smiled.

"Yes, the corporal was very helpful. Quite informative in fact! I was asking him about the accident that you're investigating. You know the one I am referring too? The one at the platinum mine! I hear that you consider it to be more than an accident. Could you perhaps explain why you came to this hasty conclusion?"

Carl explained the activities over the past few days leaving out the various parts that could be linked back to the Brigadier or to Hendrik. Lacking the substance to fill the periods spent tracking the van Vuurens and their activities, the report sounded lame and incomplete. He knew he was making a bad impression. The Brigadier just sat and listened quietly, sipping his coffee now and again. He didn't nod or show that he wanted to hear more or less. Carl could have been talking to a wall for all the feedback he received. He felt more and more uncomfortable. Why was the man here? Had he actually recognized him at the pub? Did he know that he had been followed? He finished his explanation and waited for the Brigadier to say something.

"I am not impressed Detective," the man started, "Firstly you take a routine accident case and blow it up into a suspected murder case, then you spend such an excessive amount of time on it, so much that if I didn't know your record I would think this was a deliberate attempt to swindle the public out of your services while you laze in some pub somewhere, then I hear you have been spending a fair time in Priggles Bar during working hours as well."

Carl felt a cold anger growing in his gut. That information could only have come from one person. His constable! His eyes flicked over to Gerhard who was looking out of the window into the distance as if something on the horizon had his full attention. The Brigadier saw the look.

"You shouldn't blame your constable for your inadequacies Detective. Rather you should blame yourself," he paused for a second. "You're immediately suspended from further duty pending an inquiry into your activities over the past few days. It will take some time to get the correct people together to hear your case. In the mean time, you're to hand over all information that you have to Gerhard. When you leave this office you're to take nothing with you. Is that understood?"

Carl nodded. Darkness seemed to sink down over him and threaten him with a suffocating fear. He resisted it.

"Permission to speak Sir?" he asked.

"Yes, provided it has nothing to do with querying my decision," the Brigadier conceded.

"With all respect Sir, Gerhard doesn't have the training to investigate a murder. Possibly you should get someone from another police station to help him?"

The Brigadier slammed his hand down on the desk and sat up straight. He glared at Carl.

"You insolent bastard!" he swore. "It isn't enough to be doing your job badly. You also attempt to lower my opinion of your own staff and insult my judgment simultaneously. That is a very foolish thing to do Detective! A very foolish thing!" angrily he turned to Gerhard. "I want him out of here. Allow him to get his personal items from his desk and then escort him out. Ensure he hands in his firearm!"

The Brigadier got up slapping his coffee cup down on top of a half open file and spilling coffee over the writing. Carl saw that it was the file on the mine 'accident'. The Brigadier stalked out leaving the two men together. Gerhard looked away and Carl ignored him. He knew that if he spoke he would not be able to contain his anger. He collected his diary, a set of pens that his mother had given to him, and a few personal letters that were in his drawer. Gerhard continued looking out the window. Carl obtained a large brown envelope. As Gerhard watched he started to put things into the envelope. Carl glared at Gerhard and this caused him to turn away avoiding Carl's eyes. While he was looking away, Carl quickly pulled the fax's that referred to Hendrik from his desk drawer and dropped them into the envelope. He was glad he had been too lazy to put them into the folder on the case. Finally, he grabbed his sweater that was hanging from a hook on the door and walked out. Gerhard followed him. At the charge office desk, he handed in his handgun and got a receipt in return. When he walked out, he was relieved to be clear of the place.

A feeling of relief was followed by one of loss. He wasn't even sure if he still had the use of the police car. He just stood in the warm morning sunshine for a while collecting his thoughts. His world was crumbling around him. It seemed as if all he believed in, law, order, truth and honesty, were being challenged. For a while he felt some anger and then a small inner voice seemed to tell him to overcome his anger. Slowly he relaxed. He now realized that he was free to do as he liked. Now he could really apply himself to the case. Nobody had told him to hand in the keys to the car, so he decided to use it to visit Joshua. He knew that Tom would be busy with ZPM business and that Joshua should be taking time off. Possibly he would be able to get more information about Hendrik from Joshua.

CHAPTER TWENTY-NINE

Joshua was at home when Carl arrived. Carl could see that the past few weeks were starting to tell. Joshua looked more drawn and pale than the last time he had seen him. Carl apologized for being so short with him the previous day and for nudging his car.

"It's not a problem!" Joshua assured him. "Tell me what happened!"

Carl filled him in. When he came to the part where he had been ejected from the police station, Joshua just shook his head.

"I know how these van Vuurens work, Carl," he commiserated, "our family has had to contend with that type of pressure for years. I'm sorry you're coming under the same strain. Prayer is our only relief!" he confided. "You go to church but do *you* believe in the power of prayer?"

In the heavenly realm the angels waited for the answer to determine the path to be taken to address the attack of the enemy.

Carl pondered for a while. He was mildly annoyed that Joshua had been so direct. Embarrassment and pride were doing their best to control his response. In the spiritual world a battle was underway for the influence of his soul. Both groups of spirits were debating with Carl's soul. Carl only experienced this as a moment of confusion. He found himself remembering how infrequently his prayers had been answered but he also believed God had directed him into his current work. Assurance began to grow in his heart that this would not be the end of that work.

"Yes Joshua," he acknowledged, "I think I do!"

In the spiritual realm a flurry of activity showed the hastily departing demonic beings; fear of reprisal giving wings to their retreat.

The men eyed each other. Joshua was considering how to encourage the officer, and Carl wondered how much to tell Joshua of his secrets. Joshua decided to change the subject and suggested that they find out more about the satellite tracking station. After some discussion they concluded they would ask Tom to approach the center for information. His previous dealings with them would certainly help them. Carl asked Joshua if he had been able to get anything out of Susan regarding the reason for her fear. He suspected it was fear of Hendrik but wanted confirmation.

When Joshua related what Susan had gone through, the abortions, Hendrik's absolute control over her life, her failed attempts to run away, the way Hendrik beat her, Carl erupted with anger. He cursed Hendrik with vigor and Joshua wondered how serious Carl had been in his earlier statement on prayer. His own anger at Hendrik also burned. They would both have liked to see Hendrik in jail for his crimes. They lapsed into silence, both trying to work out how to make him pay for the things he had done. The spiritual repercussions of their anger had called the demonic hordes closer. The angels were trying in vain to re-direct the men's attention but were bound by the anger that reduced the angel's success. Beor knew he could never get Joshua to realize just how specific and just the Lord's vengeance would be and that he need not ever feel that Hendrik would get away without punishment. He radiated encouragement to Joshua but his charge failed to hear it as anger shut it out.

Carl broke the silence.

"Will she give us a statement?" he asked.

Joshua shook his head morbidly. "She'll never even admit she told me this," he said.

Carl thought back to his observations the night before while following Hendrik and the Brigadier.

"If we could speak to the person they met last night, we might figure out what's going on. I think his last name was Warmen.

After a bit more discussion, Joshua then did something he believed he should do. He suggested that they pray about it. Carl felt awkward but went along with him. The angelic company praised God. Their demonic counterparts screamed, covering their ears as they frantically left the property. When their prayers concluded Joshua phoned Tom and they arranged to meet at his home during the lunch hour.

Tom looked stressed when he opened the door and led them to his study a few hours later. There were problems at the mine that needed his attention and while he wanted to solve the murder, his first priority was to ensure the productivity of his enterprise. He listened to what the men had to say. When they were finished he pulled a box from his desk drawer. Flipping through the cards, he found what he was looking for and copied some information onto a notepad. He tore it off and handed it to Carl.

"I haven't much time available at the moment and so I would appreciate it if you could follow up on this me. That's the name of a chap that I knew at the station. Give him a call and tell him that we would like to have a tour of the satellite facility. He'll be glad to help you. The hours those chaps work are tedious and with the need to be continually vigilant. He'll be glad of some company"

Carl took the note.

"Do you know anything about this Warmen chap?" Joshua felt prompted to ask.

Tom riffled through his contacts again.

"Nope, strange though..." he commented. "I am sure I have heard the name before!"

He looked bemused for a second or two. "Hang on, I'll look in my old diary," he added and went out.

Carl read the note Tom had written. The contact name was James McFarlyn and the telephone number was also given. He didn't really want to follow-up on this lead. The complications that would arise if the Brigadier connected him to the satellite tracking station peppered his thoughts. He turned to Joshua.

"Think you could do the satellite station investigation?" he asked.

"Sure Carl," Joshua replied and took the note.

Tom returned with a well worn leather organizer in one hand and brandishing a business card. The grin on his face showed his pleasure.

"The old memory cells never forget a useful contact!" he gloated. "Here it is, Don Warmen, *SAT-IN-RAD, Satellite innovations and radio Pty Ltd.* Sounds like our man doesn't it. I can't remember exactly when I met the man, but I do have a card!"

He went over to a small copier and made a copy that he handed to Joshua. Carl smiled to himself as he realized his earlier guess about the initials in the message had been correct. Tom came back.

"Hope that helps!" He said looking at his watch. "Blast! I must go!"

They all left together. Tom hurried back to the mine offices. Carl and Joshua stood outside chatting. They decided that Joshua would try and get into the satellite station to look around. Carl would use a few friends to try and locate exactly who Don Warmen was and what he did for a living.

CHAPTER THIRTY

In Hong Kong, well below the level of city activity, in an air force command center cut out of the rock, the command staff were frantically trying to re-establish communications with a satellite that provided them with their internationally secure communication transmissions and other military information.

Known to the rest of the world as "PaciComm," the satellite was in theory simply a civilian telephone exchange in space that connected the pacific countries with Europe and America. It provided secure intelligence communications and visual pictures of activity in China for the group of highly trained military staff. The civil communications function was a cleverly designed cover enabling this activity to go undetected, at least as far as the staff could ascertain.

At 9p.m. Greenwich Mean Time, PaciComm had simply stopped functioning without warning. The huge load of international communications were automatically transferred to another network, "Intersat". "Intersat" had a contract to backup the PaciComm in just such an eventuality. This network doubled its load of communications ensuring that civilian telephone calls and fax's kept running. Billing for the calls increased costs sharply for PaciComm eliminating all profit from the operation. In addition, the military functions of the satellite were completely lost. Military command came under pressure to re-establish the communications but despite non-stop effort, not even the slightest signal could be received. PaciComm drifted silently above the Pacific Ocean ignoring human communications. Daylight hours passed and as the night communication load reduced, they had hoped to re-establish control. This also failed, reducing the satellite to an expensive but useless piece of space junk.

One of the military staff, a certain Colonel Kee was getting angry and worried. What was happening? His suspicion that Mainland China had found a way to disable PaciComm was upsetting. How had they managed this? How did they know of the true purpose of PaciComm?

In a luxury apartment in a different part of the city, a well-dressed executive watched as a news reporter on TV Channel One announced that the central communication satellite for the city had stopped working due to technical problems. He gave a satisfied sigh. The newscaster announced that the cost of phone calls could be increasing if the situation continued for much longer. He smiled again. He had been present at the confusion on the stock exchange floor earlier in the day when for a period of minutes nobody could get a telephone line out of the country. The market had reflected the situation negatively for a short while but the slight downward trend had soon rectified. He picked up a phone and called Britain and spoke briefly with Roger MacLean. The name Don Warmen was mentioned twice in the conversation.

At the Pentagon in the United States, a small team of experts were meeting to consider a two hour period during which their 15 small Star Wars prototype satellites had failed to report on their status. Leading the team was a civilian they all addressed as 'Ron'. Ron Jackson was the person who led the development of the strategic control phase of the Star Wars satellite development project. He was explaining the program to a new member of the team, a Colonel, who looked every bit a military warrior even in his non-military loose fitting golf shirt and thin rimmed eyeglasses.

"Unlike what the public expects from the Star Wars system," he said, "the way this defense system works is less like a huge laser cannon blasting missiles out the sky and more like a group of jungle tribesman, all throwing their spears into the victim at the same time. There are multiple small lasers focusing onto the same point on the missile as it follows its trajectory in space."

He flicked a switch. Blinds came down over the windows, a panel opened revealing a large screen and video started to play. With a pointer, Jackson pointed out the aspects of the system.

"Surrounding the earth is a set of 15 satellites. Each satellite has a small, highly powerful laser gun capable of melting a small hole in a metal sheet within two seconds. Another group further away from the earth have relatively small and specialized reflective surfaces. Call them mirrors if you like! Arranged in a stationary orbit encircling the earth at least seven of these satellites can track anything in space at any time. A command causes them to fire simultaneously at each other's mirrors, redirecting the beams onto a single point on the incoming missile or ICBM, and BOOM! It is no more!

Ron paused for effect.

"How is sufficient energy provided to burn through the missile's skin," the newcomer asked.

"The combined intensity of the multiple beams provides the effect. Each one adding their heat until the burn into the missile occurs within a split second."

He paused and then continued, "Should one penetration not be enough, this is repeated rapidly at several points along the missile length over a short period of time. This effectively peppers the missile with white-hot holes at regular intervals. Sooner or later, the fuel tanks will rupture, the electronics will be destroyed and our mission achieved."

Ron smiled at the crowd around the table. Most had heard this before and were waiting for the newcomer to catch up with the program.

He was still looking dubious so Ron continued.

"Are you wondering how we detect the missile in the first place?"

The newcomer nodded.

"This is with our 'Firing Elevation Range Registering Information Technology' system or 'FERRIT'. A combination of information from agricultural, meteorological, spy and other specialized scout satellites is used to detect the initial launch heat pattern. This is done in all weather conditions at any time of day or night. However, at the moment, our coverage is not yet perfect!" he informed them apologetically.

"We're still in the prototype stage!" he explained wryly.

"Accuracy in detection had to give way to more pressing details. Then once a launch is detected, the scout satellites, which circle the earth at a lower altitude than the killer laser units, locate and accurately plot the path of the missile. Then, it's a simple matter to tune the laser units. These killers aim their mirrors using low power lasers until the scout satellite notifies them that the target is in their spotlight. We are then notified and an fire at the target.

Firing is done using a radio signal trigger. This could effectively be done from any one of several places on the earth's surface. BOOM! Job done!"

Everyone looked happy with his explanation and so he got to the main point of the discussion.

"Yesterday afternoon, all the units failed to report their status at the planned time. Since then each unit has reported accurately. The other indication of something different was that a slightly lower power level occurred on the status transmission two hours later; nothing else appears to have changed. Unfortunately, during those two hours, we were unable to communicate with the satellite at all. They even failed to respond to our emergency codes. Our job today is to determine the extent of the required investigation into this minor malfunction."

The team obviously understood the situation and they waited for him to continue.

"An apparently unrelated incident also occurred during this time period with an oriental satellite know as PaciComm..." the screen flickered into life and a blurred image of a satellite appeared. "...this satellite provides communications for the east while doing some primitive spying. We have managed to determine that it provides someone in the east with ground images and specialized communication services. This satellite ceased to work during this period and has not come back on line yet."

A murmur went around the table.

Ron continued, "This tells us there was possibly an unrelated external effect causing all these problems. We have ascertained..." again he flicked the switch and the video came to life showing a succession of slides, "...that there was an active burst of solar activity followed by one or two solar flares during this period. None of these appeared to be outside the normal activity expected but it is surmised that these could have emitted radiation that interfered with communications."

"Mr. Jackson," it was the newcomer, the Colonel, that was speaking, "assume that this wasn't the case, what could it have been?"

Ron shook his head.

"We have no idea. Originally we thought it could have been a program error. The fact that all the units skipped reporting during this time led us to this conclusion. Unfortunately, when we checked the programs, we couldn't find anything to support this theory. However, nothing appears incorrect at this time."

The men around the table considered the possibility of a program problem but nobody seemed to consider situation serious.

"What are the implications if that is the case?" a General wanted to know.

"Well, from what can be determined, the best case would be another black-out period such as the one we experienced and the worst case is that we could loose communications with the units altogether," Ron reported.

"..or the lasers may start firing indiscriminately..." another civilian member interjected.

Ron looked annoyed.

"Yes, I suppose that could happen but it's unlikely. Even if did, the chances of even hitting anything in the vastness of space is insignificance. That idea can effectively be discarded."

The Colonel looked interested.

"What if a laser were to hit another satellite?" he wanted to know.

"A single hit to a satellite isn't likely to strike anything important," Ron responded. "FERRIT absorbed a fortune of taxpayers' money trying to maximize damage on space vehicles. Success in achieving this damage is still uncertain and that's why we are still in the prototype phase. Your satellites are safe!" he assured the Colonel.

One of the Generals was looking at his watch.

"Sorry, I have to go to another meeting," he informed them. "I propose that this team investigate the matter further as a low priority. Meantime, we will provide a tentative conclusion that sunspot activity resulted in a temporary break in the communications. Nothing here is new to us. It frustrates me to acknowledge that the sun factor still impacts our satellite design!" he commented.

The proposal was accepted and the meeting broke up. As they were leaving, the Colonel came up to Ron.

"Keep me informed would you. I would particularly like to know if the PaciComm comes back to life. I can't say I buy that solar flare explanation. Also, I would like a listing of all communications to and from the prototype satellites for the last week."

He shook Ron's hand and left. Ron stared at the departing figure, he was thinking rapidly. He packed up his presentation material and went to his office. From there, he went into the city to a public pay phone and made a call to Toronto.

A few minutes later Brigadier van Vuuren's police radio hissed and popped as it came to life. He was in his vehicle in the city of Johannesburg in South Africa.

"Foxtrot Lima Two, personal call on the line, shall I patch it through sir. Over."

"Foxtrot Yankee Yankee, yes, put it through and secure it! Over," the Brigadier answered angrily. That desk Sergeant would get the rough edge of his tongue when he got back. How dare she address him as "Sir" over the radio? He waited for the call to come through.

"Hi, am I speaking to the right person. This is Dagwood speaking. Who is this? Over"

The Brigadier answered, "Blondie at your service. How is the weather in the other hemisphere? Over!"

"I think there is a tornado stirring itself up. Other than that things are going excellently," Dagwood answered. "I do however have a small problem that requires urgent attention. There is a book of mine that you have. I need it urgently for a friend. Could you courier it as soon as possible? Over."

The Brigadier touched the electronic card that never left his pocket. "Yes, can your friend do without it for a day or two longer? Over" he wanted to know.

"No, it would cause our friendship to break down irreparably," was the answer.

"You will have it..." the Brigadier answered and cursed silently to himself. "...Over and out!"

The need to have the card had come at a most in-opportune time. The planning was exactly on schedule and delays now would impact the delicate balance. He was glad that they had built a few days leeway into their planning. It would be needed.

CHAPTER THIRTY-ONE

Carl was having difficulty identifying the exact location and activities of Don Warmen. *SAT-IN-RAD, Satellite, innovations and radio Pty Ltd.* no longer existed. The telephone number from Tom was out of use. He had run the name through the police file using a friend from another region of the police force. Don Warmen didn't have a criminal record. He looked up the name in the Johannesburg telephone book and got five names. Three of these just rang and household maids answered the others. Carl asked if he could speak to Mr. Warmen and always had to leave a message. When he attempted to find out where Mr. Warmen worked, they were evasive. This he understood as it wasn't advisable to be free with numbers if they wanted to keep their employment. With the very high unemployment rate in the country, they definitely wanted to keep their employment.

He wished he knew the company name on the office he had visited when following the Brigadier. But he didn't. He was annoyed with himself for not asking. Frustration consumed him. Finally he climbed into his car and retraced his route into the heart of Johannesburg. It was a hot day and the drive was unpleasant. The heat was oppressive and the car didn't have an air-conditioner.

Although the building wasn't difficult to locate, when he tried to turn into the parking he used the previous evening, a boom blocked the entrance with a notification that only pre-paid parking was permitted during office hours. He drove around for another twenty minutes before he found a place to park.

He threaded his way through the crowded sun drenched streets to the building. The building was unusual in that there was no business advertising on it. The entrance was through two huge oak doors and led into a plush interior. He noted the reception wasn't where he had been the other night. It was located behind armored glass and the information he was looking for was ornately woven in brass letters imbedded in the glass above the receptionist's booth. "NUSat Global Enterprises" the name announced itself. Carl walked up to the receptionist.

"Good day" he greeted her thinking of what he was going to say, "I am trying to find out if a Mr. Van Vuuren works here?" He pulled out his police identification. "The tax department has asked us to check on his employment record."

The receptionist arranged for him to speak to someone in the human resources department. He spent a successful few minutes in conversation with the personnel manager over the phone determining that over time they had six different Van Vuurens working for them but none were employed there any longer. The most recent employee of that name had left in the spring of the previous year. Carl drifted the conversation towards the company and found that this was the headquarters for a group of companies with a Mr. Warmen as the Managing Director. They covered three main business sectors- finance, communications and heavy engineering. Carl concluded the conversation by asking for the office telephone number of Don Warmen. The manager was reluctant to give it to him but when he explained it was merely a formality for his report to the tax department, he provided it. After thanking both the manager and the receptionist Carl left.

His next stop was the Star newspaper where he phoned a contact he had made there many years ago. Aaron Smithson had been the editor in the early eighties. Although retired, Aaron still kept his hand in by writing the occasional articles for the paper. Pleased to hear that Carl was in town, he agreed to meet him for drinks at the Old Edwardian Club that evening. Carl asked him to gather any information he could find on Don Warmen of NUSat Global Enterprises before they met.

With time to kill, Carl went to a shopping mall and bought himself a beer and the Star newspaper. He thought it would be wise to know about current events as reported by the Star before he spoke to Aaron.

Back in Johannesburg, Brigadier Van Vuuren received a phone call from his brother who was at work at ZPM. Hendrik had determined that his daughter was no longer living at her apartment. He had seen that the door was sealed by police tape and when he had asked what had happened, he had been told that this information wasn't being released to the public. When he revealing that he was her father, they had simply apologized and still refused to tell him where she was. He hoped his brother would help.

The Brigadier listened patiently and promised to take action as soon as he could. It was an annoying intrusion and he had other problems that he had to take care of. He was in no mood to bother with his brother's inconsequential problems. However, since it was his brother, he placed a call to the Zinaville police station and asked for the desk sergeant. Following the correct protocol he asked for information in regard to Susan van Vuuren telling them who he was and that she was his niece. Soon he was told where she would be found and was amazed that she had gone to stay at a church manse. He called Hendrik back with the information.

The evening was slowly settling down on the land and the red orange glow of the warm sunset lit up the sky. Carl was sitting in the garden at the Old Edwardians Club in Johannesburg, cooling off in the evening breeze and drinking a Coca-Cola. Out on the cricket field, the muffled comments and jibes of players were a pleasant murmur that combined with the clamor of the birds calling on their way to their nests. Aaron arrived a little late but full of energy as always. A thin, wiry man with a blaze of white hair in amongst the gray, he greeted Carl warmly and then motioned the waiter to take their orders. Carl ordered a beer and Aaron wanted his regular brandy and Coca-Cola.

The mention of brandy triggered Carl's thoughts to the missing hobo and for a short while he was lost in his own thoughts. The old man sat there silently with a grin on his face waiting for Carl to come back to reality.

"I said, 'What is so important that it gets you following the Don?'" Aaron repeated. "I guess whatever it is, it's more important than my presence..." he joked.

Carl apologized and asked how Aaron was. For the next few minutes they discussed the good old days, changes in the newspaper industry and how the immediacy of electronic media was eroding the traditional base of readers. Then Carl asked about Don Warmen.

Aaron pulled out a sheaf of printouts from a small folder.

"Here are some of the more pertinent articles on him. They make interesting reading. He is self made, a multi-millionaire who likes to keep his name out of the public eye. Started off as an industrial chemist and small time inventor and built his name in the mining business when he made a chemical that helped in platinum recovery. He resigned from his job at a major laboratory and took one of their top researchers with him. The product gave him the capital to buy out a small electronics and radio repair business. The start of television in South Africa in the early seventies boosted him into big time business. He built up a little empire of companies that he called '*SAT-IN-RAD, Satellite innovations and radio Pty Ltd*'. When sanctions hit the country he really came into his own. He progressively bought out top men from the businesses that were leaving and produced duplicate products to those no longer supplied, at vastly higher prices. The technology he built enabled him to fill the vacuum left in the military market and ensured that he received government assistance. He is shrewd, highly competent but ruthless. His strength is that he builds a ring of men around him that are loyal to him. In addition, he has an excellent ability to forecast trends and from all reports, a huge ego."

Aaron paused for breath as the waiter placed the drinks on the table. Carl paid for them. Aaron continued, "Currently he is the chairman of the *Trivance* group. He has successively bought out most of the advanced technology research facilities in the country and attempted to meld them into a comprehensive force for development. Rumor has it that the past few years of political unrest and escalation in crime provided him with money in a big way. He expanded his operations using this money from the South African government. The attempt to develop technology to ward off the effects of sanctions, as you and I know, was a fruitless activity. Sanctions started to bite and the money started to dry up. The first of the cutbacks that occurred was in the field of research and development. "

Aaron stopped and took a sip of the brandy and coke that had arrived while he had been talking. They both watched as the players made their way off the field. Their game was finished and their noisy chatter broke the peace of the evening as they made their way to the showers. Lanterns surrounding the tables came on, and the afternoon crowd drifted away as the dark descended. They sat in silence for a while longer.

"Go on Aaron!" Carl prompted.

"It is rumored that these cutbacks hurt him badly. He tried frantically to establish ties with the incoming ANC government, which he hoped to use to further his fortunes. He attempted to advertise the *Trivance* group as the technology that would lift South Africa out of the quagmire resulting from the mess left by the previous government. Hypocritical bastard!"

Aaron smiled and Carl knew that he was getting to the crux of the matter.

"In the past few months he has been working on a deal to merge with a major overseas company providing advanced satellite communication technologies worldwide. The deals have been cleared with the new government, provided the technology can be used to supply specific services in rural communities. On receiving that assurance, they allowed him to move considerable money offshore to fund the agreement. Apparently the move provided the stockholders with confidence in *Trivance* at a critical time and provided the much needed relief to stabilize the business."

Carl was confused. He couldn't work out why Don Warmen, a self made business tycoon, would be interested in using people connected with the ZPM plant. He could envisage a connection to the Hartebeeshoek satellite station but even there the link was tenuous. Hartebeeshoek was government controlled and while it serviced industry, no private entrepreneur would be allowed to buy out the station.

"What is the name of the company that Don Warmen has bought into?" he asked Aaron.

"Starnet Communications," Aaron answered.

Carl sat back in surprise. "That's one of the biggest players in communication technology worldwide. I am sure I read an article about them in the Financial Mail."

Aaron grinned, "I am surprised to find a detective reading the Financial Mail. I would have thought '101 ways to nab a thief' would be more your flavor," he teased Carl.

Carl smiled back good-naturedly.

"Yes, and I suppose you spend your time reading up on successful entrepreneurs."

He liked the old man. They had helped each other out several times in the past. Aaron always came through with what he needed and he always made sure that Aaron got pointed in the direction of the hottest stories.

Aaron smiled again.

"Yes, that was an interesting bit of research. Mind telling me why I did it?" the older man's eyes gleamed in the lamplight. He was obviously keen to get going with his next story.

Carl contemplated the wisdom of revealing what he knew to the old man. He knew that it was risky. A good story would get Aaron pumped up and he might not be able to resist the opportunity to break the news prematurely. On the other hand, he also knew that Aaron had integrity and would not print anything until he was sure of his facts. The complexity of the problem combined with the need to get more help and information won out. He decided that he would bring Aaron up to speed on the events.

He talked for over an hour explaining the 'accidental' death at the plant, the lack of developments with locating the hobo, the connection between Hendrik and the brigadier, how he had connected Don Warmen to the others and ended with his suspension from work. He lapsed into silence. The newspaperman listened intently to the events and then sat back and thought. The night air was cooling fast and the previously warm breeze was now starting to chill them. Deciding that the lounge would be more comfortable they moved inside. Aaron ordered another brandy, Carl requested another coca cola.

Neither addressed the subject for a while. Carl suggested a game of pool. Aaron agreed and they set up the balls before the discussion continued.

"An interesting run of events!" Aaron commented. "Nothing substantial except the faxed letters. A pity we don't know what Warmen is up to with that tracking station. Something is not quite right. I've never heard of Warmen ever doing anything underhand. He may be shrewd, is not well liked and a hard businessman, but as far as I can tell he's not a crook. I'd like to know a little more of his financial situation. What are you going to do now?" He set up the balls in the triangle and both men chalked their cues.

Carl opened with an effective break, pocketing a ball with almost casual ease. He rested and looked at the older man.

"I'm not sure...one thing I do know, my problems can't be solved by my sitting on my butt and doing nothing. Got any suggestions?" He turned and lined up on the next ball.

Aaron waited until Carl had completed his shot before answering.

"Yes, in fact I do. While I look into Warmen's financial affairs, you can get me a copy of those faxes. I would also like to talk to the young man who lost his father. Next, you could introduce me to the mine manager. Lastly, you can give me a ride home this evening. A friend dropped me off here as my car is at the garage.

Carl grinned. He knew he had triggered one of the best investigative reporters in the world. Now, no matter what happened, the truth would come out. In a strange way he felt relief. He knew that he wasn't alone in his search for answers.

The rest of the pool game was a satisfying duel. The accuracy of youth pitted against shrewd wisdom of the years. Carl was glad to only loose by a small margin and reflected again how Aaron was full of surprises. He drove him home and was on the way back to Zinaville before 9p.m. He felt more certain than ever that he would solve the mystery that had enveloped him over the past few days.

CHAPTER THIRTY-TWO

In the darkness the Zinaville residents were slowly drifting off to bed all over town. Lights winked out and darkness slowly shrouded the town. The closing prayers of Zinaville Christians followed a pattern. Speaking to their hearts, God's Spirit suggested the pattern that attentive Christians discerned and followed. At their posts in the shadows the guardians protected against violence, manipulation, and a host of other undesirable spirits. A few Christians who had a wider view of the world prayed in a similar fashion for a binding of demonic forces worldwide. Joshua was sleepless and was reading a book on satellites. Remembering Tom's knowledge of the stars and astronomy, he wondered if Tom would have been able to explain some of the articles. He tossed out another prayer for Tom's soul and safety.

Tom was tossing and turning in his bed. He couldn't sleep and kept wondering what was happening to the secluded world that he had created. Having been a seaman, he was no stranger to violence or the contorted reasoning men apply to their greed. Why was he finding this murder on his mine such a problem? He was angry that Hendrik had duped him over the past years. He was also annoyed that he now needed to allow events to run their course and couldn't fire him. Mostly he was worried about the impact it was having on the work ethic that had been synonymous with ZPM.

It seemed as if the night air moved the curtain at the bedroom window allowing starlight to glitter into the room. The curtain was moved on cue by an angel on instructions from the Lord. The angelic being didn't know why and didn't even think to ask. The Lord had spoken and that was enough. Tom looked out at the night sky with his eyes that were incapable of seeing the angelic glory. Despite this, the sight of stars lifted Tom's thoughts onward and upward. He decided that his problems, compared with the immensity of the universe, were tiny. His mind imagined stars crashing together, new worlds being produced and old ones being consumed.

"Where did the universe start?" he thought.

An old resistance started to build again as he questioned the beginning of the universe. Again the programmed refrain rang through his thoughts "It never started it has always been!"

Doubt tugged at the thought. Times had changed and Tom knew that everyone of substance in astronomical circles accepted there had been a beginning. A 'Big Bang'. Also, in his heart of hearts, he knew he wanted to believe that his existence meant something to the men and women that worked for him. He wanted to believe his life was more than random probability. This slowly eroded his previous belief in emptiness after death. He thought of his mother's death and her last words, 'I am going to be with my Maker now'. The words troubled him. She had never professed to believe in a God until then. Strangely, he thought, she had never said she hadn't either. This thought lingered for a while.

An air stirring the curtains interrupted his thoughts again. Slowly he turned his thoughts back to the question of a creator.

"Was there a Maker?"

He realized he was actually asking the question in an honest manner for the first time in his life. As he contemplated his previous stance, he realized it was a reproduction of his father's words and attitudes. He grinned wryly. A pang of longing went through him as he thought of his parents. He missed them both.

The curtain fluttered.

"A Maker?" he thought. "Yes! I can accept that. Not made in one week but rather over millions of years. Yes, I can accept there is a Creator!"

He felt pleased with his conclusion. A lonely star peeped through the drapes. He was the sole remaining member of his family on earth. He was lonely again. What was he worth anyway? The new question tugged more fervently than the first.

"I wish I knew...I can never be sure..." Tom thought. "Joshua is always so darn sure! I wish I had his arrogance!"

The drapes closed again extinguishing the star.

"Is that what will happen to me?" Tom thought. "Gone, forever, as if I never was!"

The thought was followed by his realization that the star was still out there, it was just not visible to him.

"Is that death?" he thought. "Simply a closing of the drapes to those left behind. Maybe they are still out there?"

He thought of his parents and again he found himself hearing one of Joshua's comments about his own father; "Dad has just moved on for a while and I'll see him again when I get to heaven. He's better off now!"

Logic failed Tom as he considered the unanswerable question. "Had Bryan counted? Would he himself count in the overall scheme of life? Was there right and wrong?"

Until Bryan had been murdered on his plant he hadn't believed so. Now he disagreed with his earlier beliefs. "It *was* evil to murder Bryan! I *do* count!" he thought angrily.

Then he laughed at his own conclusions. Here was a self-proclaimed atheist who didn't believe in absolutes but who was making an absolute statement based on an age-old religious standard "Thou shalt not murder!" This coupled with his statement about himself based on beliefs and not based on facts, was not how he would normally have considered his world. He was cracking up for nothing! He pummeled his pillow, turned on his side and made himself comfortable again.

Again the drape opened and revealed the stars. Tom wondered if Joshua was sleeping.

In another realm Meddler was trying to worm his way into Tom's room but was being unsuccessful. On each attempt a flaming sword smashed down causing him to retreat speedily. Anxiety had managed to slip passed and enter the room, but Fear was suffering a similar fate. Meddler wondered where the lone angel was getting this power. Even in supernatural terms, it was unreal. Angrily he tried to get past again, only to be met with the same gleaming sword.

Tom's mind turned to Joshua and Bryan. These men entered his life almost at almost the same time that his mine had started. He traveled back over the years of memories of the men. He remembered just how hotly Bryan could argue any issue he believed in, and how he had resisted working on Sundays unless that was absolutely mandatory. Other men wanted the extra work because of the higher hourly wage on Sundays but both Bryan and Joshua were real believers in God. He thought of some others who put up a pretense but their heart wasn't in it. Those who like himself went to church Sundays mainly for some social interaction.

The night air gusted into the room again. He thought of phoning Joshua and asking the reason for his confidence. Flipping on the bedside light he found his diary and put out his hand to get the phone. Suddenly he felt as if he couldn't breath. His heart was pounding and his head was swimming. He lay back on the pillow and waited for the feeling to pass. Anxiety unwound the hold around his neck and soon he was breathing more regularly. This panic attack made Tom angry. He couldn't understand how anxiety had got the better of him. It hadn't given him trouble for years. Now his resolve hardened. He *would* call Joshua. *Nothing* would stop him.

The demonic forces were loosing their hold on him. They felt it. Again and again they rushed towards his room to be turned back by the flashing sword. Two more angels appeared, and demon's mad attempts became less and less effective. They watched from a distance as Tom picked up the phone and dialed. Anxiety had lost his hold.

Joshua was surprised to hear Tom's voice on the other end of the line. "Hi, Tom! I was just reading up some notes on satellites and thought you were more qualified to understand this stuff than I am."

The two men talked about the intricacies of satellite communications for a short while before Tom asked if Joshua would like to come around to his home to discuss satellites. Joshua was happy to accept and was on the way within a few minutes.

Tom was dressed and had made some coffee when Joshua arrived. They both relaxed in his study in the large comfortable armchairs, sipping the coffee and talked of the early days at the mine. They talked for a while before Tom asked the question he had been harboring.

"Josh, you're always so confident in what you do. You seem to understand exactly what you should do in circumstances and even when you have difficulties you recover extremely quickly. I have been wondering how you do it. How can you be so relaxed and confident?"

Joshua smiled.

"Tom, wasn't it you who came to get me at the police station where I went to pieces? Do you really think I am always confident?" he teased.

Tom ignored Joshua's lighthearted reply.

"Josh, even then, you did things correctly. No, Josh! I knew your Dad and I know you. You have a respect for people and an ability to understand life that is different from others. I may be successful, but I lack the happiness you generate around you. I want to know why?"

Joshua realized that Tom was serious. He wondered how this frame of mind had come over Tom and to what purpose.

"Tom, it's really simple. Worry, fear and anxiety steal happiness. We worry about things, fear the unknown and are anxious if we attach the importance of our lives to what we do and have. I don't do that. I consider that God determines the purpose of my life alone. I handed control of it to my Maker, Jesus Christ a long time back," he added, sitting back and waiting for Tom to absorb what he said.

"So, how do you know what to do if God is controlling your life?" Tom wanted to know.

"I just ask Him and wait for an answer!"

"You mean God talks to you?" Tom asked incredulously.

"Yes Tom," Joshua answered. "You may think I am crazy but I know the sound of his voice in my thoughts. If I don't hear Him, I sometimes see the answer to my queries or requests, other times he uses people to provide the answers," Joshua smiled. "He has even used you in the past to provide answers to my prayers."

"How is that possible?" an amazed Tom wanted to know.

"You offered my Dad work years ago didn't you? Did I ask you to? I just told you about him and waited to see what would happen. That was an answer to prayer. Also, I guess a more direct answer is happening right now. I have often prayed that you would want to know more about God. Here you're asking! A miracle of sorts as you have not exactly appreciated Christian talk before," Joshua smiled to rob his words of any sting they might have collected in the communication.

Tom nodded and sat back contemplating what had been said. A gentle silence settled on the study and outside the house rows upon rows of angels surrounding it, bathing it in a spiritual glow that could be seen for miles. In the depths of the demonic headquarters the first messages were filtering into the world of darkness. All hell was breaking loose. Each demonic spirit blamed the others for failing to predict the danger. Fear of retribution from higher ranks pervaded those under them, filling the area with the stench of fear. The concentration of their effort had been focused on the church and church members, with little effort being placed on those that they considered comfortably belonging to Satan. These nominal Christians in word only, but who belonged to the world, were not considered a threat. Now they saw the scary grace of God was at work. It looked as if the enemy would claim another man from the ranks of lost souls. An influential man at that! This tormented them and they shrieked their hate into the darkness. Many rushed up into the night sky only to see the angelic glow and rush down again in fear. Angels surrounding the study at Tom's home watched the evil fountain of demonic activity in the distance. Beor who stood outside the angelic group in full-reflected glory took careful note of where the demonic headquarters was located. Now he knew the position of the enemy! In their undisciplined way they had revealed it to him.

Inside Tom was considering Joshua's words.

"Yes Josh, I can't say I have. I also can't say I am sorry. A lot of those calling themselves Christians are a pain in the butt. Superiority exudes as they speak words most people don't understand. Their language isolates them in their exclusivity. On the other hand there is a need for me to acknowledge God for who He is. I have spent many years claiming to be an atheist, and now I guess I am agnostic in my approach. I know there is a God but don't necessarily accept He has anything for me. You follow my logic?"

Joshua nodded. "Yes, I can understand that. What makes you so certain God exists now?"

Tom elaborated on the facts surrounding the Big Bang theory of Universe origin that he had been following.

"You see Josh, science now supports the biblical approach that there was a beginning. I always believed in the continuity of things, that is, that there was no beginning. I believe in science and so as it changes I must accept I was wrong," Tom conceded. "Josh, you seem to have this direct relationship with God. Can't you ask Him to show himself to me somehow?"

Joshua chuckled. "I think he already has. Only, you don't yet understand what has happened."

Tom looked at him quizzically. "What do you mean?"

"Well you just said you support the biblical approach that there was a beginning and explained that you accept God created the universe. Well, if you accept that biblical approach, then you should hear what it says. Have you got a Bible around?"

Tom shook his head and then remembered he had bought a New

International Version Bible a few years ago when he started attending a church. He told Joshua about it and went up to his bedroom to get it. Joshua sent another quick telegraphic prayer to his Father in Heaven and asked for wisdom and guidance in his speech.

When Tom returned with the almost new Bible, Joshua asked him to open it to the first chapter of the first book and to the first verse. Tom read "In the beginning God created the heavens and the earth." Joshua then asked him to read from psalm 102 verse 25. Tom took some time to find it and Joshua explained it was in the center of the bible.

Tom read, "In the beginning you laid the foundations of the earth, and the heavens are the work of your hands. They will perish, but you remain; they will all wear out like a garment. Like clothing you will change them and they will be discarded. But you remain the same, and your years will never end."

Joshua explained, "That's Gods promise to you if you accept the fact that Jesus Christ is God and was here about 2000 years ago in human form. Have a look at John 1..."

Tom handed Joshua the bible, he didn't want to struggle to find the place with Joshua there. Joshua opened it and read, "In the beginning was the Word, and the Word was with God, and the Word was God. He was with God in the beginning. Through him all things were made; without him nothing was made that has been made."

"What is that talking about?" asked Tom.

"Well Jesus is referred to as the Word," Joshua explained. "He came to tell us about God the Father. This means he brought us the words that lead to our everlasting life. This is great stuff if you believe in it. Unfortunately it's difficult to understand until the Spirit of God opens it up to you..." Joshua paused and looked at Tom for a moment.

"...it also says here about Jesus, 'Therefore God exalted him to the highest place and gave him the name that is above every name, that at the name of Jesus every knee should bow, in heaven and on earth and under the earth, and every tongue confess that Jesus Christ is Lord, to the glory of God the Father.'"

Joshua put down the Bible and smiled.

"That means everyone, some only after death, will acknowledge him. My confidence is that by acknowledging him now, I get a head start on others and eternal life into the bargain."

Tom shrugged his shoulders. "If it's that easy, I may be interested, but there is one aspect of God that I want to be certain of before I even consider thinking about your God."

Joshua looked at Tom expectantly and so he continued, "From my youth I have looked up into the heavens and considered how they are formed and what would happen to them. I rejected there was a god based on my conclusions. I'll only accept a god based on knowledge that he created or sustains this universe. How does Jesus measure up to that?"

Joshua smiled and opened the bible again. "In this NIV version, the book of Hebrews starts off saying; 'In the past God spoke to our forefather's through the prophets at many times and in various ways, but in these last days he has spoken to us by his Son, whom he appointed heir of all things, and through whom he made the universe. The Son is the radiance of God's glory and the exact representation of his being, sustaining all things by his powerful word. After he had provided purification for sins, he sat down at the right hand of the Majesty in heaven.'"

"You see Tom," Joshua explained, "Jesus made this universe. Assuming the Big Bang theory is correct, Jesus' words are what initiated the Big Bang. That same Jesus, is God, and keeps the universe going. Notice however that his prime interest is in us and not the universe! Notice how it points out that he is the one that purifies sins. He was interested in mankind! Something else, do you know how the universe will end?"

Tom shook his head. "Nobody does!" he commented.

"Perhaps God does," Joshua suggested. "Slightly further on it says 'In the beginning, O Lord, you laid the foundations of the earth, and the heavens are the work of your hands. They will perish, but you remain; they will all wear out like a garment. You will roll them up like a robe; like a garment they will be changed. But you remain the same, and your years will never end.'"

As Joshua spoke the power of God seemed to double and triple. The glow of glory around him radiated to the extent that the angels pulled back to honor this presence of God.

Joshua continued, "Jesus created, Jesus sustains, Jesus completes everything and only Jesus remains constant through the whole process. Isn't he amazing?"

Tom looked stunned but recovered quickly. "Do you know about the astronomical theory put forward by a man called Hubble?" Tom asked Joshua.

Joshua shook his head.

Tom continued, "Well Hubble said if sufficient matter could be found in the universe it could be proved that our expanding universe would one day contract and disappear in the way it appeared. Do you realize that the simplistic description of that would be like rolling out a robe and then rolling it away again? That's amazing! That's in the Bible?"

Joshua wasn't quite sure of who Hubble was or what Tom was referring to but he had just read the text, so he nodded. Tom looked astounded.

"Josh, do you know men have argued about that for years. I wonder if any of them have ever read the biblical version. This is amazing. I sit in church almost every Sunday and get bored to tears with abstract terms and complicated speech, and I never hear anything like this."

Tom's look of amazement slowly turned to anger.

"Why the Hell hasn't anyone ever explained this to me before? I have wasted years looking for answers and I have never had things explained like this. Why not?" He asked the rhetorical question.

"Because it wasn't time to make your decision Tom," Joshua replied. He explained further, "You can't actually come to grip with these things unless God allows you to. The fact that you understand now is because you're ready to answer the most important question in your life. To blow it, means you blow your life, and God always waits until the correct moment..."

"So, what's this question?" Tom interrupted Joshua.

"Will you allow Jesus, the creator of the universe to control your life, to clean up forever the things that you have done that has displeased him, and to try to find out more about him. This is your decision and your answer has more power and consequences than knowing if the universe has sufficient mass or not. What do you say?"

Joshua waited for the answer; his heart was thumping so loudly he was sure Tom could hear it. The angels waited in anticipation. The room filled with power, glory and peace, and it was as if this corner of creation waited for Tom's answer.

Tom sat silently. The weight of the words penetrating his soul and his mind fought a battle. Slowly but surely God was victorious and he answered,

"Yes!"

Instantaneously demonic spirits who were sheltering in the shadow of Tom's will were exposed to the glory of God. Tom's mind and will opened to the knowledge and acceptance of God. The fire of Holy Spirit established itself on the altar of his heart and sin was stripped away from his soul as in some miraculous way the blood of Christ, alive and vibrant, changed him. The demons fled shrieking through the ranks of angels in fear of their promised demise. The angelic throng exploded into heavenly chorus of praise and honor to God.

Distantly demonic hordes shrieked and fled trying to get out of earshot of the heavenly sound.

Tom felt no change in his situation. He simply considered he had made an important decision. It was beyond him to know how important. Joshua's face exploded into a smile.

"Great Tom! You have no idea what a change this will make in your life. I have waited for the moment you would say this. Now you will start to understand the true value of life!"

The men talked on for hours and before they knew it, the sun started up over the horizon. All except two angels had gone on to other duties. The two angels that stayed were still in silent adoration of an aspect of God they could never experience. Salvation!

CHAPTER THIRTY-THREE

That orange light of day came creeping over the horizon as John Kumalo got up. Soon thereafter he was standing at the mine hostel gates waiting to get in. The gates were locked. He had been waiting for the police to find his son for the past few days and nothing had happened. When he phoned the police station they only said "We're working on it!" He was tired of the same old story. Now he was going to find out more for himself. The house was lonely without Steve and he was worried that something had happened to him. He prayed about it and felt as if Jesus, the ultimate ancestor of everyone, had said he must start his own search.

A white Landrover pulled up at the gates and blew its horn. The driver called John over. "Have you seen the person who is supposed to open the gates?" he asked with an Afrikaans accent.

John shook his head and thought to himself that it was rather a silly question. Why would he be waiting outside if he could call the person to open the gate?

The Afrikaner continued, "Here use my keys to open it for me...." He turned off the engine and handed the keys to John. John went to the gate and struggled with the large padlock for a few seconds before it opened. He pulled the heavy gates open and then handed the keys back to the driver.

"Close them after yourself!" were the words that floated back to John over the roar of the engine as the Landrover kicked up dust and shot through the gates. John smiled wryly and slowly closed the gates. He only hooked the padlock through the chain around the gates so that others could get in. If the gateman got into trouble, then it would be justice. John considered he had waited long enough for service.

In the distance he could hear the sound of voices and the clanking of tin plates. The aroma of warm porridge floated down to him on the brisk breeze and suddenly he felt famished. He had been up for over three hours and some porridge would go down well. He made his way to the bungalow of the Pedi people. He smiled as he walked past the different bungalows housing the different nations. Mr. Mandela was talking of their one nation and here in the mine hostel, where they could live with whomever they pleased, the different nations of men chose to live in separate bungalows. Zulu's, Sesotho's, Xhosa's and others. There wasn't a combined bungalow anywhere! President Mandela would have a hard task making one nation of so many.

When he entered, a large, heavily built man who was still getting dressed saw him and called out to him. "John, may it go well with you, how is your family?" John felt a rush of affection for his friend's son. "About as well as the first time we spoke. How are you and your family, Samuel?"

In the traditional manner, they exchanged pleasantries for a while. Samuel went to get an extra plate and mug. They then made their way over to the hostel kitchen. A few minutes later they each had a steaming plate of porridge and a big mug of coffee. They sat at the metal tables in the large dining hall.

John learned that Samuel had been asking about Steve all week and that nobody knew anything about him. Samuel knew a person who worked in the personnel office and called him over to introduce him. Soon the three of them were discussing the options for finding Steve. The newcomer suggested that he could take John with him when he went to work and that he would try and find out some more about what had gone on at the plant around the time of the 'accident'. They all felt that things weren't as they appeared. None of them liked Hendrik and they were suspicious about Steve going missing so soon after he had supported Hendrik's story. Many workers felt Steve had been coerced into confirming that the events of that day were an accident.

The dining hall started to empty and somewhere a siren rang out. This was the warning that the transport would be arriving to take the men to their respective workplaces. The men hurriedly washed their eating utensils, put on their work clothes and boots, and went down to the waiting area. Huge tractor-trailers drove in one after the other. They filled up with people who sat on the simple seats along their length. Once all the seats were taken the people squeezed themselves into the center area.

Samuel, John and the personnel official, Phineas, all managed to get seats on the third truck. It was a rowdy cheerful bunch. The journey was only fifteen minutes. Samuel was dropped off at the metallurgical plant. John and Phineas went on to the time office where Phineas worked. Samuel warned John not to let people know that they knew each other.

"Just tell the people at the time office that you have come to get Steve's pay. They will not be able to help you until the manager gets in at ten thirty, so that will give me three hours to look around and see what I can find out," said Phineas as they stopped at the offices. Everyone climbed out as it was the last stop and the truck roared away.

John did exactly as he had been advised, and was told to go and sit in a waiting area on a bench. They would call him when they were ready. He settled back, took off his coat and using it as a pillow against the sidewall, made himself comfortable and went to sleep.

At ten fifteen, he was shaken awake by the desk clerk. "Mr. Prinsloo wants to speak to you!" he was told.

Struggling to wake, John got to his feet and followed the clerk to a large office where a rotund middle-aged man was sitting behind a large desk. The man was balding with a remnant of gray hair neatly combed back behind his ears. He had a disapproving downturn to his mouth but strong determination in his features. Kasper Prinsloo wasn't enjoying being separated from his friend Hendrik and would have preferred to be back on the metallurgical plant.

When the clerk left John standing in the middle of the floor, Prinsloo kicked a chair out from under the desk towards John.

"Make yourself comfortable," he said and with a minimum of pleasantries he got to the point. "I am afraid that I have a problem in that we have no authority to give you your son's money. He is missing, but until the police tell us where he is, his money can't be given to anyone else. Mr. Lurie, the mine manager did however give us instructions that should you come in, we were to give you this to help you over this time period." Prinsloo picked up an envelope off his desk and handed it to John. "I am sorry that we have no good news for you but I do hope this helps."

John thanked him and was outside the time office within a few minutes. He waited a short while before Phineas joined him. Phineas had nothing to report. "As far as I can tell nobody knows where Steve is and nobody except you have asked about his money." Phineas 's brown eyes sparkled for a second. "It does appear however as if Steve spent some time with a beautiful young woman Thandi on some of his days off. Do you know her?"

John was surprised. Steve had not mentioned her. He supposed that Steve had wanted to surprise him at some time. Phineas told him where she lived. He thanked him and walked down the dusty warm road to the taxi rank.

CHAPTER THIRTY-FOUR

Heat shimmered off the road as John waited for the taxi. It arrived about thirty minutes later. He squeezed into the hot sweaty interior of the overloaded vehicle. It bumped and swayed along the road for five kilometers to a small grove of trees alongside a mountain stream.

After disembarking, John scooped handfuls of water from the stream to quench his thirst before following a footpath alongside the stream. In the distance he could hear the sound of voices. Insects clung to the grass on either side of the path and exploded in a warm buzzing cloud as he walked along. Periodically locusts leapt out of the way and he smiled as at one stage, a small frog shot out from under his foot into the safety of the stream.

The heat and the tranquility of the countryside helped him relax as he walked. All too soon he rounded a curve to see some grass topped huts alongside the stream in the distance. A crowd of woman and children were in the stream where it splashed over some rocks. He made his way to where some of the group were resting in the shade of trees at the waterside.

"*Dumela!*" they greeted him with the traditional greeting. He answered and received a cluster of sparkling white smiles in reply. The eldest woman in the group offered him some tea that they had boiling over a wood fire in a tin can. He declined and after some small talk, asked if he could speak to Thandi.

"She'll be along presently," the old lady said with a glint in her eye. "She always arrives later in the day." In the stream alongside, the younger women were washing cloths, rubbing soap onto them as they spread them over wet rocks. As they rinsed them in the water, they started to sing a local folksong. John sat back against a nearby rock in the shade of the tree and closed his eyes. Soon he slipped into sleep, encouraged by the gentle warmth of the afternoon.

The sun was settling towards the horizon when John awoke. There was nobody at the stream now and in the distance he could hear the sound of children playing. He got up and followed the path around the curve of the stream to find a cluster of mud huts with cone shaped grass roofs blackened by the weathering heat of the African sun. The children were playing a game with stones that seemed to require them to throw them up and snatch others from the ground before catching the falling stone.

Standing watching them was a young woman who was distinguishable by her high quality European style clothing. John approached her and again asked if he could speak to Thandi. She was smaller than he, probably about five foot eight but she seemed to light the environment with her smile and her presence filled the immediate vicinity.

A mischievous sparkle, almost brighter than the glittering gold earrings she wore, lit up her eyes.

"Why do you want to speak to her?" she asked.

John thought about his reply.

"My son is missing and he considered her an important person," he answered. "I hope she can help me find out where he is," he explained.

The sparkle disappeared and the young woman looked serious, then sad and then respect filled her deep brown eyes.

"I am Thandi and you must be Steve's father. I am honored to finally meet you," she added. "I wish I could help you but Steve just disappeared without telling me where he was going. I have no idea where he went. He disappeared the day after that accident at ZPM."

John could tell from the concern in her voice that she was telling the truth. A stab of fear grabbed him and he found himself praying quietly under his breath. "Lord Jesus, keep my boy safe."

Thandi invited him into her home. He was amazed to see a white BMW standing alongside her hut and his attitude obviously showed. Thandi broke into laughter and explained that she preferred a simple life but that she worked in the city every day and needed reliable transport in and out. Her joyful attitude to life impressed him and when he entered her home he found the inside to be different to what he would have expected. Instead of interior walls of packed dried mud she had what appeared to be internal walls of brick that had been painted off-white. An expensive looking chandelier hung from the rafters high in the center of the roof. When she turned it on, the room flooded with warm light supplemented by the glow of the sunset through the quaint wood lined window on the western side. A low mahogany table stood centrally surrounded by two equally low rocking chairs. A small kitchenette stood at the one side and again he was amazed to see a microwave oven on an eye-level shelf.

"How do you get electricity out here in the bush?" he wanted to know. She explained that she had a solar cell and battery installed for powering the lights and a small generator for all else. After she asked him to make himself comfortable and offered him a Coca-Cola, she politely asked him where he thought Steve was.

They talked into the night, discussing various theories about what could have happened to him. The only common conclusion that they could draw was that somehow Hendrik was connected to his disappearance. Steve had told both of them that he didn't trust the man and that he was a bad man to annoy, even unintentionally.

John found Thandi to be a delightful person to talk to and could see why his son would be drawn to this beautiful black women who was the epitome of the hopes of those wanting to combine the African and Western worlds. She had an elegant simplicity combined with an infectious smile that put him at ease and drew him away from the hurt in his life. He felt proud of his heritage as her soft voice eased his loneliness with her empathetic compassion for his son. At midnight the light started to dim and she insisted on driving him home. As she dropped him off at home, she suggested they meet again the following day. John agreed.

CHAPTER THIRTY-FIVE

About the time John was going to bed in South Africa, David Larrel was again meeting with Ron in Toronto. David handed over the electronic card that he had received from Mr. van Vuuren by courier earlier in the day.

"What is going on? Why do you need it back so quickly?" David twitched with annoyance. He didn't like inefficiency.

Ron grinned. "Worried?" he teased the older man. "Scared of loosing the potential millions of dollars?" He obviously enjoyed his associate's discomfort. "I wouldn't worry, it's simply a minor interruption. Remember we thought that this might happen. Nobody knows anything! Don't panic."

David looked at the younger man coldly. "Do they suspect anything?" he wanted to know. "Why do they want the card back?"

Ron scowled. "Just a regular security check. Nothing you should concern yourself with," he continued, "They need to do some checking after the PACICOMM incident. I want to be sure that my card is available if they want me to do specific work. I'd rather be safe than have problems!" he re-assured the older man.

They parted company, each going their separate ways, Ron to fly back to his office in Florida, David to his opulent home up north of Toronto. Each worried about their respective futures.

Back in South Africa, the following Monday, it was a warm African morning. Feathery clouds touched the tops of the grassy mountains where mottled outcrops of stunted trees hid everything except the buildings. Joshua pulled his car up to the gate of the Hartebeeshoek satellite station. The security guard came to his car window.

"Who are you going to see sir?" he asked.

Joshua explained James McFarlyn was expecting him. The guard spoke into a two-way radio and obviously was told Joshua was expected. He waved Joshua through.

Joshua drove down the winding road and parked out of the hot sun under a metal shelter. Huge photographic images of the earth covered the wall of the reception area. These included views of oceans, networks of roads and fields, infrared heat patterns and others. He was directed to a comfortable chair and waited until James came out. James was a huge man over six foot tall with shoulders of a football player. He shook Joshua's hand.

"I see you found our little hideout in these mountains," he chuckled. "How is Tom, haven't seen him for a long time? Still the mischievous sea-dog?" he asked.

"He's well," Joshua replied. "Work keeps him busy and I don't think he has much time for mischief any longer," he added.

James proudly took Joshua for a tour of the facilities. He explained how the station had been built to help with the space program and how during the sanction years, the Americans had withdrawn and left the small but dedicated team to man the station for whatever economic purpose they could extract.

"We made it through!" he said with pride. "Now we get most of our money from commercial surveys and helping with worldwide satellite control."

Joshua was shown banks of computers. Row upon row of computer monitors blinked at him. He was loosing track of the conversation as James droned on and Joshua tried in vain to see information that would help. James took him outside to show him the huge dish that was used to track the satellite.

"This massive piece of equipment is controlled by a joystick like a computer game," he explained."

This impressed Joshua. Looking past the dish he saw another building in a hollow.

"What's that?" he asked.

"Oh, that's the old station that is no longer used. Those things that you see alongside that look like pipes are the old antennae. It hasn't been used for years. No-one even goes there nowadays." James explained.

Suddenly Joshua's interest picked up.

"Can we get a look at it?" he wanted to know.

"Sure, tell you what, you go take a look. I have something to do inside. Join me in the office when you're finished. I don't think you will see much. There is nothing inside, it's just a vacant building now."

He left to do the chores he needed to complete.

Joshua walked down towards the building and excitement built up inside him. Something told him he was onto a lead that could help. An unseen angel smiled as he followed Joshua.

As he neared the building it appeared to be just as James had said. One exception was that the road up to the building had obvious markings of recent car tracks on it and the grass was worn away in the area where the wheels had traveled. "Must be some regular security check," Joshua thought. He pushed open the gate in the fence around the small complex and walked in. Vaguely in the distance he heard a bell. There was a short walk to the building and he was almost there when he heard a vehicle roar into life and saw that someone was gesturing from it for him to leave the area.

Anxiety tried to pull at him but was dealt with quickly and he turned and walked up to the building as if he hadn't seen anything. He looked through a window and saw rows of new equipment inside. The monitors looked new and so did the computers. The car roared into the area. An elderly man stepped out of it.

"You must leave immediately!" he ordered. "This is a security area and you're not allowed in here." He was red faced and obviously angry. Joshua smiled and apologized. He was given a ride back to the main building. James was there looking apologetic.

"My mistake," he said. "Sorry about that! Old man Jacobs is a stickler for rules and regulations. I ought to have warned you."

"Hey, no problem! Sorry to cause trouble!" Joshua said and after some questions he left.

Excitement filled him as he considered what he had seen. He was sure that something was up. New equipment in what appeared to be an abandoned building. He was keen to get back and discuss this with Tom. "What were they up to?" he wondered.

CHAPTER THIRTY-SIX

Tom was at the mine when Joshua arrived. He told his secretary to hold his calls and eagerly pulled Joshua into his office closing the door behind him. After Tom had poured them both coffee from a flask on his desk the men settled into comfortable chairs in the one sunny corner of the office.

"So what did you find out Josh?" Tom asked. "Is James still as fond of technology as always? That man is a wizard with radio equipment you know! I am sure he could fix a radio with string and chewing gum. I guess he told you some of the more exotic stories of my life."

"If we only had time for that," Joshua said smiling and went on to explain what he had seen. Tom listened intently and then sat back and considered what he had heard. Joshua waited. Finally Tom spoke, "So there is work going on at the station that James doesn't know about eh?" "I wonder if it's worth trying to connect this with Don Warmen?" he mused. "Now, it's about time I gave you my news." Tom went on to explain he had decided to do a little investigating of his own regarding Don Warmen.

"I called up my stock broker explaining I was interested in shares in *'Starnet Communications'* and I wanted him to make sure that the market heard of my interest," he said. "Hardly two hours later, I got a call from Don Warmen. He wanted to know if I would like to have lunch with him. Apparently my interest raised the value of the stock and he suggested we get together and discuss what I am intending to do. Naturally I agreed and suggested we meet tomorrow at the old Edwardian's Club in Johannesburg. I suppose I now have to figure out how to fudge the fact that I don't actually want the shares," he chuckled. "Hopefully I can get us some more information. The fish has taken the bait and now I'll need to play the line carefully!" Joshua was impressed and the two men discussed their experiences for another few minutes. They agreed to return that evening and see if there were any more faxes sent to Hendrik as it was important to retrieve them when nobody was in the store. Joshua left to visit his mother and contact Carl. Tom attended to the day's activities on the mine.

As the next day dawned in Zinaville, a white Ford sidled into a side street near the Pankhurst home. For an hour or two, Hendrik sat watching as people left their homes to go to work. Spouses said goodbye to breadwinners, who raced out of the houses to take up their work. Children waited at bus stops to be taken to school and finally the garbage collection truck emptied the garbage bins alongside the various homes. Jake's car stayed in the driveway and Hendrik waited patiently. Finally Jake climbed into his car and drove away about mid-morning. Hendrik took one last look around the deserted street making sure nobody was watching, and then he sauntered up to the Pankhurst residence and rang the doorbell.

Sharleen was talking to Susan in the kitchen when the doorbell rang. She walked to the door still talking to her. Susan followed and walked to the living room window to see who was outside. As Sharleen was opening the door Susan screamed, turned and ran from the room. Sharleen turned around to see Susan leaving the room and in so doing left the door half open. Hendrik smashed his shoulder into the door hitting Sharleen in the face and knocking her down. Her eyes streamed tears and as she scrambled to get up, she caught a blurred glimpse of Hendrik's back as he chased after Susan. Struggling to regain her feet, Sharleen tried unsuccessfully to wipe the tears from her eyes. Her other hand pinched her nose closed in an attempt to stop the blood that had started to flow from it. She heard Hendrik banging on what she assumed was the door to the room that Susan had been using.

"I hope she locked herself in," Sharleen thought as she made her way to where she could see down the passage to Susan's room. Through her tears she could vaguely see the man had pulled what looked like a knife from his pocket and was trying to pry the door open. Scared, she ran from her house to the neighbors to get help.

Her neighbor was shocked to see Sharleen, still in her nightclothes, bloodied nose, standing on her doorstep. She hurriedly invited her in, asking her what had happened. When told, she directed Sharleen over to the phone to call the police.

A tired Afrikaans voice answered. She tried to explain the situation and he forced her to tell him her name and address before he would listen to what she had to say. On hearing the information, he then told her to stay with the neighbor and explained that the police would respond immediately. He told her to go to a window to watch and wait.

Less than two minutes later a siren was heard and a Honda pulled up at the curb with police lights flashing. A man in uniform jumped out leaving another uniformed man in the car talking on the radio. He ran into her home and was gone for a minute before the other officer started to climb out of the car. This officer's radio started to squawk. He put it to his ear and spoke for a short time. Nothing seemed to happen for ten minutes. Every so often the officer would speak into the radio. Minutes seemed like eternity as Sharleen waited anxiously to see the outcome. Finally the older officer came out of the house with the man, whom Sharleen recognized as her assailant, slumped against his shoulder. The barely conscious man was handcuffed and had a pillowcase from Susan's bed over his head hiding his face. From the clothing color she could however identify the man. They placed him in the back of the police car where he slumped down on the seat and didn't stir. She ran out to meet the officers.

"Sir, is it safe for me to go back into my home," She asked.

He nodded. "Yes, Ma'am! Please wait there until we get this man to the police station. We will be back to take your statement. This constable will stay with you until I get back." He briefly spoke to the other uniformed man who nodded and then strolled to a garden chair on her lawn and sat down. The first officer checked on the man in the back seat of the Honda and then came back to her.

"Try and get some rest. I'll be back in an hour," he said. He told the other officer to wait outside for the detective team to arrive

Sharleen accompanied by her neighbor went back into her home. The door to Susan's room was wide open. Both the door and doorframe had been gouged around the lock and there was nobody inside. One pillowcase was missing. The pillow it had encased was on the bed. The window was also wide open so Sharleen assumed that Susan had escaped through the window. She called Jake to tell him what had happened. She tearfully explained the situation and asked him to come home. Sharleen and the neighbor waited for him to arrive. The shock began to settle in on her and she started to cry softly. The homely lady from next door put her arm around Sharleen as they waited together.

CHAPTER THIRTY-SEVEN

Hendrik, slumped in the back of the police Honda waiting apprehensively. His brother drove a block or two before tossing the handcuff keys to him and telling him to take the pillowcase off. "Hendrik, you're a stupid idiot! You have really got us into a mess now!" he complained. "Again I must save your butt! I am tired of this! Next time you're going to jail!"

Hendrik ignored him. He knew his brother wouldn't do anything about the incident.

"Right *Broer*," he said, "so how do we get out of this one?" He waited.

The brigadier scowled and then a smile crept slowly onto his face.

"I have just the idea," he said. Cover yourself with the blanket over there and lie on the floor of the car. See that steel bar! Make sure you use it effectively when the time comes."

Hendrik was confused, but his brother would not say anything else so he did as his brother suggested.

Hendrik's brother drove to Carl's home. Before he went in he gave Hendrik a few instructions. He went to the house door and knocked. Carl was surprised to see the Brigadier but agreed to immediately accompany him down to the police station to help with the investigation. Returning to the car, they got in and the Brigadier drove off. Carl briefly heard a movement behind him and before he could respond something hit his head. He slumped unconscious.

Rapidly, the Brigadier drove to a small wooded area between Carl's home and the police station. Out of sight of others, the two brothers undressed Carl, exchanging clothes between Hendrik and Carl. The Brigadier finished the job by tying Carl's hands behind his back, and placing the pillowcase over his head. Hendrik climbed into the car trunk after they had placed Carl into the back seat of the police car, and the Brigadier drove them to the police station.

On arriving at the station, the Brigadier told the front desk to call Gerard to get the prisoner from the car and place him in a cell while he filled in the paperwork of the incident. The constable got help to carry the unconscious man inside and when he removed the pillowcase he was amazed at seeing Carl. Locking the cell, he went over to find out what charge had been laid against Carl.

The Brigadier had finished entering a charge of forced entry and aggravated assault against Carl. He explained that Carl had attempted to use a knife to attack him. Together with the constable he returned to the cell to go through Carl's pockets. As they turned out the pockets of the unconscious man, Gerard pulled out the large pocketknife that had belonged to Hendrik. This was placed in a zip lock bag and handed into the charge office together with the paperwork.

The Brigadier and Gerard then returned and parked near Hendrik's car in the street near the Pankhurst home. While the Brigadier walked to the Pankhurst's home, Hendrik climbed of out the trunk of the police car, walked to his own car and drove away home to change before going to Priggles Bar.

Sharleen was pleased to see the Brigadier and gladly gave her statement. The Brigadier carefully wrote it out and at the end asked her to read and sign it. Gerard signed as a witness. They stayed a while to re-assure the neighborhood that they had taken care of the situation. The Brigadier then asked Sharleen if she would come down to the police station to identify the person who had broken into her home. She agreed on the proviso that Jake could accompany her. As they were about to leave, the constables radio crackled into life with a call to go over to Priggles Bar and break up a bar fight. The Brigadier radioed back that they would take care of it on the way.

At Priggles the bar was in chaos. Hendrik had insulted the family of a shift worker who had come off night duty and who had been drinking at the bar since it opened. The worker swung a fist at Hendrik, who picked up a bar stool and threw it at the man. It missed its target and smashed into the lineup of bottles behind the bar, breaking the shelf, and causing broken bottles and alcohol to fly everywhere. Lofty, with the help of other patrons, had subdued the two men and called the police. A few minutes later the Brigadier and Gerard arrived. They left Jake and Sharleen in the police car. After taking statements, the Brigadier arrested his brother and the shift worker. Another police van was called. Sharleen and Jake watched as the two men were placed into it.

Sharleen thought the one man looked vaguely familiar but couldn't place where she had seen him before. The Brigadier watched with interest to see if she would recognize Hendrik and was relieved when she didn't show any sign of recognizing him. As the door to the van was locked the brothers looked at each other and smiled. Both were thinking the same thing, handled correctly, crime pays.

CHAPTER THIRTY-EIGHT

On arriving at the police station Sharleen was taken to the small waiting room where they took down her information. They gave her coffee and time to settle her emotions before leading her to a small dark room. It had one-way glass viewing into another room with white walls. The Brigadier and a policewoman joined her.

After explaining that she was to attempt to identify Susan's assailant, the policewoman arranged for a group of men to file into the white room. When they turned to face her, Sharleen startled and went pale. The woman sergeant and Brigadier reassured her and asked her what was wrong.

"I know that man," she answered pointing at Carl. "He was one of the police officers who brought her to our home for safety!"

Sharleen was distraught and her mind raced wildly. The man who was supposed to have protected Susan looked as if he was her attacker. But Susan hadn't been scared of him at the time. Why would he be so nasty when he had been so pleasant the night before? Why would the policeman be dressed in the attackers clothes? Did they normally do this sort of thing to trick a witness? What should she do? Why...? The Brigadiers voice slowly penetrated the haze of thoughts being extruded by her mind.

"Ms. Pankhurst! Ms. Pankhurst! Can you identify the man that broke into your home? Ms. Pankhurst, do you understand?"

Sharleen turned to the rugged man in the uniform and forced her mind to focus on what he was saying.

"No! Possibly! No! I think so but not really! It doesn't make sense!"

"Just tell us what the problem is," encouraged the Brigadier.

"It's Carl, the third man to the left," She replied. "He is wearing the same clothes as the man I saw but as I didn't see the man's face, that is all I have to confirm it's him. However I met Carl when he and the others brought Susan to our home for her safety and she didn't seem scared of him then. I can't think he is the attacker. It doesn't seem to make sense!"

The Brigadier smiled with satisfaction. "Thank you Ma'am, we will determine that. Your identification of the suspect will do nicely," he said, and nodded to the woman sergeant.

"Please take Ms. Pankhurst back home," he asked, "Also put out an all points bulletin for Susan van Vuuren. Let me know personally when you find her and don't interrogate or question her until I get there."

The woman sergeant nodded agreement and led Sharleen out.

Sharleen was glad to leave but was more confused and scared than when she had been brought in. Unseen, her guardian angel was struggling to contain the attacks of fear, deception and confusion that aimed to attach themselves to Sharleen's soul. The Guardian was only partially successful. Prayer support from the Zinaville community was limited for the moment and the rest of the saint's prayers were too general in nature to be fully supportive. The partial success would have to do for now! This demonic detachment was too strong for a single Guardian to control completely. Limiting the spiritual damage to Sharleen was all that could be achieved unless she called on the Lord's name. However she didn't do that!

CHAPTER THIRTY-NINE

In another area of town Susan forced open a window in Joshua's home pulling herself through and half tumbling to the floor. Scared of her father and with no-where else to go she gravitated to the only person she felt she could trust. She explored Joshua's home and found the shower. Deciding to get rid of the filth clinging to her from Hendrik's chase, she showered. She rubbed dry using his towel and allowing the warm glow to rouse her spirit, she felt safer and more secure than she had felt for the past few days. As she dressed, she considered her life and where she would go. Joshua featured in much of her thoughts so she settled down on the sofa and soon her thoughts turned to troubled dreams.

Joshua left work at three. His heart jumped when, through his open door, he saw Susan startle into wakefulness at the sound of him coming in.

Confused thoughts ricocheted around his head like popcorn in a heated pot. "Why was she here?" "How did she get in?" "Why wasn't Sharleen here?" "What had happened at the Pankhursts?" "Wasn't my door locked? Where had Susan got a key?" These and a myriad other thoughts, left him with his mouth hanging open and a glazed look in his eyes. It was so comical that Susan burst out laughing. However the shock of waking and the terror of the past few hours caused her laughter to change to tears. Before the first teardrop had time to roll down her cheek, Joshua had her in his arms. Her long dark hair cascaded down hiding her face as she sobbed uncontrollably for a long time.

"What's wrong? Why are you here? Has something happened?" He wanted to know.

Over the next hour Susan poured out how fear followed her through life due to her father. She described how they culminated in this last episode that had driven her into his home. She held nothing back. A vast darkness seemed to start to disentangle itself from her soul. In pain, she described her childhood and the ritualistic incest and beatings she had endured. Scornfully she described manipulating her father into allowing her to leave home. Cuddling closer and closer to Joshua, she ended up curled up into a ball. Joshua's emotions rolled from rage, to love, to utmost concern. He knew he had to do something for her. "But what?" he thought. Disquiet flooded his soul crowding his thoughts into a spinning kaleidoscope of ideas. Slowly the whirlpool centered on the single idea of calling Jake to find out what was actually going on.

Susan cuddled up against him while he put a call through to the Pankhurst residence. The phone rang eight times before Jake answered. Jake's voice was strained. He interrupted Joshua and told him that Susan had gone missing. When Joshua told Jake that Susan was with him and that it was Hendrik's chasing her that had scared her, Jake was astonished.

"Susan told you it was 'Hendrik Van Vuuren'?" Jake exclaimed in surprise. When Joshua confirmed this, Jake told him of Sharleen's experience and Carl's arrest.

"We must get down to the police station and correct this as soon as possible," Jake urged Joshua. "Carl is being held unjustly!"

"Not so fast Jake!" Joshua retorted. "That Brigadier is tied up in this and is obviously part of the group that put Carl into this mess. Let's meet and work out a plan to clean up the situation. While you think of a solution, I'll let Susan know what is going on and then we need to meet. I suggest you come here as that will not look suspicious since they don't know Susan is with me." Jake agreed.

The Pankhurst's arrived almost before Joshua could finish briefing Susan.

It was a happy re-union. Sharleen was tearfully happy to see Susan was safe. Susan was joyful to see her friend again. The two ladies disappeared off into the living room together. Jake and Joshua went into the kitchen to find something to drink and discuss their plans.

"Could Hendrik guess that Susan is here?" Jake asked.

Joshua thought about it. "Yes," he said thoughtfully, "and it was the police knowing where she was that got her into trouble the first time." Jake stood silent for a while as Joshua made coffee. Once the pot spluttered and a rich coffee aroma spread throughout the kitchen, they came back to the subject.

"My problem is finding the safest place for her to be," Joshua continued. "Most of my friends are related to our work and so it would not be wise to use them because the police would be questioning them about my father's death. What do you think?"

Jake thought for a while. "It would be best to get her out of town if possible. Who could you trust who knows the situation and lives outside town?" Joshua shook his head. He couldn't think of anyone. They decided to ask the women. Pouring the coffee, they took the mugs into the next room.

Sharleen and Susan couldn't think of anyone either. A discussion of recent events led to Joshua mentioning Steve Kumalo. Sharleen suddenly suggested that John Kumalo might agree to look after Susan. Everyone except Susan thought it was a good idea. Susan was a bit nervous of the idea having grown up in the Apartheid era not trusting blacks. She did however agree that Hendrik would never look for her there. Finally, an unanimous decision was made to take Susan to the Kumalo home if John would accept her. The Pankhursts had brought some of her clothes to Susan's delight. She took them and put them into a small carry bag while Joshua put a call through to the mine to get John Kumalo's address. He found John didn't have a phone so they decided to drive there to see if he would help. Joshua also decided to go to the police station and see Carl after they had moved Susan.

Twenty minutes later Joshua turned into the driveway of the Kumalo home and was amazed to see a shiny new BMW parked outside. Worried, Susan ducked out of sight while Joshua went to the front door. John answered, and Joshua disappeared inside. Five minutes later he came back to the car and gestured for Susan to join him. When they got inside, John introduced Thandi to Susan. They made a magnificent pair, both were exceedingly beautiful women and Joshua sitting watching them felt proud of the new South Africa growing from the embers of the old. He had been impressed by John's immediate and humble offer of whatever his home could offer as security for Susan. Although Joshua had offered to pay all expenses to help the old man, John declined. John hadn't heard anything about Steve yet and was despondent, so having Susan there would help him keep his spirit up.

Joshua stayed long enough to see that Susan was settling in well, before he left to go and see Carl.

CHAPTER FORTY

At the police station, the desk sergeant was completing his afternoon shift when Joshua walked in. *"Middag Meneer,* Good afternoon Sir," he greeted him. Joshua asked if he could see Carl. He was taken into a small interrogation room and after a preliminary body search to check that he had no weapons or paraphernalia that could be given to their prisoner, the sergeant went to get Carl. From the sergeant's attitude and willingness to help he was obviously not happy about having Carl in the cells.

Carl arrived looking tired and worried, but when he saw Joshua, his face lit up. Joshua checked with Carl that their conversation couldn't be recorded in some way and then brought Carl up to speed on the happenings of the past few hours. Carl's face became more and more serious as the story unfolded.

"We're all in trouble now," Carl remarked. "The Brigadier has too much power in this part of the police force. I haven't even called an attorney yet. Everyone I know is linked with my work here! I can't trust them. Maybe Tom could help? I'll also use my call to contact Aaron at the newspaper and ask him to help me. Please, don't ask Sharleen to come in here on my account, as it'll put her in danger. I'll find another way out of this dilemma." They chatted some more and then Joshua went off to find Tom. Carl went back to his cell.

At John Kumalo's home, Susan and Thandi found they had much in common. John had left the two women to talk. Thandi explained how she missed Steve and how little she had been able to find out about his disappearance. Susan told Thandi about her father's anger and Joshua's kindness and how she expected Hendrik would probably try to hurt her. Both ladies lapsed into silence. John went outside for a breath of fresh air.

Deep in the Magaliesburg the demonic enclave was alive with rumors. Fear strutted around infecting the demonic horde. Poneros watched the activities from the rock throne through half closed eyes without intervening. Small flickerings of light and more angels had been seen entering the universe of time and space. This was not good! The noise quieted for a second as Kakoo swept in through the cavorting mass that parted providing him a clear path to Poneros. He settled near him, leant over and whispered something.

Meddler tried to overhear and just managed to move out of the way in time, as Kakoo's sword sliced the air near what would have been an inquisitive ear. A cackle swept the horde of onlookers. Darkness seemed to ooze an oily sulfuric smell and the air felt static. Poneros's red eyes opened wide and glared around. The huge black-velvet wings unfolded and he rolled his obese form out of the stone throne in what appeared to be a rather fast movement for the languid mood of a few moments earlier. Kakoo drew his cloak around him and in a manner uncharacteristic of his normal egocentric attitude, slid quietly into the shadows where his eyes gleamed from the darkness.

Suddenly in the center of the cave a thunderclap erupted and a brilliant white-green light flashed. The demonic herd turned tail as they tried to make way for whatever it was that was erupting in their midst. Finally they gained courage to turn, rippled black swords held high, to see what appeared to be an incredibly handsome man dressed in pure white standing in their midst. Despite this appearance, an aura of incredible evil enveloped the apparition and the little Fear had done to work up the horde was magnified a million times. The demons shrank back, Poneros cowered, and the man walked to the rock throne and sat down. Immediately Poneros bowed down low and muttered "Welcome to this stronghold your Majesty!" The demonic throng echoed, "Welcome your Majesty" mimicking their leader.

Hate flooded outwards from the perfect features of the man. "Your 'welcome' fails me?" an acid tone exuded from a perfect mouth. "This stronghold is failing to hold back the curse of the enemy!" the voice grew in strength and intensity. "The chasm awaits you should you fail!" the voice thundered, "and I'll dispatch you even earlier, if the angels don't!" the sound of the voice was now searing the demonic ears. Some tried to cover their ears to no avail as he continued; the pain stabbed at their eardrums and seemed to resound in their heads. "You will not fail me! The enemy must be halted. The humans must be controlled. Tom Lurie must return to our control, Joshua Robyn is to be hemmed in from all sides and stopped, Susan van Vurren is one of ours, but we're loosing control continually, and Carl must be neutralized. PONEROS! WHY IS CARL NOT NEUTRALIZED?" the voice thundered.

"Your planning failed your Majesty" Poneros replied.

"MY planning FAILED?" the voice reached a new crescendo, "YOU INSOLLENT WORM!" with these words the man creature transformed into a huge dragon about to consume Poneros who appeared small, insignificant and extremely scared. The serpent swung its head from side to side, gleaming eyes hypnotizing the demonic crowd into dark little statues as fear stilled the smallest movement. The sulfuric stench that wafted around the cavern increased with their fear.

Poneros fell down and groveled. "Sorry Majesty, I meant that my plan that you asked me to make, failed! Your Majesty is right as always!"

In an instant the serpent was gone and the man had re-appeared on the throne. "Stand up you abhorrent runt" a quieter voice said. Poneros stood up. The demons could see Poneros' stress. The glimmer of a perfect smile crossed the creature's features for a second. "Will you fail me again?" the creature asked.

"No, your Majesty! Certainly not your Majesty! We will definitely succeed your Majesty!" The words tumbled from Poneros's rubbery lips. Then a flickering of self-preservation glinted in the red eyes, "that is, provided Kakoo and his stronghold give us good advice and help."

The dark shadow containing Kakoo's shadow shifted and the eyes narrowed but he said nothing. "Very well, succeed or start suffering sooner than time dictates!" the voice of the man echoed in a strange quiet way around the stony walls.

Poneros wanted to reply but his voice faded into stillness, as in a microsecond the throne became empty. He turned and glared at the stronghold. "Get to work, or you will feel the cost of failure!" he yelled. The demons thought his voice was a squeak when compared to the past few minutes, but the consequences looked too real, so they complied hastily.

CHAPTER FORTY-ONE

At the Kumalo home it was late afternoon as John sat listening to the latest soccer match on the radio. There was a knock on the door. Thandi immediately hid Susan in the bedroom. When John went to answer the door he was surprised to see Phineas the personnel officer from ZPM.

"*Dumela,* Come in" John invited politely.

"*Dumelang,* Thank you," replied Phineas in the same language as he stepped into the room and waved a hello at Thandi. "I hope you're all well." In traditional African custom they discussed health and family for a while before Phineas came to the point of the visit.

"John, I can prove that Hendrik was on the plant when Mr. Robyn died and your son disappeared."

John and Thandi were listening attentively.

"I was given the job of writing up the security records for that day. They had me record the entry or exit times, the color of the marble selected and the name of the staff member from the envelopes given to us by security. Hendrik went in before the accident. He was on the plant at the time Mr. Robyn was killed. He left the plant and Steve entered. Hendrik entered again soon afterwards. That is normal but, from the records, Hendrik left almost directly after Steve before the police investigation was finished. Neither of them got searched. I thought it was strange your son and Hendrik leaving within so close to each other. They were enemies for as long as I can remember. I wonder if Hendrik was following Steve?"

John looked angry. "Yes. Hendrik was probably involved with Mr. Robyn's death and must have had something to do with Steve's disappearance! It is as we expected!"

In the bedroom Susan was watching through the door, which she had opened slightly. She couldn't understand their language, but heard the names Hendrik, Steve and Robyn clearly enough. She started to get scared. Thandi must have sensed this. She motioned an apology to the men, got up, and went to the bedroom. Closing the door she took Susan to the far side of the room. In a whisper she explained what they had found out. Susan went pale and put her hand to her mouth in shock as she heard that her father had been on the plant when Bryan had been killed. She looked even more worried when she heard that Hendrik had probably followed Steve out of the plant. The worry started to turn to panic. Thandi could see the fear on her face. She comforted her friend as best as she could.

"Don't worry, we will tell Joshua all of this and he'll make sure everything works out right." She reassured Susan. They heard Phineas leaving.

Susan was scared. Very scared! "Thandi, will you promise to keep something for me, and never let Hendrik or anyone he knows get it?" Susan asked with a desperate look on her face.

"Of course, you can be sure" Thandi replied.

Susan pulled out a small key. "There is a locker at a gym where I have membership, number 3265, this is the key for it. I have been keeping some photographs, documents and some other things I don't want to talk about in a small cardboard box. If anything ever happens to me, if I disappear for a few days, or die for some reason, or anything like that, please go and take out that cardboard box. Give it to Joshua, Sharleen or Jake and ask them to give it to somebody high up in the police force. The person must outrank my uncle who is a Brigadier. Will you do this?"

Thandi looked at Susan quizzically.

"Yes, of course. But you're not going to die!" she reassured Susan. "Why don't you take the box to them now?"

"I can't" explained Susan. There are things in it that will reveal some terrible things about my past that I don't want people to know. I'm sorry!"

Thandi put her arm around Susan.

"Never mind, I'll do as you ask," She said gently. "Let's go and make some tea!"

They went to the kitchen.

John was busy putting on his coat as they entered.

"Where are you going?" asked Thandi.

"I am sorry my daughter in spirit! I have work to do now. I must find Mr. Joshua as soon as possible. Please use my home." replied John and smiled wanly. "I am going to town to wait at his home until he returns. Please stay and look after Ms. Susan until I get back."

John looked old as he said this. The gentle creases that the aches of the world had etched into his face seemed deeper and darker than before. His deep brown eyes seemed to overflow with compassion and pain. He said farewell to each of the ladies in the traditional manner and walked off into the night to find a taxi.

CHAPTER FORTY-TWO

Early the next morning Joshua arrived at the mine office and was shown through to Tom's office. Tom rose from his desk and greeted him as he came in.

"It's early to see you here!" Tom teased as he smiled hello. "You know, I'm different since our prayer two nights ago. Something changed but exactly what, I can't say! I even found reading that old Bible interesting and exciting. Before that, it was worse than chewing dirt. Amazing what happened! Now, how are you Josh?"

Joshua sat down and explained the recent happenings. He explained what John Kumalo told him about the mine security information. Tom's face reflected the thunder in his heart as he silently absorbed this information.

"We need to understand what Hendrik is doing. He is the key to everything!" Joshua pointed out again.

The two men sat in silence for a moment and thought of possibilities.

"Let's look for any new faxes?" Tom suggested.

Joshua agreed.

Tom asked Mrs. Wold to take messages and picking up a small briefcase, walked down to the mine store with Joshua. It was a warm sunny African day with the sound of insects and birds filling the air as the bush awoke to the dawn chorus. Normally they would have driven there but both men enjoyed the fresh smells and sound of the early morning. God's glory touched each of them as walked along silently, the crunch of gravel being the only sound they generated. Locusts hopped ahead of them in the bush disturbed by their footsteps and the cicadas buzzed appreciation of the increasing sunshine.

They reached the store as the staff were busy off-loading cabling and machinery from a large truck. Greeting them, Tom and Joshua moved to the back of the store where the printer was located. After checking they were alone, they moved the refrigerator and Tom retrieved the hidden fax pages. They replenished the printer's paper from a supply in the briefcase and put the refrigerator back. A few minutes later they were back at Tom's office.

Tom asked Mrs. Wold to bring in some more coffee and both men sat down to read the faxes. When the coffee arrived, Tom in true sea-dog fashion added a good-sized drop of whiskey from the flask in his desk drawer. Joshua reading the faxes intently was startled when he tasted the coffee the first time.

"Wow, who supplies *your* coffee beans? They are definitely not lacking in energy!" Joshua put his cup aside.

Tom grunted and hardly looked up from the fax he was reading.

Over the next while Tom's demeanor visibly deteriorated. Comments like "Damn them!" "What the HELL do they think they're doing?" "Blast him! I must check up on..." were interspersed with the odd four letter word in such a way that Joshua honestly wondered if the first comment of the day applied at all. Once Tom even looked up at Joshua and commented; "I should do this more often! I'm finding out more about what happens inside my company than I do at any management meeting."

They read on.

Twenty minutes later Joshua found something that seemed suspicious. "Tom, what do you make of this," he asked.

He read the fax to Tom. "Please help to ensure Rod.A meets requirements. Imperative system is ready use within the next two weeks! Familiarization information for your visitor: Vehicle code FM1, 40 kg. Microstar class Perigee: 728 km. Apogee: 747 km. Inclination: 70.0 deg. Period: 99.6 min. Plane F. Ascending node 199.1 Frequencies to be provided telephonically. Code block Delta Lima Three...." Joshua stopped reading.

"There is a page and a half of this type of gibberish, I don't think it makes much sense what do you think?" asked Joshua.

Tom nodded, "Sounds like satellite orbital information to me, maybe even some sort of tracking information. I have a friend in Washington that's involved with something of that nature. He's a radio ham like me and we still chat occasionally. Last week he told me he's now working on some satellite job. Shall I give him a call after we finish reading and we see what he can make of this information?"

Joshua agreed and they read through the rest of the faxes. They then left to go to Tom's home to find the American's phone number. This time they took *all* the faxes with them.

It was 8-o-clock when Tom called through to America knowing his friend would be at the office as it was after lunch in Washington.

"Can I speak to Colonel Bridgewater?" he inquired.

The assistant put him through.

"Hey, Ben! It's Tom Lurie here! Time to wake up, I have a mind teaser for you to enjoy with your coffee..."

They exchanged pleasantries for a few moments.

"Ben my friend, I have come across something strange and I think it could involve satellites. Maybe it includes some of yours but I am too dumb on these things to be sure. Can I read some of it to you?"

Ben must have agreed and Tom started to read the fax. He was halfway through when Ben obviously interjected.

"Ok, Fine Ben. You think it's something about communication satellites." Tom paused. "Yes I can fax it immediately, what's the number?" He wrote it down. "When can I expect some idea of what it is?" he listened. "Ok! Sure!" He hung up and turned to Joshua.

"Ben is going to look into this personally. Apparently they've had some strange occurrence with satellites a while ago and he wonders if it's related. He says he'll call us with information when he has any. He's going to contact his friends at the Pentagon. I guess it's good to have friends in high places! Join me with a drink?" He asked. Joshua nodded but requested a lime and soda. Early morning and alcohol was more than he could stomach. He hardly drank any alcohol at all but kept to the biblical advice of "take a little wine for your stomach." The mouthful of coffee was enough of a shake-up for one day. He knew Tom had no such concern. Tom went to the liquor cabinet to pour another stiff whiskey for himself.

"To success and the elimination of troublemakers from ZPM" he toasted and they both drank to the toast silently. Then Tom took the fax as discussed, dialed the Washington number and transmitted the information to the other continent.

On the other side of the Atlantic, Ben waited expectantly for the fax. Mirar, an angel sat on the windowsill of his office watching over him. It had been a long time since the initial meeting with Beor and much work had gone into preparing this man for his tasks. The tough military man had taken a long time to overcome his pride and accept the Lord into his life. Mirar always thought that it was strange how humans fought this so much. If they could only see the Lord they would not even wait a nanosecond. This man had struggled with this simple decision for years. Benjamin was a proud man and only when his wife died did he face the truth. Mirar knew he couldn't have taken an easier path. His charge would not have acquiesced in any other way. The Lord knew best!

The door opened and a lady corporal came in with the fax.

"Colonel, urgent fax for you, Sir!" She snapped a quick salute, dropped the fax in his in tray, about turned smartly, and left closing the door softly behind her.

Ben picked up the fax and studied it. He picked up a phone and dialed.

"Colonel Benjamin Bridgewater, Zulu Three Tango Alpha" He waited and then tapped a sequence of buttons on the phone and before getting through. "General, Ben here, I have some disquieting information that I think we need to investigate with care. I am security officer for FERRIT and I would like this dealt with in a particular way. It would be better if we can track leads without allowing the FERRIT control team to know we're investigating. I also would like to have this fax processed immediately and a preliminary report to be returned within three hours. Is that possible?" He nodded after listening for a while. "I understand. Transmitting the data now, thank you."

He put down the phone and pushed a sequence of buttons on the phone. The desktop slid aside to reveal a glass panel. Lifting what appeared to the glass inset in the top of this panel, he laid the first page of the fax onto the glass panel below, took a plastic bar code out of his desk drawer and laid it on the glass underneath the fax page and closed the lid. Immediately a series of red lines shone through and around the fax and then a bright green light came on and moved down the page. He repeated this with the next page. Retrieving the pages he again typed a code on the phone and the desk returned to its previous state. He looked at his watch, got up, shredded the fax and walked out to another meeting.

CHAPTER FORTY-THREE

The Zinaville police station interrogation cell was in chaos. Carl had been woken a few minutes earlier, taken to the interrogation room where they had sat him down in the chair. A captain whom Carl didn't recognize came in to start questioning him. Carl refused to say anything and asked if he could make a call. He was tired and hungry as it was now dinnertime and he knew they would keep him going for a few hours.

"You're not getting a call, a drink of water, or a scrap of food until you talk!" the captain threatened.

"That statement is unlawful and you know it," retorted Carl. "You also know that this conversation is being recorded. Please try to remember I am not one of the petty criminals you deal with! I am a police officer and as such I know exactly which laws apply." Carl's voice was hard and icy, "So now you take your bullshit, your attitude, and your poor knowledge of law and get me a telephone so I can call my lawyer." Carl's eyes narrowed and he looked at the Captain as if he was a mosquito that needed to be squashed.

"You will talk to me and you will be happy with it!" retorted the captain angrily. "We don't baby sit people here!"

"I am aware of what we do, and what we don't do. I am *also* aware of my rights and want to talk to whoever is the Brigadier's *superior*. I wish to place a charge of false arrest against the Brigadier who arrested me. Since he is your superior officer, just get the person who outranks him!"

The captain went red with anger and looked as if he would explode. He started to come around the table as if he was going to hit Carl.

"And…." said Carl. "You stupid fool, you may have assaulted our black people, which by the way is illegal, but you will never get away with doing the same to me. I shall resist such an assault by breaking your fat little nose, and if you restrain me, the marks on my body that will occur will be pointed out by my attorney as an unprovoked physical assault which will ensure your being charged before this day is out"

The captain looked like he was going to have a heart attack but he stopped in his tracks.

"Clever words won't help you, you chicken-liver'd, snake belly'd runt!" he sneered. "You just wait!" turning to his lieutenant he snarled, "give Mr. Detective a phone. As of now, we're detaining him under the 'Internal Security Act'," Turning to Carl he snarled, "You will be aware that according to the act we can hold you without giving you any of these 'luxuries' you have just requested! I don't even need to let you call your attorney, but due to my human *decency*, I will. Not that it will help much. You're getting moved tomorrow!"

The captain sat down with a smirk on his face and the lieutenant disappeared to return with a phone. He plugged it into the wall alongside the table. Carl didn't move to make his call. "Calls to attorneys are confidential aren't they?" he asked. The Captain and his lieutenant glared at him, got up and were about to walk out when Carl spoke again. "So I suggest that you turn off that recording device, or it could be construed as another illegal act. You *do* know where the switch is? …or would you like me to show you?" The Captain ignored Carl, but the lieutenant said that he would turn it off. They went out.

Carl waited a few seconds to give them time to turn off the recording. Then he dialed, facing away from the one-way glass as he spoke. He was scared, badly scared! The thought of joining some of the crooks he had put in jail made him exceedingly nervous. Silent prayers ascended to heaven as he waited for the call to be answered. He had called Aaron as he felt that this was a case of newspaper men having power and contacts that attorneys would either not have, or would not be willing to use. Aaron answered, complaining that he had been eating breakfast.

Carl explained his situation in short succinct sentences. "Please call me an attorney and get him around here pretty darn quickly. Then call Joshua Robyn in Zinaville. Try to make as much newsworthy noise as is possible. I really appreciate your help Aaron." Aaron promised to get in contact with the attorney and Joshua. "Keep your chin up and smile," he advised. "There's nothing like that for keeping your enemies guessing! While you smile, I'll try to get something written for the early morning edition. Carl, you owe me a night's sleep." On that note, Carl thanked him, said goodbye and put down the phone. Within minutes the interrogation team returned to rob him of his night's rest. He held to Aaron's advice and never lost his smile.

CHAPTER FORTY-FOUR

In Washington, the pager on the Colonel's belt buzzed as he made his way back to work after the meeting. He looked at the number, pressed acknowledge and took the elevator up to his office. Headquarters responded far faster than he expected. Arriving at his desk he locked his door and put a call through to headquarters.

"Colonel Benjamin Bridgewater, ... Zulu Three Tango Alpha." Again he waited and then tapped a sequence of keys on the telephone. When he got through, he listened for a short while and then gave as detailed a description of his relationship with Tom as he could remember. A printer on his desk sputtered into life and churned out a report on Tom who had obviously got into a few shipyard pub brawls at various times and on various continents. Most of the information was old. There was a short bit on his mining wealth and various philanthropic activities he had started in the past few years.

"Yes Sir. I'll contact him and let him know we will be sending someone out to meet with him. Yes Sir! Definitely Sir! I'll do that immediately!"

The rather one-sided conversation ended. The Colonel carefully read the information on Tom and then called him at his home.

Tom was fast asleep when the phone rang. "You guys always forget we're on the other side of the globe," Tom complained bitterly. "So what was it all about?" he wanted to know

"We have determined that this is definitely linked to some type of clandestine satellite activity," the colonel explained. "Our people in Africa will be contacting you. A businessman will be at your office tomorrow morning your time on a pretense of being a salesman for a local oxygen supplier. Please let him have some time and help him as much as you can. On our side, we're working to find out any internal leaks. To help us, please don't discuss any of this with anyone."

Tom assured him that he would not pass on the information but insisted that Joshua who had been with him on the last call would have to know. Benjamin begrudgingly gave his permission and asked that Tom make sure that Joshua would not discuss the information with anyone else. Tom assured him of this.

In South Africa, Tom put down the phone and found that he had an excitement building within himself. "We're onto something big here!" he thought to himself and decided to speak to the CIA salesman before passing the information on to Joshua. He turned over and went back to sleep.

The phone rang in Joshua's office at nine thirty and when Joshua picked it up, the voice on the other side introduced himself as Aaron Smithson of the Star newspaper and explained that Carl was in trouble. He told Joshua that Carl had been detained at the police station and asked Joshua to bring him up to date on all the activities of last day or two.

Joshua checked that Aaron was who he said he was and then explained that the Brigadier was deeply involved in the suspicious activities surrounding the town. He told Aaron about Susan and her relationship with Hendrik. He also told Aaron that Susan was staying with the Kumalo's. Together they discussed what Carl and John Kumalo had told Aaron of Joshua's father's death. Aaron was particularly interested in the discussion about the faxes. And when Joshua mentioned to him that there was a Fax that said, "shipment will arrive Friday." Aaron suggested that maybe they should keep track of the activities at the station for the next day or two. He also explained to Joshua that he would be ensuring that the newspapers got to know of Carl's situation and suggested that Joshua should arrange for people to visit Carl consistently for the next day or two, to enable him to ask for help should he need it. They talked for a short while longer then Aaron rang off.

Joshua immediately called Tom who answered abruptly. He hadn't expected Joshua to be calling this early and on realizing who it was, he apologized for his tone. Immediately he started to relay the Colonels information. He had seen the CIA "salesman" and had been told to collect as much information as possible. A tap was to be put onto the fax line and Hendrik's home phone. Tom had been given a contact number to call with information and had been told not to do anything that Hendrik might find suspicious.

A period of silence followed as both men pondered the implications. Interrupting the silence, Joshua brought Tom up to date on the news from Aaron. When he got to the part about the fax and the Friday shipment he pointed out that Aaron had asked them to monitor the tracking station more closely.

" Darn!" said Tom, "another evening destroyed! What do you suggest we do?"

"I am not certain," said Joshua, "maybe watch the station for a few hours to see if anything happens."

Tom sighed.

"I guess I can give up an evening," he groaned. "Never say I am not supportive of others!"

He sounded decidedly grumpy.

"Thanks Tom,"

Joshua smiled to himself knowing Tom always implied that anything he had to do for others was an effort but Joshua knew that Tom had a heart of gold and would not have turned him down.

"So Joshua, what time do you suggest we go out there?" asked the older man.

"Shall we see if we can get there by eight forty-five," suggested Joshua.

"Sounds okay by me!" said Tom. "Now leave me alone and let me get some work done!"

At 8:50p.m. they met at the turn-off to the satellite station. Joshua's car was pulled into the bushes where it was hidden from the road. They took Tom's car down to near the satellite station entrance and hid it in the dark bush where they could watch and wait. There was no traffic on the road at all. They were just getting bored when a small delivery vehicle stopped on the verge of the road nearby. Joshua and Tom sat very still as the van appeared very close and they were concerned that they would be noticed in the moonlight. Fortunately, the shadows were large, and the bushes concealed them well.

They had been sitting there for an hour when a car pulled up. Tom and Joshua could see Hendrik's familiar silhouette climbing out. The individual that Carl had named "Stretch" followed him. Tom and Joshua could identify him from his nickname. He was tall, thin and seemed to have a liking for polo neck sweaters. Hendrik and Stretch climbed into the delivery vehicle with the driver whom Tom and Joshua could not see. The car disappeared into the satellite tracking station. It appeared as if they were expected since the gate was opened without discussion.

Tom surprised Joshua by pulling out a strange looking camera that he had with him. He took several photographs of the delivery vehicle, and of Hendrik's vehicle. He then climbed out of the car and made his way to the perimeter fence where he took more photographs of the establishment. Joshua just sat quietly with a quizzical expression on his face.

When Tom came back he asked him what he had been doing.

"I bought this infra red camera years ago from Russian army supplies that were being sold off to the public," related Tom. "At the time I intended to use it on the ship where I was serving. The plan was to identify warm machinery from cold machinery as a metal fatigue study. Since then I found out that it took good photographs in the dark if set up correctly. I thought it may reveal something that we may not have seen," said Tom.

Both men sat there for another few hours. It was 2a.m. when they decided to give up their wait for the vehicle to come back out. They drove off, retrieved Joshua's car, and went home to get some sleep before morning.

CHAPTER FORTY-FIVE

At 7p.m. Carl was woken and taken to the visitor's room where Joshua was waiting. His initial tiredness and confusion was dispelled and he was very pleased to see Joshua. He motioned Joshua to be quite, looked under the table and located a small microphone. Joshua watched as Carl covered it with his hand. They whispered to each relating what had happened. Carl asked Joshua to find a good attorney. He was very worried and by the end of their discussion, so was Joshua. Within thirty minutes Joshua had left the station and called a good attorney. He also called Jake to ask him to get the church to pray at the Wednesday morning prayer meeting. Jake agreed but didn't sound as if he was surprised at what Joshua told him. He suggested that he should ask the church members to call on Carl continually all day to ensure his safety. Jake also suggested that Joshua buy the morning newspaper. Apparently Carl had made the news. From his tone it sounded as if it was a good article.

Joshua bought the paper at the nearest store. He was astounded to see that the story had made the front page. "Detective Detained, Internal Shambles Act activated again!" Aaron had outdone himself with the article revealing the stupidity of the Internal Security Act. He had printed a story about detaining people without trial and had mentioned Zinaville directly. The article alluded to the danger of keeping a policeman in jail under the internal security act. The inhumanity of keeping a person not yet proven guilty, together with hardened criminals that he had convicted as part of his work, questioned the government's humanity, the police forces authority and the justice system. Joshua was shocked. Aaron had stepped across the line. He hoped Aaron would not get arrested! This was mighty strong language, about as safe as lighting a bonfire in a gas station.

He was right! At national police headquarters, the publicity control department was in disarray. The phones didn't stop ringing. Citizens had clogged the public telephone lines and even the radios were occupied with staff discussing the issue. This was completely inappropriate and the Minister of Police was fuming! The story had hit the overseas press, Foreign embassy's officials called with questions on human rights issues. The Minister of Police was furious! Angrily he demanded to know who had leaked the news and wanted to know who had failed to control the leak. Headquarters took twenty-seven minutes to find out in whose jurisdiction this originated! Those minutes took an eternity for those involved in the search. Finally Brigadier van Vuuren was linked to the incident. It took another thirty minutes to contact him, then a further thirty seconds for them to order him to release Carl and have him tailed.

The unhappy Brigadier reluctantly contacted Zinaville and relayed his command to execute the order. Twenty minutes later Carl walked out of the station totally confused about the sudden change in his perilous state. Coincidently a church member happened to be walking into the police station as Carl walked out. He offered Carl a drive home. A small swarm of unmarked vehicles followed and parked in all streets immediately around Carl's home, his phone was bugged within minutes. Carl guessed as much when he saw one of the cars that followed but he ignored it and enjoyed a shower before breakfast. He figured that with that amount of surveillance, Hendrik's brother had little chance of arranging another framing incident. Intrusion of privacy at this point improved his safety. His only concern was that a police operative could be bought as an assassin. AK47 assault rifles and 100 rounds of ammunition were easily available at a cost of less than $50. Add to that a high unemployment rate, insufficient money for the lower classes to even buy enough food for their families and little to no social security to ward off starvation in the country and he was pretty sure that someone could be persuaded to make some money quickly. He put this negative thought out of his mind as he savored the massaging hot water pulsing over him. His head still hurt and the cut in his scalp was not yet healed properly.

Carl would probably have been happier if he could have seen the CIA operatives that had followed the police surveillance team. Around the time that Carl was showering, Meddler slid across the floor in the distant cave, almost colliding with Poneros. Meddler shot back to a safe distance. The message he had to deliver wasn't going to be appreciated and he wanted to keep his leathery skin in one piece. "Your Defilement I bring news!" he said, avoiding mentioning it was bad news.

Poneros' cruel eyes opened from their apparent slumber and Meddler slid back another step or two in fear. "And?" the question exuded scornfully from the rubbery lips. "Kakoo failed, the policeman Carl is back home and no longer fully within our control."

The explosion of sulfur, expletives, threats and the flashing sword were just as the small demon had expected. Meddler ducked the shrieking sword that carved a blue streak through air that had been occupied by his body a millisecond earlier, and scuttled away, his fear diminished with the sound of Poneros's fading voice.

CHAPTER FORTY-SIX

In Zinaville the Christian community was praising God. Their praise changed the spiritual gloom of the town so that the glory was clearly seen by the enemy. The church member who drove Carl home had phoned Jake, who had phoned Frank. The leaders had each phoned key people who had a list of others to phone. In this way the news flooded the small community. There would be a church prayer meeting in both congregations that afternoon giving thanks (and without doubt to catch up on the news that individual members might have missed). The town would ring with the sound of prayer and exclamations of praise that would seriously hurt the ears of the demons in the vicinity.

Joshua received his call and then he in turn called Tom who agreed to go to both meetings. The first was at Frank's church at 2p.m., the second later at the Pankhurst's home at 3:30. Both men tried to focus on their normal daily activities but found it difficult as the time slowly drew near. Joshua was excited that Tom was joining a meeting with a serious Christian focus for what was probably the first time in Tom's life. Tom was excited because he expected that this was going to be spectacular. This "Jesus" he had just met would surely do some amazing things. In his concrete sailor way, Tom wanted to see the lightening strike and God's opposition be blasted out of town. In his simplistic view, it would have to be that way wouldn't it! Hadn't God got Carl released? Hadn't God been after him all these years and changed an atheistic sailor into a believer! Now that anything was possible, Tom wanted to see the "baddies" fried alive! He didn't give a thought to the fact that the "baddies" were sinners like him, subject to the same outpouring of God's grace.

The meeting at the Anglican Church was a quiet and controlled affair. Subdued tones and whispers could be heard as the group of mainly older ladies gathered in the seats at the front of the church. Tom and Joshua joined the few men present. Frank came in and after a brief introduction, asked Tom to come to the front and relay what he knew of the situation. Tom took a stand behind the lectern and described the happenings of the past few days. He left out the detail of who Hendrik was and the names of the people involved, but pointed out that it was now time that they did something about the situation. He was expecting a supernatural event from God, and as he spoke he wondered what this mainly geriatric crowd could in fact do. Somehow this wasn't what he expected. What he got next was even more unexpected.

"I think we should all go down to the police station as a congregation and tell them everything we know after this prayer meeting, but let's first pray" Frank responded.

Tom and Joshua were aghast. This would definitely cause serious problems for not only them, but for Carl as well!

"Rev Brenan," Tom interrupted, "This information is only for those of us that are here. It will do more harm than good if the wrong people get to hear it.

Unseen by Tom, the dark forces of anger were pulling at Frank and trying to get him to slice Tom's comment with carefully tutored religious comments. Frank's face grew strained and mildly red. Just as he was about to speak, Joshua stood up, turned around and spoke to the gathering. Beside him, unseen, Beor's sword slid from its scabbard.

"Friends, Christians" said Joshua, wondering why he was being so formal when he never was formal in meetings of this kind. "You know Tom and I are personally involved. We're here for *spiritual* warfare and not to work up support for our current police force." Turning to Frank he continued, "Reverend, we believe it's more important to focus on prayer than on taking action in our own power. Please don't endanger innocent lives by taking a non-spiritual approach to this. We need your strength and spiritual guidance."

Frank was having a hard time. Anger, was loosening its grip as Beor's presence enabled by Joshua's humility and statement, reduced its power. However, another dark presence tangled with Frank's thoughts.

Manipulation wasn't letting this saint escape so easily. He knew Brenan had given in to his brand of evil many times and was therefore weak in this area. Manipulation fired in another round of manipulative thoughts to follow the last onslaught.

Frank turned to the congregation. "I trust that we will all pray about our civil responsibilities in this regard," he responded, "and then we can decide if following the country's law, is in the direction the Lord would have us go, or not."

It was Tom's turn to go red in the face and look as if he was about to explode. Joshua sent a telegraphic prayer to the Lord, and when he saw Tom looking at him to determine what to do, he shook his head suggesting that Tom shouldn't respond. Tom returned to his seat alongside Joshua but Anger got its grip on him.

The prayer was stilted and cold as the different people prayed. Tom felt disdain rising in his heart; this isn't the power of the God he wanted to follow! He wanted a God of action! This was a group of pathetic geriatrics swayed by the Reverend, he thought.

Time marched on, the prayers raised themselves heavenwards on quavering voices, and soon Frank closed off the meeting. Neither Joshua, nor Tom uttered a word. Frank asked, "Can we have a show of hands of those that feel we should report this to the police?" When the hands started to go up, a gray haired old man who obviously had a painful back, cranked himself upright using his cane. He turned to the congregation ignoring Frank.

"I have seen much in my time," he started, "and so have many of you." He paused for breath. "I know that there are times to react, and times to pray." Again he paused and looked at Frank. "Young Reverend Brenan, I would be most appreciative if you would phrase the question differently, something like 'How many of you got direct leading from God during this prayer meeting that you should become involved in addressing this issue by a means other than by prayer alone?'" He paused for breath. The bright clear eyes gleamed out from under the bushy eyebrows and Frank visibly concurred with the older mans guidance. He knew this man was wise from past experience and felt subordinate when in his presence. The elder turned and asked again, "How many?"

Not a single hand went up.

At the old man's suggestion Frank asked that everyone keep the matter confidential and prayed a blessing over everyone. They all exited from the building.

Manipulation was being held at bay by a bright angel that accompanied the old man who hobbled out into the sunshine. Anger still accompanied Tom as he strode out, heading towards the car with Joshua. Manipulation was flitting to and fro among the crowd, but every time a likely victim seemed to become available, the ranks of the unseen guardians closed and when faced with the brilliant white warriors, Manipulation turned away snarling.

"What a bunch of useless jerks!" Tom exclaimed under Angers influence. Joshua smiled. "Not quite what you expected?" Tom shrugged. "That crippled old man was the most competent person there. That's not saying much. Is it always like this at prayer meetings?"

Joshua smiled again. "How do *you* measure the effectiveness of a prayer meeting?" he asked.

"I'm not sure, I suppose it's by what is accomplished!" Tom retorted.

"And would you have liked to see people take action on things, or should the action that occurred be spiritual and unseen?" Joshua prodded again.

"I suppose I wanted spiritual actions that I could measure," said Tom trying to weave away from the obvious implication. "Like a bolt of lightening to obliterate Hendrik" he growled.

Joshua chuckled. "Guess we will have to wait to see if that occurs. I, for one, am happy they didn't head off down to our local police station."

"That's for sure," Tom agreed. "Do we have another meeting?" he asked, "because I think I have had my full of this type of meeting for one day."

Joshua suggested a different approach. He called his mother and asked her to call John and check on Susan and tell her he would be picking her up. "Let's get Susan and meet at my mother's home," he suggested to Tom. "Maybe Carl as well?"

At 3:30 that afternoon a small group of people gathered at Karen's home. Sharleen Pankhurst opted to join the Robyn prayer meeting although Jake was leading the church prayer meeting at their home. Susan had arrived with Joshua and clung to Joshua as if he was a lifeline, which in a strange way he was. There was quite a hubbub, Susan updating Sharleen, Karen being updated by Joshua and embracing Tom regarding his salvation. It was a while before Carl joined them. He had driven himself over and watched the tag team at work following him as he did.

Carl's entrance changed the focus of the group and they were at once both inquisitive and caring, as they wanted to know what had happened to him, and if he was physically fine. Sharleen was apologetic and couldn't wait to apologize for her mistake at the police station. Carl shrugged it off with a smile.

A cacophony of warm noise encompassed the room as the saints gathered. Unseen around the room the guardians formed a protective circle. This was one area that evil was not going to intervene in very easily. Every entrance was guarded. Gleaming from the shadows were the eyes of the spirits who wanted to destroy the peace and joy of the gathering. The angelic protection was considerable compared to that of the sulphurous wraiths. Tola, Tabitha and Beor were resplendent in shining glory and fearsome for evil to look at. The wraiths didn't want to risk a short trip to the abyss by trying to intervene. They were represented in the room by a small group of demonic members that were permitted entrance on Susan's authority and were in considerable pain as they attempted to maintain their hold over Susan's will and thoughts.

This was confirmed when the prayer started and the glory of their enemy started to pour out of the room. It was as if the heavens had opened from within and a spiritual song of great beauty and scintillating power was flowing from each opening in the room to the eyes watching outside. The pain of this peace, joy and happiness caused the evil shadows to shrink back, partially to avoid detection, but mainly because the knowledge of their inability to ever experience this desirable existence drove waves of anguish through their evil twisted spirits.

The demons in Susan's life started to shriek. The humans at prayer were oblivious to the spiritual noise. Susan was feeling a huge war inside her mind. She had not been certain what to expect of a "prayer" meeting. This was all strange and very unsettling. She felt the immense warmth of the love of those around her. A tingling sensation settled on the back of her neck. Inside her head her thoughts screamed at her to get out of the building. Joshua's arm around her shoulders felt warm and reassuring, countering this fear. The power of the moment built in waves of emotion. The sound of people's voices seemed to fade as she increasingly experienced attraction towards an entity she didn't understand at one level but distrusted at another. The intensity of this and the sound of her thoughts telling her to get out now rose to a crescendo. Then a warm deluge of love flooded her soul. Deep in her spirit her created purpose started to awake and she felt herself responding. Tears poured down her cheeks and she looked at the blurred faces of those around her. Everyone had their eyes closed. Suddenly the blurred face of Tom looked up.

"Hey what's wrong?" Tom asked in a loud voice that interrupted the prayer. The prayer stopped and everyone looked up and around. Susan felt turbulent emotions within her soul. The impulse to flee was getting stronger every second.

"Susan, what's happening, can we help, tell us what's wrong?" comforted Joshua.

Susan sobbed and tried to explain but found she could hardly speak. The words didn't make sense and her mind seemed unable to accommodate the war within her, let alone conceptualize and communicate it. The group gathered around her. Karen and Sharleen came and sat along side her and put their arms around her. Joshua and Carl placed their hands on her shoulder and Tom watched from a distance confused. Sharleen led the prayer and Joshua followed. They called for the love of Jesus to console her, the power of God to bring her to Him and the peace of God to flood her heart.

The small group couldn't see the glory of God that developed within her as she struggled towards the thought that she would really like this Jesus to take away the weight and cares from her heart. As she heard someone pray, the first demon detached from her soul to shriek its way out into the darkness watched by the empowered angelic host. Joshua was talking to her. She heard "would you like to accept the power of Jesus into your life to remove your sin's, the bad things of your life, and give you a new life in His love?" Her soul overwhelmingly urged her to say yes, but her throat felt crushed and unable to utter anything. She tried to speak but no words came. Karen seemed to sense this and prayed, "Lord bind the force of darkness that is holding her tongue captive and enable Susan to speak!"

It was as if the floodgates were swept away. The words tumbled out tripping over one another. She was speaking in her mother tongue, Afrikaans, asking for the change to occur in her life and pleading for a removal of the past and telling everyone she so much wanted to understand what was happening.

It took a while before she calmed sufficiently to follow the lead of her companions. Karen led her in a simple prayer that she asked Susan to repeat. " Please Jesus, forgive what I have done, I give my life over to you to guide and protect. Enable me to do what you want me to do!"

The demonic hordes for miles around could see the effect. Again the glory blasted up high over the sleepy village, flooding the spiritual space with the news of another salvation. The remaining demons fled from Susan knowing their very existence depended on distance between them and her. In the room Tom was speechless and confused over what was happening, and everyone else looked radiant.

"What the Hell happened here?" Tom asked. "Susan, are you okay? Has this world gone nuts? Why were you crying? Joshua what's happened?" the questions flooded the room. Everyone laughed and settled back into their seats. "I guess we could say that Susan just got rid of the past and ensured her future in heaven in one simple step" Joshua explained. "Like you did the other night!"

Tom suddenly understood. "Hey, it's quite a load removed from your life isn't it?" He asked Susan, who smiled as she blinked the tears away. "That was neat!" he added. "How often does God do this sort of thing?" Everyone except for Susan and himself laughed!

They discussed this happy occasion and encouraged both of the newer Christians. It was the pragmatist Tom who brought the subject back to the problems they had at hand.

"So, how are we going to keelhaul these Van Vuuren brothers?" asked Tom. "Can we pray for God to suddenly hit 'em with a whammy of sorts, and get them changed round like He did for Hendrik's daughter and me?"

A silence settled over the group.

Joshua thought, "Would God forgive Hendrik who had killed his father? What would his reaction be if God did? Where was the fairness in that?" Karen and Sharleen had similar thoughts that were compounded by the pain of the knowledge of what Hendrik had done to Susan. Carl remembered his smack over the back of the head and the abuse in the police cell. Not one of them felt as if they wanted to forgive Hendrik in any way. This strained against their knowledge that God could change Hendrik and forgive him. One by one they accepted this absolute truth, each breaking their own bonds with the vestiges of revenge hidden in their souls. One by one the relief flooded their souls.

Joshua started and the others followed, breaking the silence with prayer asking for forgiveness for their hidden desire for revenge. Power radiated around the room. It was tangible to all present. The voices lapsed into silence and again for time immeasurable each prayed within themselves to their Savior, exposing their failings and allowing their spirits to forge a unity with the divine purpose.

Surprisingly it was Susan who led the next prayer. It was for Thandi, John and Steve. She prayed for safety, comfort and knowledge of what they should do. The others agreed. In the spiritual realm angels were descended into Zinaville by the hundreds. Demonic messengers brought the news to Kakoo and Poneros in their stronghold. They didn't stay long as it wasn't a place they wanted to be near. The evil swords had already dispatched a few evil messengers who were slow to depart.

Sharleen had to leave, and the rest discussed what to do. The men decided watching Hendrik and the satellite station would be wise and agreed to meet for breakfast to form a plan.

Carl departed with his retinue following dutifully behind him. Tom and Joshua watched from one of the windows as the group of cars parked along the street followed one another at regular intervals. "Must be an important person to have so many guards," joked Tom. Karen offered Susan a ride back to the Kumalo's and left soon afterwards.

Joshua and Tom departed soon after that. Joshua dropped Tom off at his home before heading back to his own home. Beor was staying close to his charge. Tom was followed by a huge angel, Tola. Since Bryan's death Tola had awaited a new assignment. That assignment was Tom.

CHAPTER FORTY-SEVEN

On arriving home Joshua was in for another surprise. He found the front door open with a note pinned on it. *"Mind your own business, not others!"* scrawled across a page torn from a notepad. His home was in a shambles. Somebody had emptied every drawer and every container onto the floor.

It took Joshua hours to search through the mess to find that nothing appeared to be missing. He guessed the Van Vuurens had been looking for Susan, or information on her whereabouts and had found nothing. He secured his front door with a security chain since the intruders had broken the latch and called Tom to see if his home had been vandalized as well. It hadn't. They both decided to discuss everything the next morning.

Early the next morning, Tom and Joshua ordered coffee at a small McDonalds restaurant two blocks away from Carl's home. They sat at the entrance where they would be able to see Carl arrive and discussed mine affairs. Carl would be there by about 8a.m.

Just before 8a.m. a busload of children and teachers stopped outside, and the children came scrambling into the restaurant shouting and talking, pushing one another and generally changing the surrounding peace into organized mayhem. Carl arrived in the midst of this. His demeanor was a sharp contrast to those around him. He strode over to their table.

"Tom, Joshua, we need to get everyone out of here NOW!" he said and his serious face conveyed that he wasn't joking. "A kid knocked over a garbage can and I saw a bomb inside. Right next to this window, look!" he pointed to a pile of garbage just feet away from where they were sitting. They could see what appeared to be a limpet mine hanging inside the steel can. The teachers were still milling around outside at the bus. One had seen the overturned can and they were heading towards it. "Can you get the manager and find a back entrance?" Carl shouted as he rushed outside and intercepted the teacher. He pointed to the mine on the inside of the can. The teacher rushed back to the other teachers. Carl came back inside.

Tom had found the manager, and as Carl came back inside, he roared a command over the noise of the crowd. "We have a fire drill for this restaurant. Can everyone please follow me through the back exit!" Carl and a teacher blocked the front entrance. The teacher urged the children to follow Tom. The manager motioned to her staff that everyone must leave.

Within a minute everyone was outside of the building. Carl led them away from the building as quickly as he could. The bus came racing around the corner and once they had a good distance, Carl urged the children to get on board the bus. While Tom and Joshua helped with embarking the children, one of the police cars that were following Carl came around the corner. Carl ran straight up to them. "Bomb in the garbage can outside McDonalds. Get the area clear. The second car that followed the first did a sharp U-turn. The bus pulled away. Within five minutes a huge explosion rocked the area and smoke rose into the air around the front of the restaurant.

"I wonder what my car looks like" Tom groaned. His car was parked on that side of the McDonalds building. They all started back towards the building. Police sirens and emergency vehicles were pulling up and as they tried to get back to the scene, their nemesis, Brigadier Van Vuuren pulled up. "Arrest those three men!" he shouted, and before they could protest, four burly constables had grabbed them. They were handcuffed and led off to the police van where they were loaded with other men who had been arrested for one or other reason. They looked at each other aghast at the impertinence and didn't even talk to each other as the van took them back in the direction of the police station.

On arrival everyone was placed in a holding cell and left alone. A guard sat at a desk completing paperwork. Tom suggested they use their phone calls wisely. After discussion, they decided that Joshua would notify Jake, Carl would call Aaron Smithson, and Tom would call his company attorney. Soon after the plan was in place, an officer came in and Tom and Joshua were told that they would be released but must remain in town. Carl was to remain in custody. Confused, relieved but concerned for Carl, Tom and Joshua were let out of the cell.

"We will call Aaron," Tom told Carl. "Don't worry, you will be out of here in no time."

The officer ejected them from the police station without meeting their demands for an explanation. Annoyed Tom suggested they walk down to Frank Brenan's home, which was just over a block away. Joshua agreed and they headed off in that direction to call Aaron and get help retrieving their vehicles.

CHAPTER FORTY-EIGHT

After a troubled night's sleep, both Tom and Joshua opened the Sunday newspaper the next morning to be greeted with an article at the bottom of the front page, "Hero is jailed after saving children from bomb!" Aaron had done it again! Joshua called Tom to let him know and when he put down the phone, it rang again. It was Carl. "Can you come and get me out of this hell-hole?" he asked. Joshua promised to be there in less than ten minutes.

Carl was released as soon as Joshua arrived. The Brigadier was obviously watching as Carl was given his belongings and Carl walked out with Joshua.

"Why the intense observation from the Brigadier?" Joshua asked.

"I'm not sure," replied Carl, "I think he is extremely annoyed and wanted to see you for himself. He has warned me to stop interfering with police business during my 'suspension', and would only let me go provided I called you to fetch me. I think he wanted to see who you were himself. He suggested in a Nazi type way that you shouldn't allow yourself to get involved with the Van Vuuren family affairs. In his words, 'Tell that young man to keep away from Susan van Vuuren and if he knows where she is, he must notify the police as soon as possible. To fail to do so is obstruction of justice.' Ignorant pig!" Carl ranted.

Joshua grinned. "I thought that's what you hated being called by the public? Jailhouse language rubbing off?" Carl glowered at him and then broke into a smile. "I just can't be angry around you for long," he chuckled. "Get me to a shower, you moron!"

Joshua swung the car around and headed for Carl's home. Immediately a car pulled in behind them.

"We got company again," Joshua remarked. "Pull over and let me drive," suggested Carl. They switched drivers and Carl even had the audacity to wave at the car tagging them. The occupants didn't acknowledge him.

"Let us see if they know the town as well as I do! They are not from Zinaville," Carl muttered. He pulled out across the street into the nearby apartment building. He drove in under the building, through the parking area, and directly out into the side street, turning back towards the street they had just left. He stopped, waited a few seconds then turned into the street they had come from. He turned in under the building a second time. They were just in time to see the back of the car tagging them disappearing out of the apartment parking area into the side street they had just left.

"Now for some fun," said Carl. They waited for a short while and then retraced their path back to the same road through the side street. Again they were able to see the back of the car as it disappeared down the street in the direction of Carl's home. "Looks as if they are in trouble and hoping to catch up with me at home. I can't go there now, and they will also look for me at your home. Where do you suggest I should go to for that shower?" Carl asked.

"How about asking John Kumalo if you could impose?" suggested Joshua. Carl agreed and they headed for the Kumalo home being careful to keep a watch for cars tagging them. They failed to notice a few bikers that at different times intersected with their path speaking into microphones attached to their helmets. As none of these followed them for more that one to two blocks, they could be forgiven for this lapse in their intended surveillance.

Back at the police station in an office behind a closed door, Hendrik and the Brigadier sat in a black silence staring at the wall as if it would suddenly provide an answer to their problems. They had been arguing. The Brigadier had tongue-lashed his brother unmercifully for all the screw-ups that had occurred due to his hot temper. Now there was silence!

"I'll kill that daughter of mine when I catch-up with her. She'll never, ever, have an opportunity to give trouble again!" Hendrik commented in anger.

"Another stuff-up that is likely to get you into even more trouble?" enquired the Brigadier.

"Not likely brother, you will help this time!" retorted Hendrik.

"Pity you didn't ask for my help before picking a fight with Old man Robyn!"

"Pity you didn't think before driving me to the detective's house. Now we have a real problem with that man!"

"*Ja Boet!* and we have Warmen ready to make 'war' with us if we fail!"

"*Ja Boet!*"

They both lapsed into silence.

"Shall we call him and let him know we lost track of Carl?"

"You can, I'm not doing it!"

"I guess I must," mused the Brigadier. He seemed reluctant to call, but did anyway. Relief could be seen on his face when the line went to voicemail. He left a message and rang off.

CHAPTER FORTY-NINE

John had been wonderfully hospitable again. When Carl had finished showering at the Kumalo home, both he and Joshua decided to attend the Anglican Church, as it was Palm Sunday. Carl enjoyed the pomp and splendor of the service held there on this festival and convinced Joshua it was worth attending.

When they arrived the church was full. Carl remarked that the handing out of the little palm crosses was obviously popular. Joshua felt uncomfortable in the unfamiliarity of the staid service setting. Frank was at the front in his robes and with altar servers attending to the pre-service ritual. Joshua tried to put his discomfort aside and focused on the purification and dedication prayer that he always did for himself before a service. An altar server came walking down the isle swinging an incense burner on a chain. The pungent aroma made Joshua feel queasy. He was wondering if he could manage to last through the service when there was a noise at the back and the church went quiet.

A group of bikers had arrived and were entering the church. Dark glasses, helmets, and leather attire were a considerable deviation from the norm of church dress. Joshua wondered how Frank would deal with this interruption and wondered if it would be similar to the previous occasion at his church. He instinctively looked around for Hendrik but couldn't see him. This next week would see more and more bikers riding into town. The town was part of an area the bikers used for partying during the Easter weekend. Not all were problematic but the town always had an increase in crime during these times. Beer and drugs were known to flow freely during the period.

These bikers had a BFC logo and a dove on their leather jackets as their colors. They greeted folk politely, although in a noisier manner than appreciated and the group picked a location near the front of the church since most of the congregation had seemed to fill the church from the back. They brought exuberance to the environment that was met with mixed emotions by those present. One mother sitting close to the bikers with her daughter pulled the child closer to herself. It was evident she was uncomfortable. The biker alongside her called to another biker who passed him what looked like one of their mascots. A small teddy bear with a leather jacket having the bikers colors on it. This he offered to the child. The mother was about to refuse, but the child grabbed the toy before she could do so. The child was rewarded with a big smile from the bikers and a chorus of positive comments.

Frank started the service in the traditional way, the 'Book of Common Prayer' was recited. Joshua, who had to follow the text carefully was amazed that the bikers seemed to know it all. Frank's sermon was on the Journey of Christ into Jerusalem. Humility and the inability of the masses to understand more than they could see, was the theme. As the sermon ended, Frank surprised everyone by asking the leader of the Biker gang to come up. He introduced him to them and pointed out that the BFC logo stood for "Bikers For Christ." He suggested that everyone get to know these men and women, as the group had offered help to the local communities in maintaining a good relationship between the bikers and the locals.

The mood changed considerably. The service closed off and the congregation found bikers moving amongst them introducing themselves, chatting and generally making sure people got to know them. The more adventurous even asked a few bikers around to tea.

Joshua's mind turned to the problems Carl and he were having with Hendrik and the Brigadier. As if he had read his mind, Frank arrived and said, "Think these gentlemen could help you with some of the problems we've been having?"

Carl and Joshua greeted Frank. "Maybe!" Carl replied.

Joshua could feel his heart lighten. He wasn't sure the term 'gentlemen' applied but it felt good to know they could have support if it was needed. They chatted to the men for a while and then Joshua drove Carl home as he needed a change of clothes and wanted to complete some personal errands. No sooner had they turned into Carl's street than they saw the watchdogs sitting waiting in their cars. Carl in his customary manner waved to them as they pulled up in front of his home. They studiously ignored him. The insult of loosing him didn't make them popular with their superiors and they were angry at their circumstances and the fact that they now were pulling double duty.

CHAPTER FIFTY

In Moscow, Russia, it was late in the evening when the phones began to ring in the homes of key members of the security council of the Kremlin. Each received the same short message. A meeting would be held in the morning, 8a.m. sharp and everyone was to be prepared for a two-hour discussion.

Joshua and Carl were still asleep as the morning rose over the Kremlin. The meeting was in session.

"Comrades, we have discovered that the Americans are to blame for the silencing of the PaciComm satellite." The speaker was saying. The small group of fifteen men looked to the screen alongside him as it showed a slide of what appeared to be a communications satellite.

"We managed to get a photograph of the satellite using our surveillance probe that was redirected into a parallel orbit yesterday. The damage can be seen in the following slide…" the slide changed. "…in the following trajectory along the computer housing…" the speaker pointed at a series of holes in the metal casing, "…the integrity of the satellite was compromised."

"Could this be due to a meteorite strike?" one of the audience inquired.

"No, definitely not! You can see the strikes follow a straight line, almost a precise trail. The holes show no impact on the metal during their creation. Notice no metal bend in the direction of impact. Also notice the globules of metal on this outer side of the metal sheets. These holes were created by a laser!"

The body language of the audience stiffened and their eyes narrowed.

"Are you very sure of this Comrade?" one of the older men asked.

"Absolutely, and I would like to hazard a guess that it was performed by more than one laser as well!" the speaker continued. "Notice that there is a consistent irregular shape to the hole, almost if there was an additional bite out on this one side. This is repeated exactly for all holes. My guess, Comrades, is that this is due to multiple lasers being targeted to the same point, all operating in synchronization."

"But the science and planning to get that correct is astronomical!" another Comrade volunteered. "Surely this can only be a result of that notorious American Star Wars program that they abandoned as part of our diplomacy?"

The room erupted into simultaneous discussions. The speaker stood quietly waiting for the noise to reduce.

"You're correct Comrade," the speaker concluded, "that is the reason we're here today to decide on a course of action to put before the Security Council at large."

Bedlam broke out in the meeting. Some asking for more information, others suggesting that this was the start of a buildup to an attack on the Motherland; others pointing out the satellite was not even Russian and so posed no threat.

"Comrades, order please!" the speaker continued. "As my friend here pointed out, the satellite is not ours and so this event can't be conceived as an attack against our Russian Union. It is however important to use this to query the legitimacy of the diplomacy that resulted in stopping the arming of space. This Star Wars program was meant to stay a prototype with no further development. What do you suggest we do?"

The matter was argued for an hour before they concluded that one of their members would indirectly approach the CIA and ask for an explanation. The overall attitude was of distrust but that it was better to 'let sleeping dogs lie." A communiqué was drafted and sent through the specialized channel to the Americans. One of the CIA all-night operation groups received and processed it. The priority was set to orange and a combination of pre-organized procedures was started. Key personnel would be reviewing the initial information and gathering facts from the moment it got light in the morning. For the time being they slept on oblivious to the change in world tensions.

CHAPTER FIFTY-ONE

Early in the morning in Zinaville, Hendrik was on the warpath looking for Susan. The door to her apartment had been forced open and he had gone through every personal item belonging to her. Most were now lying around the room on the floor. He broke mirrors, tore pictures out of frames, and generally destroyed anything that had even the slightest chance of harboring information of any sort. He took any cassette tapes, notebooks and anything she had written and tossed them in a garbage bag. This he took with him when he left. He didn't bother to make it appear as if a robbery had taken place, as he knew the police were smarter than to interpret his damage in that way. He did however make sure to wear a stocking over his head and wear gloves, as he did his work. No need to be stupid he thought!

The next trip was down to Joshua's home. Fortunately Joshua was at work at the mine already. Hendrik decimated Joshua's home in a similar manner to what had occurred at Susan's. This time he found and took nothing with him. His anger growing, he waited until it was time for Priggles to open as this was his next destination.

Lofty was busy packing glasses onto the shelves when Hendrik burst into the Pub and strode up to the bar.

"Morning Hendrik!" Lofty said. His smile belied the fact that he had reached under the counter for his 9mm automatic that he kept there. "You're up early today! What can I do for you? Not working today? Not planning to bust-up my bar again are you?"

Hendrik growled a greeting. "Have you seen Susan over the past few days?" Hendrik wanted to know.

"No I have not!" replied Lofty. "Do you want me to give her a message if she finally returns to her job?"

"No, just call a number. Have you got something to write on?"

Lofty slid a coaster and a pen over. "Write it on that!" he advised.

Hendrik scribbled a number and got up to go.

"Say nothing to her, just call this number. I am her father and she is in some trouble," he volunteered as he made for the door.

"And you're as likely to get that call as I am to get to be president of this country," murmured Lofty under his breath and he went back to packing glasses. He had thrown the coaster with the telephone number into a drawer that contained odds and ends to be emptied into the garbage at the end of the month.

The police station was getting used to Hendrik going in and out and most of the staff wished that the Brigadier would go back to headquarters leaving their little town alone. Unfortunately it didn't seem to be happening! The Brigadier had taken over the biggest office and made himself at home. Hendrik arrived as the Brigadier was on the phone and Brigadier motioned him to come in and close the door.

"Sure Don, I'll make sure to get our program back on track. You just get that all important card back in my pocket. Without it we're all going under in a bad way. I DON'T give a @*#! how you do it. Just do it!" he ordered and slammed down the phone.

Don Warmen wasn't used to being talked to in that manner.

"Uncultured idiot!" he raged, but silently agreed with the Brigadier. He picked up the phone and moments later the ringing awakened David Larrel in his country mansion in Canada.

"Which dumb, rear ended, squirrel brained, piggish, fish face, is calling me at this hour?" David moaned into the phone. For a second time in as many minutes, Don Warmen was angered by the lack of respect.

"The one making you into a billionaire, Moron," came the retort, "now get those brain cells awake, and listen carefully. You have work to do, and quickly!"

David swung himself around into a sitting position and looked across at the bimbo he had brought back with him from another late night social event. She was snoring and hadn't moved.

OK, shoot!" he said.

"Get Ron! Get the key card! Get it to me by Thursday, latest! Oh! Make sure Ron doesn't cause any waves about handing it over. There is no more time. We must finish the program. Time is running out!"

"Sure, can I give him details of why we need to rush?"

"No, just do it!" Warmen replied and put down the phone.

David looked at his watch; it was not even 5a.m. Eastern Standard Time! Just in time to do the same injustice to Ron Jackson! He went to the hall phone and called immediately. Ron was just as unhappy to be woken but talked less and listened more. He agreed to get the card to the Brigadier by Thursday, then rolled over and went back to sleep. David got the distinct impression Ron was expecting the call. The thought was mildly disconcerting. "That kid is a too bright for his own good" David thought.

At a more sociable time in the same time zone, the personnel at the Pentagon were alerted to the security breach in the Star Wars prototype project. First to be notified was Colonel Ben Bridgewater who had the security responsibility for the project. Simultaneously the pictures of PaciComm from the American spy satellite arrived and were securely mailed to the Colonel. A meeting was called and his presence ordered.

Secrecy being paramount, nobody on the Star Wars project was notified but suddenly all phones were tapped, all computers monitored, and everyone informed that their cards would be re-issued at 12 noon. They weren't aware that a small transponder was being placed into each card. The cards would now be tracked on a 24 hour basis by a specialized satellite. Now their physical position would be continually monitored.

Ron Jackson knew none of this but then he had expected this might occur. He had finished his work on the previous day and knew that whatever security procedures were to be established, all would be in vain. His co-workers had never suspected a thing! That was the reason he wasn't at all concerned with the call earlier in the morning; he was ready! Oh, if they could only know how ready! When he got the request to hand in his SecureCard he smiled and complied with pleasure and asked them to keep it. He was about to go on vacation. He then retrieved his vacation approval form with all the correct signatures on it and strolled out to enjoy a pleasant day.

CHAPTER FIFTY-TWO

Joshua arrived home after work to chaos. He was angry and soon his anger gave way to a smile as he realized Susan was safe. They wouldn't have trashed his home if they had found her. He settled down to a long evening of tidying and cleaning after securing the door. He considered calling Tom, or Carl, but decided it would keep until morning.

Tom Lurie was enjoying the early evening in his study with a glass of wine as he checked production plans, made notes, and caught up on the afternoon stock market activity. He would be seeing Don Warmen later in the evening and would need to know what was happening on the financial front. He was about to leave for his appointment when the phone rang. Ben introduced himself, asked if Tom had a computer with a sound card, quickly telling Tom how to activate something on the Internet. Tom agreed and found that he was looking at a screen with a request for a password. "Type our radio handles, mine first," Ben explained, "then press 'Enter'."

Tom found himself looking at Ben in a small window on the computer. "Can you hear me now?" Ben asked. Tom nodded in surprise. The voice had come from the computer and the phone simultaneously. "If you can hear me type 'yes' on your keyboard and press enter." Tom complied feeling foolish about the nod that Ben couldn't see.

Immediately Ben hung up on the phone and continued talking through the computer.

"My guess is your phone is bugged and we need to communicate this way. The password is already changed and will now be my last name followed by 1995." Ben explained. You can call me in this manner and if I am at my desk we can talk, or rather I can, and you will need to type. This mechanism uses encryption and is safe." He explained.

The image of Ben was poor and jumpy but Tom got the hang of it immediately.

"So what is so important as to get me special communication treatment?"

he typed the question. Ben filled him in on the fact that the CIA was investigating activities in Zinaville as part of a satellite crime that had by now grown to an international incident. Tom's incredulous attitude must have come through on the typing because Ben spent a fair amount of time ensuring Tom got the point and understood it. He then explained that Tom would be getting a team of geology experts that would be arriving at the mine. He wanted Tom to ensure they would not arouse suspicion, and would not get cross-questioned by 'real' geologists. "They will be doing some 'field work' in the Magaliesburg for you. Please help them, and try to stay out of their way!" he requested.

Tom agreed. "Mind telling me what they are looking for?" he typed. "Sorry, it's classified!" Ben answered. "Got to go now!" The image cleared and Tom found himself looking at a blank screen. He looked at the time and realized it was time to leave for the long drive to Johannesburg to see Don Warmen.

CHAPTER FIFTY-THREE

It was much later in the evening in Moscow when the telephone rang in the Kremlin. An unknown agent from the CIA spoke to an unknown Russian agent. Both men were dedicated to communicating on this one issue by their opposing superiors. Every word was recorded and transcribed. The Americans assured the Russians that they had not set the laser satellites into action and by way of compromise, asked for support in monitoring the satellites. The exact location of each of the satellites was given, and an invitation to monitor them extended. The Russian accepted although he wasn't happy. The information and invitation were superfluous. This could just be a play for time. He built a report for his superiors. It was their problem to determine authenticity. He knew they would only get involved the following morning. Nothing showed there was any immediate threat. That was all he had to determine. He sat back and waited again.

At Pearson International Airport, Toronto, David Larrel was climbing onto an aircraft to Heathrow in the United Kingdom. From there he would board a South African Airways flight to Johannesburg. It was time he spoke to Warmen!

At Kennedy International Airport, Ron Jackson was also leaving for Heathrow. Before boarding his flight to Johannesburg, he had to go to a British university. He needed to send encrypted code out into space. This needed to be done before end of day Wednesday. Since he was only scheduled to land in Johannesburg on Thursday, there was plenty of time.

It was midday before Col. Ben Bridgewater was notified that Ronald Jackson Jr. was his prime suspect. The CIA had already tracked him to the flight to the U.K. and wanted to know what to do. After consulting with his superiors the Colonel instructed them to follow but not to apprehend Ronald. It was important to know where he was going to, to whom he was speaking, and what he was doing. The possession of his security access card gave everyone confidence that the program's computers were safe from any further intrusion. Later they would decide on how to tighten the net and draw him in. However, wanting to keep the situation contained, it was also decided not to alert the British or ask for their assistance.

In Zinaville, Tom was finishing an evening plant production meeting with his shift bosses, Hendrik and Joshua, when his pager buzzed. He ended the meeting and left to make the call. It was from Ben by the look of the number. Tom dialed and was put through to the number. The voice on the other side was unfamiliar.

"Tom Lurie?" the voice asked.

"Yes, who's that?" Tom inquired.

"Your newest geology team leader, call me 'Greg'. We're at the airport and will be coming down to Zinaville this evening. Let your staff know we're here but will not be coming to the mine itself, as we will be working in the field under direction from yourself. Understood?"

"That I understand, but you listen here…" Tom wasn't exactly used to being told what to do. "…I do this with one provision, you keep me informed of everything you find out. If one little snippet of information reaches my ears from someone else, you can consider your efforts as public knowledge. I hope YOU understand that Mister! You're in my country, working with me. I am not working FOR you. Got it?" Tom was in a bad mood. The previous evening with Warmen had been difficult and strained, the shift bosses unhappy and he wasn't about to be told what to do by someone he didn't even know.

There was a silence.

"Please call Ben on the number he gave you. We will be in Zinaville in two hours. Thank you." and the phone cut off.

Tom looked at the handset and glowered. "Egotistical upstarts," he thought. He would have to go home to get hold of Ben who, based on the time, would probably not be at his desk. Annoyed, he let Mrs. Wold know was going home and left within ten minutes.

Tom called up his screen as before, entered the password and waited. After half a minute, a female voice said "Please, enter your home telephone number now!" he complied and then the female voice asked him to answer questions such as his radio handle, who he was calling and a few other items.

Suddenly Ben's picture appeared on the screen. Ben was in his study. "Hi Tom, what can I do for you?"

"Hi, Geologists arrived! Want to be certain they report findings directly to me, or no deal! Ok with you?" Tom typed.

"Sure Tom. Let them know you have spoken to me. They will want to meet you, and give you something to use when talking to them on the phone. Also, here is their phone number, take it down and use it to call them if you need to contact them. Use it sparingly and be aware that others will listen. Cell phones are not secure. Anything else?"

"Yes! I want an air ticket to visit you when this is all over" typed Tom.

"I'll see what I can do. Take care and good luck," the picture of Ben disappeared and Tom was looking at a blank screen with the phone number on it. He copied that to a note he put it in his wallet.

CHAPTER FIFTY-FOUR

At 7p.m. Tom's pager buzzed him with the American phone number. He called from his home phone. "Hello, is that Greg" he queried.

"Hi, Yeh! We're entering Zinaville and want to meet you somewhere. Have an idea?"

Tom directed them to Priggles and told them he would be there in an hour. He called Joshua and told him he would be picking him up in 45minutes. Joshua tried to decline but Tom insisted. Joshua said he would be ready.

When they walked in, the bar was almost empty except for a group of four men that were in an alcove towards the back. Lofty was slumped on the bar counter watching a soccer game on a noisy television. They greeted Lofty who automatically poured out a whiskey for Tom and at Joshua's request a Coca Cola for him. Tom greeted the men at the back asking if there was a Greg in the group. A man with thin-rimmed spectacles and tousled red hair stood up introducing himself as Greg. He was muscular and tanned, the typical physique of a field geologist. The men with him were similarly tanned and tough looking. Tom mused that the difference between a marine and a good field geologist wasn't that much. They exchanged names and handshakes. Lofty was mildly interested as the American accents weren't familiar and clearly Tom knew the men.

"You guys gonna be working at the mine?" he inquired with one eye on the game.

"Not really Lofty. They're doing some confidential geological field work for ZPM around the mountain area." Tom explained.

That seemed to satisfy Lofty's curiosity and he focused on the game. Greg on the other hand was cautious with wanting to know who Joshua was. Tom explained what had happened to Joshua's father and that Joshua was also involved. The Americans relaxed and Tom guessed some dossier somewhere had already provided Joshua's details. It amazed him how the United States seemed to get any information they wanted, even in foreign countries.

The meeting was comparatively short. Greg handed Tom a telephone headset that was small enough to be carried around and explained how to use it with conventional phones to secure conversation. He then asked both Tom and Joshua to explain everything that had occurred to date. The Americans explained they were CIA and their only other question was where the nearest camping spot was located. Tom directed them to it. By that time everyone was ready for sleep and left the bar together waving good-bye to Lofty.

CHAPTER FIFTY-FIVE

Tuesday morning at the Kumalo home was a somber affair. Susan had been having nightmares impacting John's sleep with her moaning and talking in her sleep. He was in an unnaturally quiet mood, tired from the disturbed night. Thandi arrived early, as it was her day off and she wanted to spend it with them. Her cheerful disposition was out of place in the Kumalo home as she put on the coffee and made porridge for her bleary eyed companions. She had bought the newspaper and Susan started to read it once she had enough coffee in her to get her mind working. They had just started breakfast when there was a knock at the door.

Thandi opened it to see a poorly dressed man who looked like he could have done with a good wash. Her immediate assumption was that he was a street person looking for food. She wondered why he would be so far out of town. "*Dumela!*" he greeted. "May I have some food and something to drink please?" Thandi turned to John who could see the man through the half open door. He nodded. "Please come in," Thandi invited him.

Susan wasn't overly impressed and wrinkled her nose at the mature body smell rising from the newcomer. She didn't understand the language and so ignored the conversation. Thandi gave him a chair to one side and handed him some coffee and a small bowl of the leftover porridge. He ate hungrily. His bright brown eyes taking in the homey scene. He explained he was a traveler going down to the coastal areas after spending some time in the bush.

"It isn't very often one finds a white girl in one of our peoples homes." He commented in the African dialect between mouthfuls and slurping some more coffee. "Is she in trouble?"

Thandi looked at John in alarm. John smiled at the man. "Maybe, and maybe, not my friend," He said. "I however don't normally discuss my house guests with others" he admonished him gently.

The traveler nodded. "That is a good path to follow!" He agreed. "It is just strange to see a white woman in a black man's house. The other day I saw a black and white man tied up together in the back of a small truck going into the Magaliesburg. It seems as if we do everything together since Apartheid is being dismantled," and he slurped some more coffee.

"A black and white man tied up together?" John asked. "Where was this?"

"I don't normally discuss my comings and goings with people I have just met," chuckled the traveler, smiling at John. They both laughed. Even Thandi broke out a brief smile. "However because you were kind and invited me in, I'll tell you." The traveler conceded.

The traveler explained how he had been traveling down the road past a general store when a truck had almost knocked him off the road as it sped past up into the mountains. It was an open truck and these men were bouncing around in the back.

"I thought it must have been very painful for them." The traveler said, "There was a driver up front but I could only see the back of him as it ascended the hill. It was night time and I don't think I would have seen them if it wasn't for the light of the opened store door. I thought it strange, but a traveler sees much and you learn to hold your tongue in these times." The traveler stopped to eat. He took a piece of bread and scooped out the remainder of the porridge from the bowl and crammed it into his mouth. Conversation stopped as the others contemplated his hungry eating habits.

They exchange looks. "When was that?" Thandi wanted to know. The traveler chewed for a bit, swallowed and then answered as he tore another piece of bread from the loaf.

"About a month ago now!" he replied.

Both Thandi and John realized it was about the time that Steve had disappeared. Without wanting to appear excited Thandi asked for directions to the store and John tried to find out if the traveler had seen anything else. He hadn't, or didn't appear to want to tell them much more. After he finished eating, Thandi gave him money for taxi fare, told him where the taxi would pick him up and sent him on his way.

When the door closed she turned to John and switched to English for Susan's benefit. "Do you think that was Steve that was tied up?" she wanted to know. John shrugged and nodded. "It's possible," he said, "maybe we should investigate?" Susan wanted to know what had been said, and so they repeated it for her. She was amazed that the traveler had been able to provide useful information.

Her amazement was nothing like theirs would have been if they could have seen the traveler disappear into thin air as he walked down the lane. In the spiritual realm, the angel rose into the air above where the traveler had been a millisecond before.

Susan would have been doubly amazed if she had known that Jake in his study at home, Joshua in his office at work, Karen in her kitchen, and a dozen of Frank's and Jake's congregations members, were simultaneously praying that something would happen to let people know where Steve was. The people praying would probably have been equally surprised to know the effectiveness of their prayers! Their guardians weren't surprised at all!

CHAPTER FIFTY-SIX

Less than an hour later, Thandi and her two companions found the store that the traveler had described. Thandi parked her BMW outside and they all went inside.

The Indian storeowner eyed them suspiciously. The combination of a sophisticated young black woman, an old black man, and a young white girl, weren't normally seen together in this dusty corner of Africa. He wasn't sure what they were up to and the owner could see Susan felt uncomfortable and out of place. The store was totally rural and Susan was a town person. There were three legged cooking pots, brightly colored blankets, beads, copper wire, candles, various farming implements, tobacco and various herbs hanging from the ceiling. Thandi and John went to the counter where the Indian storeowner had a large assortment of candy, soft drinks and magazines for sale.

Thandi's bright smile and good looks together with her buying power and carefully directed questions soon had the owner chatting to them. Thandi explained she wanted some supplies and that she wanted to camp in the Magaliesburg. She asked about campsites, purchased a paraffin lamp that was hanging from the rafters and while the owner was looking for a ladder to get her lamp, asked him if there were many public camping areas around the store, or if it was all farm area. Susan went out to sit in the car. John waited to help Thandi with her purchases. The storeowner explained that there were almost no public areas or campsites, and that most of the area was government protected natural habitat. He explained there were a few farms but along the road into the mountains. Thandi asked if any of the farmers or their workers bought items from the store.

"Not the farmers! You know what it's like; farmers only buy from the co-op and town. The workers, they buy from me and the people who live in the next village also come to buy here." He rang up her purchases. Thandi offered her credit card. "Sorry Madam, we only take cash here," He explained. Thandi gave him a few bank notes and asked him to keep the change. The owner smiled and put some notes directly in his pocket, the rest went in the till. "Do you perhaps know of someone who is being kept locked up on one of the farms?" Thandi inquired suddenly.

Immediately the storeowner looked suspicious again. "Why?" he wanted to know. "Is someone missing?"

Thandi decided to play it straight and explained that John's son, her boyfriend, had gone missing and someone had said that he was being held on a farm in the area.

The owner looked thoughtful. He shook his head. "Not really," he said, "nobody said anything about that!"

The way he made the comment, made Thandi wonder if something else had been going on. "Has there been something else strange going on here?" she asked.

"There have been many cars going into the mountains late in the evening. They are not going over the pass because my brother runs the store on the other side, and he tells me the same happens on his side. Not many cars leave, but many go in. Then, early in the morning, the cars leave again. Is that not strange?" he asked.

"That is strange," Thandi agreed, "have you noticed anything else?" "Not me!" the storeowner volunteered. "The workers who buy here, they were talking of strange lights flashing in the hills. They believe it's dangerous to go out there because there is bad witchdoctors that appear at night. They believe if you go, you will sometimes not come back." He leaned back. "But as you know, people believe in many strange things around here. Only last month, someone put a plastic snake over my door without me knowing it. Nobody would come in. It took me few days to find it and take it down. I lost a lot of business! People believe strange things around here!" he looked satisfied with his exposition. Thandi thanked him again and they left.

After brief discussion when they got back to the car, they decided to take a drive over the pass to see if they could identify some of the areas the storeowner had described. The drive was uneventful with the exception that the BMW's suspension didn't deal well with the unkempt dirt road with its ruts and bumps. There were a few farm roads leading off the road as had been mentioned. Here and there on the lower slopes, farm workers could be seen in the fields, but in the higher areas there was almost nobody. Rocky outcrops, grass and vegetation were the norm. The view as they crossed over the top was pleasant. The grasslands extended to the horizon on both sides of the small mountain range. Once on the other side they intersected with another paved highway with a store. Thandi did a U turn and they then returned. They saw nothing unusual and they were back at the Kumalo cottage by mid-morning.

Susan wanted to see Joshua, and the others wanted to get their news to him. Thandi agreed to permit Susan to take her car to visit him and so after a quick early lunch Susan drove to town. She stopped at a public phone on the way and put a call in to ZPM asking for Joshua. He was fortunately in his office and overjoyed to hear her voice. Scared the phone was bugged he cut her short soon after she announced she had news, and told her to meet him at his home. He prayed that nobody was watching his home, left a message for Tom telling him to meet him at his house, and left the plant. Hendrik was working and this gave Joshua some confidence Susan would be safe at his home until he got there.

CHAPTER FIFTY-SEVEN

Joshua went directly home. Tom got the message thirty minutes later, so he picked up some pizza on the way and arrived at Joshua's home as soon as he could. Susan and Joshua had been waiting until Tom arrived before Susan would explain the day's events.

She related them and then Joshua turned to Tom.

"We need Carl in on this. How can we do this without alerting everyone?" They thought about it for a while. "Do you think Carl can give the hounds the slip again?" Tom asked. Joshua nodded. "Then let's ask him to meet Susan at the Kumalo's home, we can arrive later, and we can plan an evening of 'excitement'," Tom suggested.

"Only if Susan approves! She knows how John feels about using his home and the potential risk to her! What are your thoughts Susan?" Joshua asked. Susan was in agreement so it was settled.

Susan then left in Thandi's BMW, heading to John's home while Joshua put a call through to Carl who was busy servicing his vintage Lotus sports car. This pastime was keeping him from going completely crazy due to boredom. The car needed work but was functional. Carl was looking forward to the complete renovation he planned. He was glad to hear Joshua but equally aware of potential eavesdropping. In a circumspect way that any listeners would find impossible to follow, Joshua told him to go to John's home. He also made a comment about no additional parties being welcome. Carl assured him that there would be none.

Tom suggested Joshua travel with him to reduce the number of cars at John's little home. They waited thirty minutes to give Carl time to evade his followers and headed out themselves. They were equally careful to watch for anyone following. Tom pulled over on the side of the road a few times to let people go passed and even went passed John's driveway, U-turning 2km away and traveling back. They watched for any sign of cars tracking them but saw none.

They arrived to see Carl sitting in his Lotus waiting for them. The BMW was not in sight and so they thought Thandi had gone home. When they pulled up, Carl shouted 'hello' and asked where Susan was. Tom and Joshua looked at each other. Concerned but not alarmed Joshua said she must be inside already as she had left a while back.

"Not likely!" came Carl's reply. "I've been inside, nobody is there."

The other two men were incredulous. "You sure?" asked Joshua.

"Help yourself!" suggested Carl and leaned back in his leather seat. "Anyone want to place a bet on what you will find?"

Neither of the men did. They did however go inside and take a good hard look around. Nothing appeared out of place, broken or damaged. "This doesn't look good!" Tom commented. Joshua took one last look around and then stepped outside.

Carl chipped in again. "Maybe you two sleuths would like to take a look at the tire marks in the dust alongside mine" he suggested.

The dust tracks showed the marking of a large off road tire that had pulled in and out. It was on top of the Micheline tire tracks of the BMW that had obviously parked and the pulled out again. The off road tires had spun on the way out by the look of the tracks.

"Maybe John has some daredevil friend with an off road truck" Carl commented.

Joshua went pale. Carl realized what Joshua was thinking and shot out of his seat. "Hey, Josh! I'm sorry! I didn't realize that this was maybe bad news. Sorry!" Joshua had sagged against the side Tom's car. Tom went over to look at the tracks.

"Lets, not jump to conclusions here," he offered. "The BMW left in no hurry before the truck took off. Maybe someone just pulled into the wrong yard?"

Carl came over and looked at the tracks more carefully. "Sorry Tom, not right! Look here, here and here," He pointed to parts of tracks. "I'm used to tracking game. These tracks tell a story. Over here..." he pointed to a set of tracks obviously made by men's shoes and ladies sandals, "is where the people got into the BMW. Over here..." he pointed to a set of sneaker tracks, "is where the person left the BMW. Notice the tracks of the man and lady overlaps those of the sneakers. That means they occurred later than the sneaker owners. Over here," he moved to a different patch of dusty earth, you can see shoes of two men heading into the house. Here they are coming out. On coming out this mans track is unbalanced and not quite in a straight line and look here..." he pointed to the ground where the tracks arrived at where the rear of the truck would have stood. "Clearly for all to see is scuffled footprints but the conclusive evidence is the shoe marks on top of a sneaker print that is part of a scuff mark." He looked up at the men.

"I'm sorry Josh! Looks like Susan arrived in the BMW and went inside. My guess is that John and Thandi left in the same car. Afterwards two men arrive, went into the house. One picked up Susan who was struggling, and they put her in the back of the truck and drove off in a hurry. Probably worried they might have been seen from the house over there." Carl shook his head sympathetically. "Sorry, I took my time getting here from town. I really hoped this wouldn't happen"

The three men stood in silence in the late afternoon. The bush hummed with insect life and the hot late afternoon sun beat down. The look of despondency on their faces was poignant. It took a long time before Carl moved. He put his arm around Joshua and looking at Tom, suggested they might as well go inside and discuss what to do. That Joshua was obviously suffering from shock again was patently obvious to both men.

Inside Joshua's mind, desolation was pulling him down. Darkness and depression seemed to be hanging around his throat. His body physically felt heavy as if the energy was being drained from it. He could hardly talk, and his thoughts merged and separated uncontrollably. He followed Carl like an automaton. One voice in his head seemed to be telling him to give up since life wasn't worth carrying on. Another less insistent voice, argued this point, pointing out his mother needed him and he needed to find Susan. The clashing voices were difficult to control. When he was sitting in an armchair in John's home he regained control of his mind. Slowly he came to himself. The other men waited patiently not even speaking. All of them were fighting depression, anger, and vengeance. The spiritual battle as best evidenced in Joshua's mind, was taxing on the three guardians who met the onslaught with singing swords. Once again they held back the onslaught enough to allow Joshua to use his own free will to decide the outcome. They would not allow the demonic creatures to run riot with his will. The Lord did not permit that, and they would ensure His will would be done. Joshua's decision was however his own to make. The Lord would not do that for him. This was another strangeness the angels couldn't understand. Why men should be left to make decisions that were sometimes bad when the Lord directed angels so exactly? That was a mystery to the heavenly beings.

Carl being a detective was more accustomed to the devastation that could be wreaked by evil men and was first to offer an idea of what they could do. "No use sitting here," he advised. "I suggest we go home, sleep on it and get together first thing in the morning. We obviously can't go to our police department as they probably perpetrated the kidnapping and I can't think of whom else to go to."

"I'll let the Americans know what happened and ask for their assistance," Tom offered. Carl looked surprised and Tom brought Carl up to date on all the interactions Joshua and he had been involved in. He also explained what Thandi and John had found.

"This is good news!" Carl exclaimed. While Carl and Tom sat discussing the news, Joshua simply sat listening and praying quietly. He knew that when he came to the end of his resources that he needed to let his Lord take complete control. He prayed and waited on the Lord as the others tried to formulate a plan.

CHAPTER FIFTY-EIGHT

Thandi and John had gone up to the mine hostel leaving Susan at the house waiting for Carl. John's idea was to get three of Steve's friends that were as bush wise as he was and that they should go and search for Steve. They planned to find out where the cars went at night.

Thandi dropped him at the gate and went back to her home to change. She returned two hours later dressed in older, more traditional clothing for their night's activity. The men waited at the gate enjoying the sunset and soon the BMW was humming along the road to the store they had visited earlier in the day. When they pulled up outside the store there was a crowd of workers enjoying the end of the day. The men were lounging around, some smoking and others drinking. The women were catching up on the day's gossip. They all stared as the BMW stopped, but soon resumed talking as the group got out. A few greeted them. Thandi went over to the women and John and the miners to the men to introduce themselves. They tried to fit into the local crowd as much as possible. Slowly the group started to drift off until the only ones left were themselves. It was now 10p.m. They sat on a log outside the store and drank beer that they acquired from the store man's 'personal' supply for a small charge. He came out to lock up and go home.

"You people going to sit there all night?" he wanted to know. The miners teased him, and then Thandi told him they were waiting to see if the cars he had mentioned would come past. "They start going passed in about an hour's time," He told them. "Maybe you want to park your car around the back?" he suggested. "People are not all good, and that fancy car draws attention. I don't want them stopping to steal your car, then deciding to break into my store!" With that he locked the store door, and made his way to his home that was set back into the bush on the other side of the main road. Thandi moved the car as he suggested, and then joined the men who sat smoking and telling stories of the African bush. The mosquitoes bothered her and she spent a lot of time slapping at them. However it was a warm wonderful evening, the stories were entertaining and soon she was enjoying the company.

The odd car drove passed but no large group that would draw attention. Then around ten thirty in the distance they heard what sounded to be a group of angry hornets. As it came closer it sounded more like a huge group of bikes. They then saw the headlights as they roared passed the store braking fast and turning down the dirt road. There were many bikers, more than half were riding two up. The lights were blinding and so it was difficult to make out what was going on. One biker didn't seem to have judged the corner correctly and rode off into the bush while making the turn. Thandi could make out yelling and hoots of laughter from some of the others and then the roar subsided into the distance.

They discussed if they should follow the bikers. John felt no, Thandi wasn't sure and the others weren't interested. They had heard stories of bikers and what they had done to some people at this time of the year while partying. They felt that waiting for the other vehicles would be a better option. Then a jeep slowed and turned onto the dirt road. Soon a small truck did the same. Over the next ten minutes an assortment of cars, trucks and some four-wheel drive vehicles turned onto the road. They decided it was time to go and got into Thandi's car, waiting for another vehicle to follow. Thandi kept the lights off. Another car turned onto the dirt road. Thandi waited a few seconds and then started, following without the lights on. After a few hundred meters she turned them on hoping that the person would think it was one of the group's cars. They wound their way over the dirt road up the mountain. The dust filled the air so much that they couldn't see the rear lights of the other car, only the dust cloud it made hovering in the night air. Thandi had to switch to a low beam to follow. They seemed to be out of the farming area on the side of the mountain and starting to get relatively close to the top, when they suddenly road out through the dust into clear night air. The bush was high and unbroken on either side for three minutes prior to this and there were no turn-offs.

Thandi didn't want to stop as the driver might have pulled over thinking he was being followed and so continued over the pass. As they started down the other side they could see three cars coming up towards them. They could see a long way and there didn't appear to be any others coming. Thandi waited until they had passed her, drove about half a kilometer, turned off her lights and coasted to a stop. They looked back. The cars were going over the rise. As soon as they were over Thandi did a fast U-turn and chased back up the pass. The dust was mostly settled and so they could see better this time. They crested the pass and had to take one or two twists and turns, again with dense bush on both sides and when they started to go down the pass, the cars had disappeared.

"They must have turned off their lights and driven fast without them to disappear so fast." John remarked. Thandi sped up to see if this might be the case and soon they had arrived at the store again. By now it was almost 11:40p.m. They waited to see if more cars would arrive but none did.

After some discussion, they decided to drive over the pass very slowly now that the dust had settled and see if they could see where the tracks left the road. John who had done some tracking as a youth in Zimbabwe sat up front with Thandi to see where they had gone. They all agreed this would be an easy exercise.

The slow drive up the pass was uneventful. John could see their own tracks and plenty of others. Just before they crested the peak John noticed something strange but by the time he mentioned it they were already past it, around a corner and almost at the top of the ridge yet again.

"Thandi, the tracks of the cars disappeared for a short time and when they re-appeared they weren't the same," John explained.

"That's not possible John! Are you sure?" she asked.

"Yes, stop! Stop!" he answered.

She stopped and he opened the door and climbed out.

"I'm going back, you follow in the car" he told her and started back up the hill following the tracks in the starlight.

She turned the car, switched on the parking lights so as not to blind John's night vision and went back in the direction they had come. He was standing at the side of the road pointing down. She stopped and they all climbed out. John was right. The tracks disappeared. Someone had dragged something across them. Only the BMW tracks were to be seen going towards the store and back. The area extended for about twenty feet. It looked like the sweep pattern was from the outside inwards to the one side. It was most confusing. John walked to the center of the area and looked at the bush at the side. It was dense, but the grass on the one side of the road was broken and flattened. He walked over, kicked at it with his foot and then gestured to the others to come and look.

The grass was real but it was dry and dead and had grown out of rock. There was an artificial rock running the length of that side of the road. Further inspection showed someone with considerable skill had built two huge gates built to look like low mountain rock, grass and thorn bushes. The thorn bushes were extended right to the roadside and were bushes of the *haak en steek* variety. These bushes had hundreds of fishhook shaped thorns with the hooks all facing inwards. They were notorious for the ease with which they accepted a hand, foot or limb, which slid in on the rounded part of the fishhook thorns and the almost impossible task of getting the same back out, since as soon as unsuspecting body part was pulled out, the hooks stabbed in and stuck. These were guaranteed to ensure anyone walking by would not go near and would pass on the other side. It made it impossible to even consider trying to open the gates. *This haak en steek* bush blended with the real version of the bush on either side of the gate. This was an impenetrable hedge, not something they could do anything about.

Suddenly they heard voices. Afraid of being discovered they ran back to the car and Thandi pulled away down the mountainous road. She drove fast not sure why. As they came around a turn they saw a man charge out of the bush behind them. He had an automatic assault rifle in his hands. They swerved around the next corner and simultaneously saw tracer bullets and heard the gunfire. Thandi forgot about the bumps and floored the accelerator. The car responded with professional ease and within seconds they were racing down the final straight of the mountain at close on a hundred and sixty kilometers per hour. Thandi threw the car around the corner hitting the asphalt road and sliding the back end out. She accelerated again. The car's speed crept to two hundred kilometers per hour and it seemed like seconds and they were at the turn-off to the Kumalo home. She slowed down fast, turned into the drive, stopped at the cottage and tuned off the engine. Then she started to cry.

The men were looking back when two cars on the main road shot passed on the way into town. It looked like as if they had been followed but had evaded detection.

"Thandi, quick, drive around the yard and park behind my house" John said. "Hey men, help me move the gate!"

There was a rusty iron gate that was locked with a chain. Thandi's crying turned to laughter when John showed them how they had to pull the one gatepost out of the ground to drag the gate open. He obviously didn't have a key. It took all four men to open it. She drove around to the back of the house and when she got back, the rusted shut gate was back in position.

"Everyone stays here tonight!" said John. The miners were in no mood to argue. "We will let Joshua know in the morning," John said to Thandi. "Let's go find Susan!"

John went to unlock his front door but when it was not locked as he expected, John exclaimed in fear. This caused everyone, including John to run for cover and hide. Nobody moved for five minutes. Then John tentatively went and pushed the door open. Nothing happened! He went in and the observers saw the house lights coming on one by one. About a minute later he beckoned them to come in. He had found the note Tom had left, explaining that they suspected Susan had been kidnapped. Demoralized John locked the doors and they collapsed into the chairs. Thandi suggested they switch off the light, as everyone would be expecting them to be asleep and they didn't want to draw attention to the cottage. John agreed and switched the lights off again. They were starting to relax when they heard a car racing up the drive.

"HIDE!" John shouted and ran to the kitchen. He threw each of them a large kitchen knife and they waited in suspense. A car slid to a stop, nothing happened for a few seconds, then it reversed, spinning its wheels and kicking up dirt as it turned and drove away.

They heard it repeat the process in the driveway at the next property along the road.

"They are looking but have not found us," John suggested. By now the usually fearless miners were looking extremely unhappy.

"Next time you ask me to help John," one complained, "I'll send my enemy! Then it will be considered true help when you get him killed! We did not expect this!"

John apologized. He told them the full story of what had happened. It was three in the morning when they went to sleep. They slept fitfully.

CHAPTER FIFTY-NINE

Joshua had almost no sleep. He had tossed and turned. He prayed for Susan's safety but couldn't shake his fear of her being hurt. The hours of darkness seemed to never end. At 5-o-clock he finally fell asleep completely exhausted. He next surfaced when he heard someone knocking loudly on his door. When he got to the door, Thandi and John were already walking away. He called for them to come back and soon they were drinking coffee in his kitchen. In true African style there was no rush to get down to the discussion of the day and John started to explain the events of the night once the second round of coffee was well on its way to being completed.

Joshua could feel anxiety rising within his soul again as the events unfolded. The concern of his friends helped as they gave him time to absorb the information before continuing. He prayed silently that he would be able to overcome his own weakness of mind and body. When John described the gates he was intrigued.

"Quite the engineering accomplishment," he commented, "Clever and simple! I wonder how they could be operated so well and so quickly. There is also the question of how they knew when to open and close them? Most interesting! I wonder if Susan could have been taken there? Maybe we should investigate?"

John and Thandi looked as if they definitely didn't think it was a good idea and went on to explain the shooting and narrow escape to John's home. They finished their story and Joshua told them how Susan's disappearance had been discovered. He suggested they drive to the mine together. Thandi pointed out they had arrived by taxi since she was scared to be seen in the BMW at the moment. Joshua agreed they should travel with him. He called Tom and told him he was coming to his home. Then he called Carl to tell him to meet them at Tom's home after he had lost his "hounds."

Carl got to Tom's home ten minutes after the others arrived. Joshua suggested starting their discussion with prayer, and Tom led them out into the garden to a set of lawn chairs gathered in the cool under tall leafy trees. It was a beautiful morning, birds chirping around them, and the final vestiges of the morning dew evaporating in the increasing warmth. The prayer was a quiet ad hoc arrangement with different parties contributing at various times. Thandi felt embarrassed. She didn't understand what was going on and was not sure how this would fit in with her ancestral gods. She decided to relax and let them carry on.

It was about thirty minutes later when they seemed to finish. They started to discuss the events, with each person bringing Tom up to date with different parts of the story. Tom in his usual way was coming up with the plans and the others were glad to let him take the responsibility.

"I think we will need to have someone in place tonight to watch the goings on at the thorn bush gate. We need to know how they open it and how they know which car to let in. I also think it will be important to watch the satellite station."

The others were in agreement. John and Thandi offered to dress in workers clothing, take a taxi to the thorn bush gate area, and carefully climb up to a point where they could see what was going on.

"We will take food and stay there for the night and watch," Thandi offered. John groaned and complained that he was an old man and this was difficult, but when they suggested that Joshua could go along with them, John pointed out that it was an area mainly frequented by blacks.

"Mr. Joshua, I am sorry to say you're the wrong color!"

The group laughed, thinking how this was the exact opposite of what would normally have been said in an Apartheid South Africa. Still chuckling they thanked Thandi and John for their contibution. Tom arranged for a mine taxi to take them home. Joshua walked out with them to the taxi rank and asked them to be careful. He gave Thandi a hug and shook John's hand as concern for them overcame him. Showing great respect for John, he asked him to look after Thandi. "You and I have lost loved one's already. Please make sure to look to your safety and don't take any chances. Please be careful! May God bless and protect you!"

After they had gone Joshua went back to Tom and Carl to bring up the question of what they would do if someone caught them at these activities.

"It seems these people are lawless and willing to do anything," he complained.

"I'll be talking to the Americans again today," Tom pointed out. "We can ask if they can help."

"I'll give Aaron a call. I think this is just the sort of story a newspaper man would love to get," Carl suggested and seeing Tom's face added, "I'll not tell him about the American involvement yet. It might however be useful if he was willing to reveal all in a newspaper story if we didn't call him before a certain time tomorrow. I have been glad of his newspaper contacts over the last while."

They agreed.

CHAPTER SIXTY

At the Pentagon, there was concern. An emergency meeting had been called very early on Thursday morning. The reason was that a radio message had been received by the Star Wars satellites. As far as could be determined from the transmission log download, it had content that was obviously encrypted and had not come from the USA. Col. Ben Bridgewater was the designated chair of the meeting.

"We will have to overwrite the programs with a historical version in place before Ron Jackson joined the program," one member suggested.

"I think we need to arrest Ron Jackson before more damage is done. Where was he when this occurred?" another asked.

Col. Ben Bridgewater asked the CIA representative present to provide the answer.

"The CIA lost him on a university campus in Britain. He apparently used the old ruse of telling a security guard they were following him. When the guard stopped our agents; he took off into the buildings and got lost in amongst the students. Since CIA coverage of universities is limited in Britain, we didn't get in contact with him again until he entered Heathrow last night. He has boarded a flight to Johannesburg, South Africa. The message was transmitted while we lost contact."

Discussion was vehement and fast. No one wanted to waste time. The meeting was adjourned within an hour with the action items; (a) to arrest Ron, (b) to replace the programming of the satellites, (c) to notify Russia of the transmission, and (d) that a mandate would be given to Col. Bridgewater to destroy the Star Wars satellites if they posed a threat to the USA, or the same satellites were not under the full control of USA defense command by Easter Monday. Ben had orders for (a), (b), and (c) ready for immediate execution and they were prepared. However when it came to (d), Ben pointed out that the only way they could achieve this, was if the satellite self-destruct sequence could be initiated. Since this was compromised, they needed to ask Russia for help to destroy them. The USA didn't have an offensive weapon capable of taking out the fifteen satellites over a short period of time. "… and any other mechanism could take a week or two," he had said. This had been the point that raised the most concern. Nobody wanted to reveal their capabilities in this area to the Russians. A General in the room agreed that the Russians should be contacted but told Ben to hold off on the last action item until the President of the USA had approved it, and could perhaps change criteria for its execution. The CIA representative agreed and said that this was something that the diplomats had to confer on before the military could get involved. The code name for the final destruction of the Star Wars satellites was "PHOENIX." The next day was already Good Friday so Ben was required to get orders prepared and U.S. Defense Control briefed by the end of the day. The Secretary of State would brief the President within two hours and Ben would receive his orders within ten minutes of their approval. They disbanded to carry out their duties.

Within an hour of the meeting Ron landed at Jan Smuts airport in South Africa to be greeted by a mob of South African Airport security officials who led him into a detention area. His relaxed attitude was in stark contrast to theirs, which was excitable and aggressive. He allowed them to jostle and pull him along after handcuffing him.

He was left in the room for over an hour and then two men arrived together with his luggage. He was less relaxed when he realized they were American and not South African. They wanted to know all about his activities and where he had been. He told them in various impolite ways to get stuffed and ignored their questions.

After twenty more minutes of this abuse, he suddenly asked for the time as with his hands cuffed behind his back, he couldn't see his watch.

"We will tell you the time when we're finished, Mr. Jackson." The CIA field agent stated and started on another line of questioning.

"You had better tell me the time, or you will find that the USA is getting the blame for a whole lot of satellites getting blown up in the heavens you idiot!" Ron answered. "Then you will get less than a pension and a dishonorable discharge for breaking down relationships between America and her allies!"

The agents looked at each other. They didn't like being threatened while they were the ones in control.

"Nice try mister," the big one said. "Why should we be listening to your fairy tale?"

"Because you idiots, while I am sitting here, I can't stop the US Star War weapons from taking out an English spy satellite. That is scheduled to occur at 12:05 this afternoon South African time. Feel free to confer with your masters on this point. I can give you a phone number to validate this point if you like. You will need to be quick or BANG!"

The interrogators looked alarmed. One left the room. The other tried to continue the line of questioning. Ron ignored him.

Within ten minutes the Agent was back looking rather pale. It had taken

less than five minutes for the relevant higher authorities to validate that the
Star Wars computers would not respond to any commands and that they were
in an arming cycle.

"What are your demands?" the harried agent wanted to know.

"You take these handcuffs off me, and put me in a taxi and when I feel I
am free and untroubled, I arrange for that this little problem of yours to go
away. Alternatively you do whatever you want with me then each hour at five
minutes past the hour, another multi-million dollar satellite of one of the USA
Allies will turn to rubble. Understand sweetie?" Ron snarled.

The agent went a pale and motioned to his buddy. "Let him go!" It took
them twenty minutes to navigate the bureaucracies and get him into a taxi.
Ron walked passed the taxi they had called and flagged down the next one.
He climbed in and took off. It was 11:45 as they drove out onto the highway.
At 11:47 Ron asked the taxi driver to pull over on the verge of the road. He
waved a car about to pass them to the side of the road. At 11:52 the agents
who had been following realized they had made a bad mistake and agreed
not to move. They also handed Ron their radios. By 11:54 Ron made a call
and at 12:00 a police car pulled up in front of the taxi and told it to pull
over. When the cab stopped, the Brigadier walked over and told Ron to get
out. Leaving the taxi driver without cab fare and very angry. Ron and the
Brigadier took off at a high speed. When the Brigadier revealed to Ron that
they would not be able to establish radio contact with the satellite before
12:05, Ron shrugged. "Too bad!" he said. "Take me to Warmen please!" and
sunk into the comfortable seat.

At 12:05 South African time, seven Star War lasers burned fifteen holes
into a British satellite having similar laser capabilities to their own. At 12:06
the British realized their satellite had been targeted. At 12:15 Ben was informed
and placed a direct call to the Secretary of State. At 12:30 both the British and
Russian Intelligence communities were informed about what happened and
that an international situation was developing. By 13:00 diplomats of all three
countries had been notified. Panic stricken, the officials in all three countries
waited for the next satellite demolition to begin at 13:05 but it never came!
By 13:30 there was so much red tape flying around the various governments,
that they were in total disarray trying to determine which procedure should
be applied to the situation. Officials were in various stages of covering their
butts, or trying to determine courses of action. Diplomats were calling in
favors as they tried to contact other government officials at an unprecedented
rate. The United Nation's headquarters was receiving calls at a rate which the
switchboard could barely handle. Clearly Ron had launched a huge shockwave
into the international community. As yet however, it had not touched the man
in the street. With care, it might still be contained.

The governments of the nations impacted would have been surprised to know that much of their hope hung in the hands of so few in Zinaville. Thandi and John dressed as workers were walking slowly along the dusty road up the little mountain pass in the Magaliesburg. Tom was preparing to call Ben but was waiting due to it being very early morning in America. Joshua and Carl were at Priggles to find out if Lofty had heard anything from, or about Susan. Jake and Frank were in their respective studies praying. Their wives and Karen together with the women of the churches were attending an inter-denominational prayer meeting.

The same governments would have being flabbergasted to see the huge spiritual forces that had converged on the Zinaville area. Demons may have the run of the world but in Zinaville, the heavenly hosts were gathering and displaying glory high into the heavens and surrounding area.

CHAPTER SIXTY-ONE

Bikers were rolling into Zinaville in groups of twenty to thirty at a time. The biker rally would be starting the next day. With the bikers came the problems of answering the calls that inundated the police station. The phone rang at Lofty's bar. He came across to Carl. "There's a call from the station for you!"

Carl took the call and came back with a bemused expression on his face. "I'm reinstated for office work," he told Joshua. I am to support the station in supporting the locals with their complaints associated with the bikers. Blast! Now I am locked in under the Brigadier's control. Sorry Josh, I'll not be able to help tonight. I'm on until twelve tonight and again tomorrow morning."

Joshua understood and they went their separate ways. Joshua went to meet his Mom. Maybe he would get some sleep at her home in preparation for the evening activity.

In Johannesburg, Don Warmen greeted both Ron and the Brigadier in a cool manner. They were told to sit and wait until David Larrel joined them. Ron's eyebrows went up on hearing that David was in town. Don ignored him, excused himself to attend to business and his administrator brought them sandwiches explaining that they would meet at two-o-clock.

David arrived almost at two and Don invited them into his conference room. Once he had closed the door and ensured they had refreshments he re-emphasized they should not come to his offices. Ron very directly and without compunction told him to "shut-up!"

Everyone's mouth dropped open.

"Let me explain, Gentlemen. The game has changed. Initially we were to buy up shares of selected companies with excellent satellite communications capabilities. These had to be those that backed up other, lesser capable networks, so that when we blasted the smaller networks out of the sky, their satellites would pick up the loads and the price of communications would skyrocket worldwide. Our shares would shoot up thousands of times in value. Warmen, you as well as David and some others were putting in the capital while the Brigadier, his brother and I were doing most of the grunt work. For that you shrewdly would give us a few million dollars while you intended to take the lion's share of a few billion. Now, I don't like that much! So I have decided, independent of how much you want, I want 50% of the profit and you get to split the rest as you see fit!"

"Who do you think you are?" Warmen shouted the question the others were thinking. "What makes you think we will not have you killed and take it all ourselves?"

Ron smiled at the glaring faces.

"Who has the security card? Oops! Oh, and I don't have it either, so you can't steal it even though that would not help you very much. Let me explain! I changed the control programs in the satellites. They now have pre-configured firing sequences. For example the British have lost an important satellite just over an hour ago. This wasn't because I did anything but because I didn't. I couldn't! My countrymen delayed me in getting out of the airport. You could say that the incident was therefore their fault!"

He paused for effect and gloated at the incredulous looks on his companion's faces.

"If I don't issue an encrypted signal by 12p.m. tonight, the French will have a similar problem tomorrow. If I am not allowed access to our facilities at Hartebeeshoek by midnight tonight, Mr. Warmen, I am sorry, but those satellites in which you have invested so much of your capital will become defunct one after another each hour. Are you following the drift of my argument? I am sure intelligent people such as you will understand that 50% is a small price to pay. You'll not notice it much as you will all have more money than you could spend if you lived a hundred lifetimes."

The demonic parties who had gathered with the human hosts were polarized. A demonic power war was on the brink of breaking out. Then, as quickly as it started, it resolved.

"I understand," said Warmen thinking quickly. "I agree. I suppose that even after the money is split, you will ensure your 'health' by keeping those satellites ready to eradicate our money source if something should happen to you?"

Ron looked around at the other men. "Look at him! There is the reason he is your leader! He is so quick to understand!" he sneered and then continued, "unfortunately, I have to give my American friends the control of their Star

Wars machines or they will simply destroy them. This means I'll relinquish control after destroying the communication satellites we need to have destroyed. They will immediately thereafter arrange to reload a previously archived version of the program to remove my 'dangerous' version. This will happen as planned but a minor modification I made to the loader ensures that you will be very unhappy if I get 'ill'."

The threat was effective. He could see that they believed him. "I intend to disappear and monitor my Swiss account from a place you will not find. Don't bother looking for me, or it may be to all our detriment." He had won without effort as planned. All except the Brigadier looked resigned. The Brigadier had hatred in his eyes. Ron wasn't worried about him. He knew the others would make him dance to their tune.

CHAPTER SIXTY-TWO

About the same time that this meeting was finishing, Tom was talking to Ben over the Internet chat line. He apprised Ben of the situation. Ben in turn explained that there was a certain Ron Jackson coming into the area. He described him in detail and explained that Ron shouldn't be made aware of any surveillance. "The consequences will be a disastrous international incident," he explained. He offered condolences on Susan's disappearance and let Tom know he would tell the CIA to look out for her. He explained that until they understood the points of corruption within the South African Police they couldn't take diplomatic action.

"Exactly how far the Brigadier is represented by others is difficult to ascertain. Do not trust the local police." Ben suggested. Tom thought this was totally obvious but did not make a comment. They said farewells and Tom logged out.

Thandi and John had made their way up past the disguised gateway on the mountain pass and tried to find a way to get to the higher mountain area on the other side of the road. The thorn bushes prevented access from the road into the bush from a fair distance back, to about half a kilometer down the road on the far side of the pass. Then they saw what looked like an animal path that cut through the bush on both sides. They followed the track as it wound up the mountainside. "Look," John pointed to a footprint on the path. "We must be careful not to leave our own tracks." He said and they both started to walk as carefully as they could. It was impossible not to leave tracks but they made it more difficult by walking in each other's tracks. The path wound up and up and soon came to the top of the ridge. They could see for miles on both sides and picked a rock with some shelter from where they could view both roads.

They had just settled when John turned to Thandi. "Someone else used this rock for the same reason." He told her. He pointed to cigarette butts that had been thrown over the edge and which littered the bush. Leaning over the rock they could see beer bottles and cigarette packs as well. "I think we should maybe find another spot to sit" John suggested. "I'll go and look, you wait here! The old man picked his way over the rocks slowly. Thandi thought him remarkably capable for his age. About ten minutes later she heard him call her from below. It sounded as if he was close by. She looked around and over the rock but couldn't see him. He called again and she realized he was below her but couldn't see him as the rock obstructed her view. "I'll come to get you" he shouted to her and arrived five minutes later. He led her around some bushes and along a rock ledge to a point just under the rock they had been sitting on. The view from there to the north was obstructed but in the opposite direction they could clearly see not only the approaching road, but also the area where they believed the thorn bush gate would be. A half dead bush formed a partial barrier to anyone looking towards their position and the indentation in the rock face gave some shelter. They settled down making themselves comfortable. It would be a long night. They planned to take turns to sleep and watch.

John was sleeping by nine in the evening and Thandi was sitting wrapped in her blanket when she heard the sound of someone coming up the path they had used. She shook John motioning him to keep quiet.

The person was noisy and they listened as he arrived at the rock above them and sat down. The squelch of a radio was heard for a second, probably as it was adjusted and then there was silence. The smell of cigarette smoke let them know he was smoking. In silence they waited. The odd car came up the road but didn't use the hidden gateway. At eleven ten they got their first change in the pattern. Two cars came up the road. One was far slower than the other. The second overtook the first and went up over the pass long before the slower car got there. The slower car rounded the bend obscuring it from the road below, before its lights flicked on and off twice. Above them they heard the man "Open North, one car!" The 'Roger' beep showed someone had heard. They could see the northern thorn bush gate swing open across the road. In the moonlight it appeared that a small tractor was used to push it open. Inside the gate thorn bushes dragged on the road. The tractor was attached to the gate by a pole. The car came up and without slowing, turned in and disappeared into a ravine out of sight. Just as quickly the gate closed and everything was as it had been and by the time the second car went past the gate was closed. They heard the pop of their neighbor opening a can of some drink. Again they waited.

The same process was repeated for the next car but this time there was no car following. Then they saw the southern gate opening in the same manner for a car coming from the opposite direction after they heard the instruction "Open south, one car" from above. Soon afterwards cars started to arrive in groups of two and three. When more cars were involved, their neighbor would call in the number.

A group of two cars coming up caused a change in the pattern. The lead car, which had a dim headlight, flicked its lights, but the one behind didn't. Their neighbor didn't say anything and the gates stayed closed. Both cars went past. A few minutes later, an "Open south, one car" allow a car with one dim headlight in.

At twelve-o-clock, they heard another person making their way up the path. The man above them threw his cans over the edge. They bounced into the bush feet away from John and Thandi. He started down to meet the person who was ascending. The two appeared to stop to talk. The sound of voices could be heard but the words were indistinct.

"This is a clever mechanism is it not, Thandi?" John whispered, "we have a problem as we can't get them to open it for us. We will have to find another way to get in!" he said. She nodded.

The sound of someone climbing up curtailed the whispering. The newcomer relieved himself over the edge into the bushes below, much to Thandi's disgust. The new neighbor then sat down on the same rock. The evening started to cool and the man stomped around above them keeping warm. John and Thandi huddled under their blankets silently.

Then at 2a.m., the radio above the hissed, "Ready to open the gate?" called a voice. Their neighbor answered. "All clear, over!" Below them the southern gate opened. A stream of ten cars exited and the gate closed. "Ready to open the gate?" came the query over the radio again. "All clear, over!" the reply was heard. This time the northern gate opened, and a larger group of cars exited south. The gate closed. "Final opening?" the radio crackled again. "All clear lets go home. Over and out!" their neighbor replied and they could hear him getting up. The southern gate opened and closed but no cars either came or left. The man above relieved himself again and then started down the mountainside.

"Why did they open that gate the last time?" whispered Thandi.

"To clear the tracks," John explained. "They have bushes and probably some sackcloth hanging under the gate to scrub out the tracks. Now I want to see how the men who were here with us get out. Let us wait a while."

They waited for another hour and didn't see or hear anything. "Now I guess we must see where the path goes," John muttered. They stretched their legs that were cramping. Yawning, John explained to Thandi that she must walk twenty feet behind him. "We must be quiet, not like those men we could hear so clearly. Walk behind and watch where I put my feet. Do the same yourself. If someone comes to me, you must duck into the bush and hide. One of us must be able to tell Joshua and Carl what we know. We should not go together as it would be a disaster if we both get caught now!" John explained.

Thandi was not happy but understood the logic and agreed to comply. The beautiful woman gave John a hug and he set out ahead of her.

The mountain path was easy to navigate in the starlight and they made good time to the road. They crossed over on the path and disappeared into the bush. John moved much more slowly after they crossed the road and seemed to be checking each time before putting a foot down. The path split. One went on down, another seemed to go off to the south. John pointed to go south. Carefully, the two of them moved quietly through the African bush, listening and attentive to the sounds of the night. Thandi kept thinking of the leopards she knew frequented the mountains. Somehow it drove the tiredness from her mind.

It must have been a while, but it felt like minutes to Thandi, when they saw the road ahead. John stopped and crouched down. Through the darkness, the sound of snoring was heard. With extreme caution John moved forward again. Then he gestured to Thandi, pointed to the ground in the path and made a horizontal cutthroat gesture with his hand. There was something dangerous in the path. He carefully stood up and stepped high over something she couldn't see. He gestured her to come. When she got there he pointed again to a thin wire stretched over the path. "Trap!" he whispered in her ear. "Step over it very carefully." She complied and they moved forward again even slower."

Thandi thanked her ancestors that John was there. It was good to have someone who understood the bush. John was thinking how the years spent with Henk Vermaak tracking cattle thieves were a gift. To think how he had hated it at the time! Once they got to the road, John motioned for her to stay, and quietly walked up the road out of sight. He came back within two minutes. "Gates are up there. A small hut is just down from the gates. One man is asleep in the hut. I'll follow the road; you follow me far enough back so you can just see me. Remember if I go down on my haunches, you must hide in the bush. When I stand up and move you follow. OK?" She nodded.

They set out down the starlit road. It wound down and around and then suddenly John went down on his haunches. Thandi slipped into the bush and strained to see. Briefly a glow of a cigarette could be seen in the darkness ahead. John motioned her to stay and slipped into the bush. She waited for over an hour and was getting worried and feeling very exposed when he reappeared in the road and came up towards her.

She stepped into the road and he motioned her back into the bush. When he was a distance ahead he motioned her to follow again. Once they were back at the path, he explained in a whisper that there was a huge cliff overhang with a cave behind it. He had been around and into the cave to where he could see another man sleeping on a makeshift bed. He didn't want to go passed as the man had a semi-automatic rifle and he may have woken. "I couldn't see Steve or Susan," The old man said. "My back is very tired. Let's go to the store and sleep there!" he suggested. "We can get the first taxi in the morning." She nodded. They retraced their path to the road and did as John suggested.

Out at the Hartebeeshoek satellite station, Joshua and Tom were taking turns to watch the activities using the infrared camera to help them. Hendrik's car had arrived at eleven and had entered the grounds. Nothing had been seen since then, except what appeared to be normal activities. It was Joshua's turn to sleep! He was in the car which was well hidden in the bush. Tom had walked down closer to the guard post and fence when Hendrik's car drove out and departed. Tom clicked a picture and then went back, woke Joshua and they went back to Joshua's home where Tom decided to stay for the night. Sleep was a welcome oblivion.

At the station Ron had preprogrammed the computer to send out the radio command to the satellites at midnight Easter Sunday. This timing had been at the Brigadiers insistence. "I want it to coincide with a special party I am organizing," He had said, "you're welcome to attend, I have also invited Don Warmen." Ron had absent-mindedly agreed as he ran the routines on the computer. He was more focused on getting everything accurate. He also programmed the computer to send a radio signal to stop the French satellite from being targeted as nobody had bothered him during the day. He enjoyed the feeling of power. He had within a few days brought some of the world's nations and one of the world's more powerful businessmen under his control. He reveled in his egotistical glory. He put the final touches to the program. A sequence of radio signals transmitted each hour over the next two days would place the target co-ordinates in the satellites memory banks. He smiled when he thought how every mind in his old unit would be trying to break in and gain control. He knew they couldn't. Every control path they could possibly use had been re-routed through his routines.

Ron's egotism would have been somewhat deflated if he could have seen the murderous intent in Hendrik's mind. The Brigadier had explained to Hendrik what this young American had done to them. Hendrik would gladly have ended the nerd's life but knew he had to wait. His time would come!

CHAPTER SIXTY-THREE

Good Friday dawned with a beautiful orange-red sunrise over the dew-drenched bush. Thandi and John awoke at the store, stiff and cold as the dew had settled on their blanket in the morning hours and made them damp. John collected sticks from the bush, and made a small fire around which they both gathered. The taxi arrived a short while later. It dropped them off at John's home. Thandi wanted to shower and change. John wanted his morning coffee. He hoped his shower would get rid of some of the aches he was feeling in his back. The previous night's activities were more than this old man needed in his life. After freshening up, they both took a taxi to Joshua's home.

It was 10-o-clock when Tom who was sleeping at Joshua's home, awoke to the sound of knocking on his door. Tom let John and Thandi in and went to wake Joshua who was still sleeping. Thandi made the men coffee and breakfast and by the time they had showered and changed, the home was full of delicious morning breakfast aromas. Joshua was mildly amused to see how Thandi had taken over his kitchen and supplies, but pleased with the outcome.

As they ate and exchanged stories, Tom and Joshua were amazed to hear what the other two had found out.

"Sounds like a small army has been going in and out of the area," Tom commented. "How many cars could be parked in the bush and under the overhang?" he inquired.

"Many! Many! Many!" John answered shaking his head. "I think there may be a hundred or more!"

"What is going on, I wonder?" Joshua asked.

Nobody had any ideas. It was obviously a well-organized and funded operation. Tom suggested he call his American 'geologists' and give them the information. He used Joshua's phone and the headset they had given him to bring them up to date. They would let Ben know via their morning situation report, or SITREP, as they called it. They told Tom that everyone should keep from doing anything unusual during the day so as not to arouse suspicions. They promised to call Tom with an update early Saturday afternoon. He gave them his pager number to ensure they could contact him.

They finished breakfast and Thandi asked the men if they could help John 'open' his gate so that she could get her car out. It some effort to remove and replace the gatepost. Joshua drove them out to John's home to do the task. Thandi drove out from behind John's house, shouted goodbye and went off home. Joshua and Tom then went out to the mine as Tom's pager was ringing continually, and Joshua needed to check on the state of the metallurgical plant.

In America, Ben's security group gathered for a review of the morning SITREP's and to plan the actions for the day. The President had been loath to provide the Russians with the authority to destroy the Star Wars system.

Instead he had requested a focus on breaking into the locked out controls. They found this wasn't going to be easy. A brute force approach with computing power was out of the question as the satellites had frequency hopping radio and the low speed communications would not have made it possible even if they could get the satellites to become active. Somehow Ron had switched the receivers off until he communicated with them at very specific intervals.

This morning they decided to switch tactics and to try to break in using his encryption codes. This meant they had to monitor the radio signals. This wasn't easy due to the highly directional nature of the signal as focused by the rod antennae. The 'geologists' had set up camp just outside the satellite station and recorded each signal that went out. They then retransmitted it to the Pentagon where powerful decryption services were set in motion to break the codes. They doubted it would be successful as Ron was highly trained in cryptography and would have applied everything they had taught him to block them.

"We have to get men into Hartebeeshoek to get a copy of the program," an advisor urged. "If we have the program, it will solve our problems."

"Unfortunately we can't stop his program running, or we will have another satellite blasted to oblivion," another member reminded them. "We don't even know how he has it set up. All he has to do is become aware and do nothing and we're swimming in pigs swill!"

"A simple look at the setup of equipment could help us in our work" another person noted.

The meeting adjourned after Ben was given instructions to draft the orders requiring a military radio expert to meet with the "geologists." They needed to get inside Hartebeeshoek satellite station with a minimum of risk. After considering his options he decided that only Tom could legally get his men in. He asked the "geologists" to submit their plan by end of day. They would need to execute it during daylight hours on Saturday. Time was getting short. The intelligence had shown that the Van Vuuren's dabbled in satanic rituals and it was likely something would happen on Easter Sunday. They wanted to be ready.

Getting the radio expert to Zinaville in time was a huge problem. There was nobody qualified in Southern Africa. The assistance of a specialist from the Air Force Special Operations was necessary. This specialist would be placed into a high altitude skydiving suit and then strapped into the transportation pod of their new subspace spy plane. He would bail out over the South African Bushveld less than an hour after takeoff. At that height he would be dropped, it would mean they would be in South African radar coverage for less than three minutes and would be out of range of the jet fighters before they could react. Detection was highly unlikely! The spy plane pilot would detach the pod by flicking a switch, allowing it to glide the first 100 000ft on a preprogrammed path. The air force specialist would then be ejected out of the back of the pod and it would continue glide to over to the Indian Ocean where it would explode to simulate meteorite disintegration. The fragments would be scattered into the sea over a wide area.

The specialist would free fall through sub-zero air for another 50 000ft. His parachute would deploy and open fully, based on computerized radar readings, at fifty feet above the ground. There was a minimal risk he would be seen but they believed that with such a low-level parachute deployment it was unlikely. The experts had calculated the higher risk was that the specialist would pass out during the free fall due to the cold. If this happened, the computer would still deploy everything correctly and the pressure suit would auto adjust his position over the landing area. They also predicted he would return to his senses before the chute deployment. If he didn't, the worst-case scenario was that he might break a leg or two, which was considered a low and acceptable risk. He could do his work from a wheelchair if necessary!

It would be quite an experience for their man! Ben was glad he was now too old to undertake these types of missions. Too many special operations seemed to be dependent on electronics that he didn't like having to trust. Ben grudgingly had to admit it was remarkable that the man could be inserted into a foreign country, almost half way across the world, within two hours! The world was changing fast!

Ben would have been even more impressed at the speed with which Beor covered the same distance, with no electronics and no risk. He had been in attendance at the meeting for its conclusion and seemed to dissolve into a spiritual light that streaked across the Atlantic to be at Joshua's side in a split second. If Ben could have seen Beor, it would have seemed as if he had vanished into thin air.

CHAPTER SIXTY-FOUR

Tom's pager buzzed insistently around mid afternoon. He was sitting back, feet on his desk and whiskey in hand, reading a journal on earth moving equipment. He ignored the first two times it went off and looked at it on the third. He groaned when he saw it was the Americans' number. He shut his office door, and called them back using the handset they had given him. It took them a few minutes to explain that they wanted him to arrange a visit to the Hartebeeshoek station for two of them and himself mid afternoon on Saturday.

"This will cost you!" Tom warned. "You had better understand basic geology because they will be discussing the geological implications of their work. I'll have to pay for an image this time. What area do you think we should ask them to photograph?"

Greg suggested that they get coverage of Magaliesburg around where Thandi and John had found the cave. Tom agreed.

"They're not going to let us get near the building we want to see." Tom warned.

"There will be a short diversion enabling us to get there," Greg explained. "It's getting out that will be difficult. We need to wait for dark before leaving. Normally nobody arrives much before 9p.m. and so we should be safe if we're out by 8p.m. Can you call me when you have the visit arranged?"

Tom agreed and hung up the phone.

It took him a while to get through to the station and it took a lot of coercion to arrange a visit by the following day. The station was on a skeleton staff due to the long weekend and did not want visitors. The money Tom was willing to pay for photographs finally ensured his success. He called Greg back, and gave him the good news. Ten minutes later, the American specialist was suiting up for the cross Atlantic trip.

In town, Carl, Tom and Joshua got together at Priggles just before sunset. The bikers and other visitors had been pouring into town all day long keeping Priggles busier than they had ever imagined. The noise was excessive and patron's were rowdy. Locals watched as bikers rolled into the bar with their leather, chains and helmets. Row upon row of bikes were parked outside with bikers lounging on the bike seats, smoking, drinking and telling jokes. The park was full of bikers and rock music blared out from a makeshift stage. People were dancing in front of the stage and at various places up and down the street radios and Walkman CD players cranked out their beats. Periodically a group of bikes would rumble up or down the street. It was a happy but chaotic environment.

Carl was actually on duty at Priggles, where he had been sent to keep an eye on the patrons. Tom and Joshua cracked jokes at how good his job was. How he got paid to sit around watching others enjoy themselves. Tom ordered beer. Joshua and Carl ordered soft drinks. Their news intrigued Carl. He'd been able to find out that the Brigadier was staying with Hendrik for the whole weekend and was only returning to the city on Monday. Carl also had seen Hendrik talking to a biker of the "Blitz-'em'" group. Carl had researched the group and found that in parts of Johannesburg they were competing with the Hells Angels for control of the drug traffic. The police had been warned to watch out for gang warfare on the weekend.

"The good news is that there's a lot of out of town police monitoring the situation," Carl explained. "I can't believe the Brigadier can influence all these guys and so we will have some real solid support over the next two days."

Joshua excused himself, as he wanted to go to a church meeting at the Zinaville Christian church. He didn't enjoy or approve of the bar atmosphere and wanted to get out of there. He also wanted to get Jake to ask his congregation to pray for their activity the next day but without giving him any specifics. Tom stayed with Carl to keep him company.

CHAPTER SIXTY-FIVE

The next day the meeting at Tom's home almost filled his living room. The four CIA agents and the new specialist, Thandi, John, Joshua and Carl were in attendance. Carl had changed shift with a friend and in exchange was working nightshift. Greg, the CIA man took charge and broke the agenda into segments. First everyone would give his or her view of the situation. Tom started and did such a good job that no one else added anything. Then Greg explained the planning for the afternoon. His demeanor showed he didn't like having to work with civilians but that he would do his job.

He explained with military precision how Tom and two agents would go to the main offices. Greg and the specialist would be hidden in the trunk of Tom's car. Meanwhile an agent would start a fire in the bush on the side of the station near the gate guard post then call the fire department to put it out. The three in the offices would stay chatting to the supervisor in the station. Their assumption was that the guard would be watching the fire and not towards the offices. Greg and the specialist would slip out of the trunk and hightail it to the building with the rod antennae. Once there, they would page Tom, who would say farewell. This would give them a few hours to work out what to do with the satellite control. The shift change at the station was at 8p.m. and they hoped that under the cover of darkness, they could get to the main offices and call for Tom. Tom would arrive letting the guard know he was going up to the office to retrieve spectacles he had dropped. The guard would check the logs and verify Tom had been in earlier and would hopefully allow Tom inside. Tom would then arrange with the new supervisor to look for the spectacles and after a few minutes 'find' them. He would thank the supervisor and drive out with the agents in the trunk of his car. If they were caught, they would say they had taken Tom hostage and made him work for them. They hoped that they would then be arrested and Tom would be able to contact Ben who could arrange to get them out of the situation.

Greg wanted Joshua and John to stake out the Magaliesburg cave entrance and monitor the evening activities as best they could. Both men agreed with this. Thandi would drop them off along the road just before nightfall. They would wait until it grew dark and move down to the cave entrance area to observe what would go on.

"Are you sure you can do this without being detected?" Greg wanted to know.

"Are you aware that most male South Africans are also trained soldiers and know exactly what to do in these circumstances?" asked Joshua who was mildly peeved at Greg's attitude. Tom looked at Joshua in surprise, as he wasn't accustomed to this side of Joshua's nature.

"All right, are we a go then?" asked Greg. Everyone affirmed they were ready and synchronized their watches. It was close to two thirty when they left to prepare for the various activities.

The plan to get the agents into the plant worked out exactly as expected. The fire started up on schedule and surprisingly instead of the fire department arriving, the guard jumped into his truck and raced to the fire. He had a water tank, hose and compressor in the back for just such an eventuality. This made it easy for Greg and the specialist to get to their target location. Then the complication arose. The guard had extinguished the fire and arrived back at his post when the fire engine arrived. Tom, as planned, was leaving and arrived at the same time as the engine. He was held up as an argument ensued. The fire department wanted to be paid for being called out, and the guard was arguing that he had not called. They called the supervisor who came down and also argued that they had not called. During the argument, the fire truck moved to let Tom's vehicle out. They left the site as the argument seemed to be reaching fever pitch.

Tom stopped, picked up the agent who had lit the fire and took him back to his campsite. He then went home to await the call summoning him.

Greg and his specialist found the office boarded up and locked. It took them a few minutes to pick the lock, cover themselves with a foil like material to fool any infrared body heat detectors and get inside. Using a night vision sight, the specialist verified that there was one infrared detector and a camera on top of a computer that was suspicious. He crawled very slowly until under the detector and then put a piece of paper in front of it. With the lights still off he did the same to the camera, this time using a piece of cardboard. They then turned on the lights and checked for additional alarms and traps. The specialist opened a small computer he was carrying, plugged it into the power and using a specialized phone, connected it to the team in the Pentagon. A camera was pulled from his pocket and within seconds he was talking to his team and showing them the equipment.

They soon isolated the main computer, which was also the one that had the camera attached. The experts advised that he not type on the keyboard as often there was only a specific sequence to release the keyboard for use. They pointed out three antennae wires coming out of the side of the computer. This wasn't usual and suggested the machine was not set up in the normal way. Instead, they suggested he open the computer up. He checked for pressure sensitive pads and then did as they instructed. The box once opened revealed what looked like a cell phone that was hard wired into the computer circuitry. In addition, the circuit board was obviously a military issue multi layer board with a molded clear epoxy layer covering the components and attached to the main board. It was impossible to get to the key components to electronically determine what was happening although each component could be seen through the clear layer. They were in a deadlock situation. To get the information they needed they had to break into the computer but to do so would result in it reporting the attempts directly via the cell phone. Closer inspection showed the same cell phone was connected to the radio circuitry to provide inputs that would drive the signals to the satellite. Other wires were connected to various pieces of electronic equipment used to establish the level of control over the array that the designers wanted. This was one sophisticated setup but was simple in design.

"I think we trained Ron Jackson a little too well!" the specialist commented. "I can't do much without trying the keyboard. Shall we give it a go?"

It took the experts about ten minutes to make that decision. Finally they decided that it could only be done just before they left so that if something went wrong, they could still get out. They had to wait until 8:00p.m., as Tom would be arriving at 8:10. They settled back to wait.

At 8:00p.m. they attached their equipment to the keyboard and hit the space bar. A screen popped up with a password request. Immediately from the look of the screen they could see it was not a standard windows PC. The cracker went to work attempting to find the password. The antennae monitor showed a signal going out at 8:05p.m. but they assumed this was the hourly signal they had been monitoring to date. Greg was watching the gate. At 8:10 he saw Tom entering. He called Tom's pager. Tom drove up to the office and then called back. Greg told him to delay ten to fifteen minutes. He would buzz the pager when they were ready.

The password cracker clicked into a sequence that was accepted. The specialist typed in a command at the prompt line assuming Linux. Immediately the same password screen came up again. He turned around, "we've been had! The password was a delaying tactic; I think they are onto us!" Greg turned off the lights immediately and they replaced everything as they found it. The door was closed and locked and they hoped Tom was keeping the supervisor busy as they ran to his car. Greg dialed Tom's pager as they tumbled into his trunk and closed it.

Tom 'found' his spectacles within the next minute and chatted to the supervisor on the way out. He climbed in and drove to the gate. The guard wasn't in a good mood.

" Sir, Would you please step out of the car?" he asked.

"What's this about?"

" Sir, Please step out of the car!"

Tom complied and pulled the latch on the trunk as he opened the car door. He hoped the guard would not notice.

" Sir, Please walk over to the guardroom and place your hand on the wall and spread your feet " the guard said menacingly and a gun appeared in his hand.

As he said this a car pulled up to the gate, its headlights shining on the situation. Tom's heart sank when he heard the Brigadier's voice asking the guard what was going on. "I stopped the car as you asked, Sir!" said the guard.

"Good! Good!" the brigadier walked up and looked at Tom. "I know you! You're the man who owns the mine. That friend of Joshua and Carl! Cuff him!" he ordered. Put him in the back of my car. "Are there any others?" he enquired.

"Not here Sir!" replied the guard.

"Then get the car out of the way I want to go up to our offices." The Brigadier ordered again.

Tom was thrown into the back of the Brigadier's car. Sitting in the passenger seat was a person that Tom could only guess was Ron.

The guard pulled Tom's car around to the back of the guard post and returned.

The Brigadier pulled in and called the guard. "Make sure that you call me if you see or hear anything suspicious!" he commanded.

While this was going on Greg and the two men climbed out the trunk of Tom's car. The Brigadier drove off. The guard was closing the gate when something hard hit him in the head and he passed out. The Brigadier parked at the locked building, unlocked the door, and the two men went inside, leaving Tom in the back seat of the car. The Americans meanwhile drove Tom's car out of the gate and blew the horn as they left. They hoped Tom would be able to stick to his story and that it would work. The Brigadier and Ron ran outside and were just in time to see Tom's car leaving. Swearing and cursing, they jumped into their car and gave chase. It was useless as by the time they got to the main road Tom's car was out of sight.

CHAPTER SIXTY-SIX

Up in the mountains, Joshua and John were by this time moving down through the bush parallel to the road to the cave. John had insisted on going first and told Joshua to follow a good way back. "Never give a man more people to see than necessary." John had said. "A good distance between us means we see twice as much, and it's more likely that one of us will get away if there is trouble!"

Joshua listened to the advice that hard years of experience had taught this old man. He followed him as John methodically picked his way from shadow to shadow.

When they got near the cave, John came back to him. He pointed out a large tree just in from the bush near the entrance.

"How good do you climb Sir?"

Joshua nodded and took a circuitous route to the bush near the tree. John gave him the go ahead and he ran to the tree and climbed up into its leafy canopy. He was able to see not only the entrance but also the approach to it. It was then that he saw the guard dogs. Two guards with Dobermans were walking along the edges of the bush. Joshua signaled to John and pointed. John started to move back into the bush watching the dogs. It was then that it happened. There was an explosion and John's body was thrown up into the air. The bush was stripped of its leaves and then people poured out of the cave. Some of them had weapons in their hands.

Horrified, Joshua watched as they walked over and kicked the lifeless corpse that had been his friend a few seconds before. A group of about twenty men gathered. Some of them started to patrol the bush perimeter. A truck reversed. The body was rolled onto a tarpaulin and thrown in the back.

"Another one for the leopards to feed on!" laughed the driver. Some of the onlookers laughed and went back into the cave. Joshua felt as if he was going to throw up but didn't. Then he felt dizzy. He undid his belt and picking a branch, belted himself to it so that he wouldn't fall out if he passed out. A man came and sat under the tree and apparently went to sleep. Joshua was feeling the attack of darkness on his soul again. It became too much and he passed out. Beor who was under the tree in the form of a human to avoid detection by the demonic hordes watched his charge. He knew this man was the key. He waited.

Joshua stirred at 10p.m. and came back to his senses. His one arm had gone to sleep where the belt pinched it. He hoisted himself into a more comfortable position. He noticed there was still someone asleep under his tree. At 10:30p.m. he saw a familiar car arrive. Hendrik pulled into the overhang, parked his car and they hauled someone out of the passenger seat. He could see the man had his hands locked up behind his back and a blindfold on. Joshua was sure he recognized the person and as the group passed by some lights, Joshua realized it was Tom. This time he controlled his emotions and sat quietly. He would ensure they paid for this but needed to be calm. He found that praying helped and started to pray in earnest for the downfall of these men. He watched until 3a.m. Suddenly he noticed his companion that had been under the tree had gone. Carefully he descended and watching very carefully for trip wires, he move quietly back to the path and to the road. He walked south for a mile and then called to Thandi who was waiting to fetch John and himself.

"Come fetch me at the store" was all he said. She said "Sure?" and he rang off without replying to her enquiring tone of voice. He didn't want to have to explain! He felt like he was a danger to all around him, and wanted to limit the time he spent with anyone he loved. They either got hurt or died!

Joshua was having great difficulty holding onto his senses. Hell was bent on bringing him down. Beor stood alongside his charge wishing the Lord would let him intervene. He never understood the Lord's will and so accepted his task unequivocally.

Thandi picked him up within half an hour. She found him walking down the road like a zombie. When she open the door to let him in he looked at her and tears started to stream down his face. Not a sound came from him, just the tears. She couldn't ask him what had happened. She knew that she didn't want to know. She drove him to his home and escorted him inside. He collapsed into a chair, put his head in his hands and said nothing.

"Shall I call Carl?" she wanted to know.

With great effort as if it took time to hear her, he looked at her for a while and then nodded. She looked through his phone numbers next to the phone and found one for Carl's home. He was asleep and at her brief explanation said he would come straight over.

Ten minutes later he knocked softly on the door and she let him in, gesturing with a nod of her head to where Joshua was slumped not even looking up. Carl went to his friend.

"Josh, Josh, how are you my friend?"

Joshua looked at him and in a strangled voice that tore at the heart of his friends said "John's dead! He's dead! Those bastards are going to feed him to the leopards! I want to KILL them!"

The utter hatred and anger in his voice made both of them recoil as if he had attacked them himself. This wasn't the Joshua they knew! Something had snapped!

Then they both perceived what he had said and realized the implications. Thandi felt dizzy and sat herself in the nearest chair. Carl was less impacted. A policeman's life prepared him for this type of shock.

"You don't mean that Josh!" he said firmly. "Stop, you're falling into emotional traps! Pull yourself together! John needs justice not a pathetic vendetta. We will see he gets justice! Do you understand?"

Joshua looked at Carl for a second and shook his head.

"You weren't there! You didn't see it! He was blown to bits by a landmine. They laughed! How can a human laugh at such a thing? They are evil! Evil deserves to die! Can't you see?"

Carl nodded. "I see and I know. I see you've forgotten it is God who judges. You know that better than I do!"

The spiritual world around Joshua was seething with a storm of angelic and demonic clashes. Beor's sword was finding its mark again and again. He would give Joshua the right to decide freely! The demonic forces would be repelled. Slowly the angels pushed the demons back.

Joshua nodded slowly. "You're right Carl," he said. "Sorry, I wasn't myself! It's been too much. Far too much!"

Thandi went over to him and put her arms around him. With tears in her eyes she told him how sorry she was. He thanked her without realizing the pain she herself was experiencing.

"What do we do?" He asked Carl.

"We get help fast!" Carl said. "Can I use your phone?"

He called Aaron and they talked for a long time. When he came back, he reminded Joshua about the 'Bikers for Christ' that had attended the service at Frank's church. "I want to get them involved tomorrow. I also want to get every congregation helping and plan to get the ministers together tomorrow. This is war Josh. Spiritual war! We will be victorious! They will be brought to justice! I need your help. This is how we will do it," he explained.

Thandi made coffee as the two men planned and prayed through to the next morning. Then they both went out and started to visit churches and people. She waited. They returned to Joshua's home at 6p.m. exhausted but with strict instructions she would wake them at 8:30p.m.

CHAPTER SIXTY-SEVEN

In the mountain cave, Tom had been thrown into a pit. They had taken his specialized headset away when they found it but had simply smashed the front of his cell phone and stuck it back in his pocket laughing. His hands were locked behind his back with tie wraps. A large tie wrap locked his feet together at the ankles. Then they pushed him onto a hole. He fell onto a pile of hay and mud at the bottom and lay winded, unable to help himself.

"They got you too Sir!" a familiar voice spoke out of the darkness. Tom struggled to sit upright. He could vaguely see an outline of someone in the darkness.

"It's easier if you sit against the side. Roll onto your knees and jump to your feet," a familiar women's voice spoke out.

He caught his breath and did as suggested, hopping towards the voice.

"Stop! Before you hit the wall! Turn around and sit," the woman spoke again.

Once he was seated, he had time to think more clearly.

"Susan? Is that you Susan?"

"Ja, care of my wonderful father and uncle!" the spiteful words seared through the darkness with hate. "I am sorry they have also got you as well."

A male voice spoke chiding, "It doesn't do us good to be angry Susan, let us rather save our strength for when we can use it to escape! I'm sorry they seem to have got to you too Sir! Do you perhaps know how it is with my father?"

Tom realized the voice was Steve's.

"I think he is fine, Steve. He is with Joshua and Thandi. They would want me to say hello from them."

Tom's eyes were becoming accustomed to the darkness and he could vaguely see them. Steve spoke, "Tell us what's been happening Sir. We have been here a long time and we hear nothing from the men upstairs. Is anyone looking for us?"

Tom asked if anyone else was with them before answering.

"There is no-one else. There was another man they called the 'hobo'. He was here for a while but I understand they killed him. They are part of a terrible satanic cult. Human sacrifice is the highest type of ritual. He was used to prepare for the event to come. They jokingly told us that they fed his remains to some leopards when they were finished with him.

We've been told we're being held here for a grand ritual of worldwide importance. This Easter they'll apparently have the worldwide convention here which will end in a black mass at which we, that is to say Susan and I, are to be the prime attraction. At the moment they don't worry about us much other than to make sure we have food, water and the basics of life. No one guards us as you need a ladder to get out and we're bound. We can talk freely."

In a whisper, Tom described the happenings of the past days. He carefully neglected to tell them that it was now Easter. He felt they would have enough time to worry about that when and if that time arrived. They talked in hushed tones for a long time and then they fell silent. Soon Tom was asleep.

CHAPTER SIXTY-EIGHT

The town hall of Zinaville was filled to overflowing by the time Joshua, Carl and Thandi got to the huge multi-denominational service that was being held. Chairs had been placed on the lawn outside and all the doors were open. Loud speakers had been placed strategically so that the service could be heard at the back and outside. Initially only about a hundred people turned up. Then the BFC biker's rode up and joined it. Their numbers had swollen to over a hundred alone. The Afrikaans churches then came as a group and suddenly all the chairs were full. Other bikers started to arrive to find out what was going on and stood around. This church service was suddenly a major event. The press turned up and they could see that national newspaper reporters were on the scene.

The service started at nine as planned. Joshua had a brand new cell phone that he checked was on the vibrate mode. He made sure it had signal. All the different church leaders went to the stage. They asked the Mayor to open in prayer. As he started to pray a few bikers thought that pressing their horns would be funny. The BFC bikers rose as group and walked outside and surrounded them. The bikers thought differently suddenly and the reporters started taking pictures. Everyone listened to the Mayor's prayer.

Out at the satellite tracking station a different scene was developing. Don Warmen, Dave Larrel, the Brigadier and Ron were seated at the computer when the door burst open, a huge shock wave hit them and tear gas was everywhere. The Brigadier, who just had time to draw his gun before the shock hit, was shot dead before he knew what was happening. The others sat there dazed. They were told to put their hands up. Don Warmen complied but the others did not. In a daze they only raised their hands after being told for the third time to put them up. They had failed to understand the first two times because the person had spoken Afrikaans. It was only when an American voice told them to do so that they complied.

Ron was the angriest, "You're making a huge mistake," he shouted. "The world will suffer due to your actions." Greg strode into the room. "Not likely," he quipped and put a bullet through the computer on the table. Warmen and Larrel jumped and Ron's mouth dropped open in shock.

Greg smiled but his eyes didn't. "The South African, Canadian, British, French and Russian governments would like to speak to you all!" he informed them.

"They will all suffer" Ron snarled. "The biggest destruction of satellites in history is about to occur! This world will not know what has happened until it's too late. You had better let us go right now or huge damage will occur!"

"Possibly, but we think not!" Greg answered. "Your cell phones antennae trick is what caused your failure. On route to being encoded, you transmitted the message with your cell phone inside that computer. He pointed to the wrecked machine. We simply recorded it, matched it with the encoded signal and broke your code. For the last hour we have reprogrammed every laser satellite and locked it out. We did this while feeding you enough return signals to convince you that you were still active. The laptop was outside under the antennae. Sorry but your scheme failed. You can thank Joshua. He was the one who asked if we couldn't record the cell phone signal. We had simply overlooked the obvious."

Ron was furious! The men were handcuffed and marched out to a waiting military transport vehicle.

Greg picked up the phone and called Joshua.

"Clear, your turn now!"

CHAPTER SIXTY-NINE

It was in the middle of the prayer that Joshua got the call. When the prayer finished, he caught Jake's eye and nodded. Jake whispered to Frank, who nudged the preacher next to him, and so on until all leaders had obviously been notified.

The sermon started. It was a fiery sermon. "Christ came to die for sinners and rose again," "We should rise with him and take up the cross," "and crime and violence are sins and must be stopped."

The first half of the sermon was delivered in Afrikaans and the second half by Frank in English. Joshua waited.

"Zinaville residents and visitors," he started. "I want to explain the very evil we have in our midst and do not know it. I am going to ask two men to speak but, before I do, I believe I can say they have the support of every man on this stage, is that not so gentlemen?"

Eyes focused on the leadership group and the leaders were all nodded agreement.

Joshua and Carl got up to speak. Quickly and in simple terms they described the events that had happened over the past few weeks. The crowd was aghast as they listened. Even the bikers drew near and for the first time since the start of the weekend the town grew quiet. The power of heaven descended and seemingly out of nowhere, more and more angels appeared. When Carl and Joshua asked people to bow their heads and pray for the souls lost and for an end to evil, the flash of glory was so great that the cave under the mountains was not impervious to the spiritual light. The demons felt the impending doom.

Carl and Joshua finished. If someone had dropped a pin, it would have made a clatter the silence was so heavy. Frank stood up.

"Now friends, it's time to act. Please follow these men to rescue our townsfolk held hostage."

A roar of agreement went up. The BFC bikers had moved to the front quietly as Joshua spoke. They picked up Joshua and Carl and carried them to their bikes. Placing them on the pillions of the front two bikes they headed out of town with almost every vehicle in town joining in behind them.

The watcher on top of the mountain controlling the gate was amazed to see a huge string of lights coming down the road all flashing their lights. He had been told to open the gate if this happened and hurriedly complied. The man on the tractor jumped off and ran when he saw the convoy bearing down on him. The army had joined behind the bikers as they passed the Hartebeeshoek station turnoff. Following after the hundred BFC bikers were six truckloads of troops. Behind the troops came hundreds of townsfolk in their vehicles.

In the cave some men had just brought Tom, Susan and Steve to the main area where candles stood lighting a pentagram. A satanic chant was beating out when the commotion started. The guards with the automatic rifles simple dropped them when they saw the huge mass of soldiers and humanity bearing down on them. The bikers drove down the passageway and into the center of the pentagram floor flooding the area with light. Joshua pointed to where Tom, Susan and Steve stood and the leader and some of the bikers encircled them. Those present tried to run but there was a human wall pressing in on them. They retreated into the furthest area of the cave quivering in fear. The soldiers formed a barrier to protect them from the angry town folk. It looked as if some of those cornered were about to get lynched by the townsfolk when the biker with Joshua revved his engine. Suddenly all the other bikers took the hint and did the same. The noise was horrendous and everyone put their hands to their ears to cut it out. With a signal, the leader told the bikers to cut the noise. Dead silence followed. The biker leader elbowed Joshua who got the hint. He stood up on the pillion.

"Thank you my friends of Zinaville. We have achieved what we needed to achieve. It is by your belief in justice, God and the love of your fellowman that we have succeeded. The troops will take these people into custody. You can now all go home knowing you have contributed greatly to making the world a better place."

The round of applause was deafening and the crowd started to disperse. It took hours to clear the traffic blockage and clean up the area.

Tom watched it happening. He felt proud of the town and humbled by the huge expression of care they had exhibited. Joshua and Susan held each other tightly. Thandi and Steve stood hand in hand. It was Joshua who finally did the right thing.

"Let us pray and give thanks," he said.

The small group held hands, stood in a circle and prayed. After a while a glorious light erupted from the group. Thandi had found her Savior!

In the heavens a crescendo of glorious praise swelled to the Father's ears as hundreds of angels joined the circle of human praise, "To God be the Glory!"